Centuries

of June

Centuries of June

A Novel

KEITH DONOHUE

Crown Publishers
New York

Copyright © 2011 by Keith Donohue

All rights reserved.
Published in the United States by Crown Publishers,
an imprint of the Crown Publishing Group,
a division of Random House, Inc., New York.
www.crownpublishing.com

CROWN and the Crown colophon are registered trademarks of Random House, Inc.

Library of Congress Cataloging-in-Publication Data
Donohue, Keith.
    Centuries of June / Keith Donohue.—1st ed.
        p. cm.
    I. Title.
    PS3604.O5654C46   2011
    813.'6—dc22   2010023574

ISBN 978-0-307-45028-9
eISBN 978-0-307-45030-2

Printed in the United States of America

BOOK DESIGN BY BARBARA STURMAN
JACKET DESIGN BY JEAN TRAINA
JACKET PHOTOGRAPHY BY ANDREAS KUEHN/GETTY IMAGES

10 9 8 7 6 5 4 3 2 1

First Edition

To Cara, Rose, Eilís, and Owen

Is it my imagination, or is it getting crowded in here?

—Groucho Marx, *A Night at the Opera*

CHAPTER ONE

Brained,
from Behind

We all fall down. Perhaps it is a case of bad karma or simply a matter of being more prone to life's little accidents, but I hit my head and fell hard this time around. Facedown on the bathroom floor, I watched my blood escape from me, spreading across the cool ceramic tiles like an oil slick, too bright and theatrical to be real. A scarlet river seeped into the grout, which will be murder to clean. The flow hit the edge of the bathtub and pooled like water behind a dam. I blinked, and in that instant, the blood became a secondary concern to the hole in the back of my head, not so much the fact of the wound, but the persistent sharpness of pain around the edges. Yet even the knot of it weighs lightly against the mysterious cause of my immediate predicament. I have an overpowering urge to reach back and stick my fingers over the wound to investigate the aperture and determine the radius of my consternation, but despite the willful signals of my brain, my arms will not obey, and I cannot alter a single aspect of my situation.

Which is: I have landed in an awkward position. My left arm pinned beneath me, my right extending straight out as if to catch something or break my fall. My legs and lower half stretched out in the dark and silent hall, and on the threshold, bisecting me neatly, would be my belt, if I were wearing any clothes. But I am, regretfully and completely, naked, and the jamb presses uncomfortably into my abdomen and hips. I have a hole in the back of my head and cannot move, although the pain is becoming a distant memory.

Just a second ago, I turned on the light, having awakened in the middle of the night to relieve my bladder, and something struck me down. A conk on the skull and my body pitched to the floor like dead weight. My left shoulder is beginning to throb, so perhaps it struck the edge of the commode as I fell. The bathroom fan hums a monotonous tune, and harsh light pours down from the ceiling fixture. Through the open window, the warm late-night air stirs the curtain from time to time.

Falling seems to have happened in another lifetime. Even as I tumbled, stupefaction began to gnaw at me and consume all. In that nanosecond between the blow and timber, my mind began to hone in on the who and the why. When the hardness struck bone, just at the base of my skull, an inch above my neck, when I began to lose balance and propel headfirst to the floor, my vision instantly sharpened as never before. All the objects in the room lost dimension, clarified, flattened as if outlined in sharp bold black, a cartoon of space. I saw, for the very first time, the cunning design of the sink, the way the dish and the soap were made for each other. The nickel handles curved for the hand, the faucet preened like a swan. A hairbrush, its teeth clogged with the tangles of many crowns, lay pointed in the wrong direction; that is, the handle was on the inside of the counter rather than the more conventional placement at the outer edge. A fine coating of mineral deposit from a thousand showers clung to the folds of the partially opened curtain, and one of the aquamarine rings had lost its grip on the deep blue plastic fabric, forlorn and forgotten on the rod. The floor sped to meet my face. Not just the pleasing geometry of tiles, but all the detritus of the human body, the hair and scruff and leavings, and as I fell, I thought a good scrubbing was definitely overdue.

Bathrooms are the most dangerous place in a house. With daily weather conditions approaching levels found in the Amazon, germs and other microbes flourish, and bacteria reproduce in unrelenting blooms across every moist surface. One could easily perish here. Seventy percent of all household accidents occur in this room and, in addition to hitting one's head, include scalding, fainting from an excess of heat and humidity, poisoning, and electrocution. Because we spend so much leisure and indulge in self-pampering—long soaks in warm baths, ablutions, digestive relief, perfuming our hair and bodies, scraping away unwanted hairs, polishing our teeth, trimming our nails, reading the funny pages—the bathroom seems as warm and wet as mother's womb, yet it is a death trap all the same.

My skin and bones smacked the floor with a kind of wet sound, and the pain shot through my cheekbone and knees and all the air inside my body escaped in a percussive puff. Bleeding does not alarm us until we see the blood. There is the famous story of a roofer who had accidentally shot an eight-penny nail into his brain with a nail gun. He did not go to the emergency room for several days until he began to suffer from severe headaches, but once there, doctors discovered the embedded projectile by taking an x-ray picture, whereupon he promptly fainted. Once the nail was extracted by surgical means, the headaches disappeared, as if nothing had ever happened. We must be shown evidence of our pain in order to feel the concomitant sorrow, but our joy comes and goes as it pleases.

By instinct, I reached for a towel to staunch the mess, but could not move. Not one millimeter. Not one grasping fingertip or one twisting toe. I could not even blink my one open eye. Given that I was facedown on the cold floor, even the expansion and deflation of my chest in the act of breathing had to be taken on faith. I believed I continued to breathe. My imagination, however, could readily float above my body, able to see the figure on the stone-cold floor and chalk an outline around the naked form. The thought occurred that someone might discover me there in the bathroom, and I would be embarrassed to death.

Just as that mortification set in, a noise in the room alerted me to another living presence. A little cough, not much more than the clearing of a throat, an *ahem* that changed everything. The existence of another soul in the room produced a strange sensation in my mind. I forgot about the wound, and all at once, the bleeding stopped. I could open and shut my free eye, and feeling returned to my extremities. Conscious of the elastic restoration of my body, I sat up, perhaps too quickly. My skull ached worse than any hangover, so I pressed my hands against the temples in order to steady myself. The cougher coughed again, this time from the vicinity of the bathtub.

He sat on the porcelain edge, clad in a terrycloth bathrobe, a pair of sandals keeping his bare feet from direct contact with the red puddle on the floor. His posture ramrod straight, the old man stared right through me. His thin bare legs hung like two pipe cleaners beneath the blue hem at his knees. In his lap, he clasped his hands together like a supplicant or a holy ascetic, and when the next cough worked its way from his lungs to his mouth, he lifted one bony fist to his lips. Jutting out from the collar, the rope of his neck strained to hold up his long head, and his face looked austere, like something by Giacometti, all severe angles, skin tight on bone, a hawklike nose holding up round rimless glasses, his eyes darkly colored of an uncertain hue but expressing a relentless sense of blinkless surprise. Atop his skull, a shock of silver hair brushed carelessly straight up and back, which added to his startled-in-repose appearance, and his ears stuck out like the handles on a ewer. When he coughed, small feathers escaped from the corners of his mouth and through the lattice of clenched fingers. Yellow pinfeathers wheeled in the air, then began to float like ashes to the tiles. A wan smile creased the lower half of his ruined mug for an instant, as if the cat apologized for swallowing the canary.

His face was like one of those I carried in daily memory, and I had known a younger version of it for many years. I could not be sure absolutely of his identity, and if he was who I thought, his physical presence and existence threw rational thought through the window. That his arrival did not surprise me can be attributed to the other startling events of the day, or perhaps he was not there at all, but rather some hallucination brought on by the concussion I had suffered the moment before. Because of the haze in my head, I put it as a question to the figure perched on the bathtub.

"Dad?"

He went into paroxysms again, that dry cough rattling up from his core, and clamped his hand over his mouth. Tiny yellow feathers popped out of both ears. "Excuse me, Sonny, but I have a powerful thirst."

Aware of the deleterious effects of moving too quickly, I eased up to my feet and held on to the sink for balance. I removed my toothbrush from the rinsing cup and turned on the tap, letting the water chill before filling the glass. The fanlight overhead played on the liquid surface, and some opaque sediment swirled and settled in the bottom of the clear cup, another reminder that a general cleaning of the room was in order. I turned and handed the glass to the old man, who had remained motionless throughout the whole procedure. He considered the contents for a moment and then passed back the water with a look of disdain.

"I never drink from anything in the bathroom." He motioned over to the toilet, indicating by dumb show some symbiotic connection via the plumbing. "Do you have anything else besides this swill from the sink?" His voice had an unbecoming plaintive quality. From historical antecedents, I inferred a preference for something alcoholic, and when asked, he nodded vigorously, a delicate smile pursing his cracked lips.

"I may have a beer in the fridge. Or a bottle of whiskey somewhere."

He raised his bushy eyebrows at the latter. "Smashing. On your way back, you may want to throw on some clothes."

The shock of again meeting my supposedly departed father, even an enervated version of the man I remember, made me forget momentarily that, except for a wristwatch, I was naked. On the hook screwed into the door hung a white robe, a constellation of fine red spots sprayed along the collar and one shoulder. I put it on and reflexively checked the time. It was 4:52 A.M. when I stepped into the hallway and out of the light and hum of the bathroom and into the darkness, which immediately compressed the visual stimuli that had set off the firing synapses. My mind cleared. With nothing to see and little to think about, I quite nearly forgot my purpose.

"I'll take that whiskey neat," the old man bellowed from behind me.

Cinching my belt, I moved ahead through a house as quiet as a grave. At the top of the stairs, I stopped and listened, and faraway came a sigh from someone asleep, so delicate it may not have been a sound at all, but only the thought or memory of a whisper from some other point in time and some space beyond the walls or perhaps within the walls themselves. I could not tell whence it came, so I delayed my trip downstairs and sought its source. Three rooms flanked the balustrade. Two bedrooms and a tiny office where the drafting table and drawings lived. The sigh might have been a puff from the computer, putting itself to sleep, but when I opened the office door, the room appeared just as usual in mad disarray, heaps of paper, rolls of plots and plans. On the dear computer, blank and quiet, a dark apple rested like a shut eye. I ran my palm along the edge of the desk, furring my fingertips with a coat of dust. Another sloughing noise crept through the walls, and I dashed over to the adjoining spare room, threw open the door, and discovered them.

The setting full moon cast a halo upon the bed. Some trick of mind allowed me, in that diffusion, to see with vivid clarity the fumble of colors and patterns, a swirl of quilts and coverlets of the most outrageous hues and designs. But I had forgotten, until that very moment, the strange naked women hidden beneath the fabric. They appeared at once and altogether, a floating cloud, flower and flesh, jumbling of limbs, hands, a bare breast, the curve of a hip, a half-dozen bare arms, skin and hair of assorted hues, some beribboned with garlands, others loose and unbound. Lips, faces at odd, unnatural angles. Eight women in a tangle, pretzeling bodies at rest. All but one of their faces were turned my way. One pair of eyes opened. Another blinked in my direction. The patterns on the blankets shimmered like colored glass in a kaleidoscope, stirring to life. The colors moved like a wave, the blankets parted like the sea. Another woman cracked alert and stared at me, caressed the shoulder of her neighbor as if to wake her, and I stepped back from the threshold and quickly shut the door. Someone sighed again, but I was not sure if this time it was not me.

Silence returned, and torn between wanting to open the door again to see and my panic over what might be there, I listened at the keyhole. Only the respiration of eight sleepers, quiet as kittens, soft as a baby's foot. A round of fierce coughing punctuated the new tranquility, and I pictured my thirsty father in the bathroom and a cloud of downy feathers swirling in the air, floating to the bath mat, sucked up to the fan, settling in the sink and commode. Right, the whiskey. Each step of the descent, I could not shake the image of those women. The sharp dissonance of patterns on the blankets, the swell of breasts and roseate nipples, a triangle of hair, a derriere turned and split perfect as a peach, faces flushed with warmth, eyes popping open as if they sensed my presence and suddenly sprang to life. The last woman, whose body lay outside the swirling colors, turned her face to the wall, and in that half-life made a crescent moon of her naked back. A film of perspiration clung to her dark skin. She resembled someone I knew quite well, though I could not place her name. Her utter mystery confounded me more than the others, whose faces revealed in the splendor of those few seconds some vestiges of intimacy. Yet I could not remember how they had arrived, what led them to my bed, why they had stripped themselves, where those richly hued covers had originated, and what, if anything, happened when I got up to empty my bladder a moment ago.

Each step seemed to take forever, as if my mind and body traveled at two different speeds. At several points along the journey, the goal escaped me, and once or twice I stopped, bound by a fog of confusion. The mental image of the bedful of naked women plucked at my cerebral cortex, but rather than clarifying meaning, the girls persisted as enigma. At the foot of the stairs, I stood still for a few minutes, trying to decide which way to turn and why. In the shambling gloom, a dark living object moved like a shadow met by shadow. A few seconds later, the cat unfurled himself against my bare leg, sending the thrill of memory straight from skin to spine. I whispered his name, and he mewed and ran away, a void in the blackness.

All the liquor bottles looked ancient and untouched, caked with a film of grease and dust. One shot short of full, the whiskey in brown glass sparkled with life when held up to the dim kitchen light. The skin around the circumference of the wound at the back of my skull stretched and tightened, as if the hole could close on its own, but the constriction produced a small double pain. For medicinal purposes, I took two glasses from the cupboard. On the way back to the staircase, I chanced upon my orange tabby cat again, eyes reflecting the moonlight. He purred at me from atop the DVD player, his tail roped over the glowing clock. I called his name again, and he whipped his tail, just enough for me to see the numbers 452. With a fingernail, I tapped the crystal of my watch.

Passing by the closed door that led to the bare ladies, I held my breath and could hear the cadence of their slumber. A floorboard creaked. Someone sighed again. A vision of mad ecstasy fluttered across my imagination. I tiptoed past the fortress and into the bathroom.

Motionless on the edge of the tub, the figure of my father sat in the exact spot. A tiny pinfeather stuck out like a flag from the prodigious wrinkle of his brow. He did not drain his glass in a single gulp as might be expected of the parched. Rather, he held the tumbler to the light, judged the liquid's clarity, sniffed its bouquet, rinsed his palate with a mouthful, and only then swallowed. The whiskey warmed him, brightened his eye, and raised the flow of blood to his pale skin. He sipped another mouthful and the dryness vanished from his breathing, and he looked almost alive. When he cleared his throat again, no feathers flew out of his mouth.

"Feeling any better?" I inquired.

With a sweeping arc of his free hand, he bade me sit down, so I rested myself on the closed lid of the toilet, face-to-face with the old fellow, our knees nearly touching. Between sips of his drink, he took me in with his stare, and the more he drank, the clearer his gaze became, so that by the time he reached the whiskey bottom, his eyes were as blue as fire at the heart of a candle flame. He iced me with that gaze, froze my brain, locked my tongue behind the prison of my teeth. I could do nothing but stare back stupidly and wait, just as I had as a child, until he deigned to speak the first word.

"The question is: are you feeling any better? That was a nasty blow to the brains."

I reached behind my left ear, but the wound had completely closed. Just old smoothness of skin and bone where once had been a hole. I strummed the spot, and it felt as if nothing in the world had happened.

My father shook his head. The blood, too, had been cleaned off the floor, and only red spots on my robe left evidence of the assault. I pulled back my fingers and checked for blood, but they were as dry as bones. My day was becoming more complicated.

"I'm feeling much better, thank you."

"Still," he said, "quite a crack to the noggin. Are you sure?"

"Tell you the truth, I'm not sure about anything. This whole day has been one inexplicable puzzle."

"The whole day, really? From the moment you woke till now? Until . . . what time do you have?"

"I'm afraid my watch has stopped."

"No matter." He poured himself another drink. "But you know, patience is its own reward, as you may have heard on more than one occasion." A low chuckle followed his remark as if he celebrated an original thought.

He had me there. Instead of stretching back in time, my power of recollection seemed cemented in place. I scratched my head, wondering if he had asked me a question. He poured himself another drink and said nothing. I thought to ask him how he came to be here, in my bathroom, a dozen years or more since we buried him, but I was afraid of his several potential answers.

At last he spoke again. "What do you make of the naked women?" He frowned at my perplexed stare, shook his head, and raised his bushy eyebrows. "Surely you remember those naked women in your bed?"

"Please don't tell me there's more than one."

"There's seven," he said, a randy grin curled across his face. "I counted."

"I counted eight, including someone that I may well know." I shook my head slowly, indicating the nullity of my consciousness.

"You seem to have forgotten everything."

All evidence pointed to just such a conclusion, but in reality, too many remembrances flooded my mind for any decent sorting and classification.

"I can understand forgetting being brained from behind; after all, you never saw it coming. And I can understand forgetting your old man," he joked. "But how could you forget the octet of naked women and how they got in your bed?"

The question awakened some ancient memory. All at once, time itself did not stretch this way and that, but it was as if that very second divided in half and halved again until the images rushed into my head the way the blood had rushed out. The women, of course, show up, arriving perhaps on bicycles.

"Today was an ordinary day in June, the kind that seems to exist permanently, coming around each year for centuries. Not too hot, not too cold. Harbinger of summer, last sweet fling of spring. When I came home today, there were seven bicycles out on the lawn, glowing in the sunshine like mirrors to the sky."

The thin man appeared to have ceased listening to my story just at the twist in the plot. Instead he focused on a spot just above my right shoulder, and at the same second, the light behind me changed ever so slightly and the room cooled by one degree. A presence had entered the bathroom, and my sixth sense tingled. As I swiveled my neck to see what lurked over my shoulder, the old man sprang to his feet and positioned himself between me and my attacker. "Put down that club," he ordered, and the raised arm lowered the weapon in a slow and resigned arc. He stepped aside and revealed one of the girls from the bed.

She had donned a yellow cotton shift that clung to her like butter on a corncob, and her arms and legs shone the color of strong tea. Her hair hung down in a black braid thick as the club she carried, and her eyes, set in the dish of her face, shone blacker still. The vision of her, perspiring slightly from her exertions and panting from the effort required by the heaving and lifting of the weapon, set my memory in motion. One of those faces to remember married to a forgettable name.

"My name is S'ee," she said, as if reading my mind, but she spoke in a language that lived on a shore distant from the center of my brain. Her exasperation she expressed in a frown, but fortunately for everyone's sake, she switched over at once to English. "But you may call me Dolly."

"A most unusual name in any language," the old man said. "Kindly refrain from swinging about that cudgel of yours. Someone could get hurt."

As long as a baseball bat but much thicker at the business end, the war club was hewn from redwood, and on the protuberant bolus at the head, the maker had carved a stylized animal in the manner of the tribes native to the Pacific Northwest. The creature symbolized some manner of carnivore, judging from the rows of sharp triangles lining both sides of a curved mouth and the madness of the wide-set eyes. I could easily imagine the terror caused by such a face rushing to hammer down upon the forehead of its intended victims. One might die of fear before being felled. It was a humbling weapon designed for crushing blows from which little hope of recovery existed, and the mere sight caused my head to ache again. Dolly modestly withdrew the club and hid it behind her skirt, taking care to keep her right hand firmly gripped around the tapered handle.

My father relaxed and collapsed like a marionette on his seat at the edge of the bathtub. I studied Dolly's face in a vain attempt to match her becoming features with those stored in the hard drive of my head, and though the search resulted in zero matches, she seemed a long-ago acquaintance accidentally erased from the files. Her black eyes revealed nothing but my own image, and her lips were drawn in a hard, straight line. She did not smile or frown at my monkeyish attempts to elicit any reaction, some sign that we were once intimates or friends.

From his perch, the old man said, "To what, may I ask, do we owe the pleasure of your delightful company?"

With her bare arm, she wiped the sweat from her brow, and in that gesture released the scent of rain and cedars, of dried fish and a musky perfume that opened my olfactory remembrance of bygone time. The old man cocked his head so the words might flow more easily into the trumpet of his ear. "You have a story for us? Do tell."

CHAPTER TWO

The Woman Who Married a Bear

Before his final daughter was born, a child he would never see, Yeikoo.shk' lived like a fish. During the last months of his wife's pregnancy, a steady, daily rain raised the waters over the banks of the creeks and streams. The trails flooded up to the village homes, and he laughed when the coho slapped their tails in the muddy pools at his doorway. Some mornings while his wife slept, Yeikoo.shk' stepped out of bed and grabbed the nearest salmon swimming on the floor, took out his knife, and slit it throat to belly, the long strand of roe glistening like berries at dawn. He would slurp the viscous mess in one long gulp, the eggs rolling off his fingers and dripping down his chin, and then throw the rest of the fish through the doorway into the street, the gravest sin. Raven and bear and the poorest of the clan fed on the corpses that floated away.

When the waters had receded, but still weeks before his final daughter's birth, the father-to-be traversed the forests to the village of Hoonah in search of spawning fish. The salty memory of roe on his lips enticed him like the smell of a woman. A few men had built a stone fish trap in the sea, and late that night, Yeikoo.shk' stole out under no moon, to borrow a few eggs. Even in the darkness, he could feel the slippery bodies wriggling in the rocks, and with delicate fingertips, he sensed the telltale bulge of a gravid female. He teethed his knife to free the huge fish. As he grabbed it by the belly, the fish snapped like a whip and with one quick blow from its tail, it knocked the blade deep into his tongue. Swearing through the blood and pain, he slipped and dashed his head against the stones as the salmon swam off. The men of Hoonah found him next morning, his blood and life drained through the mouth, running off with the tide.

"A sad story," the old man said. "Bad luck to the man who never meets his offspring, and sadder still for the daughter who never claps eyes on her old man."

I placed my index finger against my lips and indicated with a nod for the woman to continue uninterrupted.

After her father left it, the world welcomed his final daughter. Dropped to the earth from between her mother's legs, she was wet and slick as any fish. When wrapped and swaddled, she was perfect. Her parents had thought they were through with having babies and, in fact, had named the child that had been born before this baby Youngest of the Daughters. This child, when it came time to give her a name, was called Shax'saani S'ee—or Youngest Daughter's Doll, for she looked just like a doll, bound in her cradleboard, eyes wide and searching the cloudy cold sky as if waiting for someone to return. The four older sisters and five older brothers always thought of her as simply S'ee, and they spoiled and babied her all of her life, becoming little parents themselves, so that poor S'ee had to contend not only with five mothers and five fathers, but with her mother's people in the Frog clan, who treated her as a communal doll, perhaps out of sympathy for the widow with ten children. More than the others, she was a child of the village, but that does not belie the possibility that even villages can be as dysfunctional as a family isolated and on its own. She may have been better off with a little less attention.

When she came to know the true story of her father, S'ee laughed at the punch line of the man caught by the salmon. She had no fond memories—not even the sound of his voice or the smell of his skin—so he was no more than an illustrative figure in a moral tale, and thus of no consequence to her. Days and nights were spent at her mother's side, with her sisters hovering nearby and all the Frog clan at potlatch or beading blankets for their doll, a life in idleness, tempered only by the bitter rains of winter and the blackflies of short summers. As one by one the girls were married off, S'ee grew closest to Shax'saani Keek', the next youngest daughter. They went everywhere together from the beginning, and through the years Shax'saani led her doll over the hurdles of childhood, beckoned her into adolescence.

So it goes that these two sisters, young women of sixteen and thirteen, ventured forth one late summer morning to gather berries and talk of boys. A pair of dogs, Chewing Ribs and Curly Tail, accompanied them through the wilderness, trotting ahead to chase hares flushed from the brambles. The sun rose and brightened the sky to yellow, and the sisters soon wearied of their task and escaped to the shade, popping sweet berries into their mouths while they dreamt of their futures.

"They say you are destined for Man-in-the-Moon, who everyone calls just plain D'is, for his face is round as the very moon," S'ee teased her sister.

"Like an owl with a man's nose," Shax'saani replied. "Like a plate with two eyes and a bump in the middle."

"The moon in the man. He's not for you, sister. For you, someone handsome, but for me, someone strong."

"Someone like our father. Yeikoo.shk'."

Each girl fell silent at the mention of his name, as speaking of so foolish a man might disturb his spirit. Birdsong and the humming of insects relieved the silence. Far off Chewing Ribs barked at a passing curiosity, and had they been attuned to the other world rather than to their own emotions, they would have heard an ursine shuffling at the head of the trail.

"What was he like? Besides strong and stupid?"

Shax'saani glared at her and munched a handful of salmonberries. "Not stupid. He had charm. He would sing, and mother would swoon. How do you think we are five sisters and five brothers? Every time they heard that singing, the brothers and sisters watched for the furs and blankets to rustle, and if you counted the moons from the night of the song, you would only have to count nine months. And there you were, last time, little doll baby."

"So he was a great lover, but not so wise."

"Headstrong. Determined. When his father died, he stayed up three weeks straight to carve the totem. He would set his mind on a task, and it was done as he wished."

S'ee picked up her basket. "Like our brothers. Prideful." She was speaking not only of her natural brothers, but of her aunt and uncle's sons, the brothers of the clan.

Her sister rose and straightened her skirts. "Like us all."

They continued to forage, searching for the telltale flash of crimson or yellow among the green leaves, not paying any attention to where they were walking, when S'ee stepped, barefoot, in an unmistakable softness. From the smell of it, the pile was fresh and ripe with berries.

"Bearshit," she screamed. "Stupid stinking bears. Why do they have to take a dump right where people are walking?" She scraped her foot on fallen pine needles and sank to the ground. "Do they think they own the world? Bearshit, wherever and whenever." Snapping some leaves from a raspberry bush, she swiped at the excrement and swore under her breath. "Don't you know there are people here?" S'ee shouted, and her voice echoed through the trees.

Clamping a hand over her baby sister's mouth, Shax'saani grunted for silence, scanning the forest for any movement and listening for the slightest sound. "You have no sense, Dolly. What if the bear should hear you?"

"I hope he does," she shouted. "Then maybe he won't shit where people might step."

"Some respect, okay? It's their world, too." Struck by the moment, she giggled and said, "Come on, sister, we'll find some water to wash off your stink, or our mother will think I've brought home a sow."

"Who are you calling a sow, you fat, lazy bear?"

They ran off hand in hand to a stream, pulled off their clothes, and jumped in the cool water. Gnats circled in crazy clouds above their heads, and the sunlight shone in radiant waves across the rippling water. The two dogs came crashing through the brush, barking and yapping at the girls. From the bank, they whimpered and paced impatiently, not daring to jump in. Shax'saani yelled at them to scat, and S'ee splashed handfuls of water at the mutts until they gamboled away. Moments later, the leaves stirred again and S'ee thought the dogs had returned. But when the branches parted, she shrieked at the figure approaching out of the greenness, as if emerging from her dreams into the bright northern day.

"Cover yourself," she called to her sister, and they dipped in unison until the water rose to their waists.

The man strode to the edge and showed his empty hands in greeting. He paused to consider them, as if he could not find his tongue or was perhaps fearful that speech might break the spell. The sisters watched him watching them, and he was a fine, handsome man. Young and naked to the waist as they were, his skin darkened by the sun, and his features carved like a totem. He did not seem of this world, not Tlingit at all, nor of any tribe they had encountered in their travels or those from inland who had chanced upon Hoonah. S'ee looked into his eyes and, for the first time, felt her heart betray her mind.

"Don't be afraid, sisters. I heard laughter and splashing in the water and only came to see what fun I was missing."

Shax'saani scolded him. "You've seen what there is to see, now go. On your way. We are not your sisters."

"Aren't we all children of the earth? How is it that you bathe so early in the day?"

Before she could be stopped, S'ee trumpeted her explanation. "My feet were dirty, and you know why? Stupid bear doesn't know to leave the trail to take a dump." She stood, water dripping from her body, and held out her foot so the man could better see where she had stepped.

"A clean foot now, and beautiful. What is your name?"

"I am called S'ee."

"Come with me, little doll, for there is something I want to show you about that bear."

Her sister's hand grabbed her arm, holding her back, but the man on the shore kept talking in the honey voice, and she was sorely tempted.

"You can both join me. There's nothing to fear. I'm as harmless as a marmot."

"I wouldn't go with you if you were a marmot talking to us. Shoo. Go away."

"I'll turn my back and you can put on your clothes. It's just that I heard you before, shouting insults at the bear, and there is something you should know."

S'ee wrenched free from Shax'saani. "I want to go. Nothing ever happens to me." Drawing near, she whispered into her older sister's ear, "Besides, have you ever seen such a man before?"

"A man is a man is a man. Don't go, Dolly. What will I do without you?"

"He has cast a spell—"

"I will not let you go. I will send the Tlingit men after you."

"No need to send out the search party, for I will be back by nightfall. Aren't you the least bit curious about the world?"

They turned to the man, who stood with his back to them, as promised. He pawed the ground with one foot as if to keep his eyes from wandering back to the women. S'ee waded over and slipped into her clothes in one swift motion, the wetness of her skin already spreading patches where her body curved. From the cover of the stream, her sister watched, dumb and helpless, as S'ee climbed ashore and went to the man's side, touching his arm to alert him to her presence. Glancing back once, she followed him into the brush, and when the leaves ceased moving, Shax'saani muttered a prayer that she might one day see her sister again. As she dressed and gathered their baskets, she heard Curly Tail and Chewing Ribs return from the opposite direction. The dogs worried the spot where the man had stood, noses mad at the scent, whimpering softly to each other.

With the point of an elbow, the old man caught my attention through my ribs. "Do you know," he whispered, "the single biggest regret of old age?"

I glared at him, encouraging silence.

"It's nothing to do with making more money or taking better care of the old body, nothing like that. The old folk say their biggest regret is not having taken more risks. Can you beat that?"

"Will you let her tell her story?"

"That girl wasn't the least bit afraid." He smiled and shook his head. "You've got to admire her chutzpah."

Every step of the way, he hummed or sang to her, keeping two paces ahead through the dense woods and walking shoulder to shoulder as they crossed open land. The sun blazed in front of them as they began their journey, hung above their heads at their midday repast, and followed their backs as they climbed into higher country, the cedars tall and so thick that S'ee no longer smelled the salt water. She had never known the air without the sea, and its sweetness among the pines frightened her, but she marched on, enchanted by the man's songs. They made camp when the sun dipped below the timberline, and while S'ee gathered dry sticks for the fire, the man disappeared into the brush. As she warmed her hands over the new blaze, she was startled by his return. He held up a rabbit by the hind legs and grinned at his own prowess. While the dinner cooked, he told her stories, starting with the traditional tales of how the Tlingit came into the world, but stranger stories, too: "The Man Who Killed His Sleep" and "The Salmon People" and, strangest of all, "The Woman Who Married an Octopus."

"And it was the eight arms that convinced her to live under the sea and marry the octopus. Two arms to hold her feet, two to hold her hands."

He circled her wrists with his fingers and then let her go.

"One arm to stroke her hair."

She felt his hands comb her hair but averted her eyes from his.

"Two arms to hold her breasts."

With the lightest touch, he cupped her breasts and smiled when she did not flinch. The crust of the rabbit skin blistered over the crackling fire. S'ee looked at his eyes. "And where went the eighth arm?"

He put his left hand between her legs and drew spirals along her skin, pressing lightly when he reached her lap, but despite the gentleness of his touch, he frightened her with the heat radiating from his palm. He withdrew his hand and began another story, and after they had eaten, he bade her lie near the fire while he retreated to the opposite side for the sake of modesty. As they rested beside it, the fire gave up its spirit and breathed its last as embers. But S'ee could not sleep.

Darkness weighed more heavily amid the tall trees. No starlight, the moon missing from the sky, and the firs pressed all around, their branches palpable against her skin when a breeze chanced by. The typical sounds of home were absent. No gulls crying out in their dreams. No ocean sighing upon the shore. No sisters tossing in their beds. She heard the man rise, creep across the needled ground, the heat of him preceding his body's arrival. Clamping shut her eyes, she could tell he was directly above her, waiting. She willed him closer. Shivered when his hand touched her hair, then her face, but she waited, wanting and dreading the moment, and only when he said her name did S'ee open her eyes and rise to his embrace.

Her first cognition of the act had come from watching the village dogs casually mounting one another out in the plaza, but still she did not understand its purpose and only thought they were at play. Once walking home with her mother, she spied a bull moose fresh from his rutting, and when she asked her about the huge erection between his legs, S'ee's mother could only laugh. "Reminds me of your father," she said and steered her away. Her older sisters talked about sex in general terms, as some abstraction to keep men happy. In reality, she had no idea of what was about to occur.

S'ee pulled her shift over her head and was naked, and the man felt the softness of her skin, his hands in arcs and circles, kneading flesh, and turning from him, she slid and knelt, squaring her shoulders, her hands firmly on the ground. He whispered her name again and drew close behind her, stroking her legs and back, his nails tracing the contours of her body. He kissed the small of her back, ran his mouth along her spine, and licked the sharp blades of her shoulders. One hand snaked between her legs, stroking, and with two fingers he parted her labia, and then he began to kill her. Or so she thought, he was stabbing at her, forcing a blunt club into her vagina. With each thrust, she cried out and clenched her muscles, slowly realizing that this weapon was a part of him. He called to her from far above, singing her name, then began grunting in rhythm. S'ee craned her neck but she could only make out his shadowy bulk in the pitch. He pressed against her head, and she thought she felt his mouth draw wide and full of sharp teeth. No longer able to hold up her own weight under his, S'ee folded her arms and crumpled facedown to the ground, and he covered her with his body, warm as a thick blanket against her back. With a shudder and a growling roar, he came inside her, a liquid heat that filled the void, as viscous as menses. In her shock, she felt nothing more than the pressure to pee and lifted herself at once so that he would move his dead weight off her. He kissed her again between the shoulders and withdrew.

Scrambling away to a respectable distance, she squatted on the bare earth for a long time. When her muscles finally relaxed, she felt a burning sensation and caught the foulsweet smell of him streaming in her own water. The darkness pushed against her skin, chilling her. She felt her way back, desperate to find the man.

"Where are you?" she whispered.

A huff of air escaped his mouth as if he was snorting in his sleep. She followed the strange sound, her hands searching the darkness till she brushed against his hair. Thinking she had accidentally bumped his head, she mumbled an apology and when she touched what she thought was his chest or shoulder, he seemed extremely hairy, as if he had donned a fur coat.

He drew her into his arms, and she curled her back against bare skin. The puzzle over the difference between the hirsute and smooth man kept her awake well into the night. Toward dawn, he woke, aroused. Knowing what was to happen, S'ee could relax the second time and was almost enjoying herself when he climaxed and quickly rolled off her back. They spooned together in the gathering light, and she began to think of the beautiful man as hers.

Over the next two days, they traveled deeper into the forest as it rose toward far-off mountains. Each hour, the climb became more difficult, the spruce and cedar taller and thick with crepey moss, the air dense with moisture. She had never seen the inside of the rain forest or heard the riot of so many songbirds when the sun drilled a hole through the canopy. Rustling in the underbrush or the fleeting shift of shadows worried her to his side, and when a creek crossed their trail or a fallen cedar blocked the passage, he took her hand in his and led her safely. They passed the time by telling each other stories, and when she recounted the legend of her father, Yeikoo.shk', and the death by salmon, he hung his head.

"Sister salmon," he said, "was upset. Take the eggs and leave the fish is not only wasteful but shows a lack of respect. What kind of man was this?"

"A proud man. A foolish man."

"And who do you favor, little doll, your mother or your father?"

She giggled as if he were merely teasing her. His ways seemed less alien the more time she spent in his company, and they were only apart before the evening meal when he left her alone to make a fire while he scared up some dinner. Once each day, he made his toilet in the privacy of the deep woods, and each time that feral smell returned with him, as powerful an odor as that she had tried to wash away at the stream with her sister. How long ago it seemed to her. S'ee could not abide the man's scent when he first came back to her, could not imagine how so sweet a man could smell so awful.

But at night she forgot about those momentary distractions. After their first sexual encounters, it was she who initiated their intimacies, crawling to his place when the embers ashed over, kissing his face and chest until he could no longer resist, and they would roll over and he would cover her back, huffing and panting, and she, her pleasure growing, would wait for that final exclamation, a roar of release that filled her with the sense that they were to be together this way for the rest of their lives. And as he lay beside her, S'ee pictured taking him home to meet her mother and sisters, her cousins, the whole clan and moiety. She could envision their faces, filled with wonder and jealousy over how she could have landed such a king salmon, for he was nothing short of a marvel, strong, handsome, a powerful spirit.

He led her through a gap between two mountains and stopped at the apex of a descending trail, shielding his eyes against the sun as he scanned the horizon. She leaned her head against his shoulder and could feel the excitement pulse through his skin. "There," he said, pointing to a distant meadow carved in two by a winding river. "There is my clan." Perhaps the sun blinded her or perhaps she knew not what to expect, but S'ee could make out nothing more than brown specks shuffling along the shores. But for his sake, she feigned excitement. It took all day to traverse the valley, and when they arrived under darkness, she could see no more than a few feet in front of her hands in the rising river mist. As they crept among what seemed like logs, she could hear their heaving snores and was careful not to disturb their sleep.

When they had found a place to be alone, he held her in his arms and said, "Don't look up in the morning. At dawn, if you rise first, don't look up among the people."

I wonder why he says this to me, she thought, but after he made love with her, S'ee forgot, and lost in her dreams, she fell asleep and did not remember his warning. When she woke with the sun, she reached behind her for the man and her fingers touched fur. She rolled over to face him, but he looked just like a human being. Propping herself by the elbows, she rose to a sitting position and sought out the other people sleeping on the ground, but all around them were brown bears, dozing in the sunrise. She stood and pivoted on her toes, finding bears in every direction she looked. The man, when he put his hand on her shoulder, frightened her, but he was still a human being in her eyes.

"Don't be afraid," he said. "These are my brothers and sisters. They won't hurt you. And even though you insulted me—and all bears— back in the woods with your sister, no harm will come to you. Despite your curses, I have fallen in love with you. I want you as my wife."

"Gunalche'esh hó hó," she said. *Thank you very much.* "Ax téix'katix'áayi i jeewu." *You have the key to my heart.*

Next to me, the old man cleared his throat to commence another observation, but I hushed him with a curt gesture and a doleful glare.

They were in every other respect honeymooners. He did not wish for her to see him as a bear and only appeared that way under cover of darkness—when he climbed upon her back, he was as he was. At all other times, he seemed a beautiful man to her. She loved the basso trill in his voice, the black depths of his eyes, the way he stretched his spine when he stood to smell the wind. He brought her squirrel and ptarmigans and wild berries, salmon fat with eggs, and fixed a home away from the other bears in a den dug into the southern face of a hill. Her back and shoulders were hatched by his nails. His loins ached with the frequency of their wild couplings. That first winter, as he hibernated, she lived on teas sweetened with sap and the moles and mice that blundered into their cave, and she did her best to fend off boredom by imagining his dreams. Her compensation was that he held the warmth of the world in his chest, and from the time of the first frost to the thaw, she hunkered through the winter beneath a coat of fur. S'ee was happy with him, the one she called simply X'oots, or Brown Bear.

As that first winter blustered outside, she felt the alien kicks and stirrings in her womb, and until summer arrived again, she worried whether their child would be grizzly or Tlingit. X'oots roared when the baby emerged, pink as sockeye, a human boy. She named him Yeikoo. shk' after the father she never knew. With one child at the breast, but growing like a cub, she became pregnant again that fall, and in her second summer, a girl child arrived among the bears. The two small children kept her mind busy so that she forgot her people, and it can be said that love's first blush fools each of us into believing we are changed from the person we once were. Only when she was not thinking about it could her past creep in like a fox to the den. When the sun became a stranger again, X'oots prepared to find a new home, and the thought of him snoring for months while she tended to their babies filled her with dread. One morning while the children crawled and batted around a piece of dry fish, S'ee asked her husband, "Who will help me while you sleep all winter?"

"We will all sleep," he grunted. "You, me, the babies."

"No, the babies never sleep, or when they sleep I am wide awake, and when I am tired, they want to nurse or play. Your boy is all teeth and thinks my nipple is a piece of bark. And there you are in the corner on the best branches. You never open an eye, the baby could be screaming, foot caught in a hole, and now there are two."

"I am a bear, Dolly, and they are half bear. We will sleep, and you need to stop gnawing the bone. It is the most natural thing—"

"For you. But I am Tlingit, not a bear."

"I should have known when you cursed me for your own mistake—"

"And I should have listened to my sister and never followed you."

The image of her sister persisted the rest of the day, as well as the spirits of her other sisters, her mother, all of her people. Homesickness infected her heart as surely as a fever, and a delirium of memories beat like a drum through the night. She could not hold her babies without thinking of the other children in the village, running, as she had, half naked in the muddy square, chasing a three-legged dog, kicking an old seal bladder, torturing one another with spruce switches. As she stirred a stew of moose meat and roots over the fire, she saw in the steam a vision of fog rolling off the sea, enveloping the houses in the village, the people moving through a cloud, calling out to unseen cousins, and hearing the happy sound of their replies. When X'oots lumbered to a corner for his night's sleep, he left her alone with her sorrow, and while everyone slept, she cried for the first time since coming to live among the bears. Resentment broke the seedskin of her heart and shot its vines through her veins. Her husband's snoring disgusted her, and he smelled of wet fur and stomach gases. She began to plan her escape.

As the threat of snow deepened, X'oots decided that they needed a bigger home for the two cubs now wintering in with them. For three days, he searched the mountains for a suitable space, and upon his return, he ordered them to pack at once. They traveled higher into the hardscrabble country, and when the family reached the half-excavated den, he told S'ee to gather spruce branches for the floor while he finished digging. Instead of picking up fallen ones, she climbed a nearby tree and broke off high branches, enough for three beds. When X'oots saw what she had done, he confronted her.

"Foolish woman, why don't you do as I say? Now any hunter can see by the treetops that there is a den nearby. I asked you to gather only those branches already on the ground."

She shrugged her shoulders and brought their daughter to her breast. Grumbling at every step, he moved them higher up the mountain face and dug so furiously that she thought the whole hillside would come tumbling down. After their first night in the den, she snuck out early in the morning to rub her scent against the trees, and while the others slept, she made a bolus of clay and moss and spit, and rubbed it all over her skin, then rolled it down to the bottom of the mountain, knowing that, if they were looking for her, the dogs would find her scent among these pebbles and the men would figure out what she had done.

As it happens, as they must, the men of the village had been looking for her for three years. Every spring, her mother's sons and nephews would prepare for the hunt. In the first year, the brothers reached only as far as the place where the bear and S'ee had camped on their first night, but they had not figured the spell of the herbs and leaves properly, so they had to turn back. In the second year, the brothers reached as far as the place where all the bears had slept by the river, but they had made weak medicine, and the spirit abandoned them again. But come April of the third year, the boys knew how to fast for eight days with no water, how to work the leaves and not go crazy, and how to carry the dogs to search not just for brown bear, but for their sister as well. For one month, they had allowed the dog named Chewing Ribs to sleep in S'ee's old bed, among her clothes and treasures, so that he would carry her smell in his nose no matter how long the search might take.

Snows turned to the rains of spring, and the bear and his family watched from the dryness of the den. The babes crawled across the floor, harassing a field mouse, and in a corner S'ee chewed on a moose sinew to soften the leather, for she was planning on surprising her husband with new moccasins. All morning he sat at the opening trying to see how the seasons changed, and he startled her by breaking off his vigil and ambling over to her side. He sat next to her on a blanket sewn of rabbit skins, his arm looped over her shoulders.

"Restless?" she asked. "Winter's almost over, so cheer up."

"It will be the youngest one, I think. The youngest brother will kill me."

She dropped the leather to her lap, cast a quick glance at their children, and asked, "What are you talking about?"

"I dreamt last night they are coming for me. Not a dream, but a vision. Your brothers are coming to kill me. The youngest one will shoot his arrow true. They are coming soon."

"You must have eaten some bad roots to upset your stomach and give you such nightmares."

"I love you, Dolly, even if you don't still love me, but you must be brave and pay attention. Your brothers are coming, and I want you to do something for our children."

Regret seized her suddenly. She moved to his side, but he did not look at her, so she circled behind him and wrapped her arms around his chest.

"Don't be afraid," he told her. "I will not kill my brothers-in-law. After they have filled me with their arrows, have them put a fire at my head and feet. Ask them for my skin and stretch it on four poles so that I can watch the sun come out from hiding each morning and send my spirit out each new day to protect my family."

"You mustn't speak such foolishness." She kissed the back of his neck.

The afternoon's wind blew strong and carried the smell of dog, and X'oots paced on the ledge in front of the den. He stood tall, then shuffled back to her. "Where are my knives?" he asked. "I need to put my knives in my mouth." She understood this to mean he was to change into a bear, something he never did in her company during daylight. He would show them his teeth and claws. Thoughts of her brothers' safety escaped from her mind, and he read them in the air.

"Don't worry. I could kill them one by one. A slap to the face and they would tumble down dead, but I would not hurt the boys, Dolly, because that would hurt you, too. But where are my teeth? Perhaps I can scare them away?" He changed into a bear.

Below, the dogs snuffled through the spruce litter and the balls of earth and moss with her scent that she had rolled down the hill, and the man who followed the dogs shielded his eyes from the sun and searched for the opening to the den. Two brothers circled round to approach the bear from above the entrance, scrambling over the scree, and kicking stones like tiny avalanches. X'oots and S'ee could hear them coming through the ceiling.

"Remember . . ."

The other hunters clambered along the steep face, the dogs ahead on the scent, pausing with ears cocked for a sound. Chewing Ribs wagged his tail and roared toward the cave, oblivious of the grizzly, bounding between the great bear's legs into S'ee's arms. Concentrating on the approaching men, X'oots missed seeing the little dog entirely. S'ee hushed him, pushed his tongue and head away, and pinned him behind her back against the cave wall, wriggling, tail thumping a tattoo on her spine, but Chewing Ribs stilled when the bear peered into the darkness at the commotion. "Did one of their dogs come in?" X'oots asked.

"No, it was a mitten. One of the brothers threw it in to see if you were home."

When he could no longer stand the suspense, the bear poked his nose out of the cave and gave himself away. The brothers below gave a shout, and the brothers above drew their arrows. X'oots rolled back into the den, searched for his wife and children in the half-light, and spun just as the first arrow glanced off his shoulder. Soon the air whined with arrows. The bear roared and staggered, hit a dozen times, fought into open air and skidded headfirst down the rocky incline till he lay supine. He lifted his head but knew he could no longer move, then lay still and breathed his last, the edges of his fur fluttering in a passing breeze. The dogs danced around the corpse, yelping triumph and crying over their fear of death. One of the brothers braved a kick in the dead animal's ribs, and seeing no spirit left behind in the bear, he lifted his chin to the skies and began to sing.

Hearing the human voice, S'ee uncovered her children, demanded they keep quiet and gather the arrows that had missed the mark. With a strip torn from the remnants of her dress, she tied the arrows to the dog's sides and pushed him out of the den. When the arrows came back to them this way, the brothers stopped their chanting and knew that something human remained in the hole above them. They found her naked and cowering with two young children in the darkest corner of the den.

"Woman, how did you get here?"

"I am S'ee, don't you recognize me? And that was my husband you have filled with your arrows." She pushed the men aside, scrabbling down the rock face on all fours till she embraced the bear, dusty and bloodied, his spirit gone. The insects swarmed on the wounds, crawled into his mouth and lifeless eyes. She buried her hands in his fur, grabbed the broad muscles along his arm, and keened her lamentations. Young Yeikoo.shk' raced to her side, desperate to comfort, and when she saw the boy, S'ee thought of the babe left in the den and knew at once what she must do.

"Go to my mother and have her send clothes for me and my two babies, and we will need moccasins for the journey home. You are to leave the head and skin whole and drape it across four poles, facing the east, so that X'oots may see the break of each day and watch over his children."

The brothers did as she instructed, and the dogs cried inconsolably at the bearskin stretched out above them, as if alive. The brothers took the meat but would not eat it, building a pyre as soon as they left the valley, burning his body atop a mountain. For six days, S'ee woke to the sight of the bear watching the sunrise, and she cursed him for his pride.

The babies grew hungry and dirty from her neglect, and by the time the brothers returned, the children ran and hid from them. The youngest brother, the one whose arrow first pierced X'oots's heart, gave S'ee the dress and moccasins sewn by her mother, and the customary shape and style of those clothes assuaged her grief. The thought of leaving her husband behind she could not endure, so she ordered her youngest brother to roll up the skin and carry it on his back for the journey. She dressed and combed her hair with her fingers, fed the children, then followed her brothers out of the valley of the bears.

Whispers reached her ears before the family arrived in the village. Those children were not Tlingit but half bear, and S'ee herself had nearly become one from her long familiarity with the grizzly in the rain forest. Even her mother and sisters looked upon them with wonder and suspicion. S'ee overheard the eldest tell Shax'saani how their sister smelled like an old brown bear no matter how many times she bathed. At potlatch, the tribal leaders huddled together and murmured to one another as they watched S'ee's children roll and tumble in their rough play. Rumors fell like rain: that they were wild at heart and when of age would run amok; that their teeth were sharper than a marten's; that in one minute flat, they could dig a hole deep enough to hide in; that they preferred to shit on the pathways, their stools gleaming with jewels of undigested berries. By early summer, a few mothers advised their children to stay away from S'ee's "cubs." The snub spread from house to house, family to family, infecting the clan.

"I am sorry, sister," said the one who had ended up marrying D'is, the moon-faced boy, "but your boy and girl are wild things, ruining my sons."

Those children who did play with Yeikoo.shk' often goaded him to pretend to be the bear. He had grown over the summer, big enough to crawl under his father's skin and shuffle a few steps under its weight. Older boys, no longer children but not quite men, forced him to put on the bear so that they might wait in the brush and pepper him with head-less arrows. The ones that hit the hide fell harmless to the ground, but many missed the mark and struck him on his bare arms and feet.

"What happened to you?" S'ee asked her son after one such hunting game. He refused to answer and did not cry when she rubbed balm into the welts and scrapes. Petulant, he slept by himself in a corner of their house, refusing his mother's comfort and his sister's entreaties, but after that night, he did not play with the village boys any longer and often wandered off to laze away the day on a tree limb or, when the salmon ran, to thrash about the water and the rocks. Three young boys spied him there waist-deep among the rapids, a salmon flapping in his jaws. His behavior and rapid growth did not go unnoticed among the adults. Shax'saani shared the gossip with her sister: "They say he is slow, your boy. A man's body but a child's mind."

Yaan.uwaháa, the daughter, fared no better. She rapidly outgrew all of the other infants in the clan, spurted past the toddlers and young girls, and by summer's end resembled a ten-year-old version of her mother. She had a keen sense of smell and was forever hungry, and more than once, her aunties had to chase her from their kitchen door with a broom when she came looking for a second breakfast. While they shot no fake arrows at her, the girls in the village showed less mercy than the boys. Group by group shunned her. Most nights she curled beneath the bear-skin, missing her father, crying herself to sleep as the rain beat on the roof.

The two children ran away in early fall and were missing for one week. S'ee's youngest brother, the one whose arrow found X'oots first, tracked them to a nearby hill where they had dug a fresh den. He found them asleep, curled beside each other, the bearskin their pillow, and he bound their hands to a long rope and led them back to camp like recal-citrant dogs. The tribal council's fires burned late that night, and in the morning before anyone else had risen, Shax'saani visited S'ee's bed and shook her gently awake. "My sweet little Dolly," she said. "Come walk with me, and we'll see the sun sneak over the trees."

They strolled to the bayshore and watched a pod of orca swim past, leisurely hunting their breakfast. "When you followed the man, I was afraid for your life, and when you didn't come back that day or the next or many months, I was heartbroken. There was no one to talk with anymore, and even after D'is—"

"Man in the moon," S'ee giggled.

"After he married another, there was just no one left in the world. I still longed for you, and not a day went by that I did not think of you."

"I missed you, too, sister."

"When the brothers arrived with the news they had found you and then fetched our mother to send your clothes, my torment was over, and when you first walked through the door—after the smell off you cleared my head—well, my heart leapt like a babe in the womb."

The last of the whales passed by. Behind them, the sun had cleared the firs on the far shore and now light sparkled across the waters. Shax'saani took S'ee's hand in hers. "But you brought those two wild things into our family, and the men have made medicine to judge what must be done. They say the eating of the flesh of brown bear is now taboo. Only black bear may be taken for food. You may stay with us, Dolly, but your son and daughter must be exiled to the rain forest, for our own safety. They will become grizzlies one day and will surely kill a Tlingit, maybe your brother, maybe your sister."

S'ee considered her sister's words, picked up stones from the gravelly beach, and held them while she thought. "I am glad that no Tlingit will eat the brown bear from this day on, and X'oots would be happy, too. But they are my boy and girl, Shax'saani. Banish them and you banish me. Forever."

"It's not me, little sister, but the wisdom of the village."

Taking her sister's hand, S'ee forced open her palm and transferred the pebbles to her. The sun shone full on the bay. From over the ocean, a thin band of clouds gathered on the western horizon. She walked away without looking back, walked on through the village stirring with life, down the pathways that rained with salmon in the months before her birth. She walked past her mother's home without stopping at the door, past her sisters' homes, past her brothers' homes with rack after rack of herring drying in the sun. Her children stirred when she entered, and she sang as the breakfast cooked on the fire, and when they had finished their meal, S'ee told them they must go.

Because the heavy skin baked in the sun, they took turns wearing the burden and bore to the shady side of trails where the mosses made the trees look like green ghosts. The trip took much longer than S'ee had hoped. Journeying with her children over the same path traveled years ago with her young husband, S'ee felt the circle closing. His spirit lingered, fell with the rain, rose with the mist. She recollected the tender way he cradled the babies in his arms, the grin on his face when he brought back to the den some treat like cloudberries or the warm haunch of a moose. The wildness of his eyes and how it freed her to be wild. The way he'd dip his head into a river and come up gleaming, the water racing off his skin, glistening at the tips of his hair. How fat he was in December and rail-thin come April. How he roared with delight when she bucked her hips beneath him. How he chose to be a man for her.

In the valley of the brown bear, she could find no one willing to speak Lingit with her, and every word had to be filtered through the ears and mouths of her children. Her sense, after their brokered conversation, was that the bears blamed her for the death of X'oots and for bringing the humans to the rain forest, and that while her children were welcome, she could not stay among them.

"I remember," little Yeikoo.shk' said, and led them back to the den where it had happened. S'ee could barely stand to be on the hill where her husband had lain, but they had no choice but to winter in their old home. Her son was the first to leave, stealing away one night in the middle of a snowstorm, mad with hunger and confinement. Word came later that he had headed north and inland to be away from man, and some say Yeikoo.shk', the grizzly, terrorized the Yukon, fierce and smart as any Tlingit, had many cubs with many bears, and could not be tracked. Her daughter Yaan.uwaháa lasted that first winter and into spring when the cubs born that February emerged with their mothers, and the maternal pull forced her slow independence from her own mother. She was gone for good three years later, the victim of another party of hunters who, mistaking her for a true bear, shot her dead just above the headwaters of the river. One of her two orphan cubs survived, and three years later found one of the hunters sleeping in a grove and dispatched him into the next world with a swipe to the neck.

S'ee lived a long time above the valley of the brown bears. In warm months, she moved among them freely in an uneasy truce, teaching herself their ways, but they gave her wide berth. No custom or commerce would be shared. She could only watch their new families from a distance. The fragrance of foamflower and coralroot every June reminded her of the husband she had loved and lost, and in the long, cold months of winter, she dreamt of him, clinging to his skin, straining for his disappearing scent in the shabby fur. She felt as if she was becoming a bear herself as she aged. At twenty-five years, she could no longer stomach the sight of her own reflection in the water, and at thirty, she felt as if she had lived forever in the purest silence, bereft of all language she had once known. When the spirit came upon her to sing out her sorrows, the sound of her voice frightened her. On cold clear nights with the blanket draped across her shoulders and hooded over her head, she huddled on the rocks to count the stars, constellations strung like roe against the northern sky, though their names were long forgotten, praying that their lights would go away, waiting for the world to end.

CHAPTER THREE

Bicycle Girls

Lost in her story, and feeling strangely responsible for its outcome, I averted my gaze from her shining face and studied her toes, which heretofore I had failed to fully appreciate. Her feet were beautiful and soft, as if newly sculpted, and I scrutinized their graceful lines, imagining all kinds of sensual activities, with a devout attention.

"Bup-bup-bup-bup." The old man sang out a warning, and I looked up at the war club poised in her two hands lifted over her head and the mad glee in Dolly's eyes as she prepared to smash my bean. With startling alacrity, he jumped next to her and shot out his right arm like a piston and clamped his fingers around her wrist. For all his ostensible frailty, the old bugger displayed an iron grip, and the club did not budge an inch.

"Vengeance is mine," she hissed between her teeth.

"Sayeth the Lord," he corrected her, nose to nose. "You are excluding one-half of the quotation, which utterly destroys its intent. Partial quoters are the scourge of debate, and selective citation is the refuge of manipulators and charlatans. 'Vengeance is mine; I will repay, sayeth the Lord.' Leviticus, I believe. Not your place, surely, to seek revenge, and I encourage you to surrender this shillelagh of yours before it accidentally goes off. Honestly, Dolly."

Locked in immortal struggle, the two figures bristled with tightly wound energy, like two locomotives butting on the same track. Whispers of steam escaped from the corners of their clamped lips and the curlicues of their ears. Had I the slightest reflexes, I would have joined him in the fray, but some flaw of courage or instinct kept me stationary, a stoic witness to both my threat and my salvation. She panted and sneered at him, the anger pulsing at her temples. A small but distinctly metal squeak followed the tightening vise of his five digits, and she cried out sharply and let go the club, which landed with a clunk in the sink. Cradling her wrist, Dolly slumped back against the counter. She would not look at me and turned her head, though the bitterness in her eyes reflected in the medicine cabinet mirror.

My head ached again, either from my ancient wound or the complex implications of her story. The pain was not only in my mind but also two or three spots on my chest and shoulders, phantom aches of an empathetic nature. Given the tenor of her story, I found myself oddly drawn to X'oots, the bear man, and his self-sacrifice, and totally appalled by the dog Chewing Ribs. Somewhere in the house, my gentle cat practiced his diffidence. Behind the cabinet doors, pharmaceuticals promised hope and relief—an aspirin, perhaps an ibuprofen. As I was debating over which to take, it occurred to me that an hour or so must have passed since Dolly entered the room and began her story. A sleeping pill might be in order, but I did not want to take one too close to the hour I was supposed to be awake.

"Excuse me," I said to them both and left to find the correct time. Without a word, they waved me off into the darkness just outside the bathroom door. The overhead light, which I had certainly turned on when fetching the bottle of whiskey, had been flicked off. Playing with the switch illuminated nothing, and the hall dripped dark as a tomb. From the bathroom, snatches of conversation rode the air. ". . . the sixteenth century," she said. He asked, "So what have you been doing with yourself these five hundred years?" Surprised by the old man's question, I looked back and saw him standing close in front of her, nearly pinning her to the counter, his left arm extended and his palm against the mirror, and Dolly leaning back, her shoulders squared, a coy smile parting her lips. Distracted by their flirtations, I tried to fathom how and why I was alone in the darkness. The light switch failed again, but the household stairs could be negotiated even if I were blind. Closing my eyes, I grabbed the railing and lifted my toes over the abyss.

With no difficulty, my left foot found the first step, and my right the second. Thirteen to go. I remembered the thousands of journeys up and down these stairs, and the house was a great relief and shield against the aura of doom that had threatened me since I fell. In *The Poetics of Space*, the philosopher Gaston Bachelard wrote, "A house that has been experienced is not an inert box. Inhabited space transcends geometrical space." As long as I am in my own house, there is nothing to fear, for it seemed to me that the house could be trusted when everything else posed nothing but mysteries and questions. I love the *Poetics* and at the architectural firm where I work, when no one else was around, I would read it furtively at my desk. The book sort of just landed in my hands at a moment of particular despair over my future as an architect. For the life of me, I can't remember who gave it to me. Someone important, who has escaped through the hole in my head.

Despite the utter gloom of the staircase, I made it to the bottom step without tripping and killing myself. The switch downstairs had been positioned between off and on, so I corrected the situation and illuminated everything. Pupils dilating, I stumbled into the kitchen. On the digital clock built into the stove, I punched in one minute on the timer and waited. While the digits did not regress, the beeper sounded its alarm after the appropriate interlude. Certain that some electromagnetic catastrophe had stopped the power, I went to the window but saw nothing but the dead of night, not the least hint of the dawn that should have been there. I scratched my head and suppose I would still be doing so had not a sudden clunk, like a chair losing a leg or a Tlingit woman staving my father's skull, sounded in the room over my head.

The urge to flee tugged at the hem of my bathrobe, but I ignored it as one might a pestering child. This is my home after all, and I was determined to figure out what was happening here. Moreover, I had the dim sense that I was missing someone else in the house, someone dear to me, whom I should protect from harm. I could not quite place her name at the moment, but my short-term memory may have been hampered by the concussion. Someone I love may have been at risk, so I screwed on my courage and marched to the stairwell, now shrouded in darkness again, with the switch at the top stuck in the middle position.

More comfortable in the shadows, I took the steps in pairs and reached the top in no time. All doors leading off the landing were closed; behind each, dead silence. I thought of one other clock and entered my office, sat down at the desk, and pushed the start button on the computer. The flash of light and trumpeting notes that the machine played as it came to life nearly scared me to death, and I momentarily wondered if the noise had awakened anyone else in the house. A blue screen gave way to corporate graphics, and the icons popped into view like blooming flowers. In the corner, the time remained fixed, and though I could not fathom why it was still 4:52, I was pleased to know that all of the clocks in the house were in sync.

Laughter from the bathroom filtered through the ventilation ducts, a disembodied titter that sounded like a happy memory, and upon opening the bathroom door, I discovered its source. Dolly sat on the edge of the tub and standing inside, behind her, the old man ran a brush through her long black hair. Mild surprise registered on their faces for an instant when they saw me, but then they resumed without the slightest show of modesty. He appeared to be taking some sensual pleasure with each stroke, and she relaxed under his gentle attentions. Pangs of envy poked at my stomach.

"Was there an accident?" I asked. "There was a thump a while ago, like a chair that toppled over."

"A chair would be a provident addition to this room," he said, and now caressed her hair with his fingers. "Where have you been all this time? Dolly here was regaling me further with the erotic version of the 'Woman Who Married an Octopus' and other tales of her Tlingit cousins." As he spoke, his eight arms encircled her and withdrew when he came to the end of his sentence.

She opened her eyes, and on her night-black irises, two moons rose and arced across the sky, changing phases from waxing to full to waning to no moon at all. "Old stories are best," she said, "for love and truth."

"I'm not sure what to make of your story," I said.

The old man stepped out of the bathtub and interjected himself between the girl and me, and then he laid a fatherly hand on my shoulder to walk us a few paces farther. She began to sing in her native language a kind of chant that, while confined to a repetitive rhythm and scale, possessed a certain hypnotic charm. Under the sound, he spoke in a confidential whisper. "I wouldn't bring up the matter of personal tragedies, Sonny. She's been brooding over a grave injustice forever, and it's quite a grudge."

I replied in a soft voice, "But what's that got to do with me?"

"Best to change the subject." When he winked, a third eye appeared on the shut lid. Not a working eyeball, but rather a crude approximation in the thick line drawn by an eyebrow pencil or similar crayon. "Follow my lead, if you please." He ushered me back to the toilet, and we resumed the positions of our initial encounter, the sole exception being

Dolly's presence on the bathtub edge to my father's left. She finished her chant to polite applause. "You were telling me," he spoke in a loud, artificial voice, "about the bicycle girls."

My face wore a befuddled expression, a look I have seen more than once in official photographs of myself, such as those required for a driver's license or international passport, the kind of picture snapped at the subject's worst moment.

"The ladies and the bicycles," the old man insisted. The furrows of his brow, carefully etched by decades of worry and frustration, deepened to a row of crevasses, and the blue of his eyes whitened to ice. "The naked women in your bed. You were about to establish causation, man. Surely, you are one of the most forgetful little bastards I have ever met."

His clues, verbal and visual, sparked nothing. Dolly rolled her eyes. "Mind like a sieve."

"Holier than a Swiss cheese," he rejoined. "An empty beehive."

"A bucketful of holes."

Rubbing the bristly top of his hair, the old man was at a loss.

Dolly assayed another. "He uses a salmon net when fishing for herring."

"Well done," he said. Raising her fingertips to her lips, she played the coquette. On her left eyelid, the same third eye had been drawn, to match the old man's. What antic games, I wondered, occur in my absence?

He turned to me. "Your line, I believe, was 'When I came home today, there were seven bicycles out on the lawn, glowing in the something something sky.'"

"Mirrors to the sky," I said. "On the chrome handlebars and bumpers, a million little suns reflected. But that's all I can remember."

"The opposite of the elephant," Dolly said, "who never forgets."

"A leaky cauldron."

"An unwound clock."

"The cyclical amnesiac." He bowed.

"Well played." Now, she addressed me directly. "Whenever I lose something, I always retrace my steps beginning with the end and ending with the beginning. Or until what's missing is found. Shall we look for your mind? What is the last thing you can recall?"

Falling. My face smashing against the bathroom floor, a tsunami of blood sweeping across the tiles and washing against the white wall of the tub. "Checking the time on my watch."

"Good," the old man said. "Progress. So, you arrive home this afternoon at eight minutes till the hour and there were seven bicycles heaped in a tangle of spokes and chains, and then what happened?"

"I have never seen bicycles out in front of the house, but then again I am not usually here at that particular hour during the workweek, and I thought perhaps they belonged to some schoolchildren who left their bicycles and ran off to play. They looked chained and locked together, the bicycles, not the children, and there were no children. Nobody was about despite the fineness of the hour, the warm weather returning. You can feel the change in the air."

"The days are on the mend," the old man said.

Dolly patted his leg and deposited her hand upon his knee. "June. The birds and the bees, the scent of love a-bloomin' yet again. Maybe you left work early because of an assignation?"

"An illicit rendezvous with delight," he said.

"Love in the afternoon," said Dolly, and the point was won.

I was reasonably certain that was not the case, though this talk of love whipped another chain of images through my brain. A woman, surrounded by fireflies, and something I intended to do or say to her. Love, yes. I knew I was in love with someone I could not quite remember. On a spring afternoon when I opened the door of a taxi for her, she touched my arm and smiled when she got in and drove away. After she was gone, she lingered in the air. A different story unfolded in the pea of my brain.

"No, not a tryst. It was a day like every other single day. I was a bit fatigued and bored, nearly fell asleep at my desk, so having nothing pressing, I left the firm a little early. The bicycles waited in the yard in front of the house all jumbled together like a knot, and I just stood there wondering when the singing began—"

"Singing bicycles!" Bemused, he clapped his leathery hands together, sending a talc of dead skin puffing like a cloud.

"Not singing bicycles, singing from the windows."

"Even better," Dolly said. "Singing windows. Or maybe it was the house itself that was singing?"

Bachelard would allow such a possibility in his poetics, but only in a metaphorical sense, with a house so imbued with happiness that the windows could be said to sing. He speaks of the archetype of the "happy house" that young children reproduce when asked to take up their crayons and color their idea of home—a square with a peaked roof, two windows and a door that suggest a face, and around the house a tree and flowers, a line of blue at the upper border to indicate the sky, and a sun, often smiling, radiating from its tucked position in the corner. While there is no good reason to dispute the existence of a companion to such an idealized fantasy, say, a singing house, a family place so full of joy that it hums a musical score night and day, I have never seen or heard of such a space. My own childhood, as my father would attest if he is indeed my father, lacked all such song, unless one includes the dirty ditties he would sometimes croon late at night after arriving filled to the lid with drink.

"You have misunderstood me, or perhaps I did not make myself clear. It was like the opening prelude of some fantastic play or movie, and the house itself was the theatre. I was on the lawn marveling at the bicycles' sudden strange appearance and studying the light reflecting off the chrome when I heard someone singing from one of the open windows. 'Vissi d'arte' from *Tosca*."

"Verdi?" the old man guessed.

"Not so. A common mistake, but I believe it is Puccini."

"If you two are going to hide behind the screen of dead white male Eurocentric cultural references, I will take my skullcrusher and leave."

"Apologies. The actual composer is not as important as the song, and the song itself is not as crucial as the singing. And it only truly gains significance through the hearer."

The old man enjoyed my gambit, for he nodded vigorously and sprang to life. "A word is not a word until it is heard."

"A soprano floated out the melody and drew me in note by note." My audience of two appeared mesmerized by my story, for their jaws gaped and their eyes widened in anticipation. A cool breeze or, rather, an intake of air behind me tickled the short hairs on the back of my neck, and the scar tissue from the earlier hole constricted. Had a window been opened in another room to cause a sudden backdraft?

"Do you trust me?" the old man asked.

A preposterous question. Even when alive, my father earned no such confidence. Trust him? I was not sure that I even believed in his existence at all or, indeed, that he was my father and not some conflation of my imagination. A larger-than-life character from the stage. Come to think of it, my father had hazel eyes, and my inquisitor's eyes were quite blue.

"Come now, Sonny, no time to dally. If I give you the word, will you follow without reservation, no questions asked?"

"The word?"

"A command, boy-o. When I issue an order, do as I say at once, for your very life may depend upon it."

Beside him on the edge, Dolly nodded her agreement.

"Yes, I trust you."

"Good lad. Now, one, two, three . . . duck!"

I squatted immediately as above my head a projectile creased the air and smashed into the opposite wall. An irregular corona of cracks radiated from the impact against the shower tiles, and anchored deep in the center, a pointy barb of a small harpoon. From the direction whence the weapon had been chucked spewed a fount of the vilest invective. A young woman, hardly more than a girl, swore and cursed like a sailor and stomped her feet in fury. "Whoreson dog, blot, canker! Blast to Hades, I've missed."

Framed in the doorway, she shook with rage, balled her hands to fists, and agitated her head till her dreadlocks clumped and swayed like a custodian's mop. The bottled anger had nowhere to go, so out it fizzed in tears and spittle. Blood rushed to her face, darkening her complexion against the orange chiffon nightgown that twisted round her lanky frame, and when she stomped, her long legs looked like fence posts being driven into a peaty meadow. Though her frenzy obscured her features, her tantrum reminded me of such a display witnessed long ago. However, I could not place the exact location, time, or person. I turned back to confab with my associates, only to find them inspecting the spear attached to the wall. Dolly thwacked the shaft with her hand, and the vibrations caused a droning bass hum, which confirmed that it was indeed stuck.

"Hither, child," the old man said. "Come dislodge your harpoon and apologize."

"A pox o' your throat," she hissed. In three long strides, she marched into the full light of the bathroom, and beneath the tempest of her light brown hair, her green eyes darted upon the current occupants. As she walked past me, her upper lip curled into a sneer, and then she braced her foot against the tub, took hold of the weapon, and pulled. Small hills of muscle rose on her biceps, and with a great grunt, she extracted the double-flued point from the ceramic. The old man reached for the harping iron, and she handed it over without further complaint.

He touched his finger to the prick of the point and pretended it was razor sharp. Although the mere handling of the tip would not draw blood, the weapon looked fearsome in his mitts, and my eyes darted back and forth between the barbs and the barbarous woman who had tossed it headward in my direction. Hiding behind that matted hairdo, she resisted close scrutiny. Another tile, loosened by the impact, fell and shattered on the bottom of the tub.

"You could have hurt someone with this," he said. "Not a child's toy to be flinging about willy-nilly. What do you have to say for yourself, maid of the sea? Who or what are you, and why have you attempted to pin my man to the wall with your javelin?"

"Some call me by my Christian name of Jane," she said. "But I am known by many names, all of which result from my most common surname."

"Shall we guess?" the old man asked.

"Somers," Dolly said. "Gates. Newport."

"Go on, then. None of them fellas. Just take a look, and you'll guess."

The old man scratched his chin as he looked her over head to toe. "Tanglehair? Beanpole? Skinbone?"

"Long," she said. "I am often called Long Jane Long on account of my height." Raising her heels from the floor and straightening her back. "Though he may know me as Long John Long."

I confess I had no idea what she meant. I knew no Longs, John or Jane, nor could I determine why a girl would have both male and female names. There was something unforgettable, however, about the way she talked, or should I say the quality of her vernacular, an accent faintly British as if she was trying to hide or reveal her origins. The old man held on to the harpoon like a bishop's staff by the cathedral of the tub. Dolly settled in by his side, and I attended next to the toilet.

The tall woman opened the spigot on the sink, closed the stopper, and filled it with a rush of clear water. Dipping a long finger through the surface, she changed the colorless liquid to a briny blue-green and, stirring with a single digit, she created a miniature sea of sorts, waves and whitecaps, spindrift gathering like soapscum at the porcelain edges. We three witnesses peered into this ocean and beheld a miniature vessel, like a ship escaped from a bottle, beating against the swale and foundering in a storm. The old man brimmed with glee and beseeched her to begin the tale. "Go to, go to."

CHAPTER FOUR

The Woman Who Swallowed a Whale

Eight weeks out of Woolwich and seven since they left Plymouth Harbor in the glories of an English June, in the year of our Lord 1609, bound for the settlement at Jamestown in Virginia, the good ship *Sea Venture*, under the hand of Sir Thomas Gates, Admiral Somers, and Cap'n Newport and bearing the souls of fifty and one hundred men, women, and children, storm-wracked and separated from the other ships of the fleet, found itself in a watery hell. The houricane blew for four days, the clouds spit and lashed and covered both sun and moon in turn. Lightning crackled over the top of the mainmast and raced down the spars, the admiral's flag on the mizzen stiffened in the constant wind, and the wild and wasteful ocean swelled and made to swallow them. Every jack pumped belowdecks, the oakum seals peppered with holes large and small, till the leaks threatened to let in the whole Atlantic. It were Mr. Frobisher, the ship's carpenter, who suggested that the seams might be plugged with beef and biscuit, ten thousand weight in all, from the ship's stores. The common mariners and servants stripped naked in the water so as not to shrink their blouses from the salt, and only one, Long John Long, the cabin boy to the ship's pilot, refused to part with a single thread on his back. He was a beautiful lad, fair of face, and all of fourteen years, and not a hair on his cheek.

Master Ravens, the pilot, himself stripped of waistcoat and blouse, called out to his boatswain over the thunder. "Speak to th' men. Full to't lest we turtle or split."

The swain, bald as a coot and red with exhaustion, turned to the crew and gentlemen united in the cause of life. He roared over the tempest. "Yare, ye salty dogs, make haste and heave to."

No sooner had the command left his lips, all was forgot. The engorged sea spat up a wall of water that like to fall upon their heads, and so it did, washing o'er the starboard rail, and swept the decks bow to aft, filling the *Sea Venture* from the hatches to the spardeck and knocking the helmsman from the wheel. The whipstaff swung like the tail of a dog and when he tried to grab and still it, the helmsman was batted nearly into the pitching waves and by the mercy of Jesu was not rent asunder. The cabin boy upon the deck bent like a crab and scuttled to grab the helm, holding on for dear life, and were it not for that quick action, the ship and all would have sunk to the bottom of the sea.

She dipped a finger into the sink and twirled the water, making a whirlpool, and the tiny ship caught in the vortex spun like a top. I began to feel dizzy and wished she would stop.

The admiral hisself, she went on, came dripping from the hold, drown'd as a cat and to his knees in the saltwater. Those who had gained their feet gathered round. "We are quenched but not besotted, and if I am to die, I shall not perish below as in a box but under God's wide skies, in the company of these valiant mariners and my good friends." He raised his fist to the thunderclouds. "Blow ye winds and crack, give us your best, and shew ye can best these fine Englishmen."

Straining against the wheel, Long John Long listened with wonder, thinking the man a bloody fool with his false pride spewing from his mouth like the black blood of a dragon. "Men," she said under her breath, for the cabin boy was a girl, as surely you have guessed by now. She was on the cusp of the change and bound her wee breasts with a linen strap, but for ere else could easily be mistaken for a boy. "Men and their vanity, as if every jack was a stalwart son of the King. And where was he now? Could James himself still the heavens and escape such a storm?"

That night, the fire came and danced across the waves, leapt upon the deck, and tarried upon the spars, slipping up the rigging not yet torn to shreds. What the Greeks called Castor and Pollux and the French name Saint Elmo's, and every sailor knows the light foretells the changing of a storm and a shift in fortune. Friday, the sixth day of the storm, the morning revealed their fortunes had turned indeed, and for the worse. Listing to starboard, the *Sea Venture* groaned once and nearly all hope was dead. The captains and pilots clambered to the decks and bellowed orders to unrig the ship and throw o'er everything that threatened to pull them down. Trunks and other luggage were cast into the sea. Hogsheads of oil and cider and butts of small beer were staved and the barrels heaved away, and with a sigh, she lifted and righted.

"Lad, we are near finished." Ravens clapped a hand on Jane's back. They stood side by side at the stern, watching a cask of wine bob over the waves. "Cap'n Newport would have us chop down the mainmast, and surely, without sail, we would founder should this wind ever abate."

Two gentlemen and a lady joined them for a moment's respite at the rail. They were discussing among themselves how much of the sea had been pumped through the ship since the storm had begun, with Mr. Strachey arguing forcefully that the crew had quitted at least one hundred tons of water. The morning was nearly spent, and in the fabric of the storm clouds small holes and tears appeared, letting in a weak sun. One of the gentlemen passed an open bottle of spirits down the line, and even Jane drank deeply. This is my final hour, thought she, and I will take my leave of this world and steady on for the next. She cast her eyes upon her fellow passengers, all salt-sick and sore, hungry and thirsty, spent beyond endurance. As in a dream of no end, they had baled and pumped till the ropes and sinews of their arms and legs felt stretched and snapped. Even the crew, seasoned mariners all, wearied of the unending tasks and made ready to shut hope in the hatches and commend their souls to the sea. A pair of ladies sat in the corner and wept, and only Somers remained on watch through the wretched morning. 'Twas well after ten of the clock when the admiral leapt to his feet and cried out, "Land!"

All rushed forward to see the spot he had claimed, and there beyond the waves, a lump of earth appeared, and soon enough the very tops of the trees danced in the breeze. Jane went up the rigging with Mr. Chard to unfurl the sail, thanking God the while that the captain had not prevailed in his unholy plan to chop down the mainmast. The lead line was thrown and seven fathoms called, and when next ordered, the depth had fallen to four fathoms. The *Sea Venture* barreled to the shore, and Somers itched to run her aground to safety, when the ship hit white water a half-mile out and crashed into a reef, and she braked. Men, women, and all not tied down lurched pell-mell about the deck to the terrible wrenching roar of timber caught fast in the ragged coral. She would not go now no matter which way the wind did blow. Jane raced belowdecks to see the water pouring through the gash like blood from new wounds.

"We are bitten and will be chewed by the wind and the tide," said

Frobisher. "As sure as a dog fastens to a bone, this ship will never come undone."

"Murtherin' God," said Edward Chard. "To be so close and yet so far."

Great moaning prayers rose from the men and women, cries of despair and shock, and then as one, the company shoved aforedecks, bound for the ship's boat, a panic racing from person to person, be they gentleman or sailor.

Aready at skiff Master Ravens, saber drawn against assays. "We'll none of that, my good cur, but wait for orders from the admiral."

Somers parted the crowd and restored order. Eight mariners were commanded to man the oars, and the passengers arranged by class and taken over the water to the shore, the gentlemen and ladies first. Those who stayed on board cursed their lot, but once the little skiff turned back and beat against the waves, a sense of relief accompanied it. Over the course of that afternoon, one and all were transported, and then the men came back for the ship's stores, what seeds and provisions once bound for Virginia, the unspoilt food and drink, even the ship's dog, Crab, tho he be anything but crabby, made safe. Jane was among the last, arms thrown around the mastiff's neck as they were rowed the half-mile, but even with all her might, she could not stop the beast from leaping into the surf, desperate at last for land and deliverance from their deathly ordeal.

"A dog," the old man interrupted her. "A dog is the very man for displays of vertiginous exuberance. You can read their nature in their wagging tails."

Jane scowled at him, crossed her arms.

"I have often wondered," he said, "how much better off we humans would be with a tail at the end. An appendage that would betray our thoughts and feelings." Dolly jabbed him in the ribs with her elbow, and he blushed. "But do go on, my dear, with your tale."

To say that they were grateful to be on terra firma diminishes the wonder found on those islands, which the navigators and more experienced seamen knew at once to be the Bermudas, which some call Brendan's Isle after the Irishman who found it a thousand years ago, and what some call the Isle of Devils, so named for the rumours of monsters that linger there. Be that as it may, the company gave praise and thanksgiving to the Lord, and the Reverend Bucke led the evensong, reading from the *Book of Common Prayer,* while in the distance, beyond the breaking waves, the *Sea Venture* bucked, a sentinel in the ocean and symbol of all that had been abandoned, home and hope, a terrible monument to their ordeal and survival. Jane watched till the last light and the rising of the moon and stars, wondering what had become of the rest of the fleet bound for Jamestown, whether the other ships were lost, too, or lay at the bottom of the sea, or had somehow endured the tempest and rested safely in the promised land. Master Ravens found her alone on the strand and sat beside her in the moonlight.

"We have been blown off course some one hundred forty leagues," he said, "but by Jove, we have endured all, and all shall be vouchsafed. You must have faith." There was a note of disbelief to his words, a coloring that showed he was not above false promises. At the sound of his voice, she buried her face in her hands and wept. Ravens laid a fatherly hand upon her shoulder. "Come, boy, and sleep by my side. We'll have work to do in the morrow. For if we are to quit this place, we must build ourselves a boat."

Having little prospect of a passing vessel, the crew set about salvaging what they could from the ruined ship, sending men in the longboat to pick clean the ribs of wood and sail, iron and goods, even the bell itself, in order to fashion from misfortune a smaller portion of luck. Carpentry on the new boat began in mid-August, just after the skeleton of the *Sea Venture* broke into bones and scattered or sank. The men had decided to transform the skiff into a vessel capable of traversing the week's voyage over open waters to Virginia, and out of the remains of the old hatch, a deck began to take shape under the watchful eye of Mr. Frobisher, the ship's carpenter, and those not thus engaged endeavoured to make a small village for their needs, for tho the days were fine if hot, there is no place like a house for a home, no matter the circumstance.

The island was a paradise in every other regard, and for their feast and respite, fresh water and food were soon found. Fish abounded in the waters off the shore, and could be had by means of gigging a sharp stick, or later, a net was sewn from scraps of rigging, and when dipped into the water, it would return a bounty of mullet and rockfish and pilchard. Lobsters could be had by hand, tho quick hands were needed, so as not to be bit by their claws. In time, sea turkles arrived to lay their eggs upon the sand, and they could be plucked and eaten raw, and the turkles themselves, when stewed, produced a toothsome meat neither fish nor fowl tho never foule, and one large creature could feed them all for three meals in turn. Wild hogs, abandoned no doubt by earlier visitors to these isles, the Spanish or Portuguese or Irishmen perhaps, were rounded up in a most ingenious way. Mr. Chard had discovered a herd of swine rooting through the forest and that night, he lay down with them, next to the boar, and when the hog began to snuggle close, he grabbed its leg, held fast, and tied him with a rope, leading sire and sows and piglets back to our encampment as if Chard were the king of all hogs. Crab, the dog, kept his watch over the pen we built, and the hogs were bred and slaughtered in turn when the survivors tired of lobster or fish. Admiral Somers ordered a garden to be tilled with English seed, and within ten days, the first sproutlings shewed their green necks, tho the muskmelon and peas and onions never bore fruit, for the plants themselves were eaten by the multitudes of birds and creeping insects. But berries flourished on low bushes, and the fruit of the palm, when boiled, reminded many of English cabbage. Mr. Chard discovered that the palm leaves, when crushed and fermented, made a drink not unlike port wine.

"Have a taste, boy," he said one evening near the end of their first marooned month. Seated on the corpse of a felled cedar, they were enjoying a moment's peace at the end of ten hours' labor. Just at the waterline, they watched the rising of the moon, the appearance of the constellations one by one. Chard, like so many of the men, had failed to don his blouse, and his suntanned chest, brown as a beetle, glistened in the failing light. His whiskers and beard had grown so that when he spoke, he looked like a bear or some other fabulous beast. She took the cup from him and drank deep till the liquor spread across her belly and crept into her limbs.

"That's the stuff, lad, that will rid all cares and make you forget all about old England. *Precious stone set in a silver sea,* my arse."

The palm wine roared to her head.

"I, for one, am glad we are here," Chard said. "Glad of the storm. Glad to be off that ill-met ship. I don't care if we ever leave here. I am sore sick of the sea, cooped like a rat belowdecks, never your own master but bound to serve men of no sense, men who sail into the cheeks of the wind at full sail. Half-wits and knaves who like to drown you in their vainglory. There's them who pull the yoke." He poured another cup of wine for John. "Fish aplenty, the sun on your back, no crowds jostling and bustling. If only I was my own master, then I would show them as fools they be. For want of coins in England, but here, lad, here there is no king, and all can be had by a man's own labor. Here a Chard can be a lord, and a lord no better than a Chard. Here now, drink up, John, and be glad you are a free man. This mash will put a beard on you yet."

John nodded at the good sense of the argument, tho the wine toyed with her mind until all reason, indeed all feeling, escaped. The stars lost their places in the night sky and the white sheets atop each wave rolled in and then pulled away so fiercely that she feared the blankets would reach and drag her into the sea.

Like a great bellows, Chard yawned and drew a deep breath. "No more talk of kings and knaves tonight, for such fancies sit heavily upon the soul, and hope is more tiresome than a day's labor. I take my leave with my bottle and bid you good night till the morrow."

A crab emerged from a hole in the sand and began to fan the air with its great claw, its eyes twisting on their stalks, first one and then the other, and fascinated by its display, John laid her head upon the sand to watch more clearly. The little crab was the color of the sand itself and difficult to see in the moonlight, but she strained to catch every motion, and in so doing, fell asleep, rocked in wine-soaked slumber by the sound of the endless sea. How long she slept, she could not say, and when she woke 'twas as from a dream, or more than a dream, for the first thing she saw was the master, Mr. Ravens, seated beside her as the sun peeped over the edge of the Atlantic. And the first thing that she realized was that she had been stripped of her blouse and her bindings unwound, and then her shirts hastily thrown over her again. Bare-breasted, she knew, despite the thrumming in her head, she had been found out.

In all modesty, without so much as a sideways glance, Ravens spoke as soon as she stirred. "I am sorry. When you did not come to our home last night, I worried for your safety and set about the woods looking for you. And finding you here on the beach in such disarray, I shook and shook to wake you from your stupor, thinking you ill at first, rather than in your cups. You lay here in a pool of water, as if washed in by the waves, soaked in your own drops from the drink and hot night. I thought it best to cool you when you would not wake, for some fever or ague was surely upon you, and when I saw. . . . Who are you really, girl, and why have you hidden your true nature?"

Jane struggled to sit but every motion made her giddy and un-well. In time she managed to turn her back and dress herself. "Master Ravens, I have served you well these past months. I pray you not un-cover me to all. Keep my secret. There was no other way to come to Virginia than in some employ, for my mother is but a serving maid in a house named The Moon and the Seven Stars, and my own dear father left this world when I was but nine."

"And how long have you played the boy?"

"Cap'n Newport," she said, "came into the inn where my mum keeps us in chambers overhead. I heard him talking to the mariners there, a joint of mutton in his hand, saying he needs a crew of able men for an expedition to Virginia to save the company settled there from their penury. I found these here breeches of my older brother who had left home and, being in the habit of listening to the sailors' tales, was able to convince Newport I was fit for cabin and to wait upon the pilot or some other navigator. Had I known, Master, of your kindness and good nature such deceit I never would have parlayed, but I feared to be found out and thrown to the whales or sharks or shut up in the dark belly of the *Venture*."

"Foolish child."

"You will not uncover me now, Master Ravens, I prithee. I promise to make myself known in Jamestown."

He faced her, the light behind him creating a halo around his head. "You are a bold sprite. Tell me: is your brother soon to follow to re-claim his pantaloons?"

She laughed, and in so doing, began to think that he would not tell a soul after all.

"I came to find you, John, if John you be, tho surely not so—"

Brushing the sand from her arms, she confessed that her Christian name was Jane.

"Long Jane Long," he chuckled. "I came to find you for I am going away this very day. They have closed up and made safe the boat, and we sail on the tide. Had I not seen you thus, I would have asked you to accompany—"

"But I can still join you. Nothing has changed."

Henry Ravens gripped her by the shoulders, forcing her to look him in the eyes. "No, you cannot go. Intrepid as you are, you are still a woman, indeed a girl. But fear not, I shall keep close your confidence until we are all joined in Jamestown. Now, give me a kiss, boy," he said, "for good luck." And she kissed him on the cheek for the first and last time.

Eight men set out on a bark of aviso for Virginia on the twenty-eighth of August, being a Monday, to the great excitement of all those marooned, but the longboat returned on Wednesday evening, having attempted to find safe passage around the reefs from the north and from the southwest. They made to sea again on the first day of September, following the course that brought the *Sea Venture* into the bay, hoping to make way in open water. "If we live," Ravens said to the assembled company, "and arrive safe there, I shall return by the next moon with a pinnace from the colony. Light beacons each night thence to guide our ship safely to you."

Four weeks later, Long Jane tended the bonfire on that first night and for many nights afterward from the highest spot on the islands. By day, she watched the horizon when she could, ever hopeful, all through October and into November till the December moon, but no bark appeared, and to no eye, nothing but sea and air. What became of Ravens and the seven sailors no one ever knew.

During this time of waiting and watching, work began on another ship, tho divers mutinies took place among the mariners, some of whom were irreligious and of secret discontent, to spread disquiet regarding the colony in Virginia. Six men made themselves outlaws and outcasts by plotting to steal a boat and live by themselves on a nearby island, but no sooner had their conspiracy been hatched than the cock crowed, and all were banished from St. Catherine's Beach. Only by their petitions through Mr. Strachey would they be readmitted to the company by the mercy of Sir Thomas Gates, the governour. In January, a Mr. Hopkins hatched a plot with others, and he was arrested and placed in manacles. Were it not for pleading his wife and young childers left behind in London, he, too, would have been ensconced forever. Lastly, a man named Robert Waters fell into an argument with a Mr. Edward Samuell over the matter of a poor-cut timber, and it ended when Waters struck a shovel behind Samuell's ear and killed him. Gates ordered the two men, murdered and murderer, to be bound together and a guard of six attend them, but despite the horror of the sin, the guards cut the rope and led Waters into hiding in the woods beyond.

It was Mr. Chard who first approached Jane about being the go-between. "We need someone who won't be missed, lad, and someone who can be trusted. Take this food and follow the trail to the clearing where first we found the wild boars, and there turn east and travel about one hundred steps where you'll find a bower, and behind the palms, there is a cave, and in that cave, you'll find Robert Waters. Go to it, boy, and be quick and silent as a hare. You know Samuell had it coming."

For two weeks, she crept about the woods at morning and at night, through the winter cold and wind, to Mr. Waters a-hiding in the cave. The darkness so thick and the man no more than a shadow, she did not find him first but rather he found her, sneaking up and grabbing her, clamping a hand over her mouth. "And who be this?" he snarled at her and lifted his fingers so she might answer.

"Long John Long. I've come to bring your supper."

"Set it down, boy, and sit where you are. Move not." Waters fell upon the food, and in the pitch black of the cave, his slurping and chewing sounded like a rough beast or monster. "Tell me," he said between bites, "what news. Am I to be stretched?"

"They look for you, Mr. Waters, but cannot find you. You are hid as in a dog's belly, and the good men of the crew will not let Gates hunt and hang you."

"Zounds, child, and why should I be? For it was no crime but an accident."

"That's what they all say. Mr. Chard and the other mariners. They say Samuell provok'd the blow."

"Edward Chard is a good man and a stalwart judge. Would that he, not Gates, were king of this island."

So Long Jane played the go-between, a secret kept within her bigger secret of girl disguised as boy, bringing food and news to Mr. Waters. He often kept her long in the cave, anxious for some conversation, desperate for reprieve, and within two weeks, the governour relented, and Waters was freed. "I shall not forget your kindness, John," he told him. "There will come a day when you are repaid."

And while Gates later granted Waters and the other mutineers clemency, not all escaped his government. A man named Paine was later hanged for some offense, justice meted swiftly, and Mr. Waters felt the phantom rope for weeks afterward. Six in all remained forever on—or should it be in—the island: besides Mr. Paine and Mr. Samuell, there were Jeffery Briars, Richard Lewis, William Hitchman, and the baby girl born to the Rolfes, who had been christened Bermuda, buried there nearby Sir Somers's garden.

They were nearly a year in making two smaller ships, which Gates, he named *Deliverance* and Somers, he named the other the *Patience*, both hewn from the native cedar and the oaken remnants of the *Venture*. Jane labored as a boy alongside those shipbuilders, taking care at all times to disguise herself and keep her womanhood hid, never to wash, to hack at her hair when it grew long, to sweat, to swear, to feign to drink, and seem as black and rough as any mariner. When the cahows, or the devil birds, so called for the hellish noise of their nightcalls, a clamor of unholy voices that would set fright to any Christian, when they built their nests and laid their eggs, she joined the hunting parties, tho to call it a hunt makes more sporting the outright killing of these birds. They were so tame, so plentiful, and so curious, complete in fearlessness, that the men could wander among the nests with clubs and smite the cocks and hens, taking in a single night a hundred or more, which when cooked in water or roasted were as good as any English goose. The bird hunters would return to St. Catherine's Beach laden with their fare, and Jane among them, burdened under the weight of a score or more.

As water is in water or a palm tree in a winter fog, she vanished as a true person, hidden but still there, plain to see. No one knew her as anything but a boy without a master, for Ravens had flown away, and she had no true friend but Mr. Chard, who sought her out once again as April gave way to May and the new ships were judged ready for the sea. He approached her at evensong, took her arm and led her away from the others to a private spot beyond the thatched cabin that constituted Mr. Bucke's church.

"I have a mind to stay," he told her. "Why trust yourself to the mercy of these wondrous false crafted boats, these paper sailors? Think on Ravens, the best navigator among us, and he and the men and the boat at the bottom of the cold, dark sea."

She shuddered at the picture in her mind, remembering the houricane and a world made of water. Why had she left The Moon and Seven Stars, her mother, and her four baby sisters?

"And what is in Virginia that can better what we have here? I have heard tell that savages haunt the woods near James's Town, red men who go about naked and not a word of English. The people there live in fear of their very lives and suffer want of food and shelter. The winters worse than the highlands of the Scots, and the summers hotter than

Hades. Why leave this Eden for that purgatory?" Chard threw his arm around John's shoulders and drew the boy to him. "Stay with us, I entreat you, and spare the risk. If they live, they will surely send ships from England, much better beamed and planked. Mr. Carter will remain and Mr. Waters and myself."

A strange comfort to be under Chard's wing, and she thought of that night at St. Catherine's Beach when they first shared a bottle of palm wine, and how fine he seemed to her, the warmth of his bronzed skin, the wildness of his beard, his hair, his eyes. "Yes," she said, "yes. I will wait with you. Wait for rescue from an English ship and not these barks out in our own bight." Thus casting her lot with him, she longed for some sign of his affection, but Chard did nothing more than clap a broad hand against her narrow back and chuckle with approval.

Great ceremony attended the launch of the *Patience* and the *Deliverance* on the fair day in May of 1610 when the marooned company departed from Bermuda for the bays of the Chesipiak. Gates had erected a cross made of timber from the wreck and to it nailed a twelvepence coin and a copper sign Jane could not read. 'Twas Christopher Carter who told her the words were of the *Sea Venture*'s arrival upon this shore a year ago, and how this fair cross was praise for their great deliverance. Despite the pleadings from the Rolfes, from Mr. Strachey, and Somers himself, she would not join the sojourners but hid herself with the other three upon a promontory to watch the ships set sail and diminish to mere toys before falling off the edge of the world.

A kind of desolation fell upon us all in the bathroom, as we witnessed the ships sail away across the sink, and from person to person passed a profound loneliness of spirit as if we, like those left behind in Bermuda, were the only four people in the wild world. Dolly fidgeted next to the old man and sighed in a drawn-out manner, and he had a faraway look, contemplating a horizon visible only to the inner eye, gathering in the monotonous waves on the vast and endless ocean. In her gaze, Jane, too, seemed to be recalling a distant time and the prospect of those stranded mariners, not knowing what fate awaited but certain that they were now most desperately alone. As for myself, I was astounded by the girl's feckless bravado.

"Were you unconcerned," the old man asked, "to be stranded with those three salt-crusted knaves?"

She rolled her eyes and parked a curl behind her left ear.

Tho by all appearance and demeanor she was one of them, a boy among men, Long John fared no better than a woman. Not only did she must keep her sex hidden at all times, but she must play the lad. The three sailors—Christopher Carter, Robert Waters, and Edward Chard—became three masters, and where in the past she had been attendant upon Ravens, she now found herself looking after three, cooking all the meals, fetching clean potable water, tending to their meager garden, mending holey breeches, and every sundry office required by her youth and station. While she oft resented her duties, they were light, and often whole days would pass with nothing to be done but to languor upon some shaded spot for hours, the men reluctant to move or bother themselves to act at all. Crab, who was Mr. Carter's pet, could be her boon companion when the sailors were indisposed. One month gave way to the next, and when no ship appeared to rescue them before summer's end, they contented themselves to remain on Smith's Island of the archipelago, fishing the rich waters or killing a hog or brace of cahows for their supper, and poking through the woods or along the shores for distraction or adventure. Small treasures could be found—a trunk drifted in from the *Sea Venture*'s skeleton, an oyster once with a pearl inside, and all manner of shells shed from the creatures of the sea.

Of the three men, Mr. Carter kept most to himself and paid scant attention to the boy. He occupied his time with the few books left behind, seizing upon and rereading the Geneva Bible that once belonged to Mr. Bucke, complete with strange numbers at the verses and notes printed in the margins to explain the more uncertain tales. Or else he scribbled in a journal fashioned from a ship's log commandeered from the effects of Master Ravens. On those few occasions when alone in the boy's company, Carter sought to instruct him in how to distinguish the letters among the alphabet and in six months' time had conveyed an elementary understanding of the art of reading. Robert Waters, who had late killed a man, she avoided as best she could, but he was forever near Mr. Carter or Mr. Chard, anxious in his solitude, as if plagued by the memory of his foul deed and discharge of his temper. Whenever alone with Long John, Waters bore a smile upon his face, made all the meaner for the disappearance of both teeth that some call the eyeteeth and others the dogteeth, for they are pointed and sharp in some mouths. How he became untoothed Waters never said, and he also walked with a bandy-legged strut, and she guessed that upon the sea so long he had suffered the sailors' disease on a distant voyage. In all, an agreeable chap, if not for the murderous heart, and he had not one ill word for her in the entire time on the islands.

As for Mr. Chard, Edward, she found him the most fascinating of the three, for he evinced, at first, a most easy and ready character, adapting to the islands as if he had always lived there, clambering like a monkey up the palms to gather nuts and fronds, keen at spearing fish, roping hogs, digging turkle eggs. Chard went about shoeless in the long summer months, and his stockings had long since gone to tatters. At comfort in the presence of his male comrades, he soon was blouse-less, too, in hot weather, his skin baked to cedar. Whene'er he grew nosesick of his own odour, or when he simply cooled in the waters, he would strip off all clothing, his lower half pale in contrast and his pizzle in plain sight. Her discomfort on the initial occasion of seeing him thus gave way to wicked delight, so that she ofttimes wished the sun to blaze just to see him cavort, tho in his nakedness, he cajoled the others to join him in the cool ocean waters. Jane never chanced a moment in the sea save for the rare times when she'd slip away with Crab while the others dozed, and on the other side of the island, she could bathe, certain that the dog would play the sentinel and bark as if mad should anyone approach. Vigilance was her motto, and she kept herself bound.

They passed the seasons in this manner, carefree summer giving way to autumn rains and then the chilly nights of winter. No sail appeared on the sea, tho in the springtime, great herds of whales, as big as their expeditionary fleet, passed by. The four castaways gathered upon a clifftop to watch the great fish play and feed in the clear waters. From above, the leviathans seemed as small as the dolphins and porpoises that frequented the coast of Bermuda.

"'Twas one of these," Mr. Carter informed them all, "what ate the prophet Jonah." He opened his ever-present Bible and found his page. "Now the LORD had prepared a great fish to swallow up Jonah. And Jonah was in the belly of the fish three days and three nights." With his finger, he followed to the note in the margin. "Thus the Lord would chastise the Prophet with a most terrible spectacle of death, and by this also strengthened and encouraged him of his favour and support in this duty which was commanded him."

"Rubbish," said Chard. "Three days and three nights. What I eat lasts not more than a day in the belly. The most base superstition. Have you never seen a whale close up, Mr. Carter?"

"That I haven't."

"The humpedback has no teeth but a comb in its mouth whereby it brushes the water, and into the hairs many shrimps are fastened and it is these the whale swallows and spits the water through the hole in its head."

Mr. Waters laughed and spat a seed onto the ground. "'Tis true, marry, but there is whales with teeth. Have you never heard tell of the spermaceti? That man has teeth the size of yon Crab there and could swallow whole a dog or hog or man. 'Twas the sperm whale ate Mr. Jonah, I'd imagine, a brute beast, big as a church and more fearsome."

Drawing her knees to her chest, Jane wrapped her arms around her legs and considered with wonder the lives of such seafaring men. Chard plucked a blade of sawgrass and stuck the root end between his teeth. "Onct a-sea in the good ship *Forbearance,* hard off the coast of Aifric, I saw one of them monsters come roaring through the surface in a death struggle with a mighty sea spider. Huge it was, with long suckered arms wrapped around your man's massy head, its great eye bigger than a cask of ale, never blinking, and the sperm whale jaw snapping and biting like a shears, and then down they go in a splash and ne'er drew air again, so far as I can see, and Lord knows the victor."

"I'd have liked to have my hands on that whale," said Waters, "and gashed the head, for the head's where the gold is. The amber grease what foulness from which they make sweet perfume, tho the good Lord knows how, and a nugget of that stuff would make a man rich."

"A whale is just like Lord Gates, a rich man who never leaves off gaping till he swallows all."

"A pretty moral," said Carter. He had his head buried in the book and read again. "I cried by reason of mine affliction unto the LORD, and he heard me; out of the belly of hell cried I, thou heardest my voice."

Waters stood suddenly and looked at the horizon. "Perhaps we should have gone away with the rest. They are not coming back, are they?"

Carter began again to tell the true story of Jonah, complete with annotation, but the other two drifted far off to the recesses of their minds till they were gone entirely. By the end of the tale, Waters lay sleeping in the sunshine, and Chard seemed as if he had not heard a word of the sermon for the stories in his own head.

In such discourse and observation they spent their days and nights, regaling one another with tales of the sea, and it would have been a happy life had such remained their intercourse, tho every paradise has its dangers as surely crawled the serpent in the garden of Adam and Eve. To mark the second anniversary of their departure from England, Mr. Chard and Mr. Waters concocted another batch of their brew, and Mr. Carter made waste to a sea turkle and stewed it in a great vat with the berries and nuts that shewed their heads in early June. A splendid party was thrown, two days and two nights of drink and feast and merrymaking. Even Mr. Carter had his cup. "To the new world," he cried out on the second evening just before passing out on the strand next to the dozing Mr. Waters, who slept with his head on the dog's belly. Seeing his boon companions in Morpheus's snare, Chard roared out to the wide Atlantic. "I'm afire," he cried. "Imagine, John, hot on a night in June. We aren't in England anymore."

She pulled back her long hair and wiped the perspiration from her neck as she watched him strip of all clothes and wade into the surf. "Come, boy, and keep me company. Cool yourself. No need to worry, old Chard won't bite." Seeing no consent, he strode from the water and grabbed her by the wrist, dragging her across the sand and into the ocean that rose to their knees. The half-moon threw light upon the waves, silvering them in their rise and fall. Palm wine scented his every breath as he whispered to her. "I shall not hurt you, John Long." He drew her toward him, gathered her hair in his free hand and bared her neck. "I have been too long without company," he said, and pressed his lips against her nape. She trembled at the strength in his grip and felt him stiffen against her. "No more unnatural with a boy. I am so fond of you—"

"I am no boy," Jane said, the wine pulsing in her temples. "But a woman hid these two long years." Taking his hand, she guided him to her secret proof, and a wide grin split his beard in twain.

"Boy, woman, what are thou?" He fondled her and said, "More's the better, for what we are about to—"

She clamped her mouth against his to stop his words and begin all else.

Thus love in idleness was born, and they kept the matter secret between themselves the next morning and in the weeks to come, sneaking away from the others when they could to enjoy each other's passion in dark places, and careful when the others were near to put on the weeds of boy and master. At first, Jane thought him Janus-faced and most mercurial but soon came to realize that he was but playacting around Carter and Waters, merely feigning to treat her more severely than heretofore. The gruff commands to clean or cook or fetch were but his way of shewing that nothing passed between them, for he would wink or smile at her the moment their backs were turned. Entwined in a private Eden, he played most sweetly, whispering his love, tracing the curve of her naked hip with the tips of his fingers, cooing as a dove, laying his bushy head upon her breast like a little boy lost. The more Chard plied her with tenderness when alone, the more he bellowed like a tyrant when all gathered, and truth be told, the difference thrilled her and strengthened the bond of their shared confidence.

As surely as every good thing must end, their secret could not last. Thinking themselves most alone and far from their camping grounds, Jane and Edward lay side by side on a sandy strand, bared to the sun, their sport ended and sweet fatigue overtaken them. Eyes closed, she dreamt of their rescue, sailing off to Virginia and marrying Chard to start a family there. But a shadow broke across their forms and startled her with its coolness. Looking up she saw at once it was a man, the sun bursting in a corona behind his head, and she did not know his name until he spoke hers. Waters, out looking for cahows, had chanced upon them. "Is it John?" he asked. "Long John Long?"

She curled to a ball to hide and cover her nakedness. "It is Jane," she said, "and please sir, I entreat you turn your eye."

"Do mine own eyes lie? Zounds, a woman, is she? I have not seen a woman so since the whores of Woolwich." He plucked a shell from the sand and threw it at Chard, striking him on the leg. "And you, Edward, like mine own brother, only more selfish. How long have you kept this to yourself, you mottled dog?"

Chard sat up and blinkered his eyes from the sun. "Envy does not become you, Robert." A weary resignation colored his words and gestures. "Unfurl your sails, brother, for I seen your mainmast is a-ready risen. What's mine is yours. Heave to."

It happened so quickly that she had only time to cry one No, and Waters was upon her. Lying beneath the ramming man, she turned her face to Mr. Chard to plead her cause and was horrified to see his intense stare and pleasure at studying the spectacle unfolding within arm's reach. After Waters had finished, he rolled off her and kicked the trousers from his ankles. The three stretched out under the summer sky like sails set out to dry, thoughtful of the strange fate that had brought them thus together. The men did not notice that Jane was in tears, and Waters only said, "We must never tell Mr. Carter," whereon he and Chard laughed like schoolboys ripe with mischief.

And so they continued that June to make three out of two. At times, it would be as it once was, she and Chard together, and at other times, Mr. Waters would visit to take his pleasure, and still other times, they would all three go off together in ways she could not fathom until the men explained their intricate plans. More shocking still, the acts encouraged Chard and Waters to visit each other without her present, as she had heard men long at sea were said to do, tho she could not bear their seeming preference, for Jane found herself loving one and then the other, wishing one away, longing for the other's return. In her feelings, they were two halves of one man. Whereas Mr. Chard was still gentle in private and coarse in public, Mr. Waters was most kind in public but like a wild man when they made the beast with two backs in private stolen hours. Waters's passion excited her, and she recollected his promise when in the cave, and Chard, tho oft cruel, had the advantage of being first, and thus, in some way she could not reconcile even unto herself, best.

In those rare moments when neither man bothered her, she wished for some way to make one man out of two and sometimes no man at all, for tho she knew not any before leaving England, Jane felt certain that moral law concluded sharing her bed was wrong, and moreso, she found herself preferring the other when one was upon her, missing the absent man, and thinking him the better of the two. She feared as well the ire of God for her fornication, and more than once resolved to confess her sins and rid herself of the men. She sought out Mr. Carter and found him alone on the beach, Bible in hand, and the other two men gone, off tupping one another, she supposed. In a casual manner, she approached and begged him to walk with her upon the strand so that they might talk, for some heavy thing rested in the heart. The mastiff Crab gamboled in the surf ahead of them, barking at the crashing waves, and fetching a stick thrown on the waters. Carter clutched the book in his crossed hands behind his back and walked like a great heron, long-stalked, his gaze fixed upon the ground, as gentle as a vicar gone a-courting, and Jane struggled to keep pace, her thoughts awhirl in her head, her eyes darting to the man's inscrutable face, to the dog playing in the sea, to the strange visions present in memory of her two seducers. Where to begin my prologue, she thought, how best to tell the tale? Thanking Carter for his confidence, she leapt ahead, rehearsing the dark secret, wondering how he might react to her unsexing; would he understand and treat her as Ravens had, or would he, too, fall upon her like a savage?

As she parted her lips to speak, Jane heard the dog bark instead and then come bounding from the sea, wagging its stumpy tail in circles as if to tell them something as dogs are wont to do by primitive means. Crab raced back to the object of its consternation, speaking loudly and with great excitement, and there, wedged within a trio of large stones, what appeared to be a dead man, tho they could not see to tell at first. As Carter and Jane made their way, wild surmises flitted across her senses: perhaps one of them, fallen from a boat or wandering on some hilltop and tumbling down, had drown'd in the ocean, and she feared it might be Waters, hoped it would be Chard, but just as she speculated, both men appeared from the opposite direction, running on the same shore, alerted by the dog's alarums, so that all four arrived at the same spot more or less at the same time, and of the four, Chard seemed to know at once what had stopped in the crevasse. He hallooed them all and danced a jig upon the sand. "Rich, rich, I'm rich. It is the amber grease spat up from a whale."

Big as a man and heavy, too, the white-gray lump of ambergris loosed itself with much effort from the mariners who dragged it from the water. Weighing about thirteen stone, the chunk looked like the torso of a giant, sans head or limbs, and caught as well among the rocks were several smaller pieces. Laughing and shouting the while, the men danced with one another, and Jane could not resist the temptation to taste a small pebble of the stuff, but it were most foul, and she spat out the speck in her hands.

"Hah!" Carter said. "The whale can swallow Jonah, but Jonah cannot swallow the whale."

Offended by the tone of his quip, she popped the nugget into her mouth, chewed it twice, and swallowed. The men cheered her derring-do, and Carter clapped her on the back. "You must know, sirrah, that you have et more than a whale, but a small fortune."

With the sharp end of a stick, Chard drew some numbers in the sand. "If memory serves, the Virginia Company offered fourteen shillings fourpence for a troy ounce, and we must have enough for two thousand English sterling. Rich, rich, I tell you, rich. The king of the Bermudas—"

"Aye, and so are we all," said Carter. "The four kings."

Jane thought of her mother back in England making do with three shillings sixpence each week for herself and four daughters. They would live like queens.

"All we need do," said Waters, "is hie this stuff to England . . ."

His words shimmered in the sunshine, the blue waves never more endless, the horizon never more distant, the ache for home never more acute. Jane thought of The Moon and the Seven Stars, her mother fending off the men who supped there, the smell of ale and mutton, her little sisters underfoot, the youngest surely walking and talking now; did the child even know her tall sister gone to the New World? And what good is the New World and its riches if no ship would ever come?

On his feet, Chard played the tyrant. "Hove, you dirty bastards. We must find some hiding place to store our treasure, and should Somers or some other English rescue come—or worse, the ungallant Spaniard—we will smuggle the goods aboard. This is mine—our discovery—and not the Virginia Company's. Come, dogs, and make haste, let's carry off the fruits of this isle and keep the bounty, for by this amber grease we shall one day be covered in gold."

They found a dark, dry cave in which to stow the whale's perfume, and there it remained through the long summer, tho not undisturbed. Once a week or more oft, they made an expedition to assure no harm had come to it nor any man alone had dared move the ambergris. Always in the company of one or the other, and no man alone, for each suspected his fellow castaways, and none could be trusted. Edward Chard thought of little else, and when he spoke of the treasure, said "I" and "me" when he intended "we" and "us," or "mine" when "ours" was preferred. As well, he seemed to have forgot Jane and took no interest in their dalliance, nor offered so much as a kiss, an embrace, a telling look, or even one kind word. As the fog hides the morning, the idea of riches obscured his nature and rolled o'er him until he had but vanished. He did not notice, as time wore on, how Jane drifted to Waters or how Waters had become enchanted with Long Jane. As she lay unbound, she became more bound to him.

"When we are safely home and our fortune secure, I shall make an honest woman of you, for methinks I love you." They nestled in a bower of palm fronds, sweet talking their dreams. Jane rested her head upon Robert's arm and stared at the moon awink in the August sky. "We will sail back here if you like and build the finest house and be lord and lady of these islands when an English colony is here set. You shall have a proper bed—long enough for you to stretch head to toe—and a kitchen, too, and perhaps some Moorish girl to help govern our children, for I wish at least four of 'em, each taller than the next, and they shall not want for anything. We'll have old Carter marry us, should he become a vicar from carrying the Good Book so."

She sighed at the prospect and draped her bare leg over his. "And I can bring my mother to live with us here and make a home in paradise for my sisters, too."

"Aye, bring the whole Long clan, and we shall make a forest of ourselves. We are rich, my girl, beyond the dream of richness."

With a kiss, she sealed the matter. "Robert Waters, you are my secret love."

"Aye, and you mine." He rolled off his back and lay atop her, a cracked smile on his face. "The boy who was a woman, and the woman who swallowed the whale."

Thus, many a happy hour they spent dreaming and plotting as the calendar turned awhile Mr. Chard chewed on how to get the ambergris—and himself—off the isle. Day by day he attended to the horizon, desperate for sail, and nights he took to building blazing fires on the shore lest any passing vessel creep by unnoticing. Admiral Somers had left behind a small fishing boat when the *Patience* and *Deliverance* departed, and Chard toyed with the notion of crafting a mast and cloth to sail the six hundred miles to Jamestown, but he dared not risk the treasure to the mercies of the Atlantic, not alone at least, and there was no one with whom he wished to share the voyage or the spoils. His speech grew thick with curses and in his temper, he lashed out to man and beast and God at the cruelty of fate and circumstance. He would feign to kick old Crab when he could, tho dared not chance a bite in the ankle. To Mr. Carter he was most uncivil, tho his cruelty was benign against his holy shield. Chard saved his most bitter rancor for the two lovebirds who had come to exclude him from their intimacies. For Waters, nothing but sneering disdain as Cain looking upon Abel, and for Jane, most deep contempt, her mere presence an itch, a burning coal in his breeches. Vats of palm wine he brewed and drank alone, and many a morning, he would be found muttering to himself to untangle a riddle that plagued his addled brain. Too late he realized he had given up one prize to speculate upon another.

On Michaelmas, being a day to celebrate the harvest and eat the fatted goose, they proposed to Chard an excursion to Smith Island, so it was named, to find fit repast for their evening supper, a turkle perhaps, or a few cahows. The isle was also the spot whereon Mr. Carter had once found an old Spanish gold coin, and Chard accepted at once on the chance that more might be buried there. Off they set in the little fishing boat, Chard and Waters at the oars, Jane turned in the bow to face them, her collar loosed, the day fine and the sea calm. Their excursion reminded her of happier times when the three had been genuine friends. Beneath the bright sun, Waters broached the subject that was torturing them all. "Do you ever think, Mr. Chard, had I not happed upon the ambergris that our present enmity may have been avoided? For it seems the promise of riches, sir, hath caused a great change unto you."

At once Chard drew in his oar and stopped rowing, obliging Waters to do the same lest they commence traveling in circles. The little boat bobbed on the swell as Chard fixed his glare upon him. "You? You happed upon the whale? 'Twas I what saw it first."

"Come now, Edward, let us be friends," Waters implored. "We have good news to share this morn—"

"You cannot say so. I found the amber grease, and by rights, I own the whale's share of the whale."

"Jane and I, we have decided, we shall be wed—"

"Mine!" he shouted. "And what's this, wed? You cannot have her, Robert, nor the money either. I found her out first, just as I discovered the treasure."

"Mr. Chard, please," Jane said. "We are in love."

"Love, is it? Love? You are mine, too, Jane Long, and I'm ne'er done with you. How dare you lay claim to what is mine, girl or amber grease." With the butt end of the oar, he poked Waters in the ribs.

"Leave off," Waters shouted. He fingered the knife belted at his hip. "Once more, and I'll cut your t'roat."

Leaning forward in the boat, Jane set it rocking upon the waves. "Good sirs, I entreat you."

"Entreat me not, thou jot. You are no better than a thief and a whore, you scarescrow." He spat in the ocean. "He may have you, all I care, but that fortune is rightly mine, as I saw it first, damn you."

She reached to lay a hand upon his knee and calm him, but then drew back. "A quarter is yours, Mr. Chard. And half belongs to us."

The oar struck her so quickly and surely that Jane had no moment to raise a hand in defense. The blade of the wood hit the bone of her brow and split the skin like an overripe melon, a string of blood dribbling from the wound, and the blow knocked her upright where she sat. 'Tis said that in the moment of death, all of life passes through one's final thoughts, and she did think in that split second of her mother with the youngest brat at the breast, thought of how she grabbed the wheel and saved the *Sea Venture* from drowning in the houricane, thought of Ravens smiling o'er her like a father, the men and women waving good-bye from the decks of the *Patience* and *Deliverance,* thought of Chard's first kiss and the dream of life with Waters, all these contained in one moment, itself cleaved in two and both halves split further still, for what measure of time cannot be thus divided? There was no pain but the shock of the clock suddenly stopped as Long Jane Long slipped from the rowboat and into the Atlantic, and the world turned upside down, the sky now below her head, the waves above her feet. When she opened her mouth to cry out to the men in the boat that now looked as if it were beneath her sinking body, "Come save me," she drew in the whole sea to her lungs, felt herself swole and pressed for air, as if both men and Carter, too, and the whole Virginia Company were upon her chest, and hoped some great fish would swim by and swallow her, the Lord save her, in the hour of her death, as she quit this world by one man's fit of anger and by his most grievous envy.

CHAPTER FIVE

The House of the Singing Windows

By the end of her story, she had trapped us in the pathos of our own imaginations. The curtains framing the narrow window stirred a breeze redolent with salt-heavy sea, smelling of fish fries and steamed spiced crabs and oyster shells baking in the heat, though the sunrise, judging by the bruised color of the sky, was an hour or two away. Water gurgling in the sink broke the peace, and I peered into the bowl to find a little rowboat circling in a whirlpool that soon sucked down all: boat, water, a small island complete with miniature palm trees and what appeared to be a barking dog the size of a flea. Craning my neck and placing my head in the bowl, ear turned toward the drain, I thought I heard the distant refrains of some sea shanty, the voices thinning into a dreadful emptiness. The disappearance of Crab, in particular, filled me with a profound sorrow of the vicissitudes of fate that spare nothing, the innocent and the guilty swept away in one tide. This seems deeply unfair to me, an accident of design. The others huddled together on the porcelain edge of the bathtub, Dolly and the old man on either side of Long Jane, their arms draped over her wide shoulders, offering comfort as she quietly sobbed, her chin resting on her chest.

"But it was an accident," I said. "Probably."

They lifted their heads. Three sets of eyes stared accusingly awaiting explanation.

"That is, he—Chard—was probably aiming for Mr. Waters and hit her instead. Clearly, Waters made him lose his temper. He didn't mean to . . ."

Jane glared as if I had just fractured her skull with an oar. A thin red scar appeared on her forehead, pulsing like an artery, and then abruptly disappeared. She bent her head and thick coils of slubbed hair hung like ropes toward the floor. I silently withdrew the manslaughter defense and offered no new theories, and we again retreated into the dark thoughts of our own minds. After a while, the old man asked, "Out of curiosity, what ever became of the fine young man who beat the girl to death?"

"Two years they waited for rescue, and only through the intercession of Mr. Carter did they not murder each other over the ambergris. He hid the gun the admiral had left behind and hid their knives and made them swear oaths after the 'accident' and gave them promise of salvation. If not in this world, then the next. All hope had been but abandoned when they espied the redcross sail of an English ship on a fine day in July of 1612. 'Twas the *Plough,* with sixty on board under the hand of Governor Moore, sent by the Virginia Company to make a settlement in the Bermudas from those survivors of the Somers expedition who had made it safely to Jamestown. To those on board, the three men were a strange sight. Nearly naked, brown as Indians, bedraggled, and hairy as apes, the mariners were a kind of legend, living proof of the grace of God."

"Chard and Waters kept secret their hidden treasure and hatched a plot with Captain Robert Davies of the *Plough* to smuggle the ambergris on board and then so on to England, and it was Davies who recruited Edwin Kendall, a man privy to Governor Moore's council, to join the conspiracy. As all such plots, it was spoiled by their greed and fear, and they were turned in by Kendall and made to give over their treasure to the Virginia Company."

"While Davies was forgiven upon his promise to sin no more, Chard was sentenced to the gallows. A scaffold was erected, but it was a ruse by the governor to ensure that order be kept. Chard was let off without severe punishment, and the ambergris was sent back to England upon the *Plough,* though truth be told, Mr. Davies and Mr. Kendall managed to steal some little chunks and sell them for 600 sovereigns, and though a warrant was writ for their arrest, Davies escaped to Ireland and Kendall to Scotland and then to Nova Scotia with settlers of 1622."

Shaking her head, Dolly exclaimed, "Men." And then she spat on the floor. "Whatever happened to the real rogues?"

"Carter and Waters were named to the council of Governor Moore, and after Moore departed for England three years later, Mr. Carter was one of the leaders of the colony. Mr. Waters left for Virginia and built a farm, only to perish on Good Friday of 1622 at the hands of the Powhatan."

The old man asked, "What became of Mr. Chard?"

"Moore kept him in hard labor till 1615, and then he went off to the West Indies on a pirate ship, plundering in the Caribbean and as far east as Tunis. A mate of his, a Frenchman named du Chene, killed him one drunken night for coveting a girl he had taken from west Africa."

I offered a bromide at the conclusion of her tale. "A kind of poetic justice, don't you think?"

In two strides, Jane reached the corner by the toilet and grasped the pole of the harpoon, brandishing the broken end like a battering ram. "Justice?" She reared back as if to poke the ragged splinters through my chest. "What justice can you possibly see in the life of a young girl cut short by the greed and envy of one man?"

Had not my protector stepped between the two of us, she would have impaled me on the stick, but the old man stopped her with a gesture and soothed her with a word. Her purple face paled to pink as the blood rushed out of her head, and dizzy, she again handed over the harpoon and collapsed to sit on the toilet.

"My friend." The old man took me aside. "Perhaps your temporary absence would diffuse this tempest. What say you, ladies, that we retire for the time being?"

Dolly and Jane sidled up to him, hooked an arm in the separate crooks of his two elbows. They took turns whispering some startling words into each ear.

"Do you have a place where we might enjoy a private interlude?"

My first thought was of my bedroom, but then I remembered the various women still slumbering, presumably, on the bed. I suggested my office two doors down, but he seemed wary of leaving the ladies behind, and instead, sequestered them in the bathtub behind the shower curtain. He spoke once more to me in a low, suggestive tone. "They are going to teach me . . . certain things."

"Certain things?"

"You know. . . . Certain things of a delicate nature. Certain things suggested by her story. Discreet matters."

"I see. Certain things."

"Not all of us are men of the world, like you."

"You're kidding me."

"I come from a very respectable family. I've often speculated, however, as to other certain things."

Completely baffled by his reasoning, I could only nod.

"Be a good lad," he said, "and fix us something to eat while we are indisposed. We are bound to be famished."

"Do you have anything particular in mind?"

He stroked his chin as if contemplating a small Vandyke beard. "I am not picky, though if you had some turtle soup."

"I think not."

"Any slumgullion will do. A little *dejeuner* to take the edge off, eh?" And with that, he pushed me from the room.

Old Mother Hubbard went to the cupboard. The line from the nursery rhyme attended my way past the closed doors on the upper floor, and down the darkened stairway, but when I reached the bottom landing, the rest of the ditty had escaped my mind, and furthermore, I had forgotten the reason for my journey. Perhaps it was the bump to my coconut, or perhaps the visits from these strange people with their twisted histories had jarred my short-term memory, or perhaps events from long ago now jostled with contemporary thought, but the purpose of my presence in that spot at that hour had vanished. As often when searching for a missing item—my wallet or watch or keys—I tried to reason my way out of confusion by going back in time.

Our memories are best recalled by the houses of our lives. My parents' home, where my brother and I were raised, holds within its walls the memories of childhood, and any attempt at reconstructing my younger self also requires rebuilding that home in my mind. As a boy, I used to sit for hours at my father's desk in his study and draw. My mother would leave these huge sheets of brown paper, the kind you get at the post office for wrapping parcels, maybe four feet long. So that the edges wouldn't curl, I'd stack building blocks to hold down each end. Every day after school, I filled every inch of that space. One time I drew a whole city block. Every window and door, all the bricks perfect and in place. Or I would make a map of invisible countries, mystery cities. Lay out where the park would be, the baseball stadium, all the roads and bridges. Later, as a college student and then as an intern and junior associate, I lived in a series of apartments, boxlike studios or once a charming pied-à-terre, but those cells were not conducive to anything but a few hours' sleep. When my brother and I bought this house to share, I had at last some dreamscape. Attached to this house are the reveries of a woman. Even now I can picture her here, moving like a phantom through the labyrinth of rooms, gracing the space with her laughter. At rest on the sofa on a Sunday afternoon, her feet beneath the curled and napping cat. Drying her hair in the kitchen after being caught in the rain. Surrounded by constellations of fireflies on a warm night in June. I have everything of her but a name. Where is she now, and what has become of her? Who is she? For that matter, who are these strangers in this space? The possibility that the man who met me in the bathroom is the ghost of my father seems less and less likely, and if not, then who is he and what does he want?

Something to eat, of course. The old man was, at that moment, upstairs with Dolly and Jane doing who knows what. But I remembered: he was hungry and wanted his dinner. The cobwebs cleared, I paused at the front door, the kitchen to my left, and to my right the living room sat like a tomb. The cat cried out softly, so I poked my head around the corner to see him atop the television, the end of his tail a perfect circle around the LED clock. With a kiss I beckoned him, and he came straightaway, arching his back and rubbing against me in a comforting manner. I picked him up and walked to the kitchen.

The second line came to me: *To fetch her poor dog a bone.* I switched on the light and the room radiated in stark clarity. Someone had come in during the middle of the night, in the interim between this and my previous visit, and had cleaned the joint, a thorough scrubbing, the countertops glistening, the stovetop sparkling, and every appliance, breadbasket, knife rack, and all else neat and ordered, giving the kitchen an artificial quality as if a model one or a prop set for the stage or a photo shoot. Behind the facade of cupboards and cabinets, all was bare, not one box, bag, or can of food, not so much as a spice jar or box of baking soda. The refrigerator, too, had been emptied and sanitized. "Sorry, puss," I told him. *"When she got there, the cupboard was bare, and so her poor doggie had none."*

The cat mewed hungrily. I scooped him in my arms and headed for the basement where I kept an additional store, canned goods, coffee, tea, and a freezer filled with food that did not normally fit in the pantry or the cupboards. Under the weak light of a hanging bulb, the room was dim but reassuringly recognizable: the washer and dryer, the stack of old design and architectural textbooks and other mementos of my former life, and on the table next to my toolbox and odd pieces of wood sat the surplus foodstuff. I spied a can of tuna and pocketed it for the cat. A dizzying array of canned soups and fruits and vegetables rose in a pyramid. "What did the old man want?" I asked myself. "Not turtle soup, but something else . . ."

"Slumgullion," said the cat.

Without hesitation, I began to scan the labels. "Never heard of slumgullion—" And then it occurred to me that the cat should not have spoken. He crouched among the pears and beans in the normal, catlike manner, his ears pricked as if listening. His tail twitched under my scrutiny. "What did you just say?"

A low, mocking purr issued from deep inside him like the gears and cogs of a clock. I redoubled my search for slumgullion, but it obviously was not there, so taking a can at random, I held it up for his consideration, but the cat looked first at it and then at me with a blank and incurious stare, and I began to feel a little foolish for thinking that cats could read. With a flick of the wrist, I turned it round to look at the label: cream of mushroom.

"Ick," said the cat. "Try the mulligatawny." His lips—do cats have lips?—did not move as the syllables exited, and he seemed to be communicating telepathically in a high feline voice that sounded vaguely Australian. Clearly it was the cat talking and not merely the echo of my imagination.

"How did you do that?"

Once again, he adopted a passive mood, and his expression remained sphinxlike. I found a family-sized can of Trader Joe's Mulligatawny Soup and then went to the freezer for a package of heat-'n'-serve naan to accompany it, and with a nod to Harpo, I went back upstairs to the kitchen to heat the meal. A few minutes into the preparation, the cat followed me into the room, creeping underfoot in expectation. The soup bubbled in the pot and the oven timer ticked off the minutes till the bread was hot. "What is it, boy? Cat got your tongue?" The bell dinged, and I fished out the tuna in the pocket of my robe. I opened the tin and plopped the whole mess into a dish and set it on the floor for him. Loading three bowls and three spoons on a tray, along with the pot of soup and a basket of bread, I swept it up on my hand and shoulder like a waiter to bring dinner to my guests.

"Thanks for your help," I called out over my shoulder.

"Thanks for the tunafish, mate," Harpo said.

Breathless and stiff from the heavy load, I arrived at the bathroom to find the threesome waiting patiently. They appeared just as I had left them, the old man bundled into the terrycloth robe, and Dolly and Jane in their nightgowns, composed and unruffled, as if they had merely taken a brief stroll in my absence. Dolly and my father still had the third eye drawn on their eyelids, and Jane had bound her wild braids into a single coil held in place by another rope of her hair. Her long elegant neck lay bare. Tattooed along the left side was a small Chinese dragon, its fanged mouth open beneath her ear as if to strike. Drawn to the scent of chicken and curry, the three crowded around and triggered for me a wee bit of claustrophobia. No logical place existed for me to lay down my burden, so I covered the sink with the tray and lifted the lid to the pot of soup. "I hope you all like mulligatawny."

"Excellent," the old man said.

I asked, "Would you not be more comfortable dining in the dining room? Perhaps the kitchen, which is now spotlessly clean?"

Dolly ladled a heaping bowl while Jane attacked the naan, tearing a piece in half and shoving the warm bread into her mouth. With the wiggle of a crooked finger, the old man bade me come closer. We huddled under the open window. "A word, bucko, if you don't mind. It's not me that wants to eat in the bathroom, but the girls. They're allergic to cats. If I'm not mistaken, there's one of them beasts on the premises."

"Harpo? How did you know?"

"Have you ever heard of an aura, mac? Every living thing has a wave of energy they carry with them. As much a living part of you as your skin or your hair. Or in the case of a cat, its fur. And as you move through the world, you shed bits and pieces—"

"Like dandruff? Or cat dander? Many people are allergic to cat dander."

"More like the scent of a woman who just left the room, or the memory of a person brought back upon hearing some old love song. The sound of mandolins, or Proust's madeleines, or the taste of boyhood in a peach ice cream cone. The ineffable essence. The cat's been here."

"Well, he doesn't shed."

"The aura you leave behind is not the same thing as forensic evidence."

The discussion of the cat reminded me of our conversation in the basement, and the old man seemed a likely source for explanation. "But the cat can talk," I said. "He recommended the mulligatawny. What do you think of that?"

The old man peeled back the window curtain and looked intently at the black night. "I think there's something wrong in your head."

"That's the first sensible thing you have said all night." In fact, the knock on my nut could explain a great many of the events of that early morning as an elaborate sequence of hallucinations, from the man with feathers in his mouth to the talking cat to the mystery of 4:52. I stole another peek at Dolly and Jane, both barefoot in their diaphanous nightgowns, seated face-to-face in the empty bathtub, eating curry soup. The dragon on Jane's neck had changed positions, so that now the head pointed to her bosom and the tail wound round her ear. The women appeared real enough. And the man with his back to me, who peered out into the fathomless night, he seemed quite solid. I tapped him on the shoulder to confirm my suspicions, but I may have hit bone for he felt hard as stone and fixed as a statue. When he finally acknowledged my persistence, he spoke as if suddenly remembering a broken-off conversation.

"So you were telling me about this house."

I was not following his train of thought and was still at the station when he was miles down the track, but I sputtered and started. "Well, I know it's not quite the house you'd expect of an architect."

From the bathtub, Dolly chimed in, "I had no idea you were an architect."

"Would we know," Jane added at once, "any of your designs? A house of cards, perhaps?"

The sad truth was that nothing I had planned had ever been built. "I guess I should say I work in an architectural firm, but I'm kind of a finishing man, doing the small details of big plans. Home offices, day care playrooms. I once did a prototype of the office of the future . . ."

Dolly and Jane giggled like schoolgirls. "Frank Lloyd Wrong," Jane muttered to her friend.

"We bought this house when the market started going up, an

investment really. My brother and I—" My own sentence stopped me. For the life of me I could not place my brother, not his face nor his name nor anything about him, though he must exist, for how else could I have afforded to buy this house? Brushing the matter aside, I continued. "There's nine rooms in all, your standard center hall colonial, built around 1922. The master bedroom and the nursery, which as you know, I converted into a study. I put in that archway myself. And then the bedroom upstairs in the front, which was my brother's—" What had become of my brother? Where had he gone, like my mother, like my father? Like the woman I love? "And downstairs, the living room, dining room, and kitchen. Then there's the basement and the attic, not a room proper, but nine spaces in any case. If you count the bathroom we're in, which at the moment seems to be the heart of it all. Cozy, not much, but home—"

The old man cleared his throat and set down his empty bowl, the spoon clattering against the sides. "Very trenchant, but I was referring to the one distinctive architectural detail of the place, the unusual feature you earlier mentioned."

Like a four-year-old, Dolly leapt to stand and raised her arm, waving her hand like a butterfly. "I know, I know," she said. "Tell us about the singing windows. You said you came home last night and heard singing coming from the windows."

"The bicycles heaped on the lawn," the old man said, "like an orgy of chrome and rubber. And the house with singing windows. Verdi, I believe you said."

The beginning of the story seemed so long ago and longer still the events it narrates, so that I had trouble, momentarily, remembering where I had left off. "Not the house itself, but a person inside the house singing that could be heard through the windows. And not Verdi, but the 'Laughing Song' from *Die Fledermaus,* to the best of my recollection."

"You're absolutely sure it was the Strauss?" Dolly asked.

The old man simply ignored my uncertainty. He gaped at the mirror over my shoulder and flicked with his fingertip at a spot on his forehead as if trying to remove some fleck on his skin which he noticed in the reflection. Facing him, I saw nothing but a deeply furrowed brow, free of all dirt or blemish.

"There was a piano playing," I said. "And a woman singing that very distinct song—'Mein Herr Marquis'—with the laughing chorus, and she rode the register with such delightful inflection that it was, well, infectious, and I found myself laughing, too, as I came to the door, despite the fact that the presence of someone inside the house was both puzzling and disconcerting. I followed the melody up the stairs and into my brother's room. My former brother's room . . ."

Jane offered her help. "Your brother's former room?"

"That one," I answered. "Opening the door, I was taken aback by the sight of a recital going on in that space. A woman, the mezzo, stood next to the piano, her hands folded under her breast as she sang, and another woman played the piano, her back to me and the audience, which itself was composed of a number of other women seated in two rows of chairs arranged in a semicircle. A span of a few seconds intervened between the moment I entered and when everyone noticed me and stopped what they were doing. Stuck in the threshold, I was simply stunned. It seemed like they were putting on a show for my benefit. Elaborate stagecraft, fancy costumes, and the striking beauty of every woman onstage."

"Sir, you are too kind," said Jane.

Dolly nudged her in the ribs and whispered an aside. "He was always the flattering sort of man. Silver-tongued fox."

Frantic at the imaginary spot on his forehead, the old man rubbed his skin with the ball of his fist. "Pardon my interruption, but is there something in your mirror?" He put his hand on my shoulder and spun me around to face our reflection. Between our images in the glass, a small brown spot about the size of a half-dollar swelled to the size of a coffee cup. I touched the mirror to determine whether some blotch spread sandwiched in the layers, but the object existed somewhere behind the surface, and its diameter continued to increase.

"What is that?" I asked. "It seems to be getting bigger and bigger."

He grabbed my sleeve and pulled me toward the door. "May I suggest, in that case, we get the hell out of the way."

All at once the looking glass exploded, shards and slivers raining upon impact as a stick launched into the room. A thick wooden pole, deadly as a missile, protruded from the medicine cabinet and hung perpendicular to the floor. The far end of the shaft, broad and bristled, was lodged in the space where the mirror once had been.

"Looks like an old broom," I said and grasped it with both hands, ready to pull.

"I wouldn't do that if I were you," said the old man.

But curiosity got the better of me, and with a tug I freed what turned out to be an old handmade broom, its sweeping end composed of rough bristles hewn from rushes, and the handle gnarled and weatherworn, with two greasy black stains marking its pockmarked top.

Wrapping her arms around her chest, Dolly said, "Now he's gone and done it."

Jane just pointed back to the mirror. Where the hole had been, a new layer of glass now shimmered darkly. A wild human cry emanated from the distance, some far-off place inside the reflection. A figure, small as a doll, tumbled in the air, arms and legs flailing, bright auburn hair twirling madly, red dress billowing as she rolled end over end. Steadily growing larger as she approached, the woman screamed as she burst through the surface, sending another shower of glass upon us all, and landing herself in a heap underneath the window.

CHAPTER SIX

The Woman Who Swung with the Devil

C rumpled in a heap on the floor, she did not move. Her bare feet were backward in relationship to her head, and her arms had come unglued. The woman who had flown through the mirror seemed irredeemably dead. The speed of her flight and the impact with the wall had most likely broken her neck. Covered in silver shards, she made for a poignant picture: a cracked ornament beneath the Christmas tree. Fortunately, the blast had left the rest of us unscathed. We brushed bits of glass from our clothes, and the old man picked up the discarded broom. I thought he would sweep up a bit, but instead, keeping his distance, he poked the body with the tapered end of the stick.

She sputtered and gasped, a trail of drool bubbling from her lips. Blinking to life, she stirred and placed her hands on the sides of her head and twisted her neck with a crackle of vertebrae. A sigh escaped from her chest, and then she sat upright and pushed the long red hair from her face. Bright green eyes emerged from the mass of curls, and along her alabaster skin, a congregation of faint freckles dotted her cheekbones and the bridge of her nose. Her whole aspect was vaguely reminiscent of the first Elizabeth before the virgin queen had been ravaged by smallpox. She was stunning. She smoothed her gown and rose to her feet, a short woman of her late twenties or early thirties, and once composed, she possessed a regal bearing, proud, almost haughty. I expected her to sound just like Bette Davis, but she spoke not a word and merely glowered at me as if I had done her some wrong. So I bowed slightly at the waist, out of some habit, and she, by habit, too, extended her right hand decorated with rings. It was soft and white and when I bent to take and kiss her hand, my lips brushed against a chalky dust. Covering every inch of exposed skin, this powder left a residue upon contact with the windowsill, the blue tiles on the wall, and my own fingers. The grains felt like irregular bits of paper, the kind found in old, brittle books or documents that crumble at the touch. A faint rustling of turning pages accompanied her movements as she glided with sureness of purpose to the commode. Clutching the broomstick to his chest, the old man cowered in the corner while Dolly and Jane huddled in the safety of the bathtub.

With the confidence of a safecracker, she lifted the lid to the water tank and set it on the floor next to the toilet. Straightening her hands into two spatulas, she reached into the tank and lifted out a bone-dry gray rectangular box, about ten inches by twelve and a half inches and five inches deep, braced at the corners, with a hinged flap about six inches from the top. Glued to the narrow end, a small label read "The Trial of Alice Bonham." She set the box on the toilet seat and replaced the lid to the tank, and then rubbed her hands on the skirt of her dress. Red paper rust, as if from leather bindings, floated in the air and fell to the floor.

"Are we to call you Alice?" the old man asked.

"She don't talk," said Jane.

"Don't or won't," Dolly added. "You'll not get a word from her."

The old man cleared his throat. "Well, then, I shall call you Alice since you seem to be the scriniary, or the keeper of that archive."

Alice nodded to her comrades across the room, and with delicate gravity, she donned a pair of short white gloves that had been hidden in the fabric near her décolletage. The box itself was crammed from front to back with documents and papers. Taking a small brown book from the front, Alice handed it to me. A water stain in the shape of Cape Cod or a bent arm marked the cover, and antique typefaces belied the design conventions of the seventeenth century: a mix of fonts for emphasis and that strange custom of substituting an *f* for an *s*. I had to correct the text as I read it aloud to my companions:

THE DISPLAYING OF SUPPOSED WITCHCRAFT. Wherein is affirmed that there are many sorts of Deceivers and Impostors, And Divers persons under a passive Delusion of Melancholy and Fancy. But that there is a Corporeal League made betwixt the Devil and the Witch, Or that he sucks on the Witches Body, has Carnal Copulation, or that Witches are turned into Cats, Dogs, raise Tempests, or the like, is utterly denied and disproved. Wherein also is handled, The Existence of Angels and Spirits, the truth of Apparitions, the Nature of Astral and Sydereal Spirits, the force of Charms, and Philters; with other abstruse matters. By John Webster, Practitioner in Physick. London

Printed by J. M. and are to be sold by the Booksellers in London, 1677.

"That's rich," said Jane. "The part about raising tempests."

Dolly smacked her on the meaty part of her arm. "And how witches can turn themselves into cats or dogs. I had a little dog once, what was his name?"

Peering over my shoulder, the old man read the title page for himself; the whispering movements of his lips reverberated like a flight of hummingbirds. "Ah, but you miss the point, ladies, by concentrating upon the sensational. That book is a treatise on how the whole matter of witchcraft is but a deception, and how witches are really just hysterics, and our belief in such matters a case of melancholy and fancy, is that not so, Miss Bonham?"

I had never believed in all that hocus-pocus, ghost stories, fairy tales, and had long ago prided myself on being entirely rational and having an orderly mind, so I was pleased to hear the old man refute such claims and to discover long-ago works, like Mr. John Webster's, devoted to drawing attention to, and exposing, the fraudulent and irrational. As if she could read my mind, Miss Alice Bonham stood in the center of the room and began to spin, slowly at first, but soon pirouetting like a ballerina, then dizzy as a dervish, her dress flashing like a siren, her hair whipping across and hiding her face. And as she spun, she attracted the shattered glass on the floor like metal filings to a magnet, or a reverse centrifuge. The jagged splinters did not skewer her, but clung to the fabric of her skirt till it glistened and was festooned with reflected light. As she slowed her revolutions, the pieces leapt from her body and back into place on the medicine cabinet until at last the mirror was restored, the shards coming together in an elaborate jigsaw puzzle, the seams fused as if nothing had ever disturbed the perfect surface. Steadying herself, Alice sighed deeply, steam escaping from her heels like an old-fashioned locomotive come to rest, and we were dumbfounded by the trick.

The old man took me aside. "Perhaps," he whispered, "I spoke in haste."

With the room restored to its former state, a hush descended as we waited and watched for Alice's next move. She stepped to the gray box and produced a single sheet of paper covered with writing in a fine hand, and giving it to Jane, she encouraged her with a nod to read it aloud.

Salem Village
6 June 1691

Loving Sister,
I wear your knitted favours about my neck and shoulders as

cold Winter sets in, which lets me forget you not, though this is but meager remembrance and in no way makes up for your painful absence. Dear Sarah, I received thy tender lines long since I lay in. Several things prevented me from answering thee sooner, which I hope thou will pass by. I was very weak a long time and it hath pleased the Lord to take away my little one when it was but two weeks old. It was near dead when it was born and ne'er recovered. Then came over me a sore melancholy with a fit of black tears and much sadness, though it pleased the Lord to take me up again, and though I am not wholly come to strength yet.

Mr. Bonham hast not took the loss of our child so well as I, and he is an old man, near enough the hour of his own return to the Lord, so it may be so accounted. My own neighbors, the minister Mr. Parris and his wife, abiding next door have been especially generous, sending their own Maid, an Indian woman named Tituba to be my care for the household during my laying in. I have not before been in such close quarters with such a woman, and she speaks with the music of the Spanish islands whence she was brought with her man, John Indian. They do amuse and deflect all care with their fancies and songs and stories, though I suspect them not true Christians, but heathen beneath all else. Perhaps God has some especial place for the innocent and ignorant, though I vouchsafe I know not where or what that may be. The Parrises' Maid is a Godsend to me, not only in the care and feeding of Mr. Bonham, but for the two children she oft brings with her, Betty Parris who is the daughter and all of eight years and her kinswoman Abigail who is but ten, for they fill the empty house with their childish games and laughter, a merrymaking that remedies the loss of mine own infant girl, which I had named for thee. Write to me and tell me of thine son, and I shall take thy example unto my breast and rely upon the Lord to one day bless

me again with what thou now enjoy. I keep thee and thy family in
my prayers.

Your loving sister,
Alice

At the conclusion of her recitation, Jane clasped Dolly's hand and together they stepped over the lip of the bathtub and then threw their arms around Alice. They huddled in the middle of the room, sharing empathy over the sad loss of the Bonham child, and I was struck by their gesture of solidarity. Three sisters under the skin, they excluded from their bonds both me and the old man. We were interlopers on this scene, a couple of Peeping Toms, and could only stand by, hands in our pockets, till the moment passed. The women enjoyed a kind of natural affinity and felicity for emotional solace that men rarely express, as we are put off from public demonstrations of our inner feelings and must endure sorrows on our own private islands. I felt bad about the child stolen so soon from her, but could not bring myself to say anything, and when I looked to the old man for some sign of fellow feeling, he merely waggled his eyebrows and shrugged his shoulders as if this, too, was beyond understanding.

They broke from their huddle like a football team, and I wondered immediately what play had been called. Alice took from the box a small, hand-sewn book marked with red tape flags. Handing it to the old man, she indicated that he, too, had a role in relating her story. He opened the cover and read the words penned on the flyleaf: "The Journall of Nathan Bonham, being an Account of the Troubles and Tryal of His Wife." Quickly scanning the first few pages, he flipped to the first marked passage:

13 Nov. 1691
I am beginning to wonder if I have done dear Alice harm, for she is, these long months after loss, still in mourning for it,

though we know God's will and trust in His judgment and mercies. I have not pressed her on another Child, for her spirit is still sour and mean on it. Perhaps, however, the fault goes deeper that I have took her from her family and brought a convert unto the Faith. They are much addicted to Popery and to Papistical fancies, and she often speaks of feeling unlucky and other strange unheard-of superstitions. Oft I question whether she truly believes or only says so out of duty to me and to commodious marriage. That is to ask, would she be happier still had she not said yes when I pressed the case? I worry that she will ne'er be well again.

He flipped to the next red bookmark and continued:

4 Dec. 1691

Came home this even and espied thru the window, the Servant Tituba and four more besides, the Parris girl, her cousin, and two older girls, near my wife's age, gathered round the table. One had brought a round green glass and layd it down upon a letter and rubbed the glass upon it, and held it up against the firelight and bid Alice come see, apparent some magick by which to divine the future. When I announced my presence, they quick hid their fortune-telling charms. Retired in sore distress. Alice was late in comming to the bed.

25 Dec. 1691

The heathen's Christmas day. Methinks she pines for home in Casco Bay and such Papist celebration as a-wassailing, though begging at our neighbors is sure the mark of the Devill. At the lesson with Teacher Noyes, Alice wept that the birth of our Lord was not read in verse, and some struggle goes on in her soul. I am much displeased by the constant presence of the girls in our home or to find Alice about at the Parris house. Something wicked in the air.

With a frantic guttural grunt, Alice waved her arms and signaled the old man to stop. Though tempted by the other red flags taped in the journal, he respected her wishes and closed the book, keeping his finger embedded to mark his place. Fishing two more papers from the archives, Alice handed one each to the other women. They knew at once their parts, and Jane began, giving voice to the Salem girl.

Salem Village
14 Feb. 1692

Loving Sister,

Much has happened since last I wrote thee at Christmas day. The Indian woman Tituba has shewn me what has become of my dear child. She took a green-colored glass and covered a lock of hair that I had saved from it and peering through she could divine that the babe is in heaven with our father and two brothers, despite that I have not baptized it. My sorrow lifted at this sign, and I do not care what Arts were invoked, for she has comforted the grieving and is known to heal the sick of those possessed by sadness.

Young Betty Parris, whom I have written thee, has most recently been struck afflicted with a strange malady that spread to her cousin Abigail who stays with her in the minister's home. The girls have been beset with aches of no cause nor cure, disturbances that visit in the night, and frights that come in the day. The physician has come and says that they are under an evil hand, and some say BEWITCHED. Tituba had them take some of their urine and mix it with rye meal and a hen's egg, and baked it over a fire to make a witch cake to see if the poison in the girls could be so evinced in their little dog, Nick, and it did gobble the cake in two bites and was watched for signs of the devil's plague. But, Sister, it did not dye or so much as howl in pain and shewed nothing as though every morning it broke the fast with such a witches' cake. When the Elders of the village learned of this, they made first to accuse the Indian woman who many have long spoken of amongst themselves as being an odd sort of chick, and the girls, too, began to complain that Tituba did visit them in spirit when she was not there. In the night, her apparition does afflict them and pinch their arms and legs, that she did prick them with iron needles and torment them by twisting and biting their arms and necks and legs. Little Betty Parris was struck dumb, her throat seized and mouth stopped, and Abigail her cousin was wracked with mysterious pains, much like in all things that John Goodwin's children sufferen in Boston three year ago, which we all have heard of, and the torture they endured at the hands of Satan. Some others in the village were called to give their advice, and they, too, conclude the girls struck by devils.

Two other girls have been so afflicted, Elizabeth Hubbard, near mine own age, and Ann Putnam, the little girl of Thomas Putnam, who Mr. Bonham says hath grievance against half the town. I am friend to all these girls, and to the Indian woman, and am sore afraid of what may come. Keep us in your prayers.

Your loving sister,

Alice

When Jane had finished, Dolly began at once to read Sarah's reply:

Casco Bay

1 March 1692

Dearest Alice,

    Your letters and the news that travel the roads of New-England

*do send a chill thru my bones. First, you should always know that
God brings these short-lived children straight unto His breast, no
matter if baptized or no, and I do not hold with the Church teaching
of any kind that says otherwise of the Innocent. There is no need to
consult conjurers or trust cheap Tricks or false Divinations. No one
can see the future or guess what is to come. Though I daresay your
dalliance with these girls and simple Maids will come to no good
and, I, too, have heard of the Goodwin case and others so afflicted,
for I have seen often enough the Fits and Seizures some poor souls
are stricken by, and there are a thousand diseases and ailments we
know not the cause. But I am not convinced such maladies are the
work of the Devil, for if he could do as much to one, would not
Satan afflict every Innocent?*

*You would do well to shun the Company of your friends and
steer wide of these girls, who if they are not all suddenly strick by
the same cause, may well be spreading childishness and pretense.
Do not fall into such foolhardy games. Stay away, stay away, and
trust your husband over these girls. I keep you in my daily prayers.*

Yours as God wishes,
Sarah

At the conclusion of the foregoing, Dolly and Jane handed over
their documents to Alice, who filed them in the proper places in the
archives. Taking the old man by the sleeve of his robe, and nodding to
the women, I whispered a private query. "I don't understand the meaning of this. Why are you playing the husband here? Shouldn't I be reading the part of Mr. Bonham?"

"It appears you have some other role." With a wink, he bent close
and I inclined my head so his words might better pour into my ear.
"All in good time, lad. But I do think you are on to something. Good
of you to have figured out the central conceit. I had not deduced as

much, and that only goes to show how exceptionally bright and insightful you are."

His compliment pleased me immeasurably, for I had heretofore thought he found me somewhat slow. Blood rushed to my head as I blushed, and a drop trickled down my scalp where the hole had once been. "Tell me," I answered, "what is my place in Alice's tale?"

"Are you saying you don't remember her? A fine young woman like that?"

I stole a glance over his shoulder and saw her in three-quarter profile listening to the other two women. One of them said something funny, and she brought her hand to her mouth, her lips and fingernails the same shade of red. He grabbed me by the elbow and steered me toward the women. "We shall allow some patience in you for the passage of time and memory. Methinks the answer comes anon."

But instead of handing me my part, Alice returned the journal of Mr. Bonham to the old man and instructed him to read the next few marked pages.

5 MARCH 1692

My wife consorts with a WITCH. The girls named Tituba as she what taught them to make the witchcake and other magick. They say she took a Jug of Beer and a green glass and that looking in the glass saw the shape of many persons and what they were doing though they be far away in their homes or in the town. They named the beggar Sarah Good and stout Sarah Osbourne, too, as the cause of their ailments, claiming them WITCHES and saying they do visit in spirit and prick and bite and torture &c them in their beds and ask them to fly on broomsticks through the windows and into the black woods. The Barbadoes Woman has confessed to her sin and is sent to prison, as are Goody Good and Goody Osbourne, though they confess no sin and are sore distressed by such accusations. Woe betide us should the girls accuse Alice.

25 MARCH

The devil runs like wild fire thru the Village and there is a conflagration of witchcraft spread this side of Salem. Though Betty Parris has been sent away to recover with her kinsmen in the wilderness of Maine, the other girls continue to find more tormentors among the erstwhile goodwives of our town. Martha Corey has been so-named, as fine and God-fearing a woman as ere met, as well. Little Ann Putnam pointed the finger at Sarah Good's little four-year-old waif, and the child, too, now joins her mother in the jail, and my heart breaks at the thought of the poor girl in a dark cell. Mrs. Putnam herself begins to suffer an affliction, and she is soon to name more WITCHES. When shall this madness end? I dreamt last night that the same Black Man what haunts the girls was in the room aside my wife and me, beside the spirit of Thomas Putnam come from his house. As in all pictures that I have seen, He had him Cloven feet and Claws and would have me sign in blood his fowl Book. When Alice woke me in the morning and saw me ill and the bedclothes soaked with the Sweat of my night's terrors, she knew I knew her secrets, and did all she could to rid me of my fears with many kisses and caresses. I sometimes wonder if I, too, consort with a WITCH.

"Just like a man," Dolly said, "to not trust his wife and think the worst of her."

Jane hid beneath her coils and added, "Yet he was willing to lie with her though she was possessed. What does that say about the kind of man he was?"

Softly Alice walked to the old man, who was resting his hip against the edge of the sink. She pressed her palm against his chest and lifting herself on tiptoe, she kissed him softly on the cheek and brushed the other side of his face with her open hand. His bright blue eyes widened in surprise and pleasure, and the faint trace of a smile parted his lips. He whispered a phrase—*I am sorry* or *Do not worry*—that could not quite be deciphered. Slowly she parted from him and fished again in the Hollinger box till another document she produced. The four of us wondered who should be next, and I was taken aback when the handbound pages were placed in my hands with the silent order that I was to read.

NOTES AND SUNDRY ON THE AFFLICTED
BY NICHOLAS NOYES
Being a Record in Preparation
Of the Writing of a Book; or Account of:
The Witches of Salem Village
Part, the Second

Several of the Afflicted saw on the 20th of March, the Lord's day in Meeting, Goodwife Corey suffer the most unusual evidence of witchcraft. A yellow bird, seen only by the girls, had entered somehow the Meetinghouse, first landing upon the minister's hat hanging on a peg and then—*mirable dictu*—it could be seen betwixt the fingers of Martha Corey. And then her spirit flew and perched atop the ceiling beam like a man riding in the saddle, high above the church, though she herself be in the congregation. Both Abigail Williams and Ann Putnam swore to it, and moreover, they claimed Goodwife Corey was the newest cause of their affliction.

The following day, the 21st of March, we were summoned as magistrates to examine Mrs. Corey as bewitched and causing afflictions on the girls and the other accusers. Despite being twelve of the clock, a throng of one hundred or more from here the Village and Salem Town assembled.

I began with a prayer for all those gathered that the Lord guide us in our deliberations, that the tormented girls and the women to whom the terror has spread, that they be relieved and that God shew the truth and his Will be done. The accused asked that she be allowed to pray, and a murmur rose amidst the assembled, several voicing their objections. I cast my eye about the room: the afflicted rocked and moaned as though an evil wind blew through the rows, and several others— Goodwife Bishop and Goodwife Proctor and Goodwife Bonham—took notice as well and made to copy the girls, but this was mere sympathy. Thomas Putnam, too, watched with one eye on the congregation and another on the accused. Quite rightfully, I believe, I told Goody Corey that she was not there for prayer, that there would be plenty of time to make Peace with the Lord, and that she was to submit to the Questions of the Magistrates.

Mr. Hathorne took the role of inquisitor, right enough. "Goodwife Corey, why hast thou afflicted those children?"

"I do not afflict them," she said. "I scarce account any of them, but they are some chance accountered in the Village."

"They saith they are so afflicted," Hathorne pressed her. "If not you, then who does so torment them?"

"I do not know. How should I know?"

From the corner where she perched, Alice moaned, first a low hum like a cat's contented purr, and then her lips parted and the sound intensified to a full-throated O, and a tremor ran from her fingertips and hands to her shoulders. She shook her head violently and then snapped into a quiet trancelike state, her gaze focused on some scene invisible to the rest of us. Through the open windows, the smell of decay drifted. I cleared my throat and continued.

"How should I know what ails these girls?" Martha Corey demanded. She knotted her fingers and twisted her hands.

From the rows where the girls were seated, a pained scream rang out. "Why dost thou torment me?" One of them, Ann Putnam, leapt to her feet and said, "See, her yellow bird pecks my hand." She held up her fingers so the Assembled might see the red marks on her palms.

I asked Goodwife Corey if she had some familiar spirit, in the shape of a yellow bird, that attended upon her.

"Yellow bird? I know no such thing."

To which Mr. Hathorne ordered the woman to be searched for such sign, and the girl who had seen the yellow bird shouted that it was too late, the bird had flown. Ann Putnam, Sr., the girl's mother, said, "However she did stick my child in the head. Come examine her for any sign." The bailiff approached the child and found an iron pin sticking upright through the child's cap and standing straight in her hair. Mr. Hathorne stuck his spectacles atop his head and put down the deposition he had been reading. "The child says: 'And she bade me sign the book, a book writ with blood.' What of this book of yours? Even your husband has said you do sometimes hide a book when he comes upon you in surprise."

"I have no such book. I am a gospel woman."

"You are a gospel witch," Ann Putnam shouted from her seat. "I was at prayer with my father at my own house, and there came the shape of Goodwife Corey praying to the devil and entreat me sign the devil's book."

The members again whispered among themselves, and

many turned to their neighbors what hidden thoughts escaped their countenance. I did espy Mr. Corey muttering to himself and beating his fist against his breast, and next to him, Alice Bonham staring at me as if to make me stop.

"What say ye to this deposition?" Mr. Hathorne enquired.

Drawing herself full and straight, Martha Corey said, "I do not know what to say, other than this child suffers from some fancy. They are all poor, distracted children."

I told her, No, they are bewitched, so say we all. At that she bit her lip, and the children cried out that she does bite them, and they shewed the Marks upon their bare arms. Mrs. Pope, who is also afflicted, begged her stop, for she said Goody Corey did twist her in the bowels whenever she wrung her hands, and she threw her muff at the accused. When that did not reach its target, Mrs. Pope took off her shoe and threw it, striking Goody Corey in the head.

Abigail Williams cried out, "Do you not hear the drumbeat? Why do you not go join the devils assembling in the woods beyont?"

"Make her quit stomping her feet," Ann Putnam said. "She is paining me in my own feet and will break my bones." The little girl stamped her feet with great fury until Mrs. Corey stopped, and then so did the child.

"The woman is a Witch," Mrs. Putnam said. "She came to me in the night and told me that she hath signed a covenant for ten years, with six gone and four to come. Even now, The Black Man whispers in her ear, can you not see? Ask her the catechism and trick the devil."

My heart full of terror and pity, I strained to find any Black Man or Devil, but not being bewitched, all that appeared before mine eye was a frightened old woman. She seemed bewildered by all around her, and on the faces of her accusers and, indeed, on most of those gathered ran a look of hunger or anticipation. They strained to hear her words and would that they strain so much during our sermons or teaching, or even prayers. Searching for a proper question, I settled on a simple matter, asking, "How many persons be there in the Godhead?"

Her visage changed from agitation to peace, as though she knew the answer, and the correct answer—three—was on her lips, but her eyes clouded as she turned over the question in her mind. Perhaps she thought it a conundrum for which there was no correct solution, but no ruse was intended on my part. "Oft have I heard you teach, Mr. Noyes, on the matter, and I think there is but one person only in the Godhead and yet there is the Son of Man, the Holy Ghost, and the Father, and this is three, but only one come as a person."

"A simple answer," I said, "would reassure us of your meaning."

"But there is no simple answer to the riddle of the Trinity, and I have spent my long life in understanding."

Those assembled argued softly amongst themselves until Mr. Hathorne called for order. "I have read the depositions against thee, Goodwife Corey, and heard the testimonies of the Innocents, and am most dissatisfied by your answers—"

"You have no proof against me but the words of the misguided," she said. "I am no witch."

"The magistrates find otherwise, and I beg you confess."

"How might I confess to that which is not true? Which is baseless Gossip?"

"By my order, you are to be sent to Salem prison and remain there until you confess your sin of witchcraft and consort with the devil and to testify against all those who worship him."

After she had been led away and the meetinghouse cleared, I took up my hat and cloak to make my way for home. Outside the door stood Mr. Corey with Alice Bonham, who did falsely say to me that she saw Mrs. Putnam place the iron pin in her own daughter's cap, and she adamantly proclaimed the innocence of the accused. Mr. Corey, too, pleaded for my intercession, but the hour was late, and I had to hurry home for my tea.

Having come to the end of this account, I paused and looked to Alice for some signal to continue. She stood in the center of the bathroom and held out a washrag, revealing that it was ordinary terrycloth, flat as a flag, and containing no secret compartments or hidden pockets. With a theatrical flourish, she gathered the cloth at one end and proceeded to bunch it into her closed fist, and with a wave, she mimed some hocus-pocus and opened her hand to disclose the cloth now formed into a small tent. With two fingers, she lifted the point to uncover in her open palm a small, yellow bird that nodded its tiny head and spread its wings and tail feathers. This bird—some sort of housefinch—hopped to the faucet on the sink when she gently prompted it to freedom. Alice shook the wash-rag and another bird emerged from the folds, as if born from the petals of a large flower. In a quick, snapping motion, she raised her arms to a perpendicular position and from the sleeves flew two more finches, one of which landed on the old man's silver hair. Smiling now, she reached to lift the hem of her red skirt, and a whole flock of birds escaped, a dozen or more, and the bright yellow flash of feathers filled the room. One perched on the shower curtain rod and began to sing. Two hung onto the toilet seat. Another pair scrabbled on the toothbrush holder. Alice held out one hand, and the birds converged upon it as if drawn by scent or seed, dancing the length of her arm, delicately nibbling at her fingernails and tasting the salt on her skin. With no warning, Alice suddenly dropped her limb, and they vanished as mysteriously as they had arrived. My comrades burst into applause, but I was too stunned to move or speak.

"So are you a witch or just a magician?" Dolly asked.

Alice glowered at her and raised her auburn eyebrows for a split second, answering neither in the affirmative or negative, indicating only amusement at the question. She handed Jane the next batch of documents.

> *Salem Village*
> *10 May 1692*

> *Loving Sister,*
>
> *The jails of Salem are full of WITCHES.*
>
> *Half the village stands accused and Half must be afflicted, or so it seems. Mr. Bonham says that, in addition to those I have writ thee, there are two dozen more in the jail, and no one is spared. A beggar child, no more than four years, is the youngest, and the elders include Goodwife Corey and Goodwife Nurse, whom thou have met when last thee visited. No more devout Christian woman have I ever met. The affliction has spread from those who knew the Indian maid to Women of honour and distinction. Mrs. Ann Putnam and her young daughter swear against many, and Mr. Thomas Putnam has sent the legal complaints to the magistrates.*
>
> *We in the Village now look upon each Neighbour with a suspicious eye and are studied by our former Friends for any errancy. It is like living in a house made of Straw and waiting for the wind to blow or some stray ember burn down the whole and all. I am very afraid. What if those girls name me?*
>
> *Sarah, I cannot speak of this to Mr. Bonham or tell my secrets to him, for did he know of my late dalliance with these girls he would beat me or send me home or, who knows, turn me over to*

these Witch Hunters. I cannot say. Nor can I escape this place,
but must bear all in silence and sanguinity.

> *Your loving sister,*
> *Alice*

Postscript. You said you might come for a visit and bring your little
boy. Pray do, and soon.

More passages followed from Mr. Bonham's diary, as read by the old man.

1 MAY

What madness infects us? So terrific the unceasing Stench of Hypocricy, one would think the clouds befoul the earth. I put Putnam behind this. May please God to bring relief from this plague of Mendacity. Though she says naught, Alice is afraid by so many ordered into jail, and rightly so, for those girls call out every one without discrimination.

25 MAY

By my count, there are 60 in the jail. Poor Giles Corey joins his ancient wife, and Goodman Proctor and his Elizabeth, old Bridget Bishop, and too many to catalogue. Would the new Governour come and settle matters and be shewn the travesty of bearing of false witness. We are relieved that Alice's sister arrives next week, so at the last, the poor thing can find some comfort and commiseration.

He stopped at that red flag and closed the book at Alice's command. She extracted a letter for Dolly.

Casco Bay
1 June 1692

Dearest Alice,

With a heavy heart, I write to say I cannot travel as planned, for our little William has come down with some ailment that turns him scarlet and wracks him with a dreadful cough. He burned with fever for three days, though the worse be over, but the physician says he is not fit to journey, and I am loath to leave him thus. Perhaps we shall see you later in the summer when he is mended, and I write in haste so as not to leave him too long unattended. Say a small prayer for his health, and I shall write again soon. I am so sorry to disappoint you, and only urge you stay resolute. All things must pass.

Your loving sister,
Sarah

"Did the boy get well?" Dolly asked. "Little William?"

The red-haired woman nodded and then turned to me to continue the story as Nicholas Noyes.

NOTES AND SUNDRY, *continued*
Part, the Fifth

Bridget Bishop, accused of witchcraft by her husband and others, and accounted in testimony of several witnesses who swore whereto, was put to trial by Court of Oyer and Terminer, chief judge William Stoughton, our Deputy Governour, and examined by the women who found several excrescences or witch's teats upon her body that hurt her not when lanced with a pin. Thus proved a witch she confessed that some "folks counted her a witch," and did threaten Mr. Hathorne in saying, "If I were such a person, you should know it." She was sentenced to death, and on the 10th of June, she was hanged by the neck on Gallows Hill in front of many witnesses to God's judgment upon her, and when at last she ceased to breathe, a clamor rose that demonstrated the will of all to have such Evil exterminated. Governour William Phipps, upon learning that some of the magistrates objected and that Mr. Saltonsall resigned as judge in protest, has called upon Increase Mather and his son and other ministers of Boston to advize him how best we proceed these trials.

The old man interrupted, at her instruction, my discourse with another passage from Nathan Bonham.

11 JUNE

The most unusual event in all my life happened this last night. My wife was severely disturbed after witnessing the execution of Goody Bishop, and when it came time to go to bed, Alice would not, saying instead she would sit a while by the fire, and thus I bade her goodnight. A fitful sleep had I, visions of the body swinging from the rope, and after mid-night but before the dawn, I awoke in discomfort and found myself alone in the bed. I called for Alice, but she did not answer, so I shook off the blankets and went to look for her, finding herself still before the fire. You startle me, she said when I came into the room, but I am glad you are here. I beg you look upon me, she said, to see if you might discover any mark unnatural. She stood before the fire and undid her shift, letting it fall to the floor, so that she was Naked as an Infant, and I had never seen her thus before, for she was so modest, and was amazed by how fine she was in her nakedness, a young woman, and I am ashamed to say my passion rose, but holding myself in check, I examined her skin closely as she had asked, and the bold woman was not afraid to be thus seen, instead holding her gaze upon me as I inspected every aspect, running my fingers over any suspicious bump. Do you fear you are a witch? I asked, and she laughed and said No, but she feared others might call her so, and she wanted no blemish or mole to be construed as a witch's teat. I found nothing, and she was so happy that there before the fire, she lay with me for the first time since the child was lost, and I was overcome with sensation and a fullness of wickedness. For if she is a witch, she is a bonny one, and if this be sorcery, I am most consumed by pining, even as this I write, for such visions before my mind.

Red as her dress, Alice blushed so intensely that she threatened to disappear entirely within the fabric. A far-gone memory took hold of her, and she moved next to the old man, embraced him, her head pressed against his chest, and laced her fingers in his hair. With mischief in her gestures, she reached into the wild forest atop his head and extracted a large sewing needle, displaying it for all to see and wonder, and after we admired her prestidigitation, Alice rolled her eyes and indicated that we should follow her gaze.

Stuck in the ceiling, glistening like razor blades, a thousand such needles loomed, the sharp ends pointed directly at our skulls. We barely had time to comprehend the full danger before she clapped once and down they rained like a thousand tiny daggers, and by instinct, we all covered our noggins with our hands. Each needle struck as softly as drizzle, evaporating when the point struck skin, as if we were standing in a sudden shower without ever getting wet. Until the needles actually hit and proved harmless, we were frightened, and in that momentary interval, a slight cackle escaped from her lips.

"She really is a witch," said Dolly.

"Or a magician," Jane said. "That was quite a trick."

"Aye," the old man nodded. "She is a magic woman no matter what else she is."

I went back to the Noyes journal and turned the page. Tucked between the leaves, several documents needed to be unfolded and read into the record.

INDICTMENT

Anno Regis et Reginae Willim et Mariae nunc: Anglia &c Quarto
Essex ss. The jurors for our Sovereign Lord and Lady the
King and Queen presents that Alice Bonham of Salem Village
and Farms within the province of Massachusetts Bay in New-
England, the sixteenth day of June, in the fourth year of the
reign of our Sovereign Lord and Lady William and Mary, by
the Grace of God, of England, Scotland, France and Ireland,
King and Queen, defenders of the faith etc., divers other days
and times as well before as after, certain detestable arts called
Witchcraft & Sorceries, wickedly and ferociously hath used,
practiced & exercised, at and within the township of Salem in
the county of Essex & aforesaid, in, upon, and against one Ann
Putnam, Jnr. of Salem Village, single woman, the sixteenth of
June, by which said wicked arts the said Ann Putnam was and is
tortured, afflicted, pined, consumed, wasted, and is tormented,
also for sundry other acts of witchcraft by the said Alice Bonham committed and done against the peace of our Sovereign
Lord and Lady, the King and Queen, their crown & dignity and
against the form of the statute in the case made and provided:

WITNESSES
Ann Putnam
Abigail Williams
Elizabeth Hubbard
Ann Putnam, Sr.

Three other indictments, concerning the other witnesses, were included, and folded next to these were four separate depositions.

DEPOSITION OF ANN PUTNAM JUNIOR
v. ALICE BONHAM

Ann Putnam, aged about eleven years, saith
I being in the home of Betty Parris did see Alice Bonham practice sorcerie with the Maid Tituba, that they did conjure with a green glass an infant child and the baby could be heard crying though she be dead. That Alice Bonham did make a poppet that came alive when charmed and that this doll, in the shape of a child, did come visit me in the night and torment me. And that the child's mother, Alice Bonham, would also visit in the night to claim her little girl and did find the poppet in my bed and was angered and did afflict me with pains by sitting upon my chest and biting me on my arms and legs.

DEPOSITION OF ABIGAIL WILLIAMS
v. ALICE BONHAM

Abigail Williams, aged about eleven years, testifieth
That the shape of Alice Bonham does and hath visited in the night and brings a great book and asks me to sign my name in blood and when refused, does torture me with an iron needle pricking me about the legs, and another night did bring the poppet with her who does cry and torment me.

DEPOSITION OF ELIZABETH HUBBARD
v. ALICE BONHAM

Elizabeth Hubbard, aged about seventeen years, testifieth
Alice Bonham has entreated me to come to her home and to lie with her husband so that another child might be born and saith

this child is owed the Devil. She also flies through the window in the shape of a yellow bird and bids me do the same to join the witches who do coven in the woods outside Salem Farms. Alice Bonham also makes claims upon me to follow the custom of the Papist and go to Mary-land and to abandon my masters here.

DEPOSITION OF ANN PUTNAM SENIOR
v. ALICE BONHAM

Ann Putnam, nee Carr, about age thirty-eight, saith
I woke one evening in May to see the shape of Alice Bonham covering my husband Thomas, baying as if a hound, and when I reached out to strike and drive her from the bed was met with form insubstantial, though he, too, cried out her name and beat the air with his fists. When I confronted her and Mr. Bonham outside Salem Village Church, she denied all and claimed she was a true Christian, though I know she once was a Papist. I later saw her shape in the shed, suckling a hogget, and the ewe bleat in the corner at the unnatural act, and Alice Bonham sung to the lamb as if it were her own child.

NOTES AND SUNDRY, *continued*
Part, the ninth

Near three weeks ago, on the 29th of June, six were put to trial at Court of Oyer and Terminer: Sarah Good, Rebecca Nurse, Susannah Martin, Alice Bonham, Elizabeth Howe, and Sarah Wildes. We were encouraged by Increase and Cotton Mather, in their letter to the Village, to be cautious but proceed with speed and vigour to try these accused. The day was long in going, for these women must be examined separately, though all proved guilty. At every trial, the afflicted behaved exactly: when in the presence of a witch, they blanched and fell to

terrible fits and protests, but when the witch was made to cover
her eyes with a cloth and led to lay hands upon the afflicted person, the fit stopped at once: thus proving the causation. Rebecca
Nurse, heretofore judged most holy, was acquitted by the jury,
though the afflicted out-cried at the verdict. When I expressed
myself dissatisfied, the chief judge said we would not impose
again upon the jury. When another prisoner, who has confessed
to being a witch, was brought into court to witness against her,
Goody Nurse said, "What, do you bring her? She is one of us."
When asked to explain her remarks, she said nothing, and the
verdict was later changed to guilty, though she later claimed she
meant merely that the witness was a prisoner like her, and that
she had not understood the charge. So say all. Each failed at
their catechism, and we were most sure the jury was right.

In the docket, Alice Bonham protested that the girls
and other witnesses were deceiving and in collusion, that they
did prick their own skin, or bite one another, that they did hide
tokens and talismans in the accused persons' homes. When
confronted with the Devil's poppet she had made to conjure
her own dead child, Goody Bonham wept so as to break stout
hearts, but the jury found she was dissembling. She even cried
to me, asking if I recalled the trial of Martha Corey and the
pin found in the child's cap, but I could not remember at the
moment such an occasion and only now, in reading over what I
have wrote, realize that Alice had made such claims of perfidy
against the afflicted long before she stood accused.

But why would the children tell untruths, or neighbors
bear false witness against neighbors? Are we not all good
English men and women, under the same King and Queen, and
guided by the Lord? It is the guilty who doth protest loudest,
and wrong to accuse the poor Innocents who have no reason

but to rid this place of Evil. Did not the Lord himself say, Suffer the children. I cannot believe her, and moreover, did think she tried to seduce even me with her greenish eyes and the hair escaping her bonnet. Did not Judas Iscariot have a red beard? Perhaps there is something to be said about the old admonition against the Red-Haired.

On 16th of July, the six were taken from Salem Prison to Gallows Hill, and the folk along the way treated the spectacle with more disdain than called upon. Old Sarah Good called out to the houses as we passed for a small beer, and at one such, the neighbor, taking pity, handed her a mug, which she drank along the way and did feel much better. Emboldened, perhaps, by the drink, she cursed me as I said the final prayers. "Thou art a witch," I told her, hoping she would confess and save her life, "You know you are." She spat out, "You are a liar, and if you take my life, God will give you blood to drink." Such a wicked spell I cannot forget, and Alice Bonham, too, had turned into a most wretched soul. She saith upon the gallows, "And I am an innocent woman, no witch, and God will punish you and all for your wickedness and falsehoods. I hope Goody Good is right, and more, and your head swell in pain as mine is about to do."

It took no more than seventeen minutes for the last to kick once and then pass from this world. Some had their necks broken, and others strangled to death. I turned to Mr. Hathorne and Mr. Putnam in attendance and commented upon the woeful sight of those six bodies hanging in the summer sun. God have mercy upon those who sought forgiveness, and may the families and friends of those who insisted wrongly on their Innocence find some solace in the church and in knowing the will of the Lord be done.

. . .

We fell into a measured silence, stunned by the finality of her story and the image of the six hanged women and the mob of witnesses. I could not look at anyone and did not notice how Alice had caused the doll to materialize. Strung on a single thread, the simple puppet was fashioned from a washcloth—with an elementary head and limbs, no features on its face, yet strangely lifelike. Through some manipulation of the string, Alice caused the doll to toddle across the tiles, and then give a little curtsy, and quite extraordinarily, to jump up on the sink and straddle my toothbrush like a miniature witch upon a broom. With a flick of her wrist to snap the noose, the puppet collapsed into plain terrycloth. She then reached into the archival box and handed one more document to the old man.

Boston, Massachusetts
20 September 1706

Dearest Sarah,

God's blessing on you and your children, and forgive me for not writing in so many years, but I have heard some news today that I share with you, though I know not how to say it. Word has come from Salem that Ann Putnam, one of the girls who accused our darling Alice, has confessed to her sin. She recanted all and said before the congregation that it was a "great delusion of Satan" and that it was not done "out of any anger, malice or ill-will," but done ignorantly, and she begs forgiveness of God and from the relations of those she condemned. We have some consolation, at last, that Alice was both truthful and right in reasoning that some base motive caused those girls to tell such dreadfull Stories and send twenty to the Gallows, not to mention poor Goodman Corey, who was pressed

to death with stoneweights on the chest, and to stir the people of
Essex county into a frenzy of witch hunting. I now believe that
there is no Witches, and I am comforted to know she is truly with
the Lord. I hope this finds you well. My new wife, not so new any
more, is with child, and I feel like Abram, I am so old, and if it be
a girl, I shall ask to call her Sarah, after you.

Sincerely,

Nathan Bonham

No further records existed, and her story ended. She filed the last document in the box and shut the lid. A pause, pregnant with sentiment, interceded as we each contemplated this sad chapter from history. I expected her to lift the broom in attack against me as the other two women had done with their weapons, but she merely slumped against the wall and slid to a seated position, her red gown rustling like a sigh. The old man, some thought wrinkling his forehead, sat on the toilet and rested his chin in the cup of his hand. Dolly and Jane exchanged whispers in the bathtub, and I alone strove to make sense of it all. "At least, in the end, the girl apologized. It was not out of anger, but ignorance."

"Ignorance?" Alice spoke. Her high thin voice colored echoes of New England. "She was a clueless pawn in a far more dangerous game. The wrath of righteous neighbor against neighbor, the old against the new, the status quo versus change. The anger of values upended, the petty grievances of the true believer meeting the unknown threat of the Other. Red, boiling anger. Not from the children, but out of their parents. The girls themselves may not have even known what tipped their game into madness, but they surely felt it in the long-simmering wrath of their parents and their ministers. A kind of institutionalized, socially acceptable political anger that struck out against the old and powerless, ripe targets for the venting mob. The worst kind of ignorant, misplaced anger. I am surprised that it took you so long to understand, being an educated and religious man."

I did not understand the meaning of her last remark, since I do not consider myself particularly religious, but my confusion was superseded by the surprise of her gift of speech. We were all shocked.

"You can talk!" Jane and Dolly said together, and then to each other, "Jinx!"

"I told you she was a magical woman," the old man said. "What concerns me most, however, is: whatever happened to the minister Noyes?"

Her green eyes flared like a wild animal's as she spoke, and had I not known better, I would have thought Alice was casting a spell. "Justice delayed is sometimes the sweeter. Nicholas Noyes lived for twenty-five more years after the Salem trials, enjoying a good reputation and coming to regret and apologize for his role in condemning the innocent, but in the end, Sarah Good's gallows prophecy came true. One morning he woke, coughed once into his pillow, and saw the first red drops. An aneurysm in the brain, a hemorrhage that sent the blood gushing out of his nose and mouth, and he lived just long enough to comprehend the meaning of the red stain spreading on his gown and bedclothes."

As if thunderstruck, my head pounded again with the ferocity of a migraine, and the room began to spin, so I had to go lie down.

CHAPTER SEVEN

Crumpets with Strumpets

Sometimes there is no place I would rather be than under the covers in my own bed in my own house. In *The Poetics of Space,* Bachelard says, "If I were asked to name the chief benefit of the house, I should say: the house shelters day-dreaming, the house protects the dreamer, the house allows one to dream in peace." By extension, then, the bedroom and, more particularly, the bed in which we spend a third of our lives function as a kind of protective haven for the true self, the subconscious refugee from the assault of the external world. The bed, in situ, becomes the restorative womb, where the imagination is nurtured while our resting bodies are safe. Eyes closed, one drifts in warmth, the blankets pressing gently against the body, one's own breath as regular as a mother's heart, and one becomes free of all care. The familiar bed—I can never truly sleep in a strange hotel—is a comfort unlike any other. She—and I cannot help but feminize her—is the house inside the house, the locus of all that renews, and when I am tired or sick, as with a violent headache, into her tender arms I fall. Of course, a bed is many other things, and, as Bachelard also says, "Sleep opens within us an inn for phantoms. In the morning we must sweep out the shadows." But for its restorative power, I sought my dear bed when I stumbled from the bathroom, my poor skull squeaking with pain.

Unfortunately, I had forgotten about the women slumbering there. Light from the hallway spilled across their recumbent forms when I opened the door to my bedroom. The remaining five had scarcely moved since last I saw them jumbled in a crazy quilt of bare limbs and quiet faces, with one of the women turned away to face the wall, her bare body curved like a cello. Not daring to wake them, I closed the door in a swift, silent motion, the soft click of the lock against the plate sending a rail of pain to my sinuses. A nap in my own bed was impossible under the circumstances, and the only sensible alternative was the living room sofa.

Now a couch is no equal to a bed, but I can attest to its soothing power, for many a Sunday afternoon have I fallen asleep stretched out in front of the television, some sporting event going on without me, and an occasional all-nighter with a black-and-white movie long since over or a book tented on my chest or dropped to the floor. I could picture the seductive cushions, the warm afghan folded over the arm, and the throw pillows casually, yet artfully, positioned, and I entered the darkened living room with a lover's anticipation. From his customary perch atop the VCR, the cat mewed once and pointed his tail to the LED clock. I was glad to see some things had not changed and was grateful for the reassuring presence of another living being. Arranging myself on the sofa, I closed my eyes and waited for sleep and some relief from the hot poker pressing behind my eyeballs.

I must have dozed off, though for moments or centuries I cannot say, for I was awakened quite suddenly by the sensation of being smothered and deprived of air. A surge of gasping panic overwhelmed me, and I swatted at the thing on my face, realizing in the same instant that I was striking the cat. He screamed to be so rudely handled and leapt to the coffee table. "Harpo," I called for him and sat up to apologize. Diffident, the cat slunk to the throw pillows, and I had to grab him before he escaped completely. I held him in my lap, stroking him between the ears, whispering sweet nothings, and trying to make amends. Now, the old wives' tale about cats smothering people, particularly sleeping babies, is based upon the notion that when a child is completely out of it, the cat, attracted by the scent of milk, will sit on the face to suck out the baby's breath, but the plain truth is that cats dislike the smell of human breath. There is a report from a doctor in Helsingborg, Sweden, who wrote about his cat and new baby. Seems the cat had just given birth to kittens a few days before the infant son was brought home from the hospital. Upon hearing the child's first cry, the cat went to the nursery to investigate, and later that night, she moved all her kittens into the cradle. The crying baby, the doctor surmised, attuned the maternal instincts of the cat, and since she could not move this giant "kitten" to her litter, she brought the kittens to the baby. But no, it is not generally true that a cat will smother anyone intentionally, and in Harpo's case, he bothered my rest only if he wanted to be let out of the house.

As we walked to the front door, the cat weaved between my legs at each stride, and when I let him out, he scooted across the porch into the yard, disappearing in the darkness. For some reason, I thought I heard him say "So long," but soon realized the words were merely the play of my own thoughts on the radio of my imagination. I stood on the threshold watching the quiet early morning. On the lawn, where the tangle of bicycles should have been evident as a dark heap, there was nothing but smooth grass and empty space, and I began to question my memory of having seen them that afternoon. No traffic passed, and no one strolled along the sidewalks. In both directions, the lampposts glowed in a line that followed the curve of the street, and above the rooftops and leafy trees, a corner of the National Cathedral loomed, my private parapet. An airplane cut across the heavens, red lights on the wingtips in contrast to the faint white stars. A mockingbird sang in some treetop blocks away, the changing patterns of its stolen melodies designed to attract a mate to the nest. Crickets kept time. But all else was still as if painted on some universal mural, and I felt unable to enter into this outside world, for if I did I would be trapped by the landscape and would vanish forever when the moment passed. One step forward, and I would be swept out like Bachelard's dreams. The house, despite all of the strange things happening here, felt safer, and I retreated behind the door. My headache abated at once, but I just stood motionless, trying to sort through the events of the day. A woman moved through my mind, insisting upon being remembered. Her face began to take shape like an unfinished portrait on a canvas.

A cry broke my reverie, sudden and sharp, almost inhuman in its urgent intensity. At first I thought the skirl emanated from Harpo, for he often sounded like the bagpipes when he was desperate to come back in, but the sound repeated itself from inside the house, upstairs in the vicinity of the bathroom, judging by the echo. I took the steps by twos, anxious at the cause of such distress.

Huddled around the bathtub, the old man, Dolly, and Jane had their backs to me, and only when I stepped closer could I see the object of their rapt attention. Seated on the rim, Alice held to her breast a baby, not the cloth poppet, but an actual newborn, the soft spot on its bald head beating in rhythm as it nursed and one tiny fist clutching a long red tendril of its mother's hair. Mashed against her skin, its tiny mouth sucked with gusto and then paused to catch its breath, repeated the process, slowed, and then stopped. Alice pinched the tiny lips to break the suction and then slid her nipple out of the child's mouth, and by reflex, it gulped once or twice, the mouth pursed as if imagining what it had been about, and then the little one fell asleep. My eyes lingered on

Alice's bare breast as she tucked it inside her dress. Tattooed just above the nipple appeared the tiniest of witches, astride a broom, as if flying over a full moon.

"Isn't he adorable?" Jane asked. "A perfect little boy. Ten fingers and ten toes."

Alice handed the baby to Dolly, who laid him upright against her shoulder and began patting him gently on the back. Rearranging her dress to its standard position, Alice sidled up to me and said, "He'll have red hair, too, when it comes in, but he has your eyes."

"Pardon me?"

All three women grinned and gawked at me as if I were a specimen in a zoo.

"I have no idea what you are inferring," I said. "Where the devil did that baby come from?"

The old man clapped a bony hand on my shoulder. "Ah, Sonny, you don't mean to tell me you are uncertain as to the workings of the birds and the bees? When a man and a woman love each—"

I shrugged out of his grasp. "Not that . . . I understand the mechanics, you old fool. What I want to know are the particulars concerning this particular child of Alice's. It wasn't here when I left just a minute ago."

"Nine months," he said. "Or more precisely forty weeks, if all goes right."

"The details of human gestation are quite well known, even to a single man such as myself."

The little boy burped, loud as a trucker, and the rest of them giggled. Dolly handed the baby to his mother, and Alice laid him to sleep in a magazine rack where I usually kept my bathroom reading material, old issues of *Architectural Digest* and noteworthy issues of the weekly "Home" section of the *Washington Post*. The newborn fussed upon leaving his mother's arms, but soon settled into a deep sleep.

Mesmerized, we all watched for several minutes as if there was nothing more fascinating than a baby at rest, seeing perhaps in the child's complete surrender some capability lost to our world-weary adult selves.

I whispered to Alice, "You had no baby when you flew through the mirror."

"No need to keep your voice down," she said. "That child could sleep through a tornado if he has a full belly."

"But you had no baby when I met you last night."

"Perhaps your memory is at fault," said Alice. "Or perhaps your sense of time?" She winked at the old man, and on her closed eyelid, the third eye appeared, just as it had on all of them. The witch tattoo streaked across her bosom and disappeared behind the red fabric over her opposite shoulder.

The old man gathered his robe more modestly and sat on the toilet seat. "Yes, you were telling us about last night. Something about a theatrical performance in your former brother's former room? A woman singing."

"Oh, yes, I remember where I was. I followed the sound of music and entered my house, drawn upstairs by the beauty of the singer's voice and the unmistakably live piano, though as far as I know, there's never been such an instrument in this house. There were seven women: the singer and her accompanist, and five more sitting in two rows of chairs, listening to the performance. But I don't remember any baby."

Dreaming of the breast, the child in the magazine rack sucked in his sleep, as real as any of us.

"The women took scant notice of me when I entered the room. The singer flinched but she did not stop her singing, and the pianist did not miss a note. Some in the audience halfheartedly looked my way, a quarter turn of the head and a glance over the shoulder. To a person, they were stunning, though they seemed oddly out of date. Dressed in the kind of costumes seen in old cowboy movies, where the fella comes into a saloon and there'd be dancing girls in petticoats and velvet, bright crinoline, fishnet stockings, and long gloves. Like Marlene Dietrich in *Destry Rides Again,* or Lili Von Schtupp in *Blazing Saddles.* Open trunks spilled over with sequined dresses and feather boas. In the scenes, the girls would be laughing, sitting on the cowboys' laps, running their fingers through brilliantined hair, or perched atop an upright pianoforte, or leaning over the poker table, watching the action, waiting for some sap to buy them a free drink."

"Barflies," said Dolly.

"Working girls," said Jane. "Remember Madeline Kahn: 'Who am I kidding, everything from the waist down is kaput.'"

The old man slapped his knee, sending a cloud of dust and a pair of dazed moths into the air. "Tarts? Harlots? Ladies of the night?"

"Now, now," I stammered. "They were more like cancan dancers."

"It's all code, boy," the old man said. "Back in them days the films couldn't come right out and say so, but those were pros. Flirt with the boys to buy more liquor, then a romp upstairs on some ramshackle cot with the old cowpoke. What you saw were seven strumpets."

With an exaggerated curtsy, Alice flared the skirts of her dress. "Strumpets," she said. "Oh, I like that. How wonderfully old-fashioned and misogynistic of you." When she laughed, she exposed a set of flawless white teeth and a tongue that flared and fluted along its thin perimeter.

"Don't get the wrong impression," I said. "They weren't prostitutes, just dressed that way. Like they were playing a part. Actually, aside from the costumes and makeup, they acted very refined. A spread had been laid out on the sideboard. Cakes and pastries, petits fours, a silver samovar piping hot with tea, and bone china cups. Cake forks and demitasse spoons. White cloth napkins. Bottles of cold ale clotted with drops of condensation. It was very formal and elegant and showed a great deal of careful preparation."

Jane opened the medicine cabinet and drew out a small tray laden with leftover crumpets, which she passed around the room. When it reached the old man, he dithered over the options till choosing a mille-feuille, drizzled with chocolate, which he sampled with a delicate nibble. The moment the sweetness hit his taste buds, his eyes widened with pleasure, and he popped the whole thing in his mouth. Flakes of pastry sprinkled from his lips as he spoke. "So, these cancan dancers in their petticoats rode their bicycles to your house—pardon my dust—and they set up this piano recital in your former brother's former room—this napoleon is to die for—and brought in full service for high tea?" He licked the icing from his fingertips. "And crumpets?"

I nodded meekly. A short cough allowed him to swallow the last and address Jane with a parched throat. "You wouldn't have a spare bottle of that ale in the medicine cabinet, would you? Try behind the shaving cream."

Anticipating his logic, I volunteered an answer to his next query. "Of course, such a strange situation ordinarily would provoke a more immediate reaction on my part: what kind of show is going on here? Or: what are you women doing in my house?"

"Precisely. A perfectly natural line of reasoning. Indeed, I was expecting such interrogatories well before this point in your narrative. Why didn't you ask such questions right away?"

My provisional answer was a shrug of the shoulders. "I was dumbfounded—"

"Bewitched," said Alice, with a laugh.

"Yes, bedazzled, confused. Like walking into a real daydream. And besides, I wanted to hear the song through to the end."

Dolly smiled as though I brought her some maternal satisfaction. "He was only being polite."

With a crisp snap, Jane uncapped a bottle of ale for the old man. As she handed it to him, she added, "He was raised to follow etiquette and decorum. You can always tell a gentleman by his manners and whether he was brought up proper."

The old man drank deeply and then stood, the crumbs in his lap tumbling to the floor. "You were a good boy. Listened to your parents, kept your room tidy. The kind of boy who could occupy himself with a book or a pencil and some paper, always off drawing buildings and such in the corner of the bedroom. And then, following the rules: always stay on the outside of the sidewalk when strolling with a lady, hold open doors for strangers with packages, help old women across the street, and that sort of thing. You were a good boy, perhaps to a fault."

His sentiments encouraged distant memories to unmoor from my hippocampus. "You seem to know a great deal about me and my life, and I've been meaning to ask you all night: are you my father?"

The three women in the room sniggered at either the naïveté or the audacity of my question, and some whispered bit of editorial gossip raced among them. From the magazine rack, the baby stirred in his sleep as a vision knitted his doughboy features and troubled his tender soul. He kicked both legs together like a tree frog and then raised a protective fist, only to let it drop in slow motion as he relaxed again. What dreams could such a young person possibly have? What dreams might visit us in the womb? If Bachelard is right about the need to sweep out the phantoms and shadows of our dreams when we rise each morning, what is swept away when a child is born and first awakens to the world? Can he remember anything of prior existence?

"Will you not answer a direct question?" I asked again. "You do not look exactly like my father, or at least what I remember of him, but you share some familial characteristics and you appear to be the right age, had he lived, and you have treated me like a son, with a mix of love and disdain. Will you make me guess?"

He quaffed the dregs of his ale and set the empty bottle on the windowsill. A few crumbs stuck to the collar and sleeves of the terrycloth robe, and he picked and rolled them between his thumb and middle finger only to drop the crumble to the small rug in front of the toilet. With the toes of his left foot, he rocked the magazine rack like a cradle, humming under his breath a short, well-known lullaby, all the while glancing upon each person, though never looking me in the eye, before settling on his wizened reflection in the mirror. Startled by his own appearance, he combed his upswept silver hair with the rake of his fingers.

"Are you deliberately avoiding me?" I asked.

He rolled his eyes and suddenly stopped to focus on a spot directly above my head. "Not to change the subject," he said, "but do you have a small electrical fan built in to this room, of the kind designed to exhaust fumes and circulate the air?"

Petulant, I answered, "Yes. A ceiling fan."

"Ordinarily, is it black and made of cast iron?"

I looked up. Where the ceiling fan had always been, a much larger black disk appeared to be working its way through the plaster. Instead of the usual hum of the fan, the surface began to groan and splinter.

"Would you kindly," the old man asked, "take two steps either to your right or to your left?"

The object above expanded in size and circumference, and from the twelve o'clock position a handle emerged just as the frying pan loosened from its moorings and fell, crashing to the floor with a bang, cracking the tiles, and clattering as it bounced until it settled on a spot. The skillet, large as a hubcap and blackened with the seasonings of thousands of meals, was solid and heavy, and had I not moved, the weight might have fractured my skull or broken my neck. The old man reached out with a bare foot to assess its density, but he could not budge the cast iron so much as a millimeter.

From the direction of my bedroom, an angry voice roared some unintelligible curse, a door flew open, and someone stomped into the hallway. She arrived in a fury, gaped at the pan-shaped hole in the ceiling and then at the skillet on the tiles, and spewed another torrent of gibberish, which sounded like swearing in the French language or some personal patois spiced with Spanish and English. Her dark brown eyes fixed upon me, and I could see the anger flare and then recede. Acknowledging the absurdity of the moment, she began to laugh in a tone rich as coffee sweetened with sugarcane.

She was a beautiful young woman of African descent, her skin shaded to rich brown, and tall and slender limbed. Like the others she wore an elegant dress, hers a royal purple wrap trimmed with a trail of golden lionesses at the collar, sleeves, and hem. Rings of gold decorated the fingers on both hands, as well as the second toe of her left foot. A thick golden chain encircled her ankle, and enormous gold hoop earrings, round as saucers, hung to her shoulders. Hiding her hair, a cloth not unlike a turban was knotted at the base of her skull. *"J'arrive trop tard,"* she said. *"Il n'a pas reçu la casserole sur la tête. Merde."*

"Ah, you are French," the old man said, and then seeing the confusion on my face, he asked, *"Parlez-vous anglais?"*

"Speak French to me. It is the universal language."

The old man chuckled softly to himself. "Once upon a time," he said, "but now you are in modern America. *Ce fou-là ne sait rien du français.*"

Clearly exasperated by his reply, she said nothing, but simply undid the clasp of her gown and let it fall to the floor. Naked and unashamed, she closed her eyes and reached back to untie the knot of her headdress, and as she lifted the cloth, a torrent of black ink washed down her face and covered her body like a waterfall. When the last drop dripped into the dress at her feet, a pattern remained behind on every inch of her skin. "Don't be suddenly modest," she said in halting English. "Come closer and have a look. Don't tell me you have forgotten your Marie."

Written on the surface of her body were thousands of words in a small and spidery hand. I studied the sentence running along her collarbone before surrendering to my ignorance. "I'm sorry, but I don't know how to read French."

"I do!" the old man shouted, rubbing his hands gleefully. He approached and stood in front of her, his nose inches from her forehead, already inspecting the beginning of the story stamped there. "I will translate for you," he told me, and then he kissed the first phrase inked on her skin and exclaimed, *"Avec plaisir!"*

CHAPTER EIGHT

The Woman Who Danced the Vaudoux

He began in French. "*Il était une fois* . . . Are we to have a fairy tale?"

"No," she shook her head. "This is a true story. Every word."

From the breast pocket of his robe, the old man retrieved a pair of wire-rimmed spectacles and perched them on his nose and, peering through the lenses, he leaned in closely, inches from her skin, and translated as he read.

"Once upon a time there was a crocodile so hungry he could eat the world. Along the bank of the river, the crocodile would hide in the water and when the other animals came to quench their thirst, for it is very hot all the time in the old motherland, wham, he would catch them in his enormous jaws and chomp, chomp, eat them for his supper. First the zebra, but the crocodile did not like the taste of stripes. Then the giraffe, but he did not care for the spots. He even tried the poppo—"

The naked woman said, "Hippopotamus."

"Ah, I see. But the poppo was too fat and the crocodile's mouth was too tired after all that chewing. He would like to try the elephant, but no elephant ever came to this part of the motherland.

"All of the animals came to fear the crocodile with the enormous appetite, and they hesitated to go to the river, even though the sun shone brightly in the summer sky and no rain would fall. A great thirst fell upon them. We cannot be free, said the animals, until the tyrant is vanquished. In desperation they approached the king of the jungle, the lion, but he could not be bothered to leave the shade or disturb his nap. Only a pair of lionesses, who had been listening nearby, were moved to pity, and they agreed to see what could be done about the terrible crocodile.

"The two beautiful lionesses, who happened to be mother and cub, went down to the river to spy upon the monster as he dozed in the mud. A hundred daggers stood in his jagged mouth, and scaly bark, thicker than that of a monkeybread tree, covered him in armor. If those defenses were not dangerous enough, he had a tail most formidable that could knock a gnu off its feet. A dry throat overcame the daughter, and she dared take a sip. At once, the crocodile stirred from its slumber and like a flash was at her nose, the water white and churning with his fury. Just in time, she jumped away, roaring in surprise. Off they went back into the bush to discuss their strategy. He is too fast, said the mama. And too hungry, said the baby. Maman said then we shall fatten him until he becomes lazy and slow.

"So they took a share of all they hunted down to the river. Wild pigs and antelope, and he grew bigger still. And then they had the monkeys gather mushmelons and yams by the score and cook them up with spices, and the crocodile loved their recipes and ate and ate. Now bloated like a thundercloud, he slept all but one hour of the day and then rose only to eat some more. He grew so big that his belly dragged on the bottom of the river and his petite legs and feet could not touch the ground, and still they fed him, those lionesses, more and more till he was just like a fat log idly floating on the surface. He no longer had the speed to catch so much as a turtle, and then they had him. The mama jumped on his back, but he could not even turn his head, he was so fat, and she sank her teeth into his snout and clamped shut his great jaws, and the daughter seized his formidable tail, which he could not so much as swish, he was so lazy, and stilled it with her great paws, and the old crocodile, he thought gallant thoughts, but he was no match, and so, phtt!, the end of him. When they heard the news, the animals danced in jubilee, for they were now free to come to the river whenever they pleased."

The tale, written across her face, disappeared into the hair at the base of her skull, and the old man had to search a moment to pick up the narrative at its proper place, circling the woman as the words wound around her neck.

"This is the first story I can remember. My mother's face appears before me when I tell it, for I heard it first at her knee, and my mother had learned the tale as a girl in Africa, before she had been stolen and transported to Senegal and sold into slavery and shipped to the new world. She was a girl herself, aboard a ship of 150 Africans, that landed first in Habana to unload half and then in Saint-Domingue to discharge the rest. So many stories my mother told, and the songs of the Bambara people were on her lips day and night whenever the Buckra folk were not around. She was a household servant . . ."

He turned to the woman. "Do you wish me to say slave?"

"This or that," Marie answered. "In those days, we called ourselves servants, though in truth we were common property with no more rights than a barnyard hen and often not treated any better." She chewed on her bottom lip. "Yes, slave is the bon mot."

"And the Buckra? *Comment est-ce qu'on dit en français?*"

"The Frenchmen," she said and turned her face so that I might feel the brunt of her stare. "The whites."

"She was a domestic slave on the plantation of Monsieur Delhomme in Saint-Domingue, and my papa was a slave in the sugarcane fields, and he fathered me and my younger sister Louisa, though for the youngest, Claire, who knows, perhaps my papa or perhaps Monsieur Delhomme, impossible to say, though even as a baby, Claire looked lighter than the rest. Makes no difference, I suppose. The master never claimed her as his own, and my papa never treated her as anything but his. Madame Delhomme may have suspected that her husband had something to do with the pickaninny, though truth be told, when you are young the attitude of adults is difficult to measure, being so subtle, especially for a girl like me whom every adult, black or white, mystified. Their moods changed as quickly as the late summer sky, bright to cloud-dark, in a trice, and best to be neither foul nor fair yourself, but on constant alert.

"Madame had few opportunities to come in contact with Claire or Louisa, for they had no natural place in the household, while I was constantly there as the companion to the Delhommes' baby child, a girl named Anna about my age, or a year or so on either side. In all the world, she was my only friend, and I hers. For eleven years, we grew up together, playing, sometimes eating the same meals, even bathing together, and sharing a bed on the nights when she could not bear to part with me and would beg her mother so. Under the netting, she read me fairy tales and Bible stories, and while we were alone the many years, she taught me how to read for myself, though servants were not supposed to know, but we had our school behind the privy or hidden among the canes as they grew, and it was in the dust of Saint-Domingue where I first wrote my own name and more. Anna loved me more than the little dog who followed us around everywhere, and she dressed me and held my hand and nursed me whenever I fell ill. She treated me like a *poupée*—"

"Doll," said Marie. "Though sometimes like a confidante, too, but as we grew older she came to realize that I was hers to do with what she pleased."

The baby in the magazine rack fussed in his sleep and then fell back into dreamland. Finding his place on Marie's naked left shoulder, the old man resumed his translation.

"She treated me like her doll, and I was blissfully unaware, as most children are, that things could or should be otherwise. This is the way of the world. All of that changed suddenly when Monsieur Delhomme fell ill to the fever and died in the sugarcane fields and was gone from this world without notice. He was a good man and treated us most kindly, and the slaves of the plantation mourned him not only out of duty but with some genuine affection. My mama cried all afternoon, and even my papa shed a tear, though perhaps, in hindsight, not only out of grief but with the knowledge of the change to come. Sure enough, the ranger—who is that?"

"Like the overseer," she said, "but a slave. A slave above the slaves."

"The ranger came to our house not one month later with the news that Madame Delhomme, now the widow, was to sell the property and return to France, for she was dearly homesick and felt also that her little Anna had missed all proper society by living in the new world. I ran straight to the big house. Anna had heard that we, too, were to be sold. Can you not take me with you to France? I cried to her, and she cried that she could not, and it was like to break our hearts, and when we parted I sobbed myself to sleep and thought life would be best to end right there. I cannot forget my mother's face that night at supper when she told us that we would be taken to auction in Port-au-Prince, to go to the man willing to pay the highest price, and that God willing we should not be parted, but parted we were. The auction took place in the town square. My papa went first, sold to another sugar farmer, and though I was shocked to see him go, I did not really know the man all that well for he was rarely at home. And then my mama and her three girls went on market. Louisa and Claire were still young enough that the man who purchased my mother took all three as a lot, but I was made to bare myself and be pinched and prodded by several Buckra men who kept shouting numbers, until at last a price of many sols was reached, and suddenly I was handed over to a fat man in a white suit with a waistcoat colored apricot. He asked, How old is this negress? Fifteen, the auctioneer said, perhaps seventeen years.

"Fourteen, I said to the man, who seemed to be glowing in the bright sunshine. I am fourteen years old. Just as I spoke those words, I saw my mother and two sisters being led away by their new master, and I broke free, running to them, anxious not to be parted. My mother wailed when I embraced her and she hugged me to her breast. Please don't beat her, she said to the auctioneer. *Ma chérie*, she cried, be a good girl. Do as you are told, and then the man pried me out of her arms, screaming in tears, and I did not ever see her again, though I can still picture the three of them walking away until all that remained were their bare footprints in the dust, and then I felt the hand of the master fall upon my shoulder.

"M. LaChance was his name, which made me smile against my will, and he said he was sorry to have only enough money for one and asked if I had lived all my fourteen years in Saint-Domingue, and I answered, *Oui*. He asked if I had ever ridden on a boat, and I answered, *Non*. We climbed into a cabriolet and were whisked off to the docks, and when I began to weep once more, this strange round man patted me on the knee. He said, We shall have an adventure in that case, for we are bound for Orleans, and I asked if that meant we would be going to France, thinking that at least I should see Anna again, but he just laughed till his face turned red. No, M. LaChance said, New Orleans in Louisiana, and I burst into bitter tears at the cruel irony embedded in the very name of our destination.

"The journey across the Gulf was a long one, and I traveled be-lowdecks with eight other blacks, slaves one and all. In the daytime, we were allowed to stand on the deck across the open waters, but once we neared the port at the mouth of the Mississippi, the mosquitos would like to assassinate a body with their bites and they showed no pity upon any breathing thing. Clouds of gnats, too, would swarm and some flew into my mouth and nose and lodged themselves in the corners of my eyes. I was relieved to be off the ship. Waylaid in the country of the Tchactas, we disembarked in an Indian village, and the chief there dressed just like a Frenchman and spoke the language of the traders, as do many other tribes along the river. In the chief's cabin, a white man from faraway Canada looked stricken when he first joined eyes with mine. He could not stop from looking at me. He was the biggest and tallest man I ever did see, with a red beard that made his face look afire, and I heard him offer M. LaChance a good price if he could buy me and make me his bride. Had not the master thought the whole matter a mere peccadillo, I may have had a different history, but he just laughed at the Cajun, and we moved on in the morning and reached Nouvelle Orleans in a week's time."

The old man stopped abruptly, for the last phrase had been written along the length of the little finger on her left hand and the chapter ended in midair. He had to locate the beginning of the next part of her story and so began to delicately search along her skin for the proper place. Perhaps by accident, he stepped too close and lost his balance, and reaching out to break his fall, his hand landed squarely upon her breast. *"Pardonnez-moi,"* he said, but she just chuckled softly and re-plied, *"Je connais la chanson."* He withdrew his hand and resumed his investigation by sight.

Outside the small window, something thumped and fluttered against the glass, and when I lifted back the curtain, I saw an enormous pale green moth struggling to reach the light inside the bathroom. A dozen little ones were pasted on the screen. Beyond them the late-night shadows revealed nothing. All of the houses in the neighborhood stood dark and silent as a mountain range, their occupants asleep in their comfy beds. I envied them their peace and dreams, and for the first time since my head had been struck and I had fallen, I wondered if I, too, were not merely sleeping in my bed next to my beloved and the whole night some hallucination brought on by a lunchtime burrito. The old man, Marie, Alice, Jane, Dolly, the baby at our feet, all mere players in some elaborate dream. Perhaps even the bicycles on the lawn, the entire June day stretching into this bizarre night. To check, I pinched my thigh, as one is always told to do, but the sharp pain was real enough.

"Voilà!" the old man exclaimed. The story continued across her clavicle and next ran down the length of her right arm.

"We arrived in the biggest city in all of Louisiana on the 8th of December, 1768. Some folk in the old part of town followed the Lyonese custom of celebrating la Fête de la Lumière, for on the windowsills of their houses burned candles in colored glass jars, a magical sight, like stars glowing red and yellow and blue. It was like walking in a rainbow at midnight. On the corner of a pretty little street stood the house, two storeys high, with an iron rail fence running the width of a mezzanine, and facing the street, a black walnut door opened to a front parlor. He lit a candle and placed it in my hand. The flame danced like a phantom in the darkness. No one greeted us, perhaps because of the lateness of

the hour and our unpredictable arrival date, but the quiet inside un-
settled me. M. LaChance had told me all about his family and the domestic situation during our long travels from the island, and I had hoped
for some greeting other than this ghostly absence. Instead, the Master
whispered a good night and pointed with his walking stick to a room
beyond the kitchen. You will find Hachard down there, dead asleep, he
said, but you rouse her and she will show you to your bed. We will
get to work in the morning. With that, he toddled toward the staircase.
With each step, the floorboards creaked and groaned beneath his prodigious corpulence.

"Is that you, my angel? Hachard asked when I entered the tiny
room and shook her from her slumber. No, it is me, Marie, the new girl
the Master has brought back from Saint-Domingue. She stepped into
the candlelight, close enough for me to see the gray in her hair and the
dark circles around her eyes. Four of her front teeth had escaped from
her mouth, and the wind whistled in her words. Confusion danced in
her gaze, but at last she figured out just who I was. I have been waiting
for you, she said, but you are just a young girl. Old enough to marry,
I said, old enough to care for myself. Hachard laughed at my audacity,
revealing more empty spaces at the back of her mouth. We shall see, but
first some rest after your long journey. Taking the candle in her claws,
she guided me to a cot at the foot of her bed, and I fell into the blankets
without undressing. I was nearly asleep when I heard her disembodied
voice rise in the darkness. Do you know how to cook? *Oui*, I answered.
We shall see, we shall see.

"In the morning, we rose and dressed before the dawn, and I met
the rest of the family LaChance. The mistress of the house, Madame
Dominique, proved the opposite of her husband in every respect.
Where he was fat and jolly, she was thin and dour. Where he favored
white linen and played the fop, she dressed in black. *Revêche*. But perhaps all the children made her so, for though she could not have been

but thirty, she had squeezed out six, the oldest a boy two years younger than me, and the youngest but a baby. One and all they were round like their father, little balls of dough."

Dolly laughed. "The Roly-polies."

"Your description," said Jane, "reminds me of a Botero painting. The fat man and his six little dumplings."

Marie watched the old man, making sure that his wandering eye stayed fixed upon her right forearm. "Of course! I had not thought of Botero before, but the children and their father could have stepped right out of his canvas. Plump pullets, but good dears when they were young and had been fed."

This time the old man had kept a finger on the spot, and when their colloquy had ended, he was able to resume without further pause.

"My job was to be a nanny to the children and to apprentice to Hachard in the housekeeping. She had been in service to the family from the childhood of M. LaChance and was now an old woman near fifty and could not move about as quickly for the pain in her joints and a stiffness in her hands and feet that left her fingers and toes twisted and gnarled. The Mistress insisted that Hachard continue to cook the meals, but every other household chore fell upon me—the cleaning, the slops, sweeping, washing, and serving the dishes, and besides all that, to help look after the little ones. That duty was my easiest burden. Lazy creatures on even the finest days, they barely moved when the rainy season arrived, and come July and August, in the oppressive heat, they lounged behind the heavy draperies, reading their books or quietly playing cards or other games of chance. The two little girls had their dollies, and the boys would sometimes chase each other with wooden swords, but mostly they ate and slept and did their lessons with an old white woman who came to the house. The babies napped in the shank of the afternoon up until they were five or six years. But the mere presence of the children was a blessing, for they reminded me of my own Anna and my sisters and thus relieved in small measure the anguish in my soul.

"Very quickly—that first day in fact—I realized why Madame made Hachard to continue preparing the food, for she cooked most exquisitely in the French manner, unlike many of our neighbors who seemed to ape the worst of English—or merciful God, colonial—cuisine. No, Hachard performed magic with simple, fresh ingredients, and drew on a kind of cooks' club of her neighbors in the Quarter. Old slaves who actually ran the homes would be entrusted to visit the stalls in the square to buy fish or meat or produce from the cartmen who rolled along the street calling out their wares. Hachard above all was the best, cooking with touches of the Creole and Cajun, of France and Africa. I had not eaten so well in Port-au-Prince and, I imagined, not even King Louis himself ate so well in Paris. Though my heart was empty, my stomach was full.

"In this way the days turned into weeks, and the weeks into months. I was kept very busy. All that Hachard could no longer manage, she assigned to me. The simple things—the sewing and mending, plucking a hen or shucking corn, cleaning the dishes or dusting and polishing—did not trouble me, for my mother had shown me and often enlisted my assistance. Even the ordinary washday was tolerable, if, with so many children, never-ending. Worst of all, when we stripped the beds and took down the curtains and the soiled linens, perhaps once each season of the year, my back would like to break from the heaviness. Poor Hachard could not bear to steep herself in hot water, which would linger in her joints and pain her fiercely. Recompense for every odious task was time in the kitchen as sous chef to Hachard—chopping ingredients or making the sauces or roux. As she cooked, Hachard spoke aloud each ingredient, every step—a pinch of salt, three spoons of butter, keep stirring till the sugar melts and thickens, and I seized every word, memorizing in spite of myself all of her secrets. Perhaps she was consciously passing the traditions, or perhaps she was merely grateful for the company. Someone to talk with despite having little to say.

"Once a month, Madame LaChance granted Hachard a day to herself, and the old girl would spend half the morning making herself ready, changing from her work clothes into a dress of faded cornflower, then having me comb out her hair, and she'd powder beneath her arms till she smelled sweet as a baby. I asked her the first few occasions where she was going and if I could go with her, and she just hushed me and said, Never you mind, child. Or, Maybe when you are old enough to keep yourself clear, Marie, but those rascals would be on you now like wasps on a sugar stick. Late those Sunday evenings, she would return and sneak in through the back door, careful not to make a sound, hair wild and unkempt, her dress circled with sweat, her mouth bruised and swollen as a ripe peach. A few times she smelled of spirits and smoke, and once, in that first year, she cried out as she lay her body down upon the bed. Oh, the brute he would have liked to kill me. I sprang to her side to see if she was indeed hurt, and in the darkness, she touched her rough palm against my cheek and whispered, *Ma chérie,* I would not quit this kind of night for anything. With him, I am *toujours gai* and it is the only reason to keep on living.

"The next morning she woke early and had me draw a bath outside, despite the torpid weather. Even at dawn in July, the air hangs heavy and presses down upon a body till you can hardly breathe. She undressed slowly and eased herself into the water, mindful of every aching bone. I sat beside her on the lip of the trough and dipped a cloth into the water and wrung it onto her hair, rubbed the knob of her spine, and massaged her shoulders. That feels nice, child, you are a good girl. For the first time, I noticed the scars on her skin. Where did you get these welts, Miss Hachard? From being whipped, she said. Why did they whip you? For asking too many questions, she said and slid farther into the water. We are to have a new governor, she said at last. The Spaniards are to send someone to replace Ulloa at last. The whole town will be overrun with the Spanish.

"The lords of misrule were in charge, yet rumors persisted that the Spanish king would send in a new man, and indeed, the Master and Mistress spoke of the prospect nearly every week. I asked Hachard in the tub, Who do the men say it shall be? *Mon Dieu,* she spat out the words, they say it is an Irishman. She shivered in the cooling water. Now help me out of this bath before I die of pneumonia."

The old man had come to the end of another little finger, but this time he thought to ask where to look for the continuation of the story. Marie pointed toward her heart, and he could see the first line rise and fall along the curve of her breasts. The giant moth beat against the screen and settled on a patch nearer to the light. We all leaned closer to listen. Feigning a storyteller's professional disinterest, the old man stared at the words inked on her chest and began again.

"A dozen ships came sailing up the river, flying the Spanish ensign, and the whole town turned out to the levee to make them welcome. The Master and Mistress wore their finest linen suits, despite the heat, for they were to be on the dais with the other gentry in a place of honor for the official ceremony. Hachard and I were to bring the children along later and watch with the assembled on the grounds overlooking the square, and I never saw such a spectacle and a throng. As the Spanish arrived, there was singing and dancing and drinking and smoking and

gaming and Lord-knows-what going on, the lid off the pot and the ra-
gout boiling over. The youngest baby, Georges, raised such a fuss that I
must needs carry him in my arms the whole time, so I was tamed, and it
seemed like forever for that first ship to dock. While we waited, an older
man sidled up to Hachard, and they exchanged habitual pleasantries,
and I am sure I saw his hand upon her shoulder more than once that
whole time. I wondered if this Big Fella was the man who made her *toujours gai*, but I dared not ask. The first to disembark from the ship were
black sailors, and I said to the Big Fella, I did not know they allowed
slaves to sail the boats. And he said, They are not boats, but ships, and
they are not slaves, but freedmen from Habana in Cuba. How can this
be? I asked, and he said, Little Chick, not all black men are in chains.

"I pondered this assertion as the sailors and soldiers spilled down
the gangway, and last the entourage of the governor made its way to
the stage that had been erected in the center of the square. From my
vantage, I did not get a close look, but I could see the Irishman at last,
no powdered wig but black hair like a raven set against his pale skin,
and the fine coats and breeches of a gentleman, festooned with ribbons
and medals on his chest. Warm applause greeted him, a few rowdies
hooting in the anonymity of the crowd. M. LaChance and the others sat
to listen to the speech, and the rest of us held our space and strained to
hear. The new governor spoke to us first in Spanish, and a few words
that echoed our own language made sense to me, but then he repeated
his oration in French, bestowing upon the people of New Orleans bless-
ings from God and felicitations from King Carlos, a surprise to hear
that name, and to announce not only a new prosperity ahead but a return to law and order as well. And then he started again his greetings,
but the third language made no sense, though his voice bore the words
as if in a song both natural and sweet. What is that tongue? I asked. Is
Governor O'Reilly speaking Irish? The Big Fella laughed at me and
said, No, that is the language of the English passed through an Irish

mouth. Sort of like a fart passed through a flute. Hachard slapped him on the shoulder at that remark, but she was secretly smiling. We all were happy that day, though it was the only time I ever laid eyes upon O'Reilly, yet I was to hear more of him in the months ahead, and he was to change my life entirely. He gave me hope."

A low chuckle from Marie interrupted the old man's recitation, and he straightened his back and raised his eyes to inquire as to the source of her levity. He had been poised at a spot just below the curve of her breast. "I'm sorry," she said, "but your hair was tickling me."

He flattened the silver cock's comb sprouting atop his head. "A thousand apologies, Mademoiselle." When he removed his hand, his hair sprang straight up, and all of the women giggled. Something about that wild hair and those wire-rimmed glasses reminded me of a public personage whose face had often appeared in photographs once upon a time, but still I could not attach a name to the man. With a curt, proper bow, he bent to his work.

"Not four days after the arrival of O'Reilly and his black freedmen, soldiers from Cuba posted the broadsides around town announcing the arrest of the Acadian ringleaders of those who had chased the former governor Ulloa from New Orleans. I had to beg the Master to be let go into town for the execution, and at first he refused my request, saying it was not fit for a colored girl to see. More clever by far, Hachard simply informed the Mistress that she must needs go into the markets that morning and I was to accompany her to fetch home the parcels. What is that you are buying? Madame asked. Is it so heavy that you need the girl? Tabac, said Hachard, from Habana, and my friends tell me *coquille d'huître* big as a small hen are to be found, and you know how the Master loves *des huîtres*."

Puzzled by the word, the old man stopped.

"Oysters," Marie volunteered.

"Yes, Madame answered, every time he eats the oysters, he fills me with another baby. She reached into her purse and produced another coin. If you must buy oysters, she said, buy a surfeit of fat ones so the old goat will be too stuffed to move and will leave me alone tonight. *Merci*, Hachard curtsied, and we were on our way.

"The French thugs had been quickly tried for crimes against the Spanish king when they kicked out his governor, and O'Reilly had ordered some rebels exiled for life at Morro prison in Habana, and their lands were confiscated by the government. The five ringleaders were executed, perhaps—I don't know—as an example to others with treason in their hearts. We were desperate to see the firing square. A great crowd shielded the scene as we arrived, but word ran from person to person that the prisoners were bound and blindfolded and made to stand like stalwarts against the wall. No sooner had this news reached our ears than the loud volley of muskets, several shots all at one command, and then another solitary ball as if some man who suffered the first round had been dispatched with a second. The crowd parted in a moment, and the troops marched past, their elegant uniforms clean and menacing, and I was shocked to see that three of the eight musketeers were black like me and two others mulatto of some mixed blood. A black killing a white was unthinkable, but such are the changes brought by the Spanish Irishman.

"From that moment on, he became known as Bloody O'Reilly, though I do not know how he is called in Spanish. Eight slaves dragged away the bodies from the wall until all that could be seen were pocks in the soft plaster where the balls had either missed their targets or passed through the victims. A few handfuls of sawdust blotted the blood on the ground, and I confess that my heart was sore for those men, whatever sin on their souls, and in my imagination, the Irishman darkened any sense of liberty I may have felt at being at the market.

"But do not judge the chess match by an opening gambit. Stories about the governor's actions sifted through the whites and eventually settled upon our people, where the news was most welcome. He would stand no disrespect from the French and expelled the foreign merchants from the city with the sole exception of Oliver Pollock, another Irish. How they stick together. But most of all, the governor seemed to be on the side of the downtrodden. The Big Fella explained to Hachard, who passed the notion to me, that O'Reilly, being a member of a long-suffering people, could not bear to join the service of his nation's oppressors, the English, and so he became a Wild Goose and flew off to Europe, first to Austria and then to Spain. Hachard said, He is like us in one respect, to have known the heel of the boot.

"The Master and Mistress quarreled often about the man and whether the Spanish or French were better for Orleans. In all my years with the family LaChance, little else caused such rows. The Master was a genial sort; keep him fed and laid in bed, and nothing would ruffle him. We cannot change kings at will, he would say. Better to prosper in New Spain than pine for Old France. But Madame behaved like the *nombril du monde* . . .

The old man asked, "What would we say?"

She shrugged and pointed at her belly button.

"Let's say she was 'the center of the universe,' and for her it was French or nothing. She would say, Who does O'Reilly think he is, that great Ass of Dublin. I had to hide my laugh behind my hand at her words, for she did not like any show of understanding on our parts.

"After the Creoles were put down, O'Reilly sent many of those black soldiers back to Cuba, but those remaining behind made their presence felt every morning and evening with a drum tattoo and the playing of their fifes and horns. Many times the troops marched down our street, and through the window, a smarter and finer dressage was not to be found. And they went to work supervising gangs of men to shore the levees and build a bridge and to construct the banquettes so folks would have someplace to walk without dragging their hems through the muck and mire. In short, the governor brought a sense of discipline that had been missing to the fair city. It was so good to see law and order imposed upon those who for so long imposed upon us. Even the Master has his Master to obey."

With a creak and a groan, the old man unhinged his spine and slowly straightened from his crouch to a full standing position. He had been bent over to read the part of the story that began at the hip and ran into the problem of the nether lands, the words disappearing into a thicket covering her pubis. I empathized with the delicacy of his conundrum as he looked my way for moral support or some technical instruction, but all I could do was shrug. The women in the room offered no assistance, nor did they seem particularly aware of the nature of his predicament. Obliviously chatting among themselves in the interlude, Dolly, Jane, and Alice could have been three sisters at a wedding for the fourth, throwing an invisible shield about the bride, subtly resenting the attention paid to her while acknowledging her role as the center of attention. The bride herself, Marie that is, rolled her eyes as she intuited the cause of the old man's indecision.

"*Zut de flûte!* You have been ogling and objectifying me thus far. Be a man and read on." She reached out and grabbed him by the ears, and then tugged him to his knees. He cried out and accepted his subjugation. Clearing his thoughts with a long sigh, he read on from hips to toes without hesitation.

. . .

"The greatest change, however, was to the Code Noir—the legal protocols by which the French kept control of their slaves. O'Reilly, governed by the precepts of the Spanish code—Las Siete Partidas—and by his long experience in Puerto Rico and Cuba, gradually liberalized the rules. As with every other civic law that made our lives better, we only learned of this by word passing mouth to ear, yet in time, four things became clear even to us slaves.

"First, he freed the red man. No Tchacta, Tanikas, or Natches, or any other Indian would be enslaved—"

Dolly clapped once and said, "I like this Irishman more and more."

"There was a woman of Hachard's acquaintance, who lived farther along the levee, long thought to be African, and she made her claim by speaking without stop in the mother tongue of her tribe, and her master, whether from guilt or merely to shut her mouth, freed her on the spot. For the second part of the new code allowed masters to free their slaves without obtaining permission of the *cabildo* or governor or anyone at all. Under the Code Noir, an official decree for just cause was required for emancipation, but this put the matter in the master's hands. The third great change was to allow the person to own their own property and not, as the French had it, forfeit their rights to the master. After O'Reilly, we could now own money, make a contract with anyone for services on our own time, and receive an inheritance. A girl of my own age, the daughter of a freedman parted from her and living in Pennsylvania, was sent a note upon the unfortunate man's demise that she was now the owner of a farm larger in acreage than her own master's plantation. The irony would have been unbearable if not for the fourth part of O'Reilly's reforms. She was able to buy her freedom by selling a parcel of land and paying her owner. The governor had granted the right of *coartación* to all slaves in Louisiana, just as the blacks of Cuba had enjoyed.

Contracts were allowed with our masters to set a price for our freedom, and in essence, we could now purchase ourselves. A special council had been established to hear our cases and take our complaints and judge any abuse. If a master refused a contract of manumission, he could be brought before the court. If a master overstepped his bounds most cruelly, he could be ordered to sell that slave to someone kinder who might treat us as genuine humans and not mere chattel.

"One year after I had first met Hachard, on the night of the Festival of Lights, we talked in her little room about our plans for freedom, with our voices low, so as not to wake the children, but she could scarce contain her enthusiasm. The Big Fella, she whispered, says there are many people who would pay a king's ransom for the treat of a Sunday dinner from the pot of old Hachard. And he says that Mr. Pollock, the Irish merchant who is friend to the governor, will pay a handsome price to unload the ships when the wheat comes in, or the cider barrels. We have made a pact, Marie Delhomme, the first to acquire the money shall save for the other. He must love you very much, I said, and you him. A quick laugh lit the darkness. My dear, you are a child with a view of life that is too romantic for an old crow, but we like each other well enough. I felt foolish, but excitement overpowered my shame. How much will you need to pay to buy your life? Phtt, I am an old woman of little use, and the Master should pay me to go. She mentioned a figure in French money, and I asked her for the amount in Spanish currency, for I no longer understood the French sums. We shall see, said Hachard, what M. Foiegras has to say, but I hope the price is low.

"The matter was settled at Christmastime, after the children had been sent to bed, and the Master and Mistress lingered over the roast goose. Madame LaChance sat like a stump, her arms crossed over her breast. But his lips and fingers glistened with grease, and Monsieur wore on his face a look of utter contentment. Perfect, he told Hachard as we cleared the bird from the table. Delicious, as usual. *Merci,* she said. Since it is the day of thanksgiving for our Lord's birth, she said, perhaps you have given thought to our conversation? With the sharp point of a knife, he picked at his teeth and sucked in the bits of meat as he talked. Our conversation? The *coartación*? The price, Monsieur? Leaning back in his chair till he nearly toppled over, he said, We could never let you go, Hachard, for how then would we eat so well? But Master . . . One hand rose in the air to silence her, but she pressed on: I shall teach little Marie my every secret. Fat chance, he said, but let's say you do. *Ce n'est pas un perdreau de l'année.* How is 100 piastres? A fair price, no?

"If the amount stunned her, Hachard betrayed no emotion, though of course I knew it well beyond her speculations. She simply bowed and removed more dishes from the table, wiping her nose on the shoulder of her dress. Curious and emboldened, I approached the Master and asked what price was upon me. You are but a kitten. He eyed me from head to toe. Shall we say 350 piastres? That's less than I paid for you in Port-au-Prince. I could do little more than nod, but the sum might as well have been ten times as much, for I had never heard of anything to cost as much as freedom. Back in our room, Hachard and I cried together. Such a fine Christmas.

"What else can you do when life sets such obstacles before you other than to persevere and rely upon God's will and your own wits? Hachard at least had the reassurance of her man and the secret knowledge that he toiled on her behalf. I had no one in the world but my own self. I bent to my work. There was enough to do raising six children, running the household, and squeezing every recipe from Hachard.

"Once he had shown the French and Creoles and Acadians the iron will of Spain, Governor O'Reilly departed the next February, and another Spaniard took his place. No matter. The codes had been reformed, and we were not to go back to the old ways. I had my contract for manumission tucked beneath my mattress, and on free days, took the wash of some less fortunate households to the laundry along with the LaChances', and by the end of one year, I had five piastres to my name. Since she could hire herself to cook every night she managed, Hachard fared much better and made triple my wages. More and more she brought me into the kitchen as she had promised and showed me her techniques, those acquired over long years at a hot stove, but also a touch of Cuba in some dishes, for she picked up recipes from the Habanans who now resided in New Orleans. Very hot, with lots of cayenne and other peppers, and M. LaChance loved the new flavors. The hotter the better, and when the summer came and the sun bore down in July and August, he thrived on some smoke on his tongue. His favorite dish was *écrevisse épicée . . .*"

Loudly clearing his throat, the old man paused. "Spicy, *n'est pas*? But I don't know what is *écrevisse.*"

Marie lifted her foot and stomped on the handle of the frying pan that had been lying facedown on the floor since falling from the ceiling. In one motion too quick for the eye, the skillet flipped over, and inside dozens of spiced crayfish sizzled and popped.

"Crawdaddies!" Jane exclaimed. "I'm starving." She reached into the pan and pulled out a crayfish, twisted and peeled back the shell with the nail of her thumb, and gobbled it down to the tail in two bites. "Oh, she is a good cook. Help yourself, girls."

Dolly dug in, and soon the two of them were hooting with joy over the delicious explosions in their mouths. Off to the side, Alice demurred. "I'm nursing, and I wouldn't want to give the little boy a tummyache." Her friends continued eating without care. "Oh, what the hell," Alice said. "Maybe just one." Taking two bright red crayfish, she gave one to me, and it tasted of sweetness and fire.

Still on his knees, the old man ignored our gluttony. He read on.

. . .

"Every other day, I would cook for him and thus became so skilled that no one could tell the difference between my pot and Hachard's. Just as well, for in seven years—about the time of the Americans' revolt against the English king—Hachard had earned enough to execute her contract. Of course, I had known for a long time that her savings had grown, but the day came when she showed me the money, the last piastres earned for a midsummer banquet, and the finality seemed sudden. Tomorrow, she said, I will go to the Master. Listen to me, tomorrow he will no longer be Master, just M. Foiegras. We laughed a little, but the melancholy swept over me like a late summer storm. Hachard had been a mother to me ever since my own mother and sisters were so violently taken away, and my emotions mixed the two events till I was fourteen again and alone on the docks of Saint-Domingue. Yet I was happy for her as well, for she had endured a long servitude and could now rest her bones and find some ease from care. With her thumb, she wiped the tears from my face. *Ma chérie*, she said, do not cry. We shall always be friends, and I will visit as long as the Goose and his wife allow. We will not be far. The Big Fella has a place near Pointe Coupée, and you will go now to the dances in the square on Sundays and meet us there. Look at you, all grown into a woman. Time for a little love, shake your tail feathers, and let the good times roll. And you will have your freedom yet. Who knows, maybe the Big Fella and I will get rich, and then we can buy you from the old Goose.

"Promises made in passion are the most difficult to keep. After she left, Hachard became a stranger, though I missed her as much as my own mother. We met maybe five times that first year, four the second, two the third, and then not at all. A bend in the river separated us but it may as well have been an ocean. We did not see each other for years. A few months after the Good Friday fire in '88, when it seemed like all of New Orleans burned, I brought little Clothide with me to the Perseverance Benevolent and Mutual Aid Society, for all of my money had gone up in flames, and there was Hachard, old and gray and sunken into herself. Like a dying tree, but a few lonesome leaves. She wept when I kissed her.

"Maman Hachard, I asked, what has happened to you? The spark had left her eyes. Even the child in my arms failed to interest her. I have nothing, she croaked, not a tooth in her mouth. Not one peso. All gone. Nothing to be done. Setting the baby on the bench next to her, I fetched a scupper of water. Drink, maman, your lips are cracked from thirst and it is hot enough to fry the Devil."

As he had reached the tip of her toes, the old man stood and circled around Marie, finding the continuation at her shoulder blades, the words running like stripes across her back. The other women had finished their crayfish, and in the sink, the shells sparkled like mother-of-pearl. In his basket, the baby quietly snored. Outside the window, the cypress trees dripped with Spanish moss, and from the swamps, the alligators bellowed.

"Once she had managed to swallow a few mouthfuls of water, Hachard related the events since leaving the family LaChance. I knew, of course, that she had married the Big Fella and they had gone to live among the maroons in Pointe Coupée, but I had not heard of their troubles there. He had broken down early on, the victim of too many years toiling on the docks and too much rum and sugar. All my life, she said, I've been taking care of someone. First my own papa, and then thirty-odd years for the old Goose and his children, and then ten years nursing the Big Fella, watching him shrivel like a cornstalk and die. No one would have me, and I had so little left. I went to my friends in the Tremé, and cooked the once awhile for Mr. Puckett, she said. My anger got the better of me. The Tremé? You were back here in Orleans and you never came to see me once? I was ashamed, Hachard said. And then I took ill myself and bound for heaven, and my friends were burned out like everyone else, and here I am, seeking charity. Oh, what shall happen to me? She grabbed my hands. Do you think LaChance would have me back? I shook my head. There are three of us, now, and the baby. For the first time, she seemed aware of Clothide beside her. Whose is this child? I pointed to my heart. And who is the father, surely not the old Goose? I bowed my head, *Non*. Do you remember little Georges? Phtt, he is just a young lad. No, maman, he is all grown up and full of what every man is full of. He had a little dog that followed him everywhere, and one night I heard the barking outside my door and knew it was Georges and why he had come, and I tried to say no, but he insisted himself upon me. More than once. And I thought, okay, perhaps he will keep me in *plaçage* like some other black women are kept by the whites, but no. Came to it that I heard that yip-yap and I just wanted to die. Georges is as fat and white as buttermilk, and when the baby came, his mother chased him out of the house with a broom. He's up in Baton Rouge, carrying on with some Cajun girl knows no better. But he left the little dog behind, and I'd like to kick it every time I pass by. Left his baby behind, too.

"She slid her hand and petted the baby's hair. What brings you to this place, Marie? The fire, I told her, same as you. The whole house burned, even my room and my money hidden under the same mattress you slept on. Deep sadness skittered across her features. What has become of the household? We have moved till the place can be rebuilt, but nothing can be done about my three hundred Spanish dollars, enough almost to buy my contract. Without warning, Hachard closed her eyes and kept them shut so long that I worried she might have fallen asleep or the Good Lord come in like a thief and steal her soul. When I touched her hand, she like to jump out of her skin. Don't do that to a body, she said. I was cogitating and you frightened me. Bending closely so that her words fit in my ear alone, she whispered, Do you ever go to *la Conga* in the square a Sunday evening? I laughed and nodded toward the sleeping baby. I go nowhere now, but there was a time when a young man fancied me and we danced the bamboula to hear the drums and the contredanse to show the whites how it is done, and oh, the *eau-de-vie*. You are not the only one who has a wild side, but alas, he was Cuban and back to Habana he did go, such a beautiful boy. Have you, Hachard asked, ever danced the *Vaudoux?* For years I had heard about the secret dance and the magic gained by all who dared the initiation, but I never risked go myself. Some scheme lay behind her question, her voice betrayed her, and though I knew not what she had in mind, I supposed my best course was to encourage her. No, I have not, but I should like to learn. That's good, very good, she said, for there your prayers will be answered. You shall either have your money or your freedom; we will ask the King and Queen what to do. With her gnarled hands, Hachard stroked Clothide's hair as she slept. And perhaps, you will say a prayer for me, too, not so?

"On a hot night in June, I left the baby with a neighbor and found Hachard by the Place Conga and together we went to a darker part of town where an empty stables stood and no eyes could profane the holy ceremony. Two women bound me in strips of purple cloth and put sandals on my feet, and I entered the cell with twenty others, men and women both. At the end of the room stood the King and Queen at the altar of the snake. Do you believe, said the King, in the power of the *Vaudoux?* He tapped the cage with the end of a stick and the snake slithered to the other side. Will you keep secret its most sacred magic? At each question, the assembled shouted Yes to these and to many more tests of faith. The crowd was made to bow before the snake and a fire was lit, and the Queen, she walked right through the flames without burning, and other marvelous feats were performed in the name of the *Vaudoux*. Now, I was raised a good Christian by the nuns in Saint-Domingue, but even so, such wonders cannot be explained away. When the show ended, the petitioners separated and waited patiently in two lines to confer with the King and Queen, as children will queue to speak to their mama or papa. And their wants were as ordinary as children's.

"Ask the *Vaudoux,* one young woman said, if my man be stepping out on me, and if he be, may his own snake fall off between his legs. An old man asked for three more years of life so that he might outlive his younger brother. A third person wished to be made more beautiful in the eyes of her beloved, for he finds her too plain to marry. Others asked for to be cured of their ailments, and others still wished ailments upon their enemies. When my turn came to speak to the King, I was afraid. He was no Domingue man, but out of Africa, a Kongo man, back broad as a bull and a chest wide and deep, out of which boomed his voice, even when he spoke softly, asking, What can the snake do for you, daughter? I told him my tale of transport to Louisiana in service of the fat M. LaChance and his six chubby children. And the contract of manumission, the fire that ate my money, and my ill treatment by the son Georges. Even the story of the pet dog who is a constant reminder of my shame, and the King let out a yip-yap, just like Georges's monster, and I was convinced the King knew already of my sorrows. You must take the oath, he said, are you ready? I was ready to hope in something more than what had seen me through so far, and I nodded. The King framed my face in his huge hands. Daughter, feed the master corn boiled with fat, and fry his meat and fish in mounds of butter. Sneak more andouille into the gumbo and backfat bacon for his breakfast. Make cakes and have him wash them down with ale and cider. At every meal, serve the lagniappe, the unexpected treat, but make sure it is rich or fat or clotted. Stuff the old goose and you will win your freedom. I will give you a sign of the power of *Vaudoux* this very night. Against my better sense, I said amen.

"As soon as the last petitioner finished, the King and Queen became very agitated. He took the snake from the altar and set the cage on the ground, and the grand lady who is the *Vaudoux* Queen stepped up on top of the cage and made to act as if the snake itself had climbed into her, and she began to speak in a strange language I never heard here in Orleans or Saint-Domingue or anywhere on earth. She pointed her finger at me and bade me come to her.

"The King, he drew a circle with a lump of charcoal and motioned for me to stand inside and wear around my neck a small gunnysack decorated with hair and horns. Upon my head, he struck a stick and chanted another singsong in words of the Kongo, and all the people there echoed back to them, and then I was told to dance, and thus I did, slowly at first, but then some mood or spirit came into me. I felt the weight of all my troubles drag me to the earth and I must push and pull myself out of it, and then I was moving all in a frenzy and everyone in that stables was dancing around me in that circle, urging me to stay inside. Not sure at all what possessed me, not aware in the least of how my body moved. Faster than the bamboula, driven by a drum only I could hear, I felt so completely free. Soaked in perspiration, my lungs heaving like a bellows, I collapsed in the euphoria. The Queen and one of her acolytes helped me to my knees. Dipping her thumb into the liquid at the bottom of a wooden bowl, she then laid her print across my lips. With this seal of blood, she said, you are sworn to keep the secrets of the *Vaudoux*. And then it was over, and everyone dispersed like taking leave from Sunday church, the King and Queen disappeared, and every dancer. I was alone with Hachard, who hung upon my arm, still panting from exertion. I feel better already, she said. Good to loosen the old bones.

"Monday morning at the new house, the Mistress cried out for me first thing. On the foot of her bed, the yippy dog lay stiff and cold as

February. Take this wretched creature from me, she said, quivering in her nightgown. Light raced through the window and the thin fabric of her clothes. I had not thought in some time what a scarecrow she was, and how she was becoming a bundle of twigs. Gathering the poor dog in my apron, I took it outside and dumped the body in the alley, reminding myself to ask some young boy to fetch the thing to the refuse heap or toss it over the levee into the Mississippi. No satisfaction filled my soul that morning, for I shook in dread over the power of the dark custom.

"Into the breakfast skillet, I dropped another egg to make a half dozen and another spoon of butter for the Master, and he never noticed but ate every bite and complimented me afterward. Thus commenced the stuffing of the Old Goose. Gumbo ya-ya a-swim in fat, and more fat in the roux. Jambalaya thick with hock and sausages. Étouffé brightened with the extra yellow fat of the crayfish. Cassoulet, maque choux easy on the vegetables and heavy on the bacon, sweetbreads and tripe, potato dumplings taught to me by Frau Morgenschweis on the Rue Charles. Meatpies and fruitpies, *beignets de carnaval* any time of the year. At the market, I would lay in a supply of beer and ale, and just as the King ordered, with every meal the lagniappe, which M. LaChance came to favor and anticipate as a dog longs for the meatbone or the children their sweeties. Oh, I fed him those, too, the pralines and toffees till his teeth ached. I shoveled the food into that man, but he just got fatter and fatter as the years lurched by. Let me tell you, he popped the buttons off his breeches more than once after Marie's dinners, ya, yet still I slaved. Not that I said nothing about the money. I begged him to show mercy if not for me then for my daughter, but he was steadfast as to the terms of our contract, though in truth, I think he kept me for his voracious appetite and would never let me go.

"Seven years passed this way. Clothide grew into a girl, and the Master grew into a prize hog. He even got the gout, but on he ate, hollering about his foot as he stuffed his mouth with a mess of alligator tail seasoned and slick with butter sauce. And though I went to the *Vaudoux* and danced with the snake King and Queen, nothing ever changed. There were times of waiting when I felt I could not go on, yet I went on.

"And then it happened, just like in a fairy tale. All of the children had long left the house, and the Master and Mistress dined alone, she living on red beans and rice, he facing a table crammed with bowls and dishes. Just an ordinary crust of bread caught between two fingers, his mouth open to receive the morsel, when the *Vaudoux* struck. The heel slipped from M. LaChance's grasp. His other hand shot to his chest in panic over the vise pressing his heart. Like a big snake squeezing and squeezing. The pressure. His pale skin flushed claret, and his lips quivered as if to say something—*adieu,* perhaps, and then he died before his face hit the plate. He was too fat for the household slaves to lift, and we had to call in three more men just to lay him out in the parlor, a hearse with an extra pair of horses to pull him away, and God knows how heavy the stone to stop his corpse from sinking into the swampy ground of New Orleans."

A soft belch forced its way between my lips. The girls chortled at my impropriety, and while there is never a good occasion for a burp other than in private as relief to gastric distress, it seemed particularly impolite at the moment. I could not help myself. My stomach felt bloated, my limbs gravid. Sneaking a look in the mirror, I noted the foreshadowing of jowls and a general puffiness about my face. Was I, too, getting fat? The old man, now below Marie's knee, signaled that he was going to begin again.

"All through that summer and into the fall, the prodigals returned to make their claims on their late father's fortune. First, the four girls, all of whom lived nearby, each with a dandy husband on her arm, and each one chagrined by the paltry remains of the estate. Their mother, the Mistress, had nothing but disdain for her girls and told each fancy man to go out and make his own money. Then the eldest, named after the father, arrived only to discover that there was little left in his name. We had to build a new house, his mother shouted at him. Did you expect me to live on the street? Her son left four days later, bound for the Argentine. Lastly came Georges driving in a carriage from Baton Rouge with his young bride. The poor woman, she had no idea what kind of man she had married. I kept my distance but could not avoid her when she came into my kitchen to find my daughter and me at the stove. Who is this enchanting girl? Hardly more than a child herself, she had never been told, it seems, about Georges's black bastard. Clothide bowed with a grin at the compliment. Is she yours? the woman asked. Is your husband one of the men who works here as well? Gaston? I took hold of Clothide and covered her ears from behind. I am not married, I said. Her father is a Buckra man. She took my baby's hands in hers for a moment, and then excused herself. As for Georges himself, he refused to even look at his daughter or speak one word to me. He was only here to court favor with his widowed mother, but she would have none of it. Over dinner that last night, Madame told her son and daughter-in-law, There is nothing left. I have barely enough to pay my own bills. From where I stood, facing Madame with a tureen of rice in hand, she spoke as if in a trance. Your father ate it all, she said. Like a pig, every scrap.

"Next day, after they had gone, Madame called me into the parlour. Marie, how long have you been in my employ? Near thirty years, Madame. And your girl, she is already eight, is she not? I nodded. Till this week, she said, I had not noticed how much Clothide resembles her father.

"I had no answer, for the admission of her son's behavior toward me had never before been brooked, though I was certain she knew at the time of my pregnancy and had held her tongue all along. To speak of the matter would have meant shame on her part and on mine. My husband, she said, treated you most grievously, Marie, as has my son. Both could not control their appetites. *Oui,* Madame. Had he lived, she said, the Master would have never given you the terms of your contract. Not while you kept his belly full. I made the sign of the cross as she mentioned his name and felt a brief swell of remorse over the use of the *Vaudoux* to get rid of him, but that quickly passed. How much money do you have? Nearly three hundred Spanish dollars, Madame, but I had that amount when the big fires came. Yes, I know, enough to buy your freedom and Clothide's, too. She stood before me, but I could not bear to look in her eyes. Marie, she said, we shall go to the courts tomorrow, you and I. We shall sign the papers for you and your daughter, and when you are ready, you are free to go on your own, and you are to keep what you have earned and saved, and I will make amends of one hundred more. But Madame, I protested, you said you have nothing—She held up one finger to her lips. I cannot bear the sins of my husband and my children. Now, come give me a kiss, for I shall miss you.

"Clothide and I went to the Tremé and found a place with Hachard, an ancient crow now, but enlivened by our presence. Mr. Puckett gave me her old job cooking in a tavern for the Cajun people, and on Sundays, I went back to the old church, though Sunday nights I still danced the *Vaudoux.* When the yellow fever struck the following summer and so many died throughout Orleans, I worried mostly for my child and for old Hachard, but they escaped the plague. My misfortune was to contract the fever in June of '96 and quickly wither. Do not worry, *ma chérie,* I told my daughter weeping at my bedside, Hachard will take care of you and besides, you are a free person. Don't go, she cried as I left this world, don't go, and the last thing I remember was the sight of my mother being led away as I shouted the very same words."

CHAPTER NINE

A Hole in the Whole

Marie dressed quickly, pinning the purple cloth at the shoulder, and then hid her face in the corner, her head bowed and her shoulders heaving as though sobbing at the memories. The homunculus who lived in my belly raced across the lining, grumbling and cursing as he ran. I loosened the belt to my robe, yet found no relief to my growling stomach. My feet and my hands ached and seemed waterlogged, and when I lifted my fingers to my face, the skin at my cheeks was taut and tender to the touch. The more Marie cried, the fatter I got, and when I looked in the mirror, a blimp stared back at me. I had doubled in weight, my features diminished by the beachball of my head. My belly escaped from the confines of the robe whose seams strained to stay together. My fingers and toes felt as thick as sausages, and my legs as stout as totem poles. "I am becoming well rounded at last," I joked to the old man, but the words came out in a helium squeak.

"You are a zeppelin," he said. "Entirely too rotund to contain yourself."

"I feel as if I shall pop."

In one swift motion, he stepped away from me and spun Marie by the shoulders. An enormous yellow balloon, imprinted with a cartoon version of my face, was at her lips, and her cheeks were puffed to deliver the next, perhaps fatal, blow.

"Don't you dare," he told her. She sucked in her breath and pinched the stem between her fingers. The pressure hurt my brain, and I could scarcely bear to watch for fear that she might wield a sharp fingernail or a straight pin and burst me with a casual gesture. Instead she let out the air in one long raspberry, the latex blubbering in an obscene manner, and at the same time, I deflated, the air hissing from every orifice in the most embarrassing way, though I was relieved in the end to be back to my normal self. Holding out an insistent palm, the old man demanded that she hand over the balloon. They argued for a moment in furious French, the words zipping by so quickly that I could not make out a single one. Marie surrendered reluctantly, and the old man held up the balloon for my inspection. In addition to the caricatured face, there were two stubby arms and two legs molded into the shape. He wadded it into a ball and stuffed the balloon into his breast pocket. Chagrined, Marie joined the other three women on the edge of the bathtub perched like spectators consigned to the cheap bleacher seats.

"A word, *monsieur, s'il vous plaît?*" I led him to the threshold and the illusion of privacy. "First of all, let me thank you for saving my life once again. Without you, I might have been clubbed or speared or blown into bits or who knows what."

He tapped me twice on the meat of my arm. "I wouldn't want anything to happen to you—"

"That's awfully decent of you."

"—before you finish the story of the performance of our friends in your parlor. I'd like to know how you got to where you are today."

"You and me both, brother."

Behind the glass of his spectacles, his bright eyes blinked back a film of moisture that could have been taken for the beginning of tears. His bottom lip quivered, but then he composed himself. I was growing quite fond of the old bugger. He winked at the girls. "What do you think of the most recent one?" He jerked his thumb in Marie's direction. "Took every ounce of concentration to keep reading the words on her skin and not give in to distraction."

"She is quite beautiful. Stunning, really. And that accent."

"A Frenchwoman could make the shopping list sound sultry. Must be all that red wine and cigarettes." In the bare light, he looked even more recognizable, tall and thin as a scarecrow, swept-back thatch of silver hair, the wire-rimmed glasses, and a face etched with wrinkles earned from ten thousand Gitanes and night after night of staring down a blank page. The famous French playwright.

"You remind me of someone."

"Your father."

"No, yes. Him, too, but someone else."

"I am glad it is somebody else. I was getting concerned."

"What was the name of the French fella who wrote that play? *Waiting for Godot*."

He patted the pockets of his robe. Reaching in with two fingers, he pulled out the wrinkled balloon and considered it as though he had no memory of the object. A thought tickled his lips. "Do you have a cigarette?"

"I don't smoke."

"Now would be an odd time to start then. Still."

"It is a very famous play. About nothing."

"Nothing? Everything is about something."

"Even this?"

"Especially this. Even silence has meaning and countless interpretations."

"Yes," I said, agreeing simply to be sociable. "It's about two tramps who are waiting for Godot to return."

"A French play? Sounds like a film I saw once with the poker-faced actor Buster Keaton. He had gotten into a number of jams and was awaiting the return of his partner to straighten things out. Man's name was Godot, but he never returns. Or perhaps it wasn't Keaton at all, but Laurel and Hardy."

"No, *Waiting for Godot* is a kind of existential comedy."

"But Laurel and Hardy would make a good Vladimir and Estragon, don't you think? Two tramps. Laurel and Hardy were always two tramps."

"I am beginning to feel like we're two tramps, waiting for some order out of this chaos."

"No, I am sure it was Keaton. He was much admired by your play-wright. He even used Keaton in a film without words. Not a silent film, mind, but nothing to be said."

"You even sound like him," I said.

"Your Frenchman? Perhaps he only wrote in French. Forced himself to think harder."

"That's it," I said. "Beckett. An Irishman who wrote in French first and then translated his own words into English. God bless you, Mrs. Stottlemeyer."

"Who?"

"Eleventh-grade literature class. My teacher."

"Mrs. Stottlemeyer. Funny what we remember."

"So *are* you?"

"Beckett?" He raised his bushy eyebrows. "I am afraid Beckett is dead. Some time ago."

"Beckett's ghost, then?"

"Did you not pinch yourself a while back there and conclude the evidence of your current corporeality exists? Don't you trust your own senses? And if I were mere ectoplasm, what does that make those young beauties over yonder? I can assure you, Sonny, they are as real as you or me." With a flutter of fingers, he waved to the women.

"If you are not a ghost and not my father and not the Irish playwright Beckett, then who are you?"

"You attempt to answer a positive but avert to the negative. All in good time, bucko. First, there are several more women in your bed—"

"And that's another thing," I said. "Why are they here? What are they implying with their stories? That somehow I am to blame?"

The old man laid a fatherly hand upon my shoulder. "You are overwrought, my boy, and yet as I've said—as you've said—there are more women in the bed from whom we haven't yet heard."

The very thought of those other creatures nearly drove me to tears.

"Now, now," he said. "Take your mind off your woes. You are an architect of some sort, aren't you? A builder? Why don't you patch the hole in the ceiling?"

A frying-pan-sized hole provided a portal into the attic. All kinds of junk had been stored up there over the years. Anything was liable to come spilling through the opening. He had a point. Given the chore, I felt a deep sense of relief settle in my chest. I had a job to do.

"Right, so. Off you go."

"Thanks—"

"Would it make you feel any better to give me a name? Call me Beckett or what-you-will?"

"Okay then, Beckett. I'll be up in the attic, fixing a hole. To stop my mind from wondering."

"Very cute. And I'll mind the four ladies. Now there's a poker hand for you. Four queens and a knave." As we passed, Beckett patted me once on the back, and it felt good to be getting somewhere finally.

To reach the attic, one must pull on a string that releases the door and a set of stairs that descends nearly to the floor. An ingenious contraption from another era of home engineering, but with two important drawbacks: one must use a stepladder or chair in order to reach the string, and one must step off the ladder before pulling the string for the attic steps come down quickly and without warning. I grabbed a chair from my brother's room, remembering how he wrapped his feet around the chair's legs as he worked at his desk, but forgetting the sliding stairs, which hit me square in the chest and knocked me on my keister and sent the chair clattering across the hall. I expected someone to come rushing to my aid, but there was no reaction other than a muffled "Keep it down!" from Beckett behind the bathroom door, doing God-knows-what with the four women. I picked myself up and climbed the stairs to the attic.

There was a light waiting for me that threw shadows but brightened all but the corners of the eaves, and the musty room smelled faintly of fried steak and hot metal. A persistent hum increased in volume whenever I stood still. Hunting for the source of that white noise would have taken all night and easily obsessed me, but fortunately, I thought more about my predilection for obsessive behavior rather than the noise itself and hit a plateau of absurd self-reflection where I could quit thinking altogether. Amid the clutter, some clues existed that would help me piece together a rational explanation for how I ended up this way, a long-forgotten artifact that would illuminate the recesses of my mind, but my immediate purpose was to find a patch for the hole in the floor. Against the far wall rested a framed lithograph, a gift from a girlfriend—Sita is her name, I am pleased to remember. We bought it on a date to a Gustav Klimt retrospective at the National Gallery of Art. The poster was just large enough to cover the hole, but as I slid it across the opening, I chanced to spy on the bathroom below. It was empty. There was nobody inside. No Marie, no Alice, no Jane, no Dolly, and old man Beckett had disappeared. Nothing to be done. I poked my head through the opening and scanned all four corners and over the shower curtain.

Even the baby was gone. For the first time since falling, I felt utterly bereft. Sometimes there is nothing more terrifying than being alone in your own house. I checked my watch and then carefully positioned the poster to cover the hole. No light shone from below. If possible, I was even more alone with my thoughts.

I hurried to the staircase and backed down the steps, hopping from the final one, and paused at my bedroom door to determine whether the sleeping beauties had also deserted me. The tangle of limbs and bodies had diminished to just four sets. Three of the women opened their eyes in the sudden light, and the fourth still showed her back, not having moved all night. I quickly retreated in hope that they would all go back to sleep. My fingers wrapped around the cold doorknob brought back memories of Christmas mornings when my brother and I would sneak out of bed, check if my parents were asleep behind their closed door, and then tiptoe out of their room, carefully turn the knob so that it would not so much as click, and then tramp down into the living room, turn on the strings of shiny lights on the tree, and stare at our toys and presents till well past dawn. In the stillness of those moments filled with hope and anticipation and goodwill, my brother and I were never closer. We waited with patient excitement for Mr. and Mrs. Godot to arrive, sleepy-headed, but caught, too, by the surprise of their own deep and holy joy. So many years later, the doorknob in my hand brought them back, if only in the instant before I let go.

The hallway rugs muffled the sound of my bare feet, and I was able to sneak as quietly as smoke to the bathroom door and press my ear against the surface. A woman's laughter rose and trailed off, and a low voice said something funny that made all the women howl. I could not decipher their actual words, so instead I began alternately to worry that they were speaking about me and to regret missing out on all of the merriment. I knocked twice and entered.

Caught in the middle of their party, they all turned to face me. Marie stood on the edge of the bathtub, towering over the others arranged in front of her as though an audience to an impromptu demonstration. She seemed to have just stopped shimmying, so I deduced she had been performing the voodoo dance. I launched my question full force: "Where were you?"

"We have been here," Beckett said, "waiting for you. The question is: where were you?"

"You know very well I went to the attic to fix the hole. I found an old poster from Sita that covered the whole thing—"

"The hole thing?"

"No, the whole. Whole, with a *W.*"

"The hole in the whole?"

"When I looked through the opening, there you weren't. Not where you were supposed to be. Nobody at all in the bathroom."

Dolly interrupted. "Perhaps we stepped out."

"To powder our noses," said Jane.

"Or maybe," Alice suggested, "you went down the wrong hole."

Marie took the conversational baton. "Right, like a fifth dimension."

"You have a point," the old man agreed. "If there can be a crack in time, why not a hole to some other space?"

From a corner, the baby gurgled, investigating his fingers with the inside of his mouth. He was sitting up by himself, straight as you please, as if he had aged in the fifteen-minute intermission.

"But," I protested, "I was only gone long enough to cover the hole . . ." I looked up to verify, expecting to see the vivid colors of Klimt framed by a skillet-shaped hole, but there was no painting and no opening, only the smooth white plaster and the small ceiling fan humming politely in the background. In the sink, no crayfish shells. No ruined tiles on the floor. The room had healed itself, and the only difference from usual, aside from the small mob crowding close, was the weapons stacked in the corner—the cast-iron pan, the broom, the rusty harpoon, and the bear-faced war club. I scratched the top of my head.

"You did a right good job," Beckett said. "If there ever was a hole, you can't tell by looking at it."

Nothing to be said. His compliment had a disingenuous air.

"But there is another hole, a real hole. You have left us on the precipice high above the canyon with the girls in their cancan frocks gathered about the pianoforte." Perhaps he could hear the wheels spin in my cranium, for he added: "Begin again if you must. Come home on a June afternoon to find an orgy of chrome and rubber on the front lawn. Seven ladies' bicycles, and just who are these lascivious two-wheelers? And what's that melody but the house itself singing Pagliacci—"

"Strauss," I corrected. "A woman singing the laughing song from *Die Fledermaus* in a makeshift music chamber set up in my brother's room. Odd, though, but it was my brother, not me, who cared for the classics."

"Right, so," he said and winked. There was that third eye tattooed on the lid, and the others had the same design except for Marie, whose second sight was in her hands. Each palm bore a cartoon eye, though the words on her skin had vanished.

"They were dressed in fishnet stockings and petticoats, like they just stepped out of the Old West."

"Dusty and busty," the old man said. From the bathtub, two short whoops of endorsement. I thought I heard a horse nicker on the staircase.

"Only more refined," I said. "A cross between elegance and decadence."

Marie cleared her throat. "The virgin and the whore."

I ignored her editorial. "When the mezzo finished her song and the last note of the piano sounded, the rest of the women clapped politely, and one or two began to wave silk hand fans, for though only June, summertime had come to town, and the room was close and moist. I should have thought to turn on the air conditioner, but my principle is to wait till the official first day of summer."

"Ah, the solstice," Beckett said. "The longest day of the year. Though this night rivals it, or perhaps only seems eternal. When we are waiting, every moment is pregnant. Are you sure you have no cigarettes?"

"I don't smoke."

"Never start. They're the devil to give up. And a thousand pardons for my interruption. We left the showgirls perspiring in the parlor."

"That's when they first took notice of me. The piano player stood and tapped the vocalist on her shoulder, and she motioned for the rest to stand. The music lingered in the chamber. A collective jolt of recognition ran through the group. As I may have said, they were perfect strangers to me, though young and beautiful, of all shapes and sizes pleasing to the eye. A more attractive group of women would be hard to imagine. Yet for all their novelty, they behaved in ways traditional and comforting. I had heard that pianist before and recalled her elegant phrasing. The singer, too, brought back the buried memory of the same song in another place and time, but more than the aural echoes, for the music caused deep emotions to come gasping to the surface. A lot like a love that had once been deliberately forgotten. While I did not know them, they knew me and had been waiting for my arrival, and now that I had come, they rushed forward with open arms, each racing the others to be first to embrace and kiss me."

"Kiss you, is it?" Beckett asked. "I find that difficult to accept under the circumstances."

My pride was hurt, but I showed nothing.

Beckett stepped forward and whispered confidentially, "You know I have always been on your side, right? A word of advice: do not turn around, but reach back with the bottom of your foot and shut the door behind you."

I did as instructed, and as the door slammed into the jamb, something slammed into the door. The wood splintered with a wrenching crack as a sharp metal point poked through. The weapon that had just avoided my head looked like a grappling instrument of the kind issued to mountain climbers, only larger. "A gold miner's pick," Beckett said, as though reading my mind.

A stream of blue curses flooded the hallway, and the swearing woman on the other side of the door clasped the handle and tugged mightily to free the pick and wield it again. Two clomps preceded a renewed effort, and the old man suggested with a hand signal that I should open the door to see what was on the other side. Fastened like a pit bull, a rather short but wiry young woman tugged at the pick, her bare feet propped against the door so that when it swung into the bathroom, she swung with it. Her blue crinoline rode up along her thighs, and her face flushed red beneath her dark brown hair each time she reexerted herself. Like Merlin's sword in the stone, the point of the axe lodged firmly in the wood, and try as she might, she could not budge the lethal tool. The more she struggled, the worse her temper grew, till she was little more than clenched teeth and unspent fury, a torrent of obscenities gushing from her delicate mouth in a most shocking display.

"Young lady," Beckett entreated, "you will never succeed by ignoring elementary physics."

She bundled her muscles and hunched her shoulders and strained again, to no avail. At the moment of surrender, her whole body slackened. One cold hard look at the old man gave way to resignation and abject hopelessness. For a brief second, I felt sorry for her and wished she had reached her goal, despite its dire consequences for me. In a final gesture of defeat, she let go the handle and dropped to the floor on her bum. Bending gently to her, the old man helped her to stand and held her by the elbow as she fussed with the waist of her dress and brushed the lint and wrinkles. A gentleman always, he escorted her farther into the room to a place among the other females, and with a slight bow, let go of her with a signal of one finger that she was to behave. And then, stepping up to the pickaxe, he pushed the handle, rather than pulling as she had, and once the point was thus free, he eased it from the wood as deftly as lifting a splinter from a little boy's palm. He hid the pick behind his back, and the girl in blue crossed her arms and pouted.

"Now that's no way to begin a story," Beckett said. "First, engage your audience, and besides, a scowl does not become you. Give us a smile and a tall tale, and we will give you our ears and our hearts."

CHAPTER TEN

The Woman Who Caught the Gold Bug and the Silver Fever

The number of people in the small bathroom made me feel a bit claustrophobic, and we squeezed in even tighter to allow the newest woman a stage. She drew the shower curtain behind her like a scrim and stood on the narrow proscenium of the bathtub edge. The old man sat on the toilet and bounced the baby on his knee. Flush with anticipation, Dolly fanned herself next to the open window. With a hop, Marie settled on the countertop surrounding the sink, and the rest of us took positions as groundlings, forced to stand for the performance.

"Will someone outen the lights?" our newest guest asked, and Alice complied. In the dark, I stretched to get my bearings, which did not please my neighbors when my foot or fist struck another body. I made my excuses and tried to becalm my restlessness until the spotlight silenced everything, originating from some point above the old man's head and haloing the woman who had tried to plant her pick in my cranium.

"A man is to blame," she said, "but ain't that always the case. He wasn't a bad man, not at all, especially in the beginning. But as soon as he got what he wanted, then that was it."

The women murmured their amens.

"After, he was no use to nobody, man, woman, nor child. Like a mule in the middle of an ocean or an axe in a sandstorm, just no use at all. But no sooner than I get started, but I am already ahead of myself."

I tapped Beckett on the shoulder, and he quieted the child, steadying the boy with a brace of one hand against the small back. "She's the piano player," I whispered. "A dead ringer for the woman at the recital."

"Dead ringer?" the old man asked, and then turned his attention to the spotlight and the tiny woman, carefully assaying her from head to toe. "Are you sure about that, Sonny? She looks a bit wild and unkempt for that sort of thing."

Her cornflower dress rustled when she flinched, but she betrayed no further emotion other than silent umbrage.

"I am quite sure she is the singer's accompanist."

"Miss," he addressed her. "What is it we are to call you?"

"My name is Florence. But call me that, and you'll get no further response from me. Flo, if you please, short for Florence, for only my mam ever referred to me thus."

"Since you are short, a short name it shall be. Flo, my friend here says that you are a piano player of some renown."

"I can pick out a few tunes, but I'm no Scott Joplin. A bit rusty, too, but I'll do if the piece is sprightly."

Clearing his throat, the old man sat up and spoke carefully. "Perhaps we can prevail upon you for a few melodies later. There is a lovely thing by Mozart caught in my aural memory, a song stuck in the head."

"We'd have a hard time fittin' a piano in the bathroom."

Dandling the child on his knee, the old man said, "You'd be surprised what the commodious mind can accommodate. You were about to relate the troubles and grief brought about by a man."

. . .

Raising the stake for any journey was the horns of the problem, 'cause they were young and just starting out, and he didn't have any money to speak of, and while her pap had a deal of capital, it was all tied up in the farm. He had raised up the whole lot of them from dirt poor and little better than the darkies, her pap did, through the honest sweat of his brow, and as a consequence, held his dollars till the eagles squawked. "Don't worry," Jamie says, "I will find us the way, just be ready to go when I says." "And Flo," he whispered to her since the conversation was in the bed, "don't tell no one we're going till the time comes to say good-bye."

She never knew who he stole the money from or who he promised a share of the riches to come, it may have been Pap in either case, and she never did ask, not wanting to know, but Jams come home one afternoon and says, "Pack your bags, we're off tomorrow." Scant time to say good-bye, she made a tearful farewell with kin and friends, loaded a trunk with her possessions, and found herself scrabbling over to Missouri. Like a thousand others, as pouring into a funnel.

Crazed like so many they were bit by the gold bug to cross the whole country in search of it. They were argonauts, forty-niners, and made their way overland from the basin of the Ohio River. Drawn to the swarm, they leapt acrost the plain and over the mountaintops. A voyage of utter boredom and unrelenting hardship, lost two oxen bought in St. Joe to the wretched nothingness of the Great Salt Desert, made sick by the water tasting of chalk and bonedust and the chaw of dried beef or buffalo and never a lick of corn or apple or any good thing left behind at home. Some never made it at all, perishing on the migration, boiled and bleached by the sun or frozen crossing the high ground. Wasted by the cholera or some damned accident, a misstep, a lack of judgment. Ain't that always the way, fate just over the horizon waiting to catch ye out or

bring ye reward. And all who came over the Sierras were worn and thin
and blistered and oh so tired. Jamie and Florence were but twenty and
nineteen when they started, and five months later seemed to have aged
ten hard years. She rode most of the way in the wagon-back, but he
walked or went astride on a good Kentucky gelding till the poor horse
caught a hoof in a rabbit hole and was put down by the side of the trail.
And then Jams rode on a mule. Or walked when the beast was stub-
born. All that time in the wind and sun colored him brown from the
brim of his hat to his collar till he was damn near indistinguishable from
the red niggers, begging your pardon, Indians sometimes met on the
road. Miles of walking hardened the body, too, till Jams looked stringy
and wild as a half-starved coyote. While Flo was no more ready for
the mining life than when departed from Harlan County, she marveled
at how prepared in mind and limb her man was as they fetched up in
Sacramento to outfit theyselves. None of them was full ready for the
hard work ahead, for they had heard the gold was plenty there for the
taking of, but they were all wrong. It weren't just lying on the ground
but hid like every good thing, and they wasn't the only ones looking
for it neither. Jams and Flo was panners at first, like all the other green-
horns, and a more primitive art ye won't find, but harder than it seems.

A small, unfortunate chuckle escaped the tunnel of my throat.

"Think it easy, jackanapes?" She wrenched back the shower curtain,
revealing a few inches of brackish water flowing along the bottom of the
tub as if in a creekbed. "If ye gentlemen won't mind?" She handed two
miner's pans to Beckett and me and spun a third like a pie plate on the
tip of her middle finger. "Ye'll want to scoop up some of that ere river
bottom and a slick of water on top and swirl it about, keeping an eye on
it the whole time. Ye sift and watch for the telltale glister."

The old man caught on at once, and squatted on the tiles, intent on the muck he had dredged. Less certain as to how it would work, and worried in part over the mess we were making and the future task of scouring the surface, I bent to it with reluctance. I shaved two inches of gravelly mud and a half inch of water and stared at the bottom of the pan, past the reflection of my own face, seeing nothing more than a dismal reminder of my own dull life. How had I ended up with these strangers? There was no one there to truly trust, and the questions swirled in my brainpan. A speck flashed in the dirt, and with the end of my little finger, I picked it from the silt like a surgeon. "Eureka!" I said, holding up the flake for all to see. The old man grinned at my discovery and tried to conceal his pan in the folds of his robe, but not before I could see the collection of nuggets as big and plentiful as a mouthful of teeth.

A titter tweeted from woman to woman at the sight of our comparative luck. I knew right away that Flo's story would involve a certain amount of fate and chance, as do all such stories about the acquisition of wealth. I have never been a lucky man, not in love or fortune, but more of a determined plodder. More pluck than luck. When their giggles edged toward laughter, I took the only viable option: I stuck my finger in my mouth and ate the golden speck.

"I see ye have the appetite, too," Flo said, as she pulled shut the shower curtain.

One bite—or once bitten by the gold bug—ye will not let off till ye've made your mark or it has broken both body and spirit. Many who toiled by the rivers, those who sailed half the world or beat the dusty trail, many were broke by the experience and went back home the poorer or made a new life in California, up Sacramento way or lured to the Barbary Coast of San Francisco. Could be side by side in the same river. One man becomes rich, the other remains a fool.

Flo and Jams staked a claim to a rick tributarying offen the American River, and worked it fierce in twelve-hour hanks, pausing only the Lord's day as commanded. Eked by the first four months on little more than hope and nerve, enough to keep them on the spot and not give in, one urging the other when they was low. Downstream in a natural gulley, four greasers up from Sonora way played out a rich deposit, and though they could not understand a word of Mexican, Flo and Jamie sensed enough to tell when the wheel of fortune swings someone's way.

"Them boys," Jams said, "knows somethin' we don't. We just drib and drab and they must have pulled an ounce a day out one spot over."

She cogitated for a spell, put down her pan, and walked the hillside watching the foursome in the distance. That night over their beans and rabbit, the idear hit her sudden, like the old apple offen Newton's tree. "Gravity," she announced, as if discovering it. "Ever know the notion? Says the heavier a thing is, more it seeks out the bottom. We're on the side of a hill, and they in the dip. Where the river naturally sets, that's where to look. All that gold sunk down there, like treasure at the bottom of the sea."

With the femur of that hare, Jams pointed at her like a schoolmaster driving home the lesson. "Flo, if ye are right, we will never do more at this here claim. We quit it and find a bottom spot, life becomes the easier."

In one morning, they fixed their packs to the jenny mule and went in search for a more likely site, and in three days, they found the same. First pan of river, they dredged up two nuggets big as sunflower seeds. Against the bright sun, Jams held them up between his finger and thumb and proclaimed to her, "Girl, our future is made." Out of that hole, they dug in three months to the value of $20,000 and only quit it by hiring a Chinee and his brother to continue work and split the leavings. They was two yalla men by name of Lee who had twelve words of English between them, but honester than two monks, bringing each day's labor back to the little house Jams had built not far off for an accounting. He was content with the takings and ready to quit off, live the life of luxury, maybe head back to Kentucky and run a few horses, but she would not let him. "We have our nut," she said, "and from the tiny acorn the mighty oak doth grow. We have to plant that seed, invest our money, watch it grow."

Though she herself had long left the fields, Flo kept her eye on the miners in the surrounding valley and kept her ears open for the latest chatter in the town. When sluices were introduced, she hired a carpenter and had built at a second claim up north a more elaborate system for separating mud and water from the gold. The money poured in faster than they could count it, and with each new way of mining, the rate of flow only increased. If sluices watered their bank accounts, water cannons blasted away whole hillsides with mother lodes a-hiding. They made canyons out of hillsides, valleys out of plains. Jams hired ten more Chinamen to run three more claims and then secured a man named Murphy, out of New South Wales, Australia, to collect the profits from every Lee and make sure they would not cheat, and each of the claims proved true and more land was staked, more Chinee and Americans, too, redmen and the blacks, to come work for James Worth, and it seemed to never stop. Murphy hisself hired two more men to do the job he once held, and in time, fifty-seven in all mined sixteen claims in the hills of California and wasn't every damn one of them a moneymaker. Flo hired a girl to write letters for her and to read aloud the replies, and she sent back enough money to Harlan County so that her mam and pap had nary a care and ever last sister and brother and Jamie's family besides, so much so that his youngest brother Eben, who was but a tadpole when they left, hopped the western highway and took over for Murphy, who had earned enough so's not to work another day of his life, and he didn't. 'Stead he sailed back to his wife—the kangaroo—for all Flo cared.

They built themselves a house, a mansion really, in San Francisco after the fires of '51, and went there to retire from the fields when work was too much with them. Perched atop a hill, they could look out into the Pacific, and from their rocking chairs count the masts of the tall ships abandoned in the harbor, captains, crews, and passengers all lit out for the fields with not a care for their boats. Evening times, they'd feel the fog creep in, so's that sometimes only the tips of the spars and crow's nests could be seen, like a fairyland forest.

Ever since she was a girl Flo had dreamt of such a palace, two stories high, and eight rooms in all, furnished in the finest shipped from New York and Boston and London. Because of the fire, Jams insisted on building in brick, and for a time, the red house stood out amid the general rubble, but one thing about Californians, they is quick to build what's been razed and try again, for they is the luck-seekingest people on the earth. In no time, a new San Francisco stood, better'n the last. When the babies started coming, Flo contented herself with life in the city while Jams managed the land and holdings and brought home more gold dust from the Chinee every few weeks. They named the first child Jessie, after Mrs. Frémont, and their boy John C. arrived in the same year that Mr. Frémont became the first nominee of the Republicans for the President of the United States at the convention way off in Philadelphia. It was a time to be proud of who ye were, and they were Californians by now and had washed Kentucky clean out their pans.

Now, up to the point, Jams was a perfect husband and father, industrious as an ant, and never gave her ought to complain, but a kind of idleness began creeping in once he no longer had to actually go out among the miners. And then his brother Ebenezer hired hisself a man to do the job they'd brought him west to do, and now the both of them together had little to occupy their time, and an idle mind is the devil's workshop, so says the Bible. It were innocent enough at first to be there in that Gomorrah, to have a glass of the hard stuff with your dinner or a scupper of beer at supper, and it were understandable to go pass the time in converse with men your own age and like ye, forty-niners made good or dreaming of the luck to turn. Truth be told, Flo was glad to see them join their friends the first few times, for Jams always came back in a better mood than when he left, and when Jams was out carousing, at least he wasn't pawing at her. Bad enough the babies kept coming one right on top of the other. And he never came back stinking drunk like her pap had done, and he never hit her neither, and he always said please and darling, so what harm in it? "Me and Eben are going out," he told her one Christmas night, and she should've, could've asked him to stay, but instead just inquired where they would be going on the Lord's own day. "To the hells," Jams said, with a snort. "The hells?" The youngest baby started bawling. "What is the hells?"

Eben was at his side, hat in hand. "The hells is places where a man can be a man. Down in the plaza, there are places for a drink and a smoke and a game of chance. We like the Aguila de Oro, don't we Jams, for there's a band of Ethiops there every night can sing like your mammy putting ye to sleep. A game or two of monte, nothing at risk."

They waited for her nod, which she gave reluctantly, and off the brothers went into the cool night to mingle with the Americans and Mexicans and Chiles and Chinee and Lord knows aught else, when a man should be at home with his family. Off they went for a game of cards.

The bathtub drain gurgled and sucked away the last of the water, as if waiting for her cue. With a grand flourish, she pulled back the shower curtain to reveal a tubful of gold dust and nuggets and bars and jewels and coins, a trove at least six inches deep. Despite the dim light, it twinkled ostentatiously. A sea of bling. We gathered around the bathtub as if gathering around a manger.

"Beautiful, ain't it?" Flo prodded Alice and Dolly with her elbows. "Go ahead, girls, take something for yourself. I've no use for any of it anymore. Money is the root of all evil."

From behind us, Beckett cleared his throat to draw our attention. The baby in his arms kept pawing, reaching for the wire-rimmed spectacles perched on the end of the old man's long nose. Beckett had to cock his head just out of reach and thus spoke from the side of his face. "Not money, my dear. The correct adage is: 'For the love of money is the root of evil.' Timothy 6:10. Sometimes love is translated as 'desire,' which is my own preferred reading of the Greek original. For what are we but the sum of our desires?" The baby boy stuck his fingers between the old man's lips and Beckett pretended to chew them like some rough beast. "Num, num, num," he said, and the child squealed with laughter.

As I turned, I spied the three round bottoms of the women as they bent and dipped into the treasure. Only Marie resisted the temptation to further embangle her arms with bracelets or cram more rings upon her fingers or toes. Alice claimed a necklace of nuggets, and Jane wove a chain of gold into her hair. Worst of the three, Dolly emerged from her splurge with a rime of dust flecked upon her lips and staining her cheeks, as though she had tried to feast upon it. Like a magician, Flo pulled to the curtain and hid the glitter from our curious eyes.

See, they were rich, Jams and Flo, richer than she had thought possible, and the money kept flowing into their lives like the ocean beating upon the shore. When the fifth baby came in '61, the Worths bought a bigger home on a hilltop overlooking the Golden Gate, stealing the design of the octagon house down on Gough. They dined at Delmonico's or at the Sutter House when the mood struck and paid no heed to the prices, though would ye believe, near $15 a dinner at the peak. She would regularly take all of the children on an August day to the Fountain Head or the Branch for a cooling glass of ice cream, devil-a-care the expense in dragging out a man and coach just to get them there. On Steamer Days, the thirteenth and twenty-eighth of each month, the ships would come in from the East and bring them treats from New York and Philadelphia. Buttons and bows. Whirligigs and thingama-jigs and Dresden dolls and hobby horses. Them babies wanted for noth-ing, she saw to it, and were it not for the War of Northern Aggression, she would have taken them all to Kentucky for a visit, arrive in style to show her kin and all the girls she'd a-grown up with how fine life had become for those that worked hard. She tried in her daily doings to show the Worth boys the simple truth of this lesson, but Jams and Eben preferred to let the money work for them 'stead of the right way round.

When every last dot of gold had been dug off their lands, they sold off what was played out and let their workers go, with a $20 bonus to the Chinee who so long and honestly served the Worth operations. Piece by piece, the land vanished, and their assets converted to a number in a bank account. She would have preferred to hold on to what was real, stomp on their soil, finger their cold cash, but Jams insisted the figures scratched upon the ledgers was as good as gold. "There's more to be made in making deals and trading paper," he told her, "than the capital and labor of the man of trades." In a single week in '62, Jamie made a small fortune by buying and then quickly selling the stocks of a com-pany that provided blankets to the Union army when the weather back east suddenly took a chill. His brother, too, became a rich man and lav-ished upon himself the accoutrements of wealth. Ebenezer wore bespoke suits and studded shirts, shoes imported from far-off Italy and Spain. A suite of rooms at the Parker House and three meals a day at the best restaurants in the city. Nights at the opera and days at the races. A dollar bet on everything from whether the Rebs would hold Shiloh to whether he could teach the yellaman shining his boots to speak a sentence of passable American before he finished both feet. He smoked cigars two bits apiece and had the finest liquor and whores of every color and nationality. It's a wonder that he could not figure out how to evaporate his fortune despite his best efforts.

With no more gold mines but an excess of enthusiasms, the Worth brothers began to cast about for some other scheme to make money without dampening their brows. They searched no further than over the Sierras, crossed so long ago, and there found the next wave of speculators in the silver mines of Nevada. Giddy as two schoolgirls, they read the papers and heard the rumors in the streets, and the next year set off on expedition to Virginia City to see right close the famous Comstock lode and what prospects Nevada held for men so bold as they. The silver fever was upon them, and no remedy can be had but silver itself.

Upon that aphorism, she paused. With the tweezers of her right thumb and index fingers she dug into the bustline of her blue dress and produced a lit cigarillo, took a deep drag, and blew a jet of smoke in the general direction of the open window. Beckett frowned at her and gestured with his chin to the babe asleep in his arms. "Tut, tut, tut," he said. Flo grabbed one last puff before extinguishing the cigarillo underneath a stream of water gushing from the sink's faucet. The room suddenly smelled like a boxing gym or the men's room at a horseracing track. Had I not been somehow constrained to remain in the house, I would have left, robe and all, for a quick walk around the block and some fresh air. "I wasn't always like this," she said and nodded at Alice as apology for smoking in front of the child. "All nervous and all." She clicked her nails on the edge of the sink in a rhythm reminiscent of a pianist's flourish. My brother had a similar nervous habit. After ten years of clarinet lessons, he would absentmindedly finger a pencil, performing a melody heard only in his mind. Funny what you remember. I had not thought of the clarinet in ages, despite the fact that it had been the daily music of my youth. My brother struggling to learn and then his sudden mastery, and how he would change the time of almost any song to redefine it: a melancholy Christmas tune, a syncopated Irish reel. Amidst this early morning's chaos, I can almost hear him again.

They returned, Eben and Jams, in three months' time, bringing not much from Nevada save the dust that had collected in their hats and clothes, in their carpetbags and boots, a silt of alkali that gathered even in the wrinkles around the eyes and collected in the hidden cracks and creases of a man that only the wife knows. The maid was sweeping silver dust from corners nine months after their return. For the children, Jams brought silver trinkets made by the redmen, spurs and belt buckles for the boys and combs and mirrors for the girls. Elegantly wrapped in a mahogany box, his gift for Flo was a hunk of raw silver ore, blue-black as night and heavy in the hand. "This here will double our money," Jamie said. "The ground is thick with it. Those poor bogtrotters who discovered the Comstock lode knew nothing for silver. Four Irishmen were digging for gold, and this black stuff kept clogging their rockers, and it were an accident altogether that they even bothered to ask were it of any use. McLaughlin cashed in for $3,500 which he promptly lost, and Comstock hisself traded an old blind horse and a bottle of whiskey for a one-tenth share formerly owned by the mick called Old Virginny. Give me an Irishman to dig the hole any day, but I'd take even a Chinaman to have wits enough to ask what was in it." He picked up the hunk of silver sulphite and pretended to smoke it like a cigar.

Something about his mood or manner alarmed her that morning, and try as she may, Flo could not completely shake the sense of foreboding that began to build upon her husband's return from the silver hills of Nevada. She should have trusted herself to be right. When she and Jamie had first left home for the west, she was but a girl, just married, and knew no better. But now with his latest scheme, James seemed so cocksure it was all going to work out just the same as it had in '49, but the difference now was she was a grown woman and mother of six, and his confidence grated on her common sense. "We ain't kids no more," she said. "Are ye going back into the earth? Or send that brother of yours, at least? To see firsthand what labor is necessary to find this ore?"

He dropped the silver cigar back in the box and spoke coldly. "We been under the ground and seen it, Flo, in the pit of hell with but a candle. The hole timbered and beamed like a ship's hull, and every minute a danger of the cave-in and the whole mountain landed atop ye. I been there, and I seen it. Ain't I been right before? And amn't I the one who got us all this?" He gestured at the furnishings. "Have ye no faith in me?"

"It ain't a matter of faith, but of capital and risk."

"We was there near three months, woman. I think I can find my way round a silver mine and know a good investment when I see it." One of the infants commenced caterwauling from the other room, and he frowned at her. "Ain't ye going to tend your baby?"

"Nurse can take care of her, Jams. This is a serious proposition ye made, and I need to hear it out and understand—"

"Leave off understanding to me, Flo, and to Eben. We saw for ourselves what's coming up the ground by the tubful, and we spoke direct with the owners. They has drifts and tunnels, five miles in all, and over five hunnert men in the ground. Once ye go down, ye never wish to go again, and I don't aim to. Leave it for the workingman. I'm too old for that sort of thing, and besides, the real money is in the speculation. Don't worry about it, for we will be made millionaires when this comes roaring through." Jamie held her in his arms, and for the last time, Flo felt assured there.

By some subterfuge, the houselights were extinguished and once more Flo stood in spotlit halo before the shower curtain. "Ladies . . . and gentlemen. I bring new riches from days gone past. Not gold, me dearies, but somewhat else . . ."

On Beckett's lap, the baby began to whimper, and from the folds of her skirt, his mother slipped a pacifier and popped it into his mouth. The handle of the ninny was plated in gold.

Flo cleared her throat and spoke in a loud voice, "I now draw your attention to the rewards of rash speculation." She opened the curtain and in lieu of the golden treasure, the bathtub held six inches of paper in a ragged heap. Upon closer examination, the documents were identical stock certificates, emblazoned with the American bald eagle clutching in one taloned fist a miner's pick, and in the other, Union dollars.

For two years, the Worths collected these certificates, buying more stock in the mine than they could afford, and living as they were accustomed, on credit and debt. This borrowed way of life did nothing to curtail their habits; if anything, they lived more extravagantly on the promise of the profits from their gamble. With the war's end in the spring, prices continued to rise, but despite the cost, daughter Jessie was sent to Europe with a governess on a summer's tour. Eben found a girl and asked her to marry him, and brother Jams gave him a send-off never seen before in the city, a ball with full orchestra, a meal with pheasants shipped overland by train, and flowers of every kind, all out of pocket, and damn the expense. They made a wedding gift of a full silver service, as much a token of filial bonds as to encourage the purchase and use of silver among their acquaintances. Why, they even gave away money they did not have, to various benevolent societies for the care of homeless children, for it was important to the acquisition of a place in society to behave as if the millions existed, whether or no merely on paper.

Reckoning arrived swiftly, as bad news often does. They say people no longer had any confidence, though she could not understand how ordinary people could be confident one day and not the next. The lack of confidence brought a panic, and the panic caused the fall, and the value of the stock in the mining company plunged down the shaft, and there was no hope for recovery. Overnight, the Worths became worthless. The bubble had burst and not so much as a slick of soap remained. By the time they sold their shares for pennies and accounted for their considerable debts, little was left but the octagon house and its contents and some cash Flo had in her name to pay the domestic staff their monthly wages. The servants, a-course, were let go at once, and telegrams sent to hurry Jessie back from Italy. They was ruined, and so was Ebenezer, returning home from his wedding trip to less than nothing, who had to move instead with his new bride into the third floor of the octagon house. She—the girl's name was Rebecca—was there all alone that Sunday in October when the Big One hit, the heaviest earth shocks ever felt in San Francisco to that time.

The Worths, sans Jams, was at service on Sunday morning, and when the first shock hit, the minister said stay calm, stay put, which they did for perhaps five seconds as the pews rocked violently and the stained-glass windows rattled like a carriage going over cobblestone. The second shock threw them from their seats, the whole church emptying into the streets, with the minister leading the flock to safety, the shepherd jogging past each and every sheep. A loud grinding noise followed, the brick buildings rubbing together, glass and plaster falling, and the earth itself rumbling and growling. The walls swayed and buckled like treetops in a tempest, and the windows popped out like firecrackers. Above, the bell kept ringing of its own accord even as the shock subsided, until the third tumbler tossed all around for another six seconds, and then it was all over.

Flo and her children watched in dull amazement as the cross on the steeple tottered to the left and stopped short of toppling over. A few blocks away, Jams and Eben crawled out of one of the hells with the gamblers and rummys and the hookers and that morning's entertainment all blinking in the bright sunshine and swirling dust like bats from a cave. At the corner of Seventh and Howard, the earth had opened and laid bare a sewer flowing with water. Over where an empty lot had stood was now a pond, and they watched in a stupor of cards and liquor as a duck circled and landed there, calling in grave distress. Geysers were forced up into the air on certain street corners, and here and there among the ruined and cracked buildings small fires blazed. Back at the octagon house, poor Rebecca had been having a bath and had to run out into the street in nothing but a robe as the walls began swaying and making to bear down upon her. She was not the only one thrust out into the public. Others emerged in little more than a bedsheet, and it went to show what occupied the common man on a Sunday morn.

That was the beginning of the end for Rebecca and Eben, for she wanted no more part of the quakes and shakes of San Francisco, and he would not be parted from his brother. Last anyone saw her, she had taken the train back to her folks in Baltimore. As for the octagon house itself, the inner walls were badly damaged, the windows shattered, and every room littered with plaster from the ceiling. On all eight sides, paintings had fallen to the floor or swung round to face the walls, and every good piece of glass or china on the mantels and in the cupboards was chipped or broken. A small fissure, the size of a man's arm, opened in the northwestern corner beneath the roof, letting in the air and dust, but the house survived, unlike so many others. The structure stood firm and strong, though some small damage had been done.

Not one of them was seriously hurt, but John C. had taken a bump in the church, though it made him no sillier than usual. It would have been a double blow to lose a child or lose their home on top of losing their fortune, and she was not sure she could have stood either, though in hindsight, perhaps better they had been forced to start all over and go somewheres else. As it was, the earth shakes was what did in Jams. He wandered back home that Sunday night in a daze, as if the world itself had fallen in on him.

After the rubble had been cleared and the windows replaced and the cracks mostly plastered, Jams sighed at the state of things and went to bed and stayed there for four days. He made no complaint other than feeling powerful tired, and he could rouse himself to have a meal at eleven in the morning and seven at night and to visit the jakes, of course, but otherwise he slept like a newborn. His brother could not lure him with a hand of monte or faro or the prospect of a night in the hells, and Flo herself slept on the couches in the parlor downstairs for better egress should the shocks revisit. She left her husband alone. On the fourth day, the twins, unaccustomed to having their father lay about, jumped upon the mattress and then his prone body till he fought back, wrasslin' little Zach and Jeb as though a child hisself again. "C'mon, Pa." Jeb smacked him with a wooden sword. "You can be Johnny Reb and I will be Tecumseh Sherman and march you to Atlanta." Their father roared at the boys and chased them in his nightshirt, pausing only at the top of the stairs to catch his breath.

After supper that evening with the whole family, at which he seemed to brighten and return to his old energetic self, Jams climbed back up the stairs to the room with the crack just under the roof. He sat quite still in a chair and watched the stars pass by, not greatly participant in the conversations that surrounded him, but not ignoring the others either. Jessie read from Hawthorne to the others, and Ebenezer and Flo discussed the reports of damage around town from the shakes. But Jams just sat and did nothing, and this pattern he repeated several nights in a row—to All Hallows' E'en—doing little till supper and retiring to watch the constellations turn, or if there was no stars, to stare at the clouds or the rain, and once or twice, let the fog seep through the fissure and engulf him and the chair and the whole room altogether, like they was in a dream. Through this routine he passed the time as if a man a leisure and not the head of house bound for ruin. When his brother asked him to go out for a game of poker or to hear the Mexican crooners or see the magicians from Siam now down at the hells, Jamie begged off. "Not tonight, but you go on and say whaddyaknow to the boys. I think I'll just rest a bit." And so he did, night after night, day by day.

Rising each morning well after the children had been sent off to school or their new jobs, and much later than his lazy brother, James would dress in his silk gown and come down to the table to eat his breakfast when most of California was beginning to grumble for its noonday dinner. He'd learned to read by then and would take the newspaper, usually the morning's *Examiner,* or when the steamer came, two weeks' worth of Dickens's serials in the New York papers, despite that rascal's "American Notes," and Jamie's reading would occupy mind and spirit for several hours. Then he would dress just as the eldest were coming through the door—John C. from his job as a printer's devil and Jessie late from her post in a ribbon shop on Union Street. Sometimes he and the boy would have a talk on the front porch, and Jessie was given a little dog by one of her beaus that her father would watch over and play with for hours at a time. A few times a week, Eben would go out and leave him alone in the house, and like as not, Jams would fall asleep by the fireplace or watching the stars through the crack. He was but six and thirty yet had the habits of a man twice his age.

And so things continued to worsen. With little income from the children and nothing from her husband, Flo struggled to meet the bare expenses. Bit by bit, they sold off their possessions. No carriage, no horse, no need. The silver service for Eben and Rebecca's marriage fetched enough to keep the household running for eight months. Gold and silver trinkets from their mining days went to the pawnshop or friends, who gleefully overpaid as a means of stealthy charity. New purchases were forsaken. His shirts began to fray at the sleeves and he saved the collars for the rare occasions he ventured in the city. Her dresses slipped out of and back into fashion, depending on her skills in mending. The children wore their boots and shoes to the nubbins, and the twins relied on the castaways and hand-me-downs from their elder siblings and had aught new from '65 on. Thank the Lord they lived in perfect climes where the temperatures were mild year-round, for Jeb and Zach never had more than two gloves for their four hands. How they ever got those children raised was a mystery to their mother. The three girls married young to the first gentlemen interested enough to ask, and the boys left home early to seek their fortune. Young John C. ended up with Mr. Hearst's enterprises, and one twin joined the gold rush to the Black Hills of the Dakotas in '76, though the boy met his end that summer at the hands of the Sioux. The other left this mortal coil in an opium parlor attended by a Japanese woman who claimed to be his lawful wife, though her claim earned her nothing at the Worths' home, for there was nothing to be had.

It were not for any lack of effort on Flo's part. Sure, she had coddled Jams early on, allowed him time to recover from the blows of first the stocks and then the earth shakes and the damage to the house, but in a few months, she thought to ask when he might be going to find work or some other means to money. "In due course," he would tell her. "Right now I am aiming to rest for a while." Her mam had been a nag to her pap, sending the man to moonshine, so she waited and bit her tongue till she damn near bit through it.

At some point someone, probably Eben or one of the twins, had climbed a ladder and nailed a slat across the crack in the wall beneath the roof, obscuring the night sky, but Jams faithfully watched the stars in pieces each night. After many years had passed and all the children grown and flown the nest, the pull of gravity on both sides of the fracture proved too much. The nails popped one by one from the ends, and the board clattered to the floor. Unkempt and soft and bloated and dressed in his ancient silk robe, the man in the winged-back chair broke into a satisfied smile. "At long last," he said, and the very next day, Jams woke early, shaved, and left the octagon house, announcing to his wife that he was off to seek their fortune and that she should not expect his return that evening or any time soon. She grunted a good-bye and watched the old sloth saunter down the avenue and disappear.

Days later, the little dog starts barking at the door, so she like to think it might be her husband returning. 'Stead a package arrived in the post. She opened it to find a red lacquer box filled with notes from the First National Gold Bank of San Francisco in fives and tens and hundreds, enough money to change their lives. Atop the stack of currency was a letter in her husband's hand: "This should keep you in the pink of the mode until my return. I must rest from my labors. Your Jams."

She turned to Eben, who had been speechless ever since she had opened the package, and asked, "What do you make of all this? Where did all this money come from? Where is Jamie, and when will he be coming home?"

"Nuffin in the world no longer surprises me," Eben said. "I got no answers, though that looks like a Chinese box to me. Suppose when he's done restin', we'll find out."

They waited for him to return to the old run-down house, waited night and day, week after week, watching the stars pass through the hole in the wall, pestering the postman twice a day to double-check for letters, taking turns walking the hilly streets to his old haunts, diving into the hells, and inquiring at the banks. None of their old friends could recall the last time they had seen him inside or out of the octagon house, and none of their old business partners or fellow speculators could even recall old James Worth. As the months became years, they had forfeited hope for the return of the prodigal brother and husband. He had vanished from the earth, leaving behind just enough, if they were careful, for the welfare of the pair. And for the most part, they husbanded their little egg well, though Eben pissed away a fair share gambling and dissipating. And then he lost all one day in 1881 when he crossed too close to a cable car racing down Clay Street, and he died at hospital from the injuries, leaving Flo all alone in the ramshackle house.

Like Penelope faithful to Ulysses, she waited for Jams to come home. Over the years, the frequent earthquakes had widened the fissure in the wall to the point where she no longer felt safe entering the room, but his presence lingered there in the indentations on the seat of the easy chair, the shape of his body on the sofa cushions, and the picture of the universe he loved to watch. Rain and moisture left a trail of mildew that trailed down the wall and into the room below, and the carpets and furniture were constantly damp and coming to pieces. The stove was near impossible to light. Nails in the flooring had popped and would catch her slipper when she crossed. Her bed was lonesome, and whenever the house creaked she feared it was either another quake or his return. Mice had gotten behind the plaster, and she could hear their comings and goings in the dead of night, and seagulls had frequented the southwestern sides and streaked the outer walls with their guano. Forty years had passed since they had left Kentucky and a dozen since he had suddenly left her to go rest. Had he walked through the door at any moment, she would have given him an earful, beat him for abandoning her, and then held him in her arms.

Just when all hope was lost, a Chinaman come to her door one Sunday afternoon. Ye scarce saw any Chinee since the Exclusion in '83, for they kept to themselves more or less from fear of the whites. The young man on the stoop unnerved her. She had not a word of Chinese, and he little English, though he had a message to deliver.

"Mister," he said. "Mister in the bed."

"There is no mister here. I live by myself."

"No. Mister-in-the-bed no more. All gone."

"What does this have to do with me?"

"Your mister. All gone." He handed over a packet addressed to her. *"Nee dohng mah?"* He lifted his eyebrows as if trying to convey some understanding.

She could not take his meaning, only that he had delivered it to the correct address as printed on the brown paper surface. "Thank you," she said. "Wait right here, and I'll find a penny for your troubles."

When she returned to the door, the boy was gone.

With great care, she opened the packet. Wrapped in red tissue paper were a few personal things she instantly recognized as her husband's. A silver pocket watch engraved "Virginia, Nevada" from his trip there. A tortoiseshell comb that Flo had given him on his thirtieth birthday. A straight razor with an ivory handle. A leather billfold, which she opened and found inside forty-nine dollars and a carte de visite with a photograph of the family, probably from before the silver disaster, and on the reverse, the family name and address of the octagon house. Stashed in the secret compartment was a yellowed clipping from an ancient newspaper, a brief story about the robbery of a red lacquer box filled with cash, owned by a well-to-do Chinatown importer named Li, a longtime resident of the city who had first worked the California gold fields back in the glory days.

A letter accompanied these tattered effects:

Please forgive me English.

I am returning these few things of my tenant, Mr. James Worth, who left this world peacefully some months past. He was an ideal man and never caused any trouble. Although he seemed hale and hearty during our long acquaintance, he must have been otherwise suffering, for no one could enjoy his bed and sleep more than our Mr. Worth. I do not know if he is survived by any family, but in good conscience, I send these few remainings to the last no address.

Ah Sum

Beneath the English signature, the author had printed a character in Chinese, but this meant nothing more to her than the final inscrutable sign of her incomprehensible man.

The spotlight snapped off, the houselights were raised instantly, and the shower curtain was drawn back a final time. The other women in the room gasped one by one as the golden jewelry melted from their necks and arms and evaporated from their ears and hair. All of the silver stock certificates in the bathtub began to curl and form little spheres, and as they rose, they changed into soap bubbles, exploding as they touched any surface, until the tub was clean and empty.

CHAPTER ELEVEN

Sea-girls Wreathed with Seaweed

Two young sisters, maybe ages six and three, screamed in the front yard as their parents blew soap bubbles into the summer air. Catching the falling light, the bubbles spun and danced, and with each new bunch blossoming from the wands, the girls chased after the floaters, following dizzying patterns, to capture with claps or open hands the ephemeral and shout with delight at each surprising pop. When the sun had nearly set, the fireflies began to appear, blinking their small lights on the lawn and in the boxwood and fragrant rosebush. The little sisters shadowed these insects, running after the slow erratic flights with outstretched arms to lure one to their fingers or clamp down on one struggling along a blade of grass. Their squeals upon capturing each bug sounded like ecstatic sirens, and they brought every prisoner to their waiting parents to show them the green glow in the cave of their tiny fists, and then, with a shake, released each into the June sky. From across the street, I had watched this comedy unfold, spying on the young family while I pretended to listen to one of the guests at our cookout drone on about marinades. My girlfriend, Sita, was trapped on the other end of the deck by two men from the architectural firm. They wooed her with a story about kayaking down the Potomac River. I longed for her to come join me on the chaise longue and watch the girls chase fireflies. But as the stars appeared in the night, the parents rose and called their daughters inside. My coworker began to explicate aromatic rubs and the Zen of the Maillard Reaction. Sita seemed enthralled by the pair of office goofs. The moment passed, as it always does.

Fingers long and thin and stained with ink and nicotine flashed before my eyes. The old man was fanning his hand before me to see if I was awake or had fallen into some trance. The bubbles that lately had filled the air had disappeared, though the crowd of people in the bathroom was still real as ever. Four of the women stood at the cardinal points of the room's compass, and Flo slouched, disconsolate, on the edge of the tub. She seemed to be speaking of me when she eulogized the late Mr. Worth.

"I can forgive anything but laziness in a man. Show me a man without ambition, and I'll show you a living corpse. Sure, he had his ups and downs, what else is life? But to give up like that, to crawl into bed and never try, well, it's a form of cowardice, isn't it? I'd take a crooked man, a liar, a brute, a fake, a cheat over the lazy man. Give up on yourself, okay, but give up on the rest of your responsibilities?"

Dolly leaned forward and stuck the jut of her jaw into the cradle of her hand. "So, whatever happened to her?"

"Lived for years in that house and was well known around the city as that old lady with the red box, which she carried everywhere she went. Perished, like so many, in the great quake of aught-six, and when they found her, buried in the rubble of the octagon house, she still had that lacquer box clutched in her hands, had to pry it off her. Funny thing, when they opened it, all they found was an old comb, a silver pocket watch, and a rusty straight razor. Not a cent. She'd put it all in the bank and a few stocks and made do off the interest. Left a small fortune to the Chinese American Benevolent Society."

The last bit of her story made me remorseful for the hardship and loneliness she had to endure those final decades, and at the same time, I was pleased to learn that she had held on to both the box and the money. And as an architect, I was further delighted to learn that the eight-sided house withstood nearly sixty years of earthquakes, not to mention the hole in the wall. They certainly don't make them like they used to. Almost by instinct, I began sketching in my imagination the plans for a modern octagon house of two stories and an attic, and thus engaged, I slipped away into the comfort of my mind. Perhaps it was the example of the man so desperate for nothing more than a bed, but an enormous fatigue settled into my bones, and I may have fallen asleep, for the next thing I remember was the sound of the old man's fingersnapping next to my ear.

"Wake up, Sonny. The night is young, and so are we." The five women chuckled at his remark. "You were just about to relate how the dancing dames of the Old West were assaulting you with hugs and kisses."

A sort of yellow fog occluded my vision, and when I awoke fully and shook the exhaustion from my eyes, there before me in Beckett's lap sat the child, now older by some months. He looked closer to two than to one year old, and when he smiled, eight teeth appeared in his bright red mouth.

"So that we may have no further interruptions to your saga," Beckett said, "perhaps it would be wise to find some nourishment for this young bucko. Would you have any Melba toast in the larder? Or they seem to favor dry breakfast cereal in the shape of life preservers. Circles of bananas. Cold Spaghetti-os. Any morsel, really, small enough to be picked up by tiny fingers but soft enough to avoid choking if swallowed whole." He whispered an aside. "They feel independent at this age if they feed themselves, matteradam if they make an unholy mess. Would you have some tidbit about the place?"

I informed him that a search of the pantry would be necessary.

Beckett addressed the toddler directly. "What do you say, young man, some num-yum-num in order?"

"Soightenly," the baby said.

I bowed to his wishes and backed out of the bathroom.

Grateful for the silence and emptiness of the hallway, I paused with my hand on the doorknob and considered my predicament. Although this had long been my home, it felt like a strange land in which strange things had been happening all night, ever since I found myself naked and bleeding on the floor. No, before that, strange things from the moment I arrived home to discover the seven bicycles splayed across the front yard. Or perhaps even earlier? I tried to remember the last normal thing to have happened, retracing my steps past that homecoming, but memory failed me. All I could truly recall was waking in the middle of the night and finding my way to the bathroom.

The doorknob jiggled in my hand, so I let go and hurried downstairs to look for some food for the baby. At the bottom landing, I glanced to the right and saw that everything had changed in the living room. The white walls had been painted sea green and the decor had morphed from my rather traditional Stickley to a sleek fusion of styles, the lines vaguely art deco but the furnishing a mixture of Japanese-Italian-Southwestern-Zen ethos, favoring a kind of modern simplicity. It all looked like some interior decorator's misguided vision of the future. Instead of the old television, there stood a panel thin as glass, but flexible to the touch. Worst of all, my books were missing. There was not a volume to be seen, not even *The Poetics of Space*. It looked like a wasteland.

More formal and austere than before, the dining room bore only the faintest traces of my design, and the kitchen appeared to have been dropped directly from the spaceship of an anal-retentive species of aliens. Gone were the rustic cabinets, the bread on the counter, the booze collecting dust, and the cookie jar molded into the shape of a mermaid that my brother had acquired on some Caribbean vacation. Stainless-steel cabinets and appliances in brushed nickel gave the room cleanliness and order, but the immediate effect was mitigated by the sensation of having wandered into a morgue. What lurked behind those closed metal drawers? It all looked sterile and dangerous. I opened the cupboard in the area where the cereal had once been stored, but the freakish designer who had made over the outside of the room had care-fully catalogued and labeled the foodstuffs into clear plastic containers. The cheese crackers were filed beneath the challah and above the chut-ney. Alphabetized. Talk about measuring one's life out in coffee spoons (between the cocoa and the corn chips). Imagining the baby might be thirsty after his snack, I fished around in the gigantic fridge and poured a half glass of skim milk. I also remembered that the cat was about the house somewhere, and I left a saucer of water on the floor. Not want-ing to wake anyone, I softly called for Harpo, here kitty, kitty, but no meow echoed back. Cats are notoriously independent and cannot always be bribed, like dogs, with food. I shut off the lights and made my way through the strange rooms to the upstairs landing.

The urge to peek in on them was too strong, so I softly elbowed open the door to my bedroom, just a skosh, enough to see the three bodies remaining on the bed. Two of the women groaned slightly at the disturbance and tangled themselves together in a knot, and the third had not moved all night, if indeed the night can be said to have passed at all, but she remained still, her face to the wall, and her hand resting on the swell of her hip. For a moment, I watched the rise and fall of her breathing, and not wishing to disturb her sleep, I left the room as quietly as I had arrived. The floorboards groaned at my tread, and the bathroom door flew open suddenly, flooding the space with light.

"There you are," the old man said, pulling me by the wrist into the cramped room. "What took you so long? We've been waiting for ages."

They had been up to their usual shenanigans in my absence. Someone had found a lipstick and rouge, and they had painted their faces. And each woman had a new hairstyle: Marie in a medusa of dreadlocks, Alice in a Veronica Lake wave that dipped over one eye, Dolly in twin braided pigtails of prodigious length, and Jane and Flo, tall and small, in matching pageboys. Powder caked their faces, and they looked altogether artificial. Beckett's eyes had been shadowed with kohl, making his stare starker still, and even the baby had rosy cheeks. Perhaps the little one smelled or saw the cereal through the plastic or heard a typical rattle, for he implored me by clenching and unclenching his miniature hand to give over the loot.

I pulled off the lid and offered the container, and he reached in up to his wrist and came away with little Oaty-Ohs sticking to his skin and spilling from his grasp. The tot seemed more concerned with what he had lost than with what was still in hand, and he struck me in the moment as somewhat emblematic of the human condition, not to read too much into basic greed and regret. He shoved the lot in his mouth and happily chewed and chewed. Alice took the cup of milk and set it on the sink counter, and then reached for her broom and pulled out a single strand of straw and blew on one end, forcing a hole the length of it to make a suitable tube through which the child might easily drink. The crowd in the bathroom saluted her ingenuity, and everyone watched as if they had never before seen a child take a sip. His first assay was too forceful and the boy gasped and spewed out the milk, but he soon learned his lesson, and general applause was proffered. Fondness and pride buoyed our hearts. I wondered what raising a child with Sita might be like.

Batting his eyes at me, Beckett resembled a rather gaunt raccoon, but when he fluttered his eyelids again, there was no mistaking his ploy to attract my attention. As best we could, we huddled into a corner for a tête-à-tête. He spoke in a hoarse whisper that anyone could hear. "You were gone a long time. Is anything awry?"

"Now that you mention it, the whole of the downstairs has been re-decorated, like some designer's bad dream of the future. Very modern, very austere. Someone came in and got rid of all my stuff."

He put a finger to his bottom lip in a gesture of cogitation. He was wearing pink lip gloss. "That isn't right. Much too soon."

"Do you have any ideas as to who's behind all these changes?"

"Household elves," he said, without hesitation. "Or perhaps grem-lins, or the faerie changelings or wayward angels. A pair of giant lob-sters or two tramps with nothing to be done. How the hell should I know?"

His sarcasm perplexed me, but I did not press the point. Beckett had saved my life five times, yet possessed a preternatural relationship with the five would-be assassins, cozying up to them in my absences. Nonchalant to the essence of my predicament, he seemed awfully famil-iar, yet his true identity shifted in mysterious ways. One moment he re-minded me of my deceased father, the next I was sure he was the spirit of Samuel Beckett come to wait with me for a truth that would never arrive. I could not tell if he was friend or foe, and as these thoughts raced through my mind, he smiled dumbly at me, as though content to let me stop and ponder it all. The rouge on his cheeks, the pink gloss on his lips, and the heavy black around his eyes contributed to his rather seedy demeanor. For the first time that night, he looked old and tired. I felt a sudden need to strike back at him for his cold remarks. "Have you seen yourself in a mirror? You look like an old drag queen at five A.M. on the morning after."

Brushing me aside, he stepped to consider his reflection, pulled off his glasses, and leaned so closely that the tip of his nose was touching the glass. I fear I may have hurt his feelings, for tears collected in the red bottom rims of his eyelids. Jane gave him a hand towel the moment he reached out blindly, and burying his face in the cloth, he rubbed savagely against his features, blew his nose, and handed the towel back to her. The old face had returned to the old man, and with it, the old glee and lechery. He ogled a pair in the corner and then turned to me with mischief in mind.

"So, you were saying. These seven women are all trying to hug and kiss you at once . . ."

Momentarily, I was lost in what seemed like a non sequitur, but then it came to me that he wanted me to continue the story I had begun long ago, before the quintuple interruptions, the story of what had happened before we met under such odd circumstances. I was in the process of losing that story; that is to say, the stories that each woman told, preceded by their attempts on my life, had superseded prior events. Or at any rate, the two stories were jumbling together so that it was difficult to separate what had happened and in what order. One of the functions of the old man must have been to get me to keep my stories straight. I was having trouble remembering what had happened before and then after the bump to my head, and the threat of amnesia hovered and cast a dreadful shadow.

"You left off, Sonny, with the girls in their Wild West costumes about to devour you with carnal desires?" He leered and waggled his eyebrows lasciviously à la Groucho Marx, and I half expected him to lift a cigar to his mouth beneath a greasepaint mustache.

"Don't get me wrong. The moment when they rushed to greet me was more an expression of how happy they were just to see me, and after the initial kisses, my face was dotted with lipstick impressions, and I was in a state of euphoria. Tiny stars and moons and flapping bluebirds orbited my head, and the group moved forward as one from the piano recital and into the hallway. I had no idea how I was even walking, but the women chatted among themselves, wandering to and fro, paying almost no attention to me, and we reached a crossroads of sorts. To the left was my bedroom. A sharp right round the bend was the staircase, and farther along was the bathroom. My inclination at this point was divided into two distinct and competing urges. Did I dare suggest the bedroom, or would I be a gentleman and allow the mob to dictate the rules?"

"Seven women would require a full week."

"Apparently the decision wasn't mine to make. Into the bathroom they filed, some glancing back, one or two waving discreetly, and the last, Jane here, telling me that they needed a moment to freshen up."

"A wise decision, I should think," the old man said. "I myself have been a bit, shall we say, stale, and a quick wash, brush the teeth, and a dash of talc, and you're good as new. Cleanliness is underrated as a virtue, and many people nowadays forget to scrub behind their ears."

The rest of us, by reflex, checked to feel if the space behind the ears was clean, and each of us sighed with relief when fingertips grazed smooth skin. Nobody bothered to check the baby, of course, for it is a well-known fact that small children are almost always dirty, their folds and creases the hiding place for grime, and in the summertime, they usually excrete some clammy, sticky substance that covers their entire persons. Pick up a baby of your acquaintance at a July or August picnic, and you will be shocked. They can be as slimy as a three-day-old mackerel and often smell none the better. Moreover, they swarm with germs and harmful bacteria and carry untold diseases. One of the women in the firm is the mother of twins, and she is forever sneezing or wheezing or complaining about ear infections or some bug going around the day care, and thus the contagion travels outward from child zero until everyone has a cold or the flu.

"Well, I waited," I told him. "First pacing up and down the hall, and then finally sitting on the top step. They took forever."

The old man laughed. "What is it with women and bathrooms?"

All at once he was assaulted with flying objects—a wad of toilet paper, a sliver of soap, an avalanche of cotton balls, the cap to a can of shaving cream, my toothbrush! Even the baby tossed a few Oaty-Ohs at him, thinking their protest a new game. Beckett covered his head beneath the shield of his hands and apologized in a sonorous voice, "*Désolé.*"

"There were seven, after all," I said, "but I was curious as to what was going on. The shower had been flowing for some time, and when it finally stopped, the singing commenced—"

"Ah, the same singer as when you thought the windows had been singing."

"No, this was different. Seven voices in a kind of roundelay, the women singing each to each, a melody so entrancing and bewildering that I could have listened to it all night, and yet it lured me to the door and to the keyhole."

"Why ever would you have a keyhole in the bathroom door?"

"Precisely. Furthermore, no such hole existed prior to that evening, nor is there any such key on the premises. I concluded that there was one reason only for the keyhole, and that it had been put there for me to spy on the women in the bathroom."

The old man clapped his hands with delight. "Very good, old man. Deductive reasoning at its finest. But you could have asked me for the skeleton key." From the pocket of his robe, he removed a long, black old-fashioned iron key with a skull at the top of the handle. "It unlocks all the doors in this house."

"But you weren't here at the time."

My assertion seemed to confuse him, and he scratched at his hair with the blade of the key. "Right, so. Still. You were about to place your eyeball against the perforation and behold the maidens . . ."

"That was my expectation, but when I looked through the hole, the bathroom itself had been replaced by what appeared to be an ocean and a rocky shoreline that resembled the coast of Maine or Cornwall, some rugged northerly locale. Waves rolled and crashed, and above in the pale blue sky, a gull laughed and winged beyond the frame. In disbelief, I blinked, and then the perspective shifted so quickly that my eye functioned like a zoom lens, making all appear closer or giving me the sensation of being on the sand itself and the rocky ledges near enough to touch. I heard that singing again, a dying strain, as the tune passed along a chain of voices, and then I saw the first of the seven, naked to the waist, and where her legs had been, a fish's tail. All of them were mermaids, sea-girls wreathed with seaweed, singing atop the outcropping of rocks, luring sailors to their ruination."

Through the open window, some stray music reached us, the morning medley of a mockingbird auditioning for a mate. I wondered if his cry meant that dawn would soon come, but a quick glance at my watch disappointed me. The birdsong faded.

Beckett took up his part to fill the silence. "Lonesome mariners in their longing often mistakenly believed a herd of walruses, far off on some ice floe, to be a school of mermaids, until the ship drew near to the fearsome beasts. Have you ever seen the tusks of that fellow? Two daggers, big as a man's leg. Or some say the mermaids were actually the manatee, a freshwater mammal, sometimes called a sea-cow for its placid demeanor, vegetarian diet, and prodigious weight. In India, I believe, it is called the dugong, but you would have to ask that girlfriend of yours. Sita. In either case, a rather far-fetched connection. The mermaids' song, I've heard, is actually the song of the humpbacked whale, as the behemoths wander the oceans of the world, calling one to the other. You'll not hear a more haunting song on land or the deep blue sea."

"Aye," Jane stepped in. "The humpback is a good songstress, and the beluga whale is known as the canary of the sea. But all the tales of whales and walruses is stuff and nonsense. 'Twere never thus that a grown man mistook such a creature for a woman. 'Twere the long years aboard ship that drove sailors to madness. A woman's body above and a fish's below is a matter of imagination and great longing and fear. Afore the houricane blew in on us, we had a cloudy night on the sea with no moon or stars, just the lanterns of the ship, and beyond nothing but blackness and the sound of waves slapping against the hull. Nine hours I was on watch, looking into nothing, and is it any wonder that every errant splash became a great sea monster, and every groan of wood meant the spars would soon crash down, and every sigh in a man's sleep gives birth to a ghost."

"Nine hours, hah," Dolly scoffed. "I once waited nine years in a cave for a ghost who I knew was never going to come back. Imagine the demons who visited me."

Marie shook her dreads. "Try waiting your whole life to be free, and then you will see what the imagination conjures. It is the secret of the voodoo."

"And the curse of the human race," the old man said. "Imagination is the fuel of hope. Better you should leave such fires be and see what is truly in front of you."

Red hair draped across her face, Alice rose with her baby on her hip. "Don't you dare say such awful things in front of the child. I carried him for nine months, nine months of hoping for him with every breath, imagining what he would be like, and imagining now what he will become. Imagination is no curse, mister, but what separates us from the monkey, and hope is enough to bend iron bars as though blades of grass. Never underestimate the human mind."

Placing his hand over the region of the heart, Beckett bowed slowly. "I stand corrected. You will forgive me. The young gentleman most of all." The baby gurgled at him.

Quick as a terrier, Flo crossed the room, spat in her palm, and offered her hand to the old man. "Apology accepted," she said in a brassy tone.

A loud bang on the door prevented the consummation of their handshake. Someone had thrown something hard enough to cause the wood on the inside to buckle, and the missile sounded loud as a stone. I imagined David slinging rocks at Goliath, and the next one came in harder, the impact like a thunderclap, spraying splinters into the room.

"That was a pretty good one," the old man called out. "A little higher next time."

The third throw arrived at a spot where my head would have been had the door not been closed. The wood absorbed most of the blow, but the object embossed a fist-sized impression.

"Strike three," the old man hollered. From his pocket, he produced a tailor's measuring tape and held it against the width of the door. Twenty-two inches, though I could have told him that, had he asked. Part of the occupational training for an architect is to be able to estimate with high accuracy dimensions in space. He rolled up the tape and put it back in his pocket, and then he placed his hands on my shoulders in order to address me in a direct and sober manner. "Can you be brave? Can you face the foe and not flinch, despite all instinct? You know that I am on your side, and I have taken careful measures and done the necessary geometry to reckon the angles, so I ask merely for your unwavering trust and confidence."

I nodded my approval to his unstated plan, and he positioned me just in front of the door. "Stand here, and don't move a muscle, no matter what happens after I open this door. Do you think you can do this? Good boy."

Before I had the chance to think, he flung open the door. In the threshold waited a young woman in a green dress with a baseball bat resting on her shoulder. Her eyes widened when she saw me standing there, and as if awaiting a pitch right down the middle of the plate, she drew back and swung the Louisville Slugger straight at my bean. The fat end of the barrel connected with the doorjamb, sending a stinging vibration down the bat and right into her hands. With a small yelp of pain, she dropped the baseball bat, and the old man stepped on the handle with a bare foot. He jerked his thumb into the air. "You're out!"

CHAPTER TWELVE

The Woman Who Lost the Flag

The old man examined the baseball bat and, to my surprise, gripped the handle like an experienced hitter, gave a half-hearted swing, and then tossed it in the corner with the war club, the miner's pick, and the other weapons of my destruction. The woman at the door ticked like a furnace as her anger cooled. Like the others, she was beautiful—a straw-colored blonde with verdigris eyes and pale, almost translucent skin, set off starkly against the green dress she wore. A vein snaked along her left temple, and her full lips radiated pink health against that porcelain complexion. One would deduce from her appearance that her forebears hailed from some Scandinavian town. She had a northern composure, a skim of ice around her heart.

"Your swing leaves much to be desired," the old man said. "But you have a helluva fastball."

On the outside of the door, now visible to all, two deep impressions pocked the surface, but on her third pitch, the one aimed at my head, the baseball stuck in the wood, its red stitching bright as a scar.

She laughed in a four-note measure. "Those first two were just warm-ups. I brought the high heat on the last one."

The old man asked, "Where did you learn to throw like that?"

"From watching the old ball game. From a beau—"

"Ain't that always the kick in the teeth," Flo interjected.

The other women murmured their assent, and a ripple of solidarity zipped from woman to woman and fizzled when it reached me. No rancor was directed toward the old man, only me. In fact, he seemed in cahoots with them, so I looked to the baby for moral support. He was busy trying to eat his fist.

"She's the singer," I said, suddenly recalling her face. "The one from the recital, the opera singer."

"Are you sure?" the old man asked. "The singer is usually a bit more zaftig, and Miss . . ."

"Adele," she said.

"Miss Adele is in fine shape, eh? Probably from all that baseball."

Certain now, I insisted. "Florence there was seated at the piano, and Adele was crooning 'The Laughing Song,' I believe, and later, when the mermaids sang, her voice was truer, more clear and pleasing than the others. This bird can sing."

"Is this right, Adele? You can sing as well as sling the old horsehide?"

She flushed from her chest and along her throat, and in a hesitant voice, she said, "One can love both."

"Love?" The old man looked like he was about to spit out his teeth. "One can love any number of things at once. I love a good Buster Keaton film, crêpes suzette, and flying kites in the March winds. But if what Sonny says about you is true, you have more than love. You have passion, you have a gift. And I've seen you pitch. Sister, that ain't love. That's talent."

The blood rushed to her face again, and she had no answer for him. When the initial embarrassment faded, two rosettes lingered on her cheeks. Taking her by the elbow, the old man led her to the center of the room. From his bottomless pocket, he retrieved a cream-colored baseball cap with a short blue bill and an old-fashioned blue *P* emblazoned on the peak. He jammed the cap over his silver spiked hair and then reached deeper into that pocket and procured an ancient leather mitt, barely bigger than his left hand, and he put it on and pounded the palm with his right fist. "I'm ready now," he told her. "Give us your best stuff. Fire that yarn right here, baby."

Behind her, projected on the tiles of the shower, a large sepia-toned photograph sharpened into focus. Two young men in high collars and boaters lounged on the steps of a city brownstone on a summer's day. They looked like brothers, and the older one had tossed something in the air, but the aperture of the camera transformed the object into a white blur. Only upon inspection could it be guessed that the object in motion was a baseball. Adele began her story.

She already knew he was a crank before she ever met him. He and his brother Christy were just fiends for baseball. Went to every game they could, those boys, over in Exposition Park across the river. In fact, that's where Pat courted her, in the ballpark, just one of several thousand cranks, rooters, and fans come out to cheer.

The photograph on the wall whirred into motion, and the ball that the young man had been tossing fell into his hand. Just like an old silent movie, the film jerked in time, depending upon the action of the cameraman, and scratches, flecks of dust, and moments of underexposure and overexposure darted by. A sound track started, an old-timey piano to accompany the action. But nothing much happened in the scene. The camera did not move, nor did the actors. A title card flashed on the screen: "Patrick Ahearn and his younger brother Christopher 'Christy,' Pittsburg, Penna., 1903."

Beckett piped in from the peanut gallery. "Hey, I thought there was an *h* at the end of Pittsburgh."

"Not in Aught-Three," she said. "They spelled it differently."

On the film, Christy lights a cigarette and appears to smoke it in superfast motion, as the film must have been undercranked. Pat tosses the baseball again and again till he mugs for the camera. His hair is slicked back and parted as though with a knife. He stops slouching against the balustrade and stands up straight. Confidence pours from his gaze. He tosses the ball again, and the image fades to black.

The year following her graduation from the twelfth grade, Adele helped the Sisters at St. Luke's, making sure the little ones had proper coats and gloves, mending the torn books, and teaching the children's choir. Two of her younger sisters, Katie and Grace Ann, were still in school there, and it gave her the chance to play mother during the day. Sometimes she thought of entering the convent herself, but she never heard the call, and spending time among those children, she couldn't help but want a family of her own. But that's another story, isn't it? That spring, one of the poor third-grade boys was struck by a tram and killed, and the whole class was expected to be at the funeral, but Sister Aloysius couldn't bear her grief and asked Adele to escort the students in the procession from the school to the cemetery.

The children were more unruly than had nuns taken them, and for all but a few, it was a lark, a parade in the sunshine. Two lines, the twelve girls in pairs, the nine boys paired as well, with the odd one, Frankie Day, as her companion. They had been hushed and chastened on the way to the church, but after the Mass and once that little box had been lowered in the hole, the children were a terror. Girls refusing the hands of their partners in the lines. Boys being boys, stepping on the heels of those walking in front of them, chittering like sparrows, and one boy fingering a lump in his trousers, looking suspicious as a squirrel. Turns out he had a baseball in his pocket, and whenever Adele's back was turned, he took it out and tossed it to his best friend.

The procession passed right in front of the two men on the stoop, and she noticed the older one watching her; his gaze nearly burned a hole in her skirt. Behind her, a boy cried out, and given the circumstances, of course she spun around quickly to see to his safety.

Like a flock of angels, the boys and girls materialize in the photograph on the shower tiles. Posed as though for a class picture, they appear somehow more adult and alien than the eight-year-olds of today. Perhaps it is the formality of fashion. The boys are as neat and clean as bankers, still in short pants or knickerbockers with knee socks, and their buttoned shirts shine bright. The girls have done their hair in ribbons and curls and sit primly in short dresses or simple skirts and blouses. They are poor, but appearances matter. An empty chair stands next to a dour nun, and I reckon it once contained the lost child. Written in white below the children is "St. Luke's Third Grade, May 1903."

As Adele continues her story, the image changes, almost imperceptibly at first, for it is still the same group of twenty-one children seated in the same chairs, but they have aged. In 1909, another chair is empty. By 1918, young men and women, but the nun is gone, and three boys are missing, perhaps the Spanish flu or the Great War. Three others are dressed as doughboys, and one of the young women wears a nurse's white uniform. They are in the prime of life in 1929, half the men in suits, the others working men, but all the women looking older than their years. Only fifteen of the original group remain. The years roll on, and the empty chairs increase. By midcentury, less than half the chairs are filled. In another decade, there are but two men and six women. Across the room the old man is counting, too, and I wonder if he is pulling for the survivors. In 1972, there is one boy left, a white-haired man who wears a Nehru jacket and a braided ponytail. Surrounding him are four women in shapeless dresses and sensible shoes. One by one they begin to fade from the photograph, and by 1981, one man and one woman keep company. They are holding hands. Another year passes, and he sits alone, shrunken but still too big for the children's chairs, bewildered by his longevity. The calendar turns, he waits. The final frame is the empty classroom with a single paper curling on the floor.

Straightening the collar of her green frock, Adele continued.

When the boy cried out, she was shocked, you understand, for they had just come from the graveyard and were supposed to be in their prayers, and what does she see instead, but the young man tossing a ball in ône hand, and three of her students surrounding him, silently beseeching him for its return. Cool as you please, the man just kept taunting them, for he knew full well that the ruckus would bring her over soon enough.

He took off his hat like a real gentleman when Adele approached, and the boys parted to make way, and he stepped forward and offered her that infernal baseball. "One of your charges," he said. "A bit too full of mischief." Their fingertips grazed as she took it from him, and Adele nearly jumped through her skin. Having no bag or pocket, she kept the ball in her grip. The miscreant boys wandered back into line. All of the children were spying on them. "But aren't you just a bit older than these young chiselers yourself? Sure, but you are too young to be a Sister."

"I am fully nineteen, and I am not one of the nuns. I teach the children how to sing and am only helping out today . . . with the funeral."

When he smiled at her answer, he seemed to show too many teeth, but they were straight and white. His skin was clear and bore no pocks, and his black hair was neat and lightly oiled in place. But his eyes did her in. As brown as chestnuts, his eyes fixed on hers, and she could feel him looking at her even when she averted her gaze. "The best news of the day, Miss."

"Adele," she answered. "Adele Hopkins."

"I'm Patrick Ahearn, at your service. That's quite a grip you've got on that baseball, Miss Adele. Do you play?"

The children were watching. "I must be going. They're expecting us back at St. Luke's." She nearly knocked little Frankie to the ground as she turned, for he had been beside her all along, hiding behind her skirts. With a stern look, she ordered the boys and girls to form their columns, and they were about to resume their procession.

"Are you a fanatic?" Pat asked. "Have you ever been to see the Pittsburg boys? Our Pirates?"

Blushing, she bowed slightly and then faced forward and marched her third graders as briskly as union men in the Labor Day parade. The very thought of traveling across the river to Allegheny City for a mere baseball game filled her with incredulity, and though she knew some young women—such as her best friend, Helen—who had been to Exposition Park for the spectacle, it was not altogether respectable somehow, and Adele wondered what her parents would have to say to such a proposition, and the fact that he, a total stranger, had more or less invited her moments upon first meeting heated her blood to a boil. The very idea. He was simply too brazen to further consider one jot. By the time she herded the children into the classroom, Adele felt damp and thirsty. This will not do, she told herself, but all night long she could not help speculating if he had, in fact, asked her or intended to ask her to come along. Helen would know what to do. She would have to ask Helen about this baseball man, this brazen Irishman, this Patrick Ahearn.

"Oh look," the old man said, "a new film."

The clickety-clack of the projector whirred into motion and a rectangle of light flashed on the wall before the image introduced itself. The sprocket holes on the edges fluttered madly, then disappear, and the figures lighten, darken into focus and life. Two young women in their linen dresses sit side by side on a porch swing in the good old summertime. A black-and-white mutt, curled up like a cinnamon bun, lounges just out of reach of their feet. Perched on the windowsill are a sweating glass ewer of lemonade and two empty glasses. A breeze is blowing, for a dance of shadows and light pours through the branches of a tree and onto their faces. They are as intimate as two sisters in conversation. One of these young maidens is our Adele, her honey-colored hair piled high into a bouffant in the fashion of the day, but there's no doubt of that face, those features. The other, whose dark hair rises to a mountain of curls, is her friend Helen, aptly named, for she is stunning.

"The friend is a looker," I whispered to the old man.

"A Gibson girl," he replied behind the back of his hand. "So named for the artist who drew the original. A kind of personification of the idealized female, though there's a bit of satire in it all, a poke at the masculine tendency to sexualize half the human race. Look at that waist, for goodness' sake. A wasp has a bigger belly. No surprise you think her the more beautiful of the two."

As the young women rocked on the swing and chatted, the sound of piano music filtered through the bathroom fan. Some vital bit of information was being conveyed, and the camera zoomed in. Adele on the wall grew particularly animated, and the title card stated: "I had no idea he had a brother." Helen smiled broadly, the heavy pancake makeup visible in close-up. She says something and winks. The intertitle reveals a moment later: "And he is sweet on me!"

The title card on the wall reads: "Her First Game" and dissolves into a static shot of the crowd making its way down School Street and into Exposition Park. The twin spires decorating the roof of the wooden grandstand point into the smog, but the men and boys and few women rush forward, a sea of hats and caps. Spurred on by the prospect of the duel at three o'clock against the New York Giants, the crowd is electric with happiness. The few women in the queue are dressed as finely as any gentlemen, and Helen and Adele wear matching straw toques with a peacock's feather, one in blue and one in red, in honor of the hometown team. Caught in the instant looking back at the camera, Adele holds on to her hat with one hand as she is swept away.

When the film concluded, she picked up her story.

Pure chance, though sooner or later, they were bound to meet. The Ahearn brothers were West End Irish, but they had moved into town for a place of their own nearer to work. Pat finished early in the morning, and Christy was on nights, so they had nothing to do on summer days but go to the ball games. By June, the four of them would go together, and Adele put aside her reservations just to be near the brash fellow.

At the gates, Pat paid the two-bit admission each for all four of them, as if a dollar was nothing, and he gave the man another dollar to find them seats in the grandstand beneath the shelter of the roof. The afternoon sun shone brightly, and she nearly swooned the moment she first saw the brilliant green field. Cut into the manicured expanse was a keyhole between the pitcher's mound and home plate, and the paths around the bases were similarly shaped in dirt. In their cream-colored uniforms and brown hats and stockings, the New Yorks were practicing, throwing the ball with such effortless grace and impossible speed.

Bordering the great lawn was a fence plastered with advertisements for everything from hair tonic to downtown restaurants. Just beyond ran the railroad, and beyond the tracks, barges and paddleboats sailed the Allegheny River, and on the other side of the water lay Pittsburg proper, the Point, and the hubbub of the city. She felt well away from all that in Exposition Park, almost as if out in the country for a summer's picnic. The men had asked, and permission was granted, to remove their jackets, and they sat in their shirtsleeves like two stevedores. A negro in a white coat came by and offered to sell them a bag of roasted peanuts. Every few minutes, someone would wave or shout greetings to Pat and Christy, who seemed to know all of Pittsburg and Allegheny City. One such fellow in a derby and dark suit kept passing in the aisle near their bench, uncertain as to whether he might approach, until he became a thorough distraction. Finally, he caught Pat's eye and made his way over.

"Hiya, Charlie." Pat stood to greet him and shake his hand. "Caught us with a few friends. Miss Hopkins, Miss Jankowski, this here is Charles Wells. Good to see you, old boy, hope you enjoy the game."

Charlie touched the brim of his bowler and went right to his point. "Who'd ya like today, Pats? I've a half eagle to put on the Giants." He held up the gold coin.

"Ah, you're crazy. They'll be lucky if they score at all against the Deacon."

"Phillipe's pitching? You've got yourself a bet—"

"No," Pat held up his hand. "No sportin' for me today, chum. Can't you see I've company? Ladies present."

"Go on then," said Charlie, "you're jagging me with that."

Pat shook his head and folded his arms against his chest.

"Don't be like that, old sport." He turned to address Adele. "Don't you know this old man is but a reprobate?"

As quick as a hound, Pat found his feet, stepped on the empty bench in front of them, and had Charlie's lapel in his grip. The man in the bowler squawked, and half the crowd, it seemed, turned around, and thus surrounded, Pat let go. Spry as a rat, Charlie was on his way, skittering down toward the field. One of the New York ballplayers, an older, stout fellow, was watching the fracas, and he cupped his hands in a megaphone and called to Pat, "Leave the poor sonofabitch alone, you big galoot." He feigned throwing a baseball at the patrons in the stands, and all the cranks had a good laugh. Even Pat, his temper abated, flashed that toothy smile.

"Ain't that something," Christy told him. "That's old John McGraw, the manager hisself, bawling you out."

The Pirates came onto the field in their home whites, blue caps and collars, and the blue stockings with the red stripes. A great war cry rose from the crowd. At three or four spots in the bleachers, young boys clanged cowbells, and one put a cornet to his lips and blew out a three-note huzzah. As prelude to the game itself, the players tossed around the ball, and the pitcher went to the mound to doctor the dirt hill to his liking.

Adele had scores of questions, but she deferred all until the game itself began, preferring instead to let the experience invade her senses—the smell of peanuts and grilled sausages, wool suits in the summer heat, the thwack of the ball hitting leather mitts, the sight of men as gleeful as boys cavorting in the newly mown grass. As she had been warned, a fair amount of foul language peppered the hum of conversation in the stands, a few words she thought she never would hear, and every now and then, some gentleman would feel compelled to yell something disparaging at the foe. The cranks cheered at every New York out and hooted when the umpire decided the other way. The whole first inning passed by her notice. Too much was happening, and the man beside her gave her the vapors.

. . .

Across the room, from the cramped niche between the bathtub and the sink, whispers grew louder. Jane conferred with Alice on some secret matter, but they had become animated in their discussions to the point of overtaking the unfolding narrative of the baseball romance. The old man cleared his throat as a sign of disapproval.

"And who are you to stick your beak in it?" Alice asked him.

"Yarrah, go off, old man, and take that little drooler with you." Jane flashed him a sparkling look.

Gently, he removed the child from his lap and set him on the floor. During the course of this latest story, the boy had stolen the cap and now wore it backward on his head. Clutching the lapels of his white robe, the old man straightened and bounced twice on the balls of his feet, thrusting out a defiant chest. "There is no call, ladies, for that sort of sedition. Adele has the floor as you once had, and we owe one another a modicum of respect—"

"Hear, hear," Dolly amended.

"And what, might I ask, is the subject of your private disputation?"

They both eyed Adele, a mixture of disdain and pity in their gaze. Jane threw her arm around Alice's shoulder. "We were only talking about the sad state of feminine affairs, and what a shame it was to swoon over a man, and such a man as that."

Light flickered on the tiles and the music started with a few discordant notes, like a cat crossing a keyboard, and the silent movie began again. A wide-perspective shot of the ballpark from the vantage of an overlooking hill gave way to a panning shot from the outfield and into the diamond itself. Men in baggy uniforms ran the bases, fielded ground balls, and turned a double play. Against this backdrop, Adele picked up from where she had been interrupted by her more cynical sisters.

· · ·

That first ball game, that whole June day, passed in a blur and yet in memory lasts a century. The Pirates won, 7–0, a shutout, the first of a record six in a row their pitchers were to post. She was at the ballpark for the last of the six, as well, and read all about it in the newspapers. In fact, everything about baseball could be found in the *Post* or the *Daily Gazette,* most important the scores, who won or lost, and how the runs came about, and the names of yesterday's heroes and goats. She had never taken an interest in the sporting news before meeting Pat, but now her mornings began with a quick check of the league standings and over her toast and jam she deciphered the box scores.

On the screen were shots of the players relaxing. Two men clown before the camera, monkey-faces, and the taller grabs the hat off the short, stocky fellow and rustles his thick wavy hair. Above the man runs his name in black letters: *Ginger Beaumont, outfield.* The gangly fellow holds the cap out higher and higher as the redhead paws for it. Above his grinning face: *Kitty Bransfield, first base.*

Keeping up with the news about the Pirates occupied her days when Pat failed to call. But that occurred infrequently as the month wore on. Those first weeks of June when the Pirates were in town, he would fetch a hack two or three times a week to include her on the ballpark excursion. Other days he went by himself, but he would arrive at her home on the Bluff around six o'clock and take her out to dinner or promenade on the ridge above the Monongahela River. When the team left town, he had more freedom, and once they attended an afternoon at the movies. *Alice in Wonderland* thrilled her when the girl was trapped in the small house and had to reach through the tiny window for her magic fan. But on the same bill was Edison's *Electrocution of an Elephant,* and she cried in her sleep that night, remembering the cloud of smoke and how the beast toppled at once as the volts pulsed through its body, and she wished that Pat had been with her in the bed to put his arms around her as he had done in the dark exhibition hall. She dreamt of him often, waking in the hot nights drenched in sweat, and wondering how he might touch her, what he might do to her, should they be married.

In sepia, the boys, still in their uniforms, file out of the park and climb aboard a horse-drawn omnibus. Across the street, storefronts advertise Milliners, Dry Goods, and the Benevolent Temperance Society of Chicago. The game is done, and the Pirates are on their way back to the hotel in a good mood. Two of the young men stand on the wagon's running boards, and as it jostles on, they perform a mock arabesque, as if preparing to fly. *Claude Ritchey, second base. Jimmy Sebring, outfield.*

On the morning of Independence Day, Pat showed up on her doorstep to take her to the ball game against Philadelphia, the dregs of the National League. Adele's father answered the knock, and from her bedroom on the second floor, she could hear the two men conversing in stiff exchange. Mr. Hopkins, an accountant for the city, was a small, formal man, not given to any display of emotion, but his voice, which had started out mild and pleasant, grew agitated by Pat's booming replies to his queries. No, Pat was saying, no I have not. She quickly finished tying her corset and then threw on her dress to hurry to intervene. At the top of the stairs, she heard Pat's anguished reply to her father's insisting question. ". . . but I've not had a drop today, Mr. Hopkins, hand to God. It's not even noon."

Adele flew down the steps and inserted herself between the two rams. Flustered by any sign of disagreement, she did not even see her beau but focused immediately on mollifying her father.

"Papa dear, I had no idea you were home today. How nice." She kissed the old man on his cheek and clung to his shoulder with one hand. He placed his hand over hers and returned her kiss. Then and only then did she face Pat Ahearn and notice, with a shudder, the thin vertical line that split his lip. The blood had dried into a dull red scab. She drew her fingers to her own mouth and could not find the words for a simple greeting. Neither man could muster a graceful exit to their disagreement, and they all might be standing there to this day, silent as a three-legged stool, had not the dog walked into the parlor, demanding, by the fierce circling propelling of her tail, to be acknowledged. Pat reached down and scratched behind the mutt's floppy ears, cooing thatagirl, that's a good girl. Adele stepped under her bonnet and using the glass window as a mirror, she tied the straps in a bow and kissed her father good-bye all in one motion, promising to be home in time for the celebratory supper and to hear the cannons and see the fireworks that evening as they had done every Fourth of July since she was a little girl.

A broad-faced man shows how his long crooked fingers allow him to hold in one hand four baseballs at once. *Ed Phelps, catcher.* Four young men, three right-handers and a left-hand thrower, wind up and pretend to hurl the pill right at us through the camera lens. When they finish their follow-through motions, three are smiling sheepishly: *Deacon Phillippe, Sam Leever, Brickyard Kennedy, pitchers.* Only the fourth, lefty *Ed Doheny,* remains dead serious. A strangeness in the eyes.

. . .

At the ballpark, she finally managed to ask him about the argument with her father.

"He accused me of showing up drunk to escort his daughter. I'm not drunk at all. Christy and I had a beer or two with our breakfast, but that's all. Hardly a drop."

"You should know that he's got a stir about the Irish—"

"Who don't?" Ahearn clenched his fists. "It's always the micks this, the micks that."

"Are you sure it was just a beer with breakfast?"

Pat flicked back the brim of his boater so that it made a halo around his face.

Squinting into the bright light, Adele watched the Pirates take the field and begin to toss around the baseballs. "He took the pledge is all. A temperance man." She was nearly afraid to ask about Pat's injury, but at last volunteered, "Did you hurt your lip?"

"Don't be a mope," he told her. "A gentlemen's disagreement. But you should see the other fellow. This ain't nothing."

For the first three innings she sat, petulant, barely caring herself who won or lost. In the middle of the fourth, Pat leaned closer, held her chin in the crook of one finger. "C'mon, Adele, give us a kiss." And for the first time: "Be a sweetheart. Don'tcha know that I love you?"

The house lights rose and we all blinked, adjusting our sight.

"Gag," said Flo and mimed sticking her fingers down her throat.

"Revolting," said Jane at the mirror, fixing the ends of her new hairdo. "Absolutely revolting."

The old man stretched his long bare legs and crossed his arms. "Now, ladies, your bitterness is unbecoming. We all have faith in love, especially in our youth."

I nodded my agreement, thinking the while of the girl surrounded by fireflies.

Abuzz with opinions, the women debated the merits of love, and the old man took advantage of their philosophizing to address me privately. "May I ask a personal question?" This he asks after spending who knows how long in my bathrobe, in my bathroom, and sharing as my coeval the sundry stories visited by the past upon my present. This he asks after saving my life no fewer than six times, and more to come, I fear. This he asks, though he does not realize, slender as it may be, that he is the reed upon which clings all hope that some sense and order may be restored. I thought and hoped that he might ask me about the girl and help me rescue her from my amnesiac fog. I gave him the okay.

He spoke in a serious manner that had a hint of sarcasm. "Where'd you get the money to afford a place like this? Surely not on your salary with the architects. At which, may I add, you've not designed and built more than an archway."

Perhaps it was unintentional on his part, but the words stung. He may have detected the faint whiff of self-abnegation escaping from my body. I must have smelled of disappointment. Even the baby crinkled his nose, and the women briefly paused their discussions to note the aroma of failure and, now, mortification.

"Not that you haven't got ideas, I'm sure," he said. "Great designs in the mind. Plans to plan. But this place must have cost a small fortune."

"You're right," I said. "My brother and I went in together. I never would have been able to afford this house on my own."

"Must be a helluva fella," the old man smiled and then reached out for the baby boy begging to be held.

The house lights dimmed and as the movie started once more, we fell silent to its spell. Three men in baseball caps and matching sweaters pose unhappily on a cold day. The guy in the middle mouths something to the other pair, the words emerge as clouds. Like bears waking from hibernation, they loosen their limbs, roll their necks, shrug their shoulders. The title reads: "Hot Springs, Arkansas, Spring Training." The man on the left has a serious air about him, the weight of gravitas. *Fred Clarke, outfield and manager.* In the middle stands an imp. *Tommy Leach, third base.* But the man on the right is of a kind not made anymore. Long-armed, broad hands, and long crooked fingers, he appears to be a kind of golem or man of baked clay. His legs are slightly bowed. A hooked nose dominates his face, and his gaze at first is circumspect. He shows the cameraman a pet miniature dachshund sitting nonchalantly in the cup of one hand. On command, the little dog barks and howls and then, still in its master's palm, stands on its hind legs and begs until rewarded with a morsel hidden in the man's other hand. Once it has finished the treat, the dog lifts its left hind leg and piddles down the big man's arm. The other two roar with laughter, and the man dances on his bandy legs, feigning anger, until he, too, cannot escape the humor of the moment. His booming laugh can almost be heard. *Honus Wagner, the Flying Dutchman, shortstop.*

Although she loved him, Adele fought the impulse to blurt out her feelings right then and there at the ball game in front of all those cranks. But she loved him, yes, and was so happy that he loved her, too. She kissed him quickly and for the rest of the day allowed Pat to hold her hand when she was not cheering another victory by the swaggering Pirates. He was good and kind and generous, and aside from that flash of anger at the man in the bowler hat, he had not shown a single fault. A drink now and then, but that could be hidden from her father. And, true, he liked to tease her at times, especially when Christy was around as coconspirator.

"Did I ever tell you," Pat said near the end of the game, "about our man Hans Wagner and his big shovel of a hand? Out in St. Lou it was, a batter hit a ground ball towards him, but instead of grabbing the base-ball, he scooped up a rabbit that had wandered on the field."

"A rabbit, no," said Christy.

"Aye, Wagner throws it over to first base anyway, and the runner was out by a hare."

Adele smacked the meat of his arm with her paper fan. "You boys," she laughed. "You had me going for a moment. Feeling sorry for the little bunny."

Up hopped a small hard chaw of a man, his bowler cocked forward to hide a black eye. He waited in the aisle between the rows of seats, as penitent as a scolded child, and he did not speak till Pat noticed him.

"Well, if it ain't Charlie Wells hisself. I thought I made myself clear last night when we spoke."

Tipping the brim of his lid, Wells acknowledged Adele and winced before he spoke, as though putting thoughts into words pained his mind. "Beggin' your pardon, Patsy, but I just came to apologize—again—for the fracas and to inquire after your health."

Reflexively, Pat brought his hand to his tender mouth. "Never mind all that. It's you I hope learned your lesson."

The briefest trace of resentment flashed across Wells's face, the bitterness of a small man long-suffering and put upon by bullies. He reminded Adele of her father, a man of a thousand grievances against those richer or stronger or more handsome or more confident. Or just luckier in life. She knew countless such downtrodden men, boiling under the surface, who hesitate momentarily when confronted. "Never cross the Irish," Wells said, with a laugh.

"That's the style," Pat said. He seemed unaware, Adele thought, of the little man's obsequiousness. "Now tell me, do you still think the Pirates won't finish first and win the flag?"

Let off the hook, Wells relaxed. "From what the touts say, I'd watch that Ed Doheny and see he doesn't go buggy like the rumor has it. As

Doheny goes, so goest the team. They're in first place now, but I warn you, the wheel of fortune turns for every man."

"Round and round, round and round," the little boy sang from the old man's lap. I had forgotten he could talk.

The heat that summer drove everyone slightly mad. Not just the temperatures, brutal though they were, but the heat of the city generated by the steel mills along the rivers' edges, and the coke ovens burning night and day. They called Pittsburg hell with the lid off, and as a July drought settled in, the clouds of smoke and soot thickened, so that the sun itself burned as through a woolen blanket. The new millionaires, whose homes lined Fifth and Forbes in the Oakland suburbs, would escape to the Great Lakes or the Atlantic shore. The workingman took relief where he could.

Pat and Adele would journey to the new zoo out in Highland Park or simply picnic in the groves nearby. Some afternoons they wandered among the modern art at the Carnegie Museum or in the cooled splendor of the Phipps Conservatory. It was all new, a sign of the money minted through the bars of pig iron and ribbons of molten steel, the largesse of the burghers and barons. The ball club began a monthlong western swing to Cincinnati, Chicago, and St. Louis, so the Ahearn boys were free for a little sport. Pat and Adele and Christy and Helen hopped on the train to Carnegie Lake and bathed with the crowd of swimmers gathered there. Cartmen sold sandwiches and cold beer from a keg on ice, and the brothers drank mug after mug to stay cool. The sight of the two women in their bathing costumes raised the heat in the Ahearn brothers. In the covering waters, Pat held her close, and what she felt stirring against her thigh both thrilled and horrified her, but she knew better than to pull away, so she let him press against her till he could no longer stand it and had to swim off like a lunatic, muttering oaths. Later that evening, after supper and over a game of rummy in the summer parlor of the Hopkins home, Adele and Pat passed a knowing glance when Mr. Hopkins asked how the water had been that day.

"Crowded," Christy said. "People will do anything to beat the heat."

Mopping his brow with a handkerchief, Mr. Hopkins paused at the table and waved his evening's newspaper. "Did you hear about Doheny, the pitcher? Paper says he went bughouse. Up and left the Pirates and went home to Massachusetts."

Suddenly alert, Christy said, "In the *Post* this morning, the headline was 'His Mind Is Thought to Be Deranged.' Claims detectives are following him."

Pat laid down a card. "Don't be too sure what you read in the papers. Eddie Doheny is a lefty, and you can never be sure about a lefty. He's always had a temper. Remember that bat he threw at the Giants catcher back in May?"

"Gee, I don't know, boys." Mr. Hopkins shoved the wad of his kerchief in his back pocket. "The Pirates have the look of doom. Clarke has been hurt, and Sebring goes off to get married. And now this fella has lost his mind. It's like they won't have enough boys to field a team."

"Maybe they'll sign you, Papa," Adele laughed.

"I think Doheny's just worn out with all this heat," Pat said. "Just needs to cool off a couple days at home with the missus."

His remark drew a grunt from Mr. Hopkins, who then nodded and shuffled from the parlor, his kerchief bobbing like a rabbit's tail.

"Tell the gals what Honus did last summer," Christy said, "when it was so hot."

"Last summer, the Pirates were the best. Nobody could beat 'em, talk about a team. Anyhow, comes September, and they're guaranteed to win the league championship flag, so a couple of my pals says they're going out to Carnegie Township where Honus Wagner lives and give the Dutchman a box of cigars and the best steaks they can find, just to say thanks, since those cranks were real sporting men and had made a ton of dough off the Pirates. They take the tram over to his place and the father is there—you know he lives at home with his folks—and it is hotter than Hades, and he says sure, go on upstairs. John—that's what they call him at home—is just cooling off. And what do you think, middle of the day, but the great Honus Wagner buck naked in a bathtub filled with ice he crushed with an old baseball bat, and he's drinking a bottle of beer, and he says to the fellas, sit down and have one."

Helen gave him a look. "Don't say words like that."

"Like what? Hotter than Hades?"

"No," said Christy. "She don't like you swearing in front of the women folk."

"What'd I say? Buck naked?" He threw his cards into the middle of the table. "Gee, it's so hot. That don't sound like a bad thing right now."

Pressed against her temple, the glass of iced lemonade did nothing to cool off Adele. It was a hot and muggy night.

Through the screen window, light flashed, and thunder sounded in the distance. It had been a hot and muggy night, and perhaps that explains why I was naked when I landed on the bathroom floor. Usually I wear something to bed, unless pajamas prove uncomfortable when it is too early to air-condition but too humid for a good night's sleep. The sudden spike in moisture must have made me strip. Now, with a thunderstorm threatening, I wondered if I should call the cat inside and close all the windows in the house in case of torrential rain.

"Not to worry," the old man said. "We can turn it off or on by will."

"You mean it's not going to rain tonight?"

"Special effects," he said. "Even as a little boy, you were prone to rather vivid imaginings."

How could he know about my childhood, especially if he is the Irish playwright who wrote his masterpieces in French? I began to suspect that he was not who I imagined him to be. But if not Beckett, then who? The child at his feet was pretending that a bar of soap was some kind of aircraft that he could fly at the end of his hand, and he aimed the jet straight for the face of the commode, before swiftly turning at the last possible moment to avoid a crash, all the while making the sound of a sputtering engine. The old man had become distracted by the child's play. "Bbbrum-bbrum-brum," Beckett said to the boy.

The sound of his blubbering lips transformed into the sound of a movie projector. All of us except Adele turned our faces to the light. The young men in their antique costumes trotted the bases, hit the ball with their wooden sticks, and spun their arms like windmills before delivering the pitch. The big German, Wagner, stands poised at shortstop, and the batter's hit skips sharply toward his left. He digs for it and throws a shower of dirt and pebbles out of which the baseball emerges tailed like a comet and lands in the first baseman's mitt. Behind Adele, the game goes on, unabated by her continuing narrative.

Love is sweetest as it ripens, and they were in that pleasant interlude between awkward shyness and any formal engagement, though Adele, when he pressed his case, strongly implied the necessity of such a promise before she surrendered even a hint of her virtue. From time to time, his anger bested his good judgment, but he never took out any frustrations on her. Rather, Pat boiled over and started moving, doing something, going somewhere—tossing a medicine ball to his brother, hitting a punching bag, walking the whole way from Exposition Park to Birmingham, crossing two rivers along the way, or once or twice going to a shooting range to try one of the rifles his father had stashed in the attic. But mostly, Pat was a perfect gentleman, and when the Pirates came back into town for their September games, he was readily distracted by the baseball and the chance to place bets among his fellow fanatics. Unrelenting August had given way and soon enough the heat had broken. Even the southpaw Eddie Doheny had rejoined the team after a few weeks, though all the cranks said he was not quite the same. Charlie Wells and the other sports would guy him on, but Pat would have no part of any such talk, thought the whole matter bad luck. His intuition proved correct when Doheny started acting out again and became unmanageable. His brother, a preacher, came to town on the twenty-second and took the pitcher back to Massachusetts. "Poor man," Pat said when he read the news. "Some fellas can't take the stress."

The loss of Doheny, however, was overshadowed by the Pirates clinching the National League pennant for the third year in a row, and the talk was that they would accept a challenge from the best finisher of the American League for a world's championship series.

"It's going to be the Bostons," Christy said at the ballpark. "There's nobody even close."

"The Beaneaters?" Helen asked.

"Not them," said Christy. "The ones from the American League. The Boston Americans."

"They should be called the Jumpers," Pat said. "That's all they are, that whole American League ain't nothing but a bunch of contract jumpers and money grabbers, and them boys will put the dollar above team loyalty or their fans."

"So you think our Pittsburg boys can beat 'em? Best five out of nine?" Christy asked. "Without Doheny and banged up as we are?"

"Brother," Pat said, "we'll beat them senseless. And if they go, I'm going with them. All four of us go up to Boston, what do you say?"

Helen laughed and scoffed at the idea. "Why, Mr. Ahearn, you sound as if you are making a proposal for yourself and on your brother's behalf to Miss Hopkins and myself."

"A proposal?" Christy stammered.

"How else could we accompany you on a train trip to Boston?" Helen asked. "Surely you mean to be fully respectable and take us as your wives?"

Adele stared at her shoes.

"I tell you what," Pat said. "You girls stay right here in town, but when Pittsburg wins, what say you and me tie the knot, Adele? And Christy here can marry Helen, and we'll have a swell old time."

Adele had not thought the question of matrimony would be raised like this. She had dreamt of some more romantic setting than the grandstand of the ballpark and some more private moment than in a crowd of several thousand, mostly men. She had reckoned on some more enthusiastic declaration of love in ardor, rather than the afterthought of an out-of-town excursion, when folks she knew had gone to see the Falls at Niagara or honeymoon where a man and woman might get to know each other in a more sylvan or pastoral setting. But there it was, her first and only proposal, she feared, if that was indeed what Pat intended when the words were blurted from his mouth.

"Ma, ma, ma, ma," the little boy yelled. "Da-da-da. Bap-a-doo, bapa-doo, Buddha, Buddha, Buddha."

Making a cage of his entwined fingers, the old man scooped him up and lifted the bare belly to his lips and blew a frazzled raspberry on his soft skin. The baby laughed and so did the old man, until they were content, and the child wrapped his arms around the thin neck and laid his head against the old man's shoulder. Within seconds, the child was asleep. Seeing how quickly he had conked out reminded me of the lateness of the hour, or the earliness of the morning, depending upon one's perspective. I envied the little fella's peace, his rest unburdened by adult cares. Perhaps some flaring anxiety had awakened me, not the need to empty my bladder. A worry. What had the newspaper said of Eddie Doheny? His mind is not his own? I had a few questions for the proprietor of mine, whoever that may be.

Adele and Helen wound their way through the mob gathered at the railroad station to greet the team home from Boston on an October Sunday evening. Despite the weather, the cranks had turned out in the hundreds, hoping to get a glimpse of Fred Clarke and the boys, triumphant in return, having taken two of the first three from the Americans. As they filed off the Pullman car, the ballplayers looked like farmers or mill hunks in their Sunday best, and they limped off the train like a company of soldiers, nursing the injuries of a long season. There was Jimmy Sebring greeting his new wife with a kiss. Sam Leever, old and tired, carrying his grip in his left hand, favoring his sore right arm. Little Tommy Leach and Ginger Beaumont engaged in some deep conversation. And there's Honus Wagner, rushing off to catch the outbound train for Carnegie, waving at the well-wishers, his big German face creased with fatigue.

And then came the swells. The reporters and hangers-on who rode along with the team. The owner, Barney Dreyfuss, dapper in his cravat and mustache, whispered something to Clarke, who began to make a speech. Behind him cheered the sports, the gambling men who had gone to Boston in search of some action among the bookies there, for almost nobody in Pittsburg was willing to bet against the hometown team. The Ahearn brothers brought up the rear. Christy trotted straight to Helen. Despite her mother's admonitions, Adele raced to Pat and threw her arms around his shoulders and kissed him squarely on the lips.

He held on to his hat. "There's my girl. Didn't I tell you? Didn't I say this ball club would make good?" On the trip home, he gave her a present from Boston, a stickpin with a diamond nestled on top of a small baseball pennant. For luck, he told her, for the luck she brought him. They talked the whole time about the Boston trip and made their plans for Exposition Park and the next four games of the Series. He winced when she squeezed his hand.

"What's the matter, Patsy?"

"Hurt my hand is all. Fella in Boston ran into my fist with his face."

Autumn had arrived, and a chill breeze swooped along the Bluff and forced them to shelter on the front porch. Behind the lace curtains, Mr. Hopkins stirred at the sound of their footsteps, so Adele spoke quickly. "You don't think you'll have to go back there, do you?"

"To Boston?" Pat said. "Not on your life. We only have to win three out of four here, and it'll all be over."

She nestled close to him. "And we can be married?"

"Instantaneously." He kissed her good night before her old man could knock on the glass.

"Barf," Flo said. "Gag, retch, ick."

"Don't do it, sister," Jane said. "That man ain't nothing but trouble."

"What man isn't?" asked Alice. "Ask me, they're all worth a bucket of nothing."

"A thimble of bother," said Dolly. "All talk, no action."

Marie nodded. "*Vendre la peau l'ours avant de l'avoir tué.*"

"Hey!" Dolly objected to this oblique reference to her man.

The light dimmed, the moving picture moved again. The crowds moved in and out of the ballyard. Rain fell. The ballplayers appeared

tired and out of sorts. One by one, the title cards revealed the sad outcome of the games:

> Pittsburg 5 Boston 4 (cheers)
> Boston 11 Pittsburg 2
> Boston 6 Pittsburg 3
> Boston 7 Pittsburg 3

The losses happened so quickly that she was not sure how the
Bostons had managed to go from being down three games to one to
being on the verge of ending the whole championship series. With each
contest, Pat grew angrier and increasingly frustrated. During the seventh game, the Royal Rooters and their hired band began to play and
the hundred or so Boston fans began to sing to the tune of "Tessie":

> *Honus, why do you hit so badly?*
> *Take a back seat and sit down.*
> *Honus, at bat you look so sadly,*
> *Hey, why don't you get out of town?*

The boys on the field, even the Dutchman, got a kind of perverse
kick out of the cranks' shenanigans, but in the stands, the Pittsburg
crowd howled and started singing their own ditties. Charlie Wells came
by, backing Boston and looking for a wager, and Pat nearly came to
blows with his old chum. Even his brother steered clear of Pat, and only
Adele's presence brought his temper under control. She sensed his jitters
as they waited on the platform for the train to take both clubs and their
followers back to Boston.

"Kiss me," she said. "Kiss me before you go."

He kissed her politely on the cheek. She pressed her forehead against
his cheek so hard that he could still feel the pressure days later.

"You don't understand, Adele. I put it all on Pittsburg when we were up there. All our money, not just mine, but money from Christy and from my friends and some of the sports. And then I doubled up when the Pirates went ahead. Bet more than I had. More than I could possibly raise—"

"But Pittsburg will certainly win."

"That's just it. They're all beat up. No pitchers left. Fred Clarke even sent Eddie Doheny his uniform, but the poor sap is in the nut-house in Danvers. That's where I'll end up, or worse. I'll owe a small fortune to some very angry men."

"Surely, I could help. We could sell this pin," she said and removed the diamond stickpin from her lapel. "We could find the money."

"Don't lose the flag," Pat said. "That wouldn't cover a tenth of what I might lose."

The locomotive rolled into the station, and the travelers climbed aboard. He kissed her distractedly and failed to wave from the window of his carriage, despite the fact that she waited for him and kept calling out his name long after the wheels on the train had gone round and disappeared.

"Round and round, round and round," the little boy sang.

The flick flickered to life. A car pulls up to the Danvers Insane Asylum in Andover, Massachusetts, and a solitary man exits quickly and runs to the entrance, dodging puddles. Hard to recognize Fred Clarke without the baseball cap and uniform, but his features are clearer when he doffs his hat and shakes off the rain at the front door.

The film's point of view cuts to interior, a patient's room, white and sterile, and there is Eddie Doheny in the bed. His young wife sits in a chair beside him. A small bouquet rests on the night table, courtesy of Mr. Dreyfuss. Beyond her shoulder, the window is slightly ajar, and the rain drums on the sill. The young wife twists a handkerchief into a butterfly, and the camera zooms in as she speaks. The title card: "He thought he could play when you sent him his baseball uniform." And Fred Clarke answers: "We only wanted to cheer him." Mrs. Doheny: "His nerves snapped! When you boys lost for the fourth time, he beat his nurse, Mr. Howarth, with the leg off a stove. He just needs a rest." She hands the Pirates' manager a message. Cut to interior of the Vendome Hotel, Boston, where the team is gathered in a bedroom. Clarke opens the envelope and two bills slip out. In close-up, the letter reads: "As they were taking away my husband, Eddie said, 'I owe only two dollars, and that to Claude Ritchey. Won't you pay him?'" Ritchey says nothing, leaves the money on the bedspread. A few of the boys have tears in their eyes as they depart for the ball game.

Of course they lost. No pitching. Deacon Phillippe was asked to pitch for the fifth time in eight tries, but he was out of steam. Leever's arm was hurt. Kennedy and the other pitchers, no go. Half that team was beat up, and even Wagner threatened to quit the game altogether. And Doheny was gone for good. He died of TB thirteen years later, never left the asylum. Imagine that.

For days after the Boston triumph, Adele expected Pat to appear suddenly, swaggering up the avenue, or at least to hear by telegram or letter. But the train carrying the Pittsburg team back to the city dispersed half its passengers along the way. Kitty Bransfield went home to Worcester. Ginger Beaumont lit off for a hunting trip in Wisconsin. Jimmy Sebring, the first person to hit a home run in the history of the World Series, departed near Williamsport, Pennsylvania, with his new bride. Claude Ritchey headed out to his folks' farm in Venango County. Pat could have jumped off anywhere between here and there. Of the few that made the Pittsburg area their home, none could remember seeing

Patrick Ahearn aboard the train at all. A query to the Boston police later that fall was unsatisfactory. The only unknown or missing person from around the dates in question was a tramp found in an alley behind the Vendome Hotel, penniless and drunk, and beaten to death by a baseball bat, and the hotel itself reported that Patrick Ahearn had skipped out on his bill and would the responsible party kindly remit $12. His brother Christy seemed to think, however, that Pat was too clever for such a fate, though he himself was killed two years later by a single blow to the head by a baseball bat outside of Exposition Park. He left behind a young wife, pregnant with their first child. Helen Ahearn named her boy Eddie, after the poor pitcher who had also seemed to vanish from the face of the earth.

Eventually Adele stopped waiting for Patsy to come back. Some nights she imagined the scene in Boston—Patsy confronting the Boston gamblers, trying to fight his way out of trouble, and the Boston boys ambushing him with baseball bats, and making him pay for his debts with his life. The next summer she was back at Exposition Park, but it was not quite the same. Still, a girl had to look out for herself, make the best of her prospects. When Charlie Wells proposed in the winter of '04, he offered at least some connection to the halcyon past. The Pirates finished fourth that year, nineteen back of the Giants, and did not make it back to the World Series till 1909 against Detroit. Despite Charlie's objection, she wore the diamond stickpin to the ballpark. Exposition Park was gone by that time, and the Pirates played out in Oakland at the brand-new Forbes Field in what was now known as Pittsburgh with an *h* on the end. Only Clarke and Leach and Wagner made it from that first championship club, and they were old men by the standards of the game. Adele's daughter wore the diamond flag to the 1925 World Series against Washington, but she lost it on the last rainy day, when the fans could barely see the finale, and the boys had no business playing baseball, no business at all.

CHAPTER THIRTEEN

Love and Bowlers

The baseball that had been stuck in the door dislodged, falling to the tiles with a wet splat and rolling across the room to the little boy, who picked it up at once, considered biting the sphere as though it were a red-seamed white fruit, thought better of the idea, and then threw it with great exuberance against the porcelain side of the bathtub, the ricochet sending the ball spinning back through the opening into the hallway, smacking a newel post on the banister, and bounding down the staircase two or more steps at a time, caroming off the wall, till it reached the front door where it stopped with a bang. Surprised by his own strength and the physics set in motion, the tot blinked and clapped for himself, uncertain as to what had just happened. I recognized the shocked perplexity on the boy's face and felt a sense of kinship, for I had been in that same semiconfused state from the moment I struck my head, or, should I say, my head was struck for me.

We all stared at Adele. Just above her heart, tattooed on the bare skin of her left breast, were two crossed baseball bats.

"Bad odds about your fella," the old man said. "A tough break, but at least you didn't wait your whole life like our friend Dolly."

With the heel of her hand, Adele rubbed the tip of her nose to fight back the impulse to cry. "No, I didn't wait. But I never forgot him, brash as he was, and the way he made me feel, and I never forgave him for it either. And what makes you think I wanted Charlie Wells, always on the wrong end of the bargain? Why did you go and have to lose your temper and challenge those men with the bats?"

Had I been tempted to explain, that query would have been the window to jump through. Instead, I pretended to look in the mirror, check the condition of my gums, and worry over the steady retreat of my hairline. No question I was getting older, and perhaps Sita was right to insist that I come to some conclusions and make some decisions about my life. On the other hand, I had all the time I hadn't used yet. What's the hurry?

"Makes me mad," Adele said. "To think what might have been, and how in the end, we never even had one night together. What's the use of virtue if all it buys you is regret? You men had it so much easier . . ." She stopped suddenly and pursed her lips, scrunched her brow, seething with frustration, and her face turned flame red. Something fell from the sky and struck the roof, startling me, but like the first drops pancaking on a sidewalk, the percussion quickened and intensified to a constant rippling roar. I looked through the tiny window. Outside it was hailing baseballs. Bouncing at crazy angles of destruction, the balls smacked against the roof and within minutes a single layer covered the ground.

Over the din, the old man waved and gestured for Adele's attention. "You did not miss much."

She looked right through me, as though I was gauze, as though I was nothing, and thus appeased, she stopped the storm. The last of the baseballs fell from the sky and melted into the stack. "It's like a giant ice cream sundae," Marie said, and all of the women gathered around her at the window to see the mounds of white drizzled with strawberry sauce. The old man took the opportunity of their distraction to spring to my side and offer his advice.

"Some act of contrition might be nice. An outward display of penance. Sackcloth and ashes." He could readily see the depths of my misapprehension. "If I performed a trepanning and had a peek at your gray matter, do you think I might detect the far-off glimmer of cognition flickering in your hippocampus?"

"I have no idea what you are talking about."

"Right, so." He shook his head slowly. "I suppose you would not. Relate to me, then, your memory of the she-fish and how they escaped by swimming through the keyhole."

"Hah, that's a laugh. Boy, you've got a vivid imagination."

He appeared bemused by my remark.

"They walked out," I said, "just like they walked in."

"On their fishy tails?"

"Have you lost your mind? Of course not on their tails, but on their legs. I was peeping through the keyhole when someone inside turned on the shower, hot, hot water till the whole room steamed up and I couldn't make out anything through the fog."

"I'm surprised you didn't just bust in anyhow. Can't think of a more prurient fantasy than the girls' locker room after the showers."

"It wasn't like that at all," I lied. It was a little bit like that, not entirely, but somewhat prurient; that is to say, I was interested enough to strain my sight at the keyhole, but when the room became too steamy, there was no longer the same potential. "I waited for them in the hallway like a perfect gentleman."

The kid said something that sounded like "my arse," but it could just as easily have been nonsense sounds. Or "Meyers," whoever that might be.

"How long did you wait?" the old man wondered.

"A long time. Interminable."

"Did you happen to check your watch and note the time?"

"My watch was broken when I fell," I said. He scratched his head as if pondering some conundrum. I decided to press on. "At last, the doorknob rotated and out they came in billowing vapors, as if in a dream or some cheesy horror movie with dry-ice mist on the moors. They had changed clothes, or rather lost their tails altogether, and now donned Coco Chanel dresses and cloche hats. They were Jazz Age flappers, voh-doh-dee-oh-doh and bobbed hair and long strands of pearls or floor-length scarves. Ready to do the Charleston."

"Did they provide you with a change of costume? Long tails and a Charlie Chaplin bowler hat?"

"No, just my robe. No bowler."

"That's too bad," the old man said. "I've long thought that the bowler hat is due for a comeback. We should be wearing them at least, like a pair of tramps eternally waiting in the comedy of time."

"Sorry, no bowler," I said. "I suppose this means you are not Beckett after all?"

"If I were Beckett," he said, "there would be bowlers."

"Laurel and Hardy wore them."

"They are called derbies in America. Al Smith wore one during the 1928 presidential election, and it may have cost him the job. And Mercier and Camier, and those two tramps in *Godot*."

"What were their names?"

"I can never remember," the old man said. And then after an interlude, he spoke again. "They were great comedic teams."

"Do you think we would be better off with bowlers?" I asked.

He looked at me with what can only be described as love. "I think we are a great team even without the bowlers."

Having popped out the window screen, the women were scooping ice cream from the roof and piling it in cones fashioned from old manila cardboard dividers taken from the archives boxes. Even the little boy was enjoying a taste, for his mouth was rimmed with cream and strawberry sauce.

A puppet's grin split the old man's face. "They're having fun, aren't they? Of course, they deserve it after all they've been through."

"You mean the stories they've been telling of their past lives?"

"That goes without saying. Not just the stories, but the lives themselves, those count for something. And having to entertain you—"

"They were like a floor show, those flappers. One of them, the one we haven't seen yet, played the ukulele and sang the 'Hong Kong Blues' and 'Paper Moon,' and they formed a conga line and sashayed from the bathroom to the bedroom."

The old man peered out into the hallway. "That's hardly long enough to fit seven people."

"Eight. I was at the end of the conga and there was a lot of hip swinging but very slow forward progress. Just as I got to the door, the ukulele player slammed it shut in my face, and there I was again in the hall, waiting all by myself. Behind the closed bedroom door, there was a tremendous commotion, laughter and giggling, and heavy objects tossed about the room, like they were having a pillow fight—"

Clucking his tongue like a mother hen, the old man stopped me in midsentence. I was getting good at reading his moods, and he seemed displeased with where my story was heading. "Typical schoolboy dreams. Fantasy of the most infantile sort, the nubile maids in their nighties thrashing each other with overstuffed pillows, feathers floating in the air. Skin and taffeta and more skin." As the images infiltrated his brain, his eyes widened. "By God, this is good stuff."

"After a while, the commotion stopped, and dead silence from behind the door. I looked through the keyhole, which again I don't recall being there before, but pitch darkness greeted my sight no matter how I positioned my eyeball. With one finger, I gingerly pushed the door, and it swung open slowly. The light from the hallway did not penetrate the blackness of the bedroom, but in fact, the usual order reversed and the darkness spilled into the light to the point where I could not see my feet below me and my hands disappeared when I stuck out my arms. Someone tittered in the heart of darkness and gave me the courage to go on. Not being able to see a thing, I tottered forward, following that fetching giggle."

"A case," the old man said, "of the blonde leading the blind."

Once again he was pelted with small objects for his troubles. Pill bottles and stolen hotel shampoo bottles and an exfoliating sponge. Even the boy caught the spirit and overturned his ice cream cone on the old man's bare toes. When he felt how cold it was, the old fellow let out a whoop and danced on one foot, to the child's delight.

"The farther I went, the darker it became. As a general rule, I prefer a dark bedroom, especially for sleeping, with the blinds drawn to block out the light, which always seeks out any chinks or the slightest crackling so that even a dark room has gradations, shades of black if you will, and after the eyes have adjusted, one can make out bulky shapes and masses at the very least. But this was the darkest place I've ever been. Darker than a closet in a dark room. Darker than a trunk in the closet in the dark room. Darker than a sealed box in the trunk in the closet—"

"Yes, very dark, I get it," the old man said. He was wiping his foot with a washcloth.

"All I could do in such a room was to follow the sound of their breathing. Stretch out my hands in front to sweep the air for obstacles, and rely upon spatial memory, that the bed was so many steps from the doorway, the night table to its left as I faced the bed, but that memory proved false, for I kept on walking and walked for a long time until a hand grasped my forearm and pulled me hard to the bed, where I collapsed into a sea of blankets. A spotlight came on near the foot of the bed, and there atop a piano sat one of the chanteuses, spilling from a leather bustier, legs in fishnet stockings, lips blood red, and a bowler cocked over her brow. She winked, and the light snapped off, only to spring on several paces to her left. There in the second spotlight stood another woman in a costume made of bubbles, transparent balloons strategically arranged, and when the first one popped, the light shifted to the third woman, partially hidden behind a fan of feathers. One leg, bare to the hip, snaked out in front of her fan. The fourth was a Godiva, blonde hair down to her bottom, atop a white mare, though I instantly wondered about the logistics of maneuvering that horse on the stairs. The fifth was a French maid teasing with her duster and her ooh-la-la. The sixth was a starlet in a strapless sequined gown that left nothing to the imagination. The seventh was clad entirely in form-fitting leather, even her face hidden in a leather mask, brandishing a bullwhip. She flicked it and the tip nearly took off my tip. When the last light went out, we were once more plunged into black ink, and the bed itself moaned in anticipation."

I stopped to look about the bathroom to see if anyone else was listening to our conversation, not that I feared they would contradict my account, but because I was suddenly conscious of their feelings and struck with the notion that providing further detail might be unchivalrous, particularly since the participants were within earshot. Fortunately, nobody paid any mind to me. Adele was sitting on the edge of the tub having her hair done in French braids by Marie. Flo and Alice and Dolly appeared to be engaged in a contest to see who could most quickly slurp the ice cream from the bitten-off bottoms of their cones. Jane had the babe in arms at the sink playing with some miniature plastic—at least I hope they were plastic—sea serpents in the water. Even the old man seemed glazed over, but when I caught his eye, he smirked and nodded. "So, what is it like to go to bed with seven women at one time?"

"That's just it," I said. "There were eight."

"You inconsiderate bastard. Eight?"

"Yes, the seven and another waiting for me in the bed."

"Where did you even know to begin with eight?"

"Here's the strange thing, though. It seemed like one woman with eight mouths, countless arms, hands, breasts, legs. I could not keep up with her, them, and every moment was chaos and soaked through with pleasure. I could not see a thing but only felt the curve of flesh over bone, roundness, the swell of tissue, the fissures and holes, the softness of skin, and wet hidden places. The smell of them different each to each, and yet the same musky heat and taste of mint and enamel and last night's dinner and tangle of hair and perfume. Too many hands on me. Like having sex with a goddess in a bowler hat. Eight limbs, pinned down, devoured, spent. Ecstasy, yes, but too much and too brief. All washing me out to sea before I could tell what in the world was going on. I remember falling into a stupor, a kind of sleep, wanting to stay and experience it all again, but more slowly drowning, for something was wrong with me. I had hit my head and I was out."

"Too bad you weren't wearing a bowler," the old man said. "They are usually very hard and stiff, and you may not have been hurt when you hit your head. Oh, don't look so shocked. I once knew a man named Idaho Slim who liked to have sex wearing chaps and spurs and a ten-gallon hat, and, of course, there is Mr. Meyers who could only diddle with a sash around his middle. And Mrs. Wilma Houghton-Thorne who only screws while wearing alligator shoes. Takes all kinds. What's a bowler hat in bed? A trifle, a jaunty jape, a sign that one is not too serious when it comes to the old slap and tickle."

I sat on the threshold, my back to the empty hallway and my feet resting on the cold tiles. My head ached and I was very tired at having reached the point of the foregoing story when I awoke in the early morning hours with the urgent need to relieve my bladder, which in turn led to the bump on my head and the ensuing encounter with the old man and the women gathered in my bathroom, but something was not right. Something was missing. Asynchronous. Out of order.

"There is the matter of the seventh suspect," the old man said. "Would it be wise to sit with your back to the bedroom?"

I swiveled to see if anyone approached.

"You could always confront her first, rather than be surprised like with the others. You would have the upper hand."

Rising to my feet, I contemplated his suggestion. He handed me the toilet plunger, ostensibly for my protection, and thus armed, I stepped into the darkness. Behind me the door closed with a thick click caused by the failure to turn the doorknob. Almost instantly I regretted having left behind my companions and venturing alone into the unknown. Only a few paces separated me from the bedroom door, but I was afraid of what I might find. Six of the seven had attempted to kill me, but the old man had thwarted their assassination attempts. Why would the next one not have similar intents? Only now my so-called friend had sent me to face the killer with nothing more than a suction cup on a stick. I thought of comforting myself by whistling, as my mother had taught my brother and me to do when afraid, but then reconsidered the whistle as a dead giveaway when sneaking up on the enemy. I tiptoed silently to the door and gently cracked it open.

Alone in the bed rested the familiar body, her back to me, curved like rolling hills. The other body was missing. There was only one doorway, so she had not slipped past me, and since we were on the second floor, an exit from the windows was out of the question. She may have hidden in the closet or scooched under the bed, though she had little reason to do so, and I did not wake the sleeping beauty to inquire. No, the seventh chick had flown the coop. I retreated from the darkened bedroom and closed the door with a whisper by gently turning the door-knob till the tumblers and pins slid into place. As I exited, the girl in the bed sighed in her sleep.

Where would the killer be hiding? The space of the house could be contained neatly in the space of my memory, for its rooms and traffic patterns were as habitual to me as the enchanted places of my child-hood. There were only so many secret spots, and with the plunger hanging like a weapon from my belt, I set off to find the girl.

The best places to hide would be in the basement, so I bounded down two flights of stairs and flicked on the lights. Thankfully the bottom of the house was as I remembered, more or less, though some-one had tidied the pantry and rearranged the small hand tools and jars of nuts and bolts and nails. The furnace was the same as ever, as were the washer and dryer. A collapsible rack stood near the ironing board, across which hung a sundress flocked with tiny tigers and monkeys and elephants in shades of gold and red, the kind of thing that Sita might wear. I pinched the fabric and ran my finger along the hem. A cricket chirruped in a corner, but I left it alone. Some cultures, the Chinese I think, believe a cricket in the house brings good luck, so I never bother a stray or two. When we were children, my brother ruined the story of Jiminy Cricket from Pinocchio by telling me the real story. In Collodi's original Italian, *Il Grillo Parlante*—the Talking Cricket—is the voice of reason and responsibility for the newly minted boy Pinocchio, who gets frustrated by the nagging and throws a hammer at the cricket, and that's the end of him. An accident.

The talking cricket reminded me of my cat, suddenly able to speak, whom I now remembered putting out some time ago. I trundled up the stairs and opened the door from the kitchen to the back porch, where he often waited to be let in, but no sign of Harpo. I called him once or twice but dared not step out of the house. Rather, I just stood in the doorway for the longest stretch, feeling the damp June air on my bare skin, and drinking in the smell of roses blooming next door and the newly mown lawn two doors down. While summer brings its share of miseries—the heat and oppressive humidity, the mosquitos and other flying-biting-stinging things, and the stench of trash day and the quick decay and rot—the sensual pleasures more than compensate. At least that's what I tell myself. A few calls for the missing cat floated into the soft blackness and dissipated. I stuck my thumb in the saucer of water on the floor. Still cool to the touch, as though just filled from the sink. The pet flap on the door was unlatched, so I plugged in a canary-shaped nightlight for Harpo. The cat will come back when he is ready.

Very few hiding places existed on the main floor. In the dining room, a huge oak corner bureau in the Chinese style, with the fall front carved with a pair of dragons. My brother bought the extravagance at an estate sale. "The perfect size," he said, "for hiding a body." In the living room, I checked the closets and sought the telltale shoes sticking out from some floor-length drapes. I searched the joint, thinking of what I might do should I actually find her. If she attacked me with her ukulele, I'd have to parry with my plunger. After the possibilities downstairs had been exhausted, the only option was back upstairs. The disadvantage of the design of these houses can be measured in the constant tread upon the stairway from level to level. One spends a great deal of time either ascending or descending. Good for the legs, but unless one is a sherpa or a sheep, the climb is a chore in the early morning hours. From the bottom, a million steps loomed, and what was ahead but attempted homicide upon my person followed by some story bound to make me feel bad about myself? Had sense triumphed over curiosity, I never would have pulled myself up again.

My brother's room was bare and empty, just as he had left it, the bed and dresser ready "in case I need to crash." No lady with a ukulele hid in my office either. The plans usually strewn about the place were stacked neatly on the drafting table against the wall. Out of habit, I woke the computer from its sleep and the anthem rang and blue light filled the space around my desk. The hardware chugged and the software spun, and eventually all the file and program icons filled the screen. I opened the e-mail browser and was stunned to find the memory full. Impossible, I thought, but thousands of unopened messages crammed the inbox. I checked to see if Sita had written recently, but her address was missing from the list. It will take me weeks just to organize the mail into *junk, delete,* and *read* piles. The dates on the most recent messages are wrong, too, as if they had been sent from the future, but just thinking about how to fix all this gives me a headache.

Beneath the desk, the octopus of plugs and wires lurked in darkness. In the linen closet, towels and sheets kept order. The last possibility was the attic, but the door was shut as I had left it. She had disappeared completely, if she had existed at all in the first place. The faint strains of a jazz tune slipped under the bathroom door, and above that background noise, conversation rolled and pitched, someone told a joke and the rest laughed, the sound of people having fun. I could hear ice clinking in glasses, as though a cocktail party was going on, some scene out of the late '50s or early '60s, the old man in a tux or evening jacket, the women dolled up with bright red lips and lacquered hairdos. The very thought of a party cheered me, and I was pie-faced happy as I opened the door. Pointing straight back at me was the business end of a revolver. Holding the gun in my face was the seventh sister, deadly in a menacing little black dress. Behind the pistol, she wore a devilish grin, and behind her, the rest of the gang had turned their smiling faces to me. "C'mon in," she said. "You're the guest of honor."

CHAPTER FOURTEEN

The Woman Who Fired the Gat

I found her oddly seductive, the woman with the revolver, though perhaps it was in equal part the danger of the little black dress. She waggled the barrel at me, and I obeyed her direction to squeeze into the room. We now numbered ten—the seven women, the old man, myself, and the boy. Boy, because in the time I had been away, the child seemed to have aged another few months. His baby fat was melting away to reveal a more angular facial structure, and when he smiled he had a full set of tiny sharp choppers.

While I was searching downstairs, the lady gunslinger must have snuck in from some hiding place, and the others had taken her in and included her in their usual high jinks. They were mugging for one another, winking their third eyes. Changes in hairstyles and clothes, and of course the moving tattoos. Another bit in the performance piece, or maybe it was all some elaborate game. Had I not been preoccupied with the thought of bullets, I would have inquired as to the meaning behind the cryptic symbols. Maybe they meant nothing. Maybe sometimes a slithering tattoo snake is just a snake; a cigar, Dr. Freud, is just a cigar; and a gun is just a gun. In any case, she held the power in her hand.

Through a variety of signals—a raised eyebrow, a curled upper lip, and quick glances back and forth between me and the gun—the old man sought to assure me that he had a plan to disarm the shooter, but I had no idea what role I was to play in the drama. My hands were up in the air and my reflexes are very slow. The very idea was entirely too dangerous, someone would most likely be shot, but I had no way of communicating my anxieties.

"Don't try anything funny," she said.

"I have no intention of trying anything," I said, "funny or otherwise. Do you really need to do this?"

"As a matter of fact, very much so."

"In front of the little kid? You'll scar him for life."

"Somebody pick up that kid," she said. "And avert his eyes. No, on second thought, let him watch. It'll be good for the boy to know what happens when you wrong a woman."

I lowered my arms to half-mast. "Listen, sister, I never met you before tonight. What cause you got for saying I done you wrong?"

"You got time for a story?" She laughed at herself, and the irony spread through the group till all the women were giggling.

Caught in the spirit, even I chuckled. "I've got nothing but time, though I'd feel a little bit better if you would point that piece in another direction."

She lowered the gat slowly, all the while keeping her gaze trained on me. "No monkey business, see."

I was sorely tempted to make like an ape, but under the circumstances controlled the impulse. Without the gun in my face, I took a closer look at her. No doubt, the ukulele woman, now done up in her killer black dress, stockings, pumps, and a choker of pearls. Her bleached-blonde hair was arranged in a bouffant with a saucy little flip curl, and her reddened lips set off two rows of wicked white teeth. If the bullet didn't work, she could bite. I wanted her to bite me. Like a pasha on a throne, the old man leaned back on the toilet seat. During my absence, he had acquired a red fez, now perched atop his silvery hair, which gave him an air of exotic intrigue while simultaneously making him slightly ridiculous. "Before you begin your story, Miss, may we have the pleasure and courtesy of an introduction?"

"Button your lip," she told him. "One thing you should know straight off: she that's got the gun calls the shots."

"Oh, well played," the old man said.

She pointed the pistol at him. "Seriously, chum, shut up and let me do things my own way."

Thus chastened, we settled in like schoolchildren, polite and quiet, for story time. All except for the little boy, who was busy undoing the sheets of toilet paper, spinning the roll till all he had left was the bare cardboard tube. He pointed it at the woman in the black dress and said "Bang!" She clutched her chest so quickly and convincingly that I thought for a moment she really had been shot, and then she pointed her gun at the toddler and as it recoiled, she said, "Bang!" His pudgy little hand went right to his heart, and I thought she had really shot him, but it was all a charade.

"You may call me Bunny," she addressed the child but was surely speaking to all of us. He clapped and pretended to shoot her again.

"If he's bothering you, Bunny," the old man said, "I can take that away from him."

She stood on her tiptoes and stashed the revolver atop the medicine cabinet. "You'll do no such thing. What everyone needs to do is relax."

I felt much better with the gun out of her grasp, and the old man, too, breathed a deep sigh and leaned back against the commode to hear her tale. With a snap of her fingers, she dimmed the lights, and the hum of the bathroom fan switched tempo to a Cuban jazz melody. From the registers on the floor, a cloud of cigarette smoke rose and settled near the ceiling. She reached inside the cabinet and retrieved a series of cocktails, passing the glasses one by one around the room so that we all had a drink. I put mine to my lips and felt the pleasant sting of scotch on the rocks. The old man sipped a martini and spun the glass by its fragile stem to watch the olive twirl.

Bunny commanded our attention with one deep breath.

He was so startled by what she whispered in his ear that his cigarette dropped from his lips and into his drink. When he turned his head to get a look at the woman who proposed such a thing, all he saw was cleavage, a pair of red lips, and the fleeting pass of her hand as it disappeared beneath the table and into his lap. He flinched when she touched him and banged the tabletop with his open hand, clattering the dishes and glasses and ashtrays. His three friends all gave him knowing looks, as if they could tell what the woman in the black dress was doing, even if he could not. Her fingers lingered just long enough and then she straightened and smiled at the party. "Here are the matches you dropped," she said. "Thanks for the light." She blew smoke in his face, and he was too surprised to say anything but accepted the matchbook, nodding once to the departing woman, and then pretended to turn his attention back to the rumba band and the chanteuse swaying to "El Manisero."

Bunny waited by the telephone for the call that she knew was coming. It didn't take long. She had written beneath her phone number to call after ten thirty. The big clock in the kitchen said 10:32. Maybe he didn't want to appear overanxious, but she knew better.

"Is this Bunny?" the voice over the telephone said.

"Yes. Who's this?"

"Phil Ketchum. From the Stork Club. You dropped your matches."

"How nice of you to call to say you found them."

"Dropped 'em right in my lap. I'd like to return them to you. How 'bout I drop by on the way home?"

She wrapped the cord around her finger a few times. This was her favorite part. The anticipation. "I'm afraid that's impossible. I got to get up early in the morning—"

"Oh, I won't stay long."

"If you're going to come clear downtown, you really should stay long."

"Well, long enough."

"Mr. Ketchum, behave yourself." She stood and looked out at the apartment building on the other side of the street. With her free hand, she scratched her bottom, for the flannel pajamas were clinging to her skin. Jerry always kept the place too warm.

"I'd really like to get these matches back to you," the disembodied voice said.

"Come by tomorrow morning," she said. "After nine. My husband will be at work." At that moment, she craned her neck to look down the hallway at their closed bedroom door. She could almost hear him snoring.

On the other end of the phone, the man paused to light a cigarette. "You best get to bed then," he said. "I'll be there bright and early, and you'll need to be well rested."

She giggled into the receiver. "Phil, you are such a hound."

He howled, quietly, so that nobody would hear through the glass of the phone booth, and then hung up. Back at the table, Phil Ketchum ordered another scotch and soda and told the boys that he might be coming in late the next morning. They all laughed.

Once or twice a week, Phil and Bunny played a variation of the game at a rendezvous. She would be out with the girls, and he would arrange to bump into her at some nightclub or at the flicks or, once, at the corner of Seventh and Fifty-third during the Macy's Thanksgiving Parade. Four months had passed, but the game hadn't lost its glamour or excitement, for she would delight in bringing him to the edge before retreating coyly. Once on the subway, she told Phil that she was wearing nothing under her skirt and managed to maneuver close enough in the packed car to let him discover the truth for himself. Another time at the library, she bit him so hard in the Anthropology section that he actually screamed in surprise and caused a security officer to investigate the trouble. They would meet and flirt seriously, and the next morning he would be hot and bothered, ready to burst.

Twice in the first months of the affair they nearly were found out. Rushing to her on an October morning, when everything was still new and dangerous, Phil bumped into Bunny's husband in the lobby of their apartment building.

"Phil? Phil Ketchum?"

He had pulled down his hat, but he had no choice but to acknowledge him. "Jerry? As I live and breathe."

"Why you old dog, I knew it was you the minute I saw you. What's it been, five, six years? What brings you to this neck of the woods?"

"How are you, old man? I had no idea you lived in this part of town."

Jerry sized him up and then checked his watch. "I haven't seen you since the wedding. Bunny and I moved down here from Morningside right after. There goes the neighborhood and all that. How are you, you old dog?"

"I'm just here meeting a friend of mine."

"Who's that?" Jerry asked. "We know everyone in the building."

"Friend of mine," Phil said. "Name of Meyers. Doesn't actually live here, but comes down for a visit sometimes, if you know what I mean."

He looked at his watch a second time, and then through the

sidelights on the doorway he checked the traffic on the street. "I'm not following."

"Sees a woman here, I think."

Like a conspirator, Jerry leaned in close and whispered, "Not Natalie Hoffman?"

Shaking his head, Phil put a hand on Jerry's shoulder. "You know me, old man, never kiss and tell, and I don't rat out a pal."

"Sure, Phil, I understand. Just thought, y'know, she's the type, a real looker. And her husband's kind of a schlub. Listen, I didn't mean nothing by it."

"No harm, no harm." He frowned disapprovingly.

"I'm late to work," he said. "But it's good seeing you, and let's get together sometime. Me and Bunny would be thrilled to have you and Claire over sometime for dinner or maybe drinks."

"Sounds great, Jer."

They shook hands. At the door, Jerry stopped and turned around. "Why don't you stop in and say hello to Bunny, if you've got a minute. She's up this morning, believe it or not, and she'd love to see you. We're in 6B."

"Maybe for a minute, Jer. And we'll have to make a date for drinks." He waved good-bye to his old friend, waited in the lobby for another five minutes, and then took the elevator to the sixth floor. They didn't even make it as far as the bed, for he took her behind the closed door, still in her housecoat.

The second close call happened the week between Christmas and New Year's. They had arranged to meet at a matinee showing of *The Bridge on the River Kwai,* and there in the dark, in the back of the balcony like a couple of teenagers, they stroked and petted and fumbled beneath the coats on their laps. Coming out of the theater in the late afternoon light, eyes still adjusting to the contrast, they ran into Claire's younger sister Kate and her high school friends, on line for the following show.

"Philip!" Kate yelled above the crowd.

He removed his hand from the small of Bunny's back and made his way across the sidewalk. She followed close behind, certain that she had been seen. In one smooth move, Phil reached down and kissed his sister-in-law on the cheek. "Happy New Year's, Katie."

"Imagine running into you here in the middle of the day. Sneaking out of work, are you?"

"You caught me. You won't tell your sister on me, will you?"

Bunny took the initiative. "Kate Dawson, I would have never recognized you. Look how grown up you are!"

Given the level of enthusiasm, Kate pretended to remember the strange woman.

"I'm your sister's old friend, Bunny. We went to high school together, Claire and I, and isn't it a small world, but the one day I sneak out to the movies, who shows up in the same theater but Phil Ketchum. And now you . . ."

Ducking out of the way, he eased back under his hat. "Small world. Had I known she was in there, we could have sat together and split a popcorn. It's godawful long, Kate, and kinda violent for a kid."

The gang of teenagers pressed closer to the conversation, and Katie hastened to defend herself. "I'm not a kid, Phil."

"She's all grown up," Bunny said. "You're certainly old enough to see a movie about a bridge. Why don't you be a gentleman and treat your sister-in-law?"

"That's all right," Kate said. "We can pay our own way."

"Tell Claire that Bunny says hello, would you? Nice bumping into you, Phil. Good to see you, Kate." She raised her hand to hail a cab. "Happy New Year's."

Everyone wished everyone the same, Phil walked off whistling "The Colonel Bogey March," and the crisis was averted.

The old man tugged on my sleeve and motioned for me to engage in an aside. I could not take him entirely seriously on account of that ridiculous fez. "I'm having trouble," he said in a low voice, "knowing who to root for in this one. Bunny is Bunny, of course, but who is the male lead of the drama—the cuckold or the cad?"

I shrugged my shoulders, sloshing my scotch, uncertain as to the significance of his question.

"That is to say, do you remember, do we root for Phil or Jerry here? And what do you make of the gun?"

Glistening atop the medicine cabinet, the gun seemed harmless for the moment, so I shrugged once more, indicating my general ignorance.

"Anton Chekhov asserted that if you put a revolver on the mantel in Act One, it must be fired by Act Three. A principle of dramaturgy that seems eminently sensible."

The woman in the black dress stared straight at us, hearing his every word, impatient for our interruption to conclude.

"Don't say I didn't warn you about the gun," the old man said.

In one fluid motion, Bunny lifted the hem of her skirt at her right hip and extracted, from a bespoke leather holster strapped just above her stocking, a derringer. Raising her arm in a straight line, she fired a single shot into the ceiling. The small explosion startled everyone in the room and reoriented our attention to the narrator. Bunny continued.

The morning after she groped Phil Ketchum at the Stork Club, Bunny waited for his arrival in a state of mild agitation. Her husband had left earlier that morning bundled like an Eskimo against the January cold, even though it was just under the freezing mark. His precautions she found nearly unbearable; the coat and mittens and stocking cap and scarf were emblematic of the problems inherent in his general character. Jerry was a very sensible man. Got it from his mother, probably, who had babied him through childhood, hovering over his every cough and sniffle. The zealous hen had raised him to be afraid of life. No baseball, you could put an eye out. Wait two hours between eating and a swim, you can't be too careful. No wonder her son was such a closet nebbish, not like Phil, who did not give a damn about anything and would do anything, try anything she asked of him.

He banged on the door at half past nine, careless of the neighbors, and was upon her the moment she closed the door. Bunny ran into the bedroom and he chased her, tearing off his tie, kicking off his shoes, and leaping beside her on the bed. Breathless, she undid his belt and unzipped his fly, astonished that he was already erect after little more than a kiss from her. He nuzzled her neck, fondled and licked her breasts, and kissed her on the flat of her stomach. In no time, his face was between her legs, the smooth-shaved chin brushing against her thighs, his tongue flickering like a snake's. She lost herself in such moments, abandoned her mind to the lust that radiated from his mouth and hands. He would do anything she asked, she thought, there is nothing he would not do to please me. His hands slid beneath her bottom and he pulled her whole body toward his mouth, and she grabbed his hair and held him to her, thinking how nice it felt in her hands, soft and thick and not the bald spot like Jerry's, growing wider day by day while the rest of him seemed hairier, his skin slick and waxy. But Phil, he filled her, and she moaned and pulled him up so that his fat dingus could go in, and she loved him and wished he could be hers.

Later in the rumpled soiled sheets, they rested in a languid stupor. She loved him more, if possible, afterward and took possession of his skin, his arms, the power in his hands. For his part, Phil waited to begin again, gauging the energy necessary to stir himself to arousal. She knew he was allowing her to work him up.

Bunny spoke across the pillow. "Don't you ever wish we could be together always?"

He breathed deeply and longed to rise from the bed and float away, right through the ceiling into 7B and on until he bashed through the roof and escaped gravity altogether. "I do," he told her.

"We can't go on like this." She slowly raked her fingernails against the ladder of his ribs. When she hit the right spot, he flinched and rolled away, and then sat up on the edge of the bed. Bunny leaned her head against the arch of his back. In the half-light of the shuttered room, he stumbled and found his Lucky Strikes and lighter. They shared a smoke.

"We've been over this a hundred times, Bun."

The first time was just a drunken whim, a chance meeting at the Carnegie Deli, a momentary opportunity when he saw her home and found her husband out on travel. But Jerry would sooner kill her than divorce her. He had beaten her years earlier, when he suspected that she was carrying on with an actor named O'Leary, and he swore he would never let her go. As for Phil, all of his finances were tied up with Claire's inheritance, everything in her name. He would be destitute without her money. They had been over and over the options for the past four months.

With a sigh, she slipped out of bed and extinguished the cigarette in an ashtray on her bureau. From his spot on the mattress, he watched her nude form glide through the room, and she could see the lust stitched in his gaze. She moved deliberately through the light seeping between the slats of the blinds, allowing him to watch her, drinking in his pleasure at her nonchalant sensuality. Bunny knew that Claire would never dare parade in the buff in front of Phil. To make the moment linger, she grabbed a brush from the dresser and watched him watch her in the mirror as she fixed her hair. A small laugh jumped from her throat.

"What's so funny?" He was lying down on his side to get a better look.

"Just a thought." She dared not face him. "What if they both were out of the picture?"

"Sure, that would solve everything." His voice oozed sarcasm.

In three quick steps, she was back in bed with him. "You have to take care of Jerry, bump him off. It's the only way out. He'd never give me a divorce. Once I get ahold of his dough, you take care of Claire, and we live like royals."

"Wait just a minute, Bun. . . . You're asking me to kill my wife?"

"No, silly." She rolled over and lay on top of him. "You kill Jerry, and then we get rid of Claire. You could divorce her if you had Jerry's money to look forward to." She sat up suddenly and wondered if he would actually leave his wife for her. She broke into a toothy grin and straddled him. "I'll make it worth your while."

Staring up at her, luxuriating in the touch of her fingers, Phil could not help himself. His body betrayed his true feelings.

Down in the backyard, a tomcat yowled, and I could tell by the length and timbre of the call that Harpo had returned and was announcing his presence. Had I left the cat flap unlatched?

Alice went to the window and peered into the abyss. "What on earth made that hellish cry?"

"You, my dear witch, of all people, should know," the old man said. "It is a cat."

The mention of a cat in such proximity caused quite a stir in the room. In the small space, they kept bumping into one another in a kind of flustered, mild panic. Adele could not stop shaking her head in disbelief, and Marie was ready to tear out her hair. Flo and Jane huddled near the door, debating escape. Alice approached the old man and grabbed him by the lapels of his robe. "Nobody said nothing about any cat."

The old man stood and addressed the crowd. "I have spoken to your man here about the filthy beast, and he has assured me that said cat will stay in the bottom of the house while we occupy the top. There's no need in getting yourselves in an uproar, ladies." His speech mollified them to the point where everyone returned to their places. From the corner of his mouth, he muttered to me, "Allergies." With a nod of his fez, he indicated to Bunny that she might resume, and so she did.

Things went on as they had been going with Phil and Bunny, as though the subplot had not been introduced to the everyday drama of sneaking around to be with each other. She did not mention murder at their next tryst, but thought instead to treat him to his favorite sexual favor. "I want more than this," she said to him as he left the apartment. Over the next few weeks, she repeated the performance, always with the same bittersweet good-bye at the door. Only gradually did she let him know how disappointed she was in his lack of will, canceling dates at the last minute or leaving earlier than planned or not being so compliant. But her strategies failed to work, for he took her actions as a sign of diminishing interest on her part, and she found the plot drifting away. It took an accident, an unexpected bit of bad luck, to lead him to change his mind.

Going to the icebox for some ice for Jerry's nightly Cuba libre, she pulled too hard on the handle of the stuck door, which then flew open and smacked her squarely in the face, blackening her eye and splitting her lower lip. The poor dumb thing took care of her as best he could, a steak for the contusion and a cold compress for her mouth, and she almost felt a twinge of affection for the mug, but Jerry fell asleep on the sofa watching *Playhouse 90,* so she stole away to the telephone. "He suspects something, Phil. He hit me again." On the other end of the line, he groaned. She managed to cry a little bit, too, and have him promise to come over on Friday morning.

The tenderness of his touch surprised her, as he ran his fingertips over the yellow and plum circle around her eye. Phil kissed her gently and withdrew when she winced and held her hand to the sore spot. Instead of taking her to bed, he made a pot of coffee, cracked a soft-boiled egg on toast cut into bite-sized pieces. Like a pair of newlyweds, they sat across the breakfast table and stared at each other. Bunny told her story of how Jerry had accused her of stepping out with Woody Pfahl, a fella who lived down in 2A, and when she asserted her innocence, her husband had struck her twice with the back of his hand. "He knocked me to the floor with the second one," she said. "And called me a slut and a whore and said that he'd kill me if he ever so much as caught me talking to him."

"Who is this Woody Pfahl?"

"Just some kid. A folksinger or a beatnik or something. You know the type." She hid her face behind her hands. "You must think I'm hideous."

He grabbed her by the wrists and wrestled her hands away from her face. "I'll do it," he said. "I'll kill the bastard. We'll make it look like an accident or someone else did it. Maybe that Woody Pfahl."

Her lip began to bleed again when she cracked a smile. "You will?"

"I could strangle him right now."

"And then we can take care of Claire, and be together."

Tamping a cigarette on the edge of the laminated tabletop, he seemed to be considering the proposition beat by beat. "Right. Jerry first, and then we just have to wait till it all blows over."

"A little while, and then you leave her."

There was a pause, a beat too long. "Sure," he said.

Crimes of passion are best done in haste, while the heat of the moment bubbles in the blood. Too much planning for the perfect crime often leads to overanalysis and weakens the nerve necessary to make the kill. Instead, they dithered. For months, they went over possible scenarios of how Phil might stage an accident. A push from the subway platform into an oncoming train was dismissed over potential witnesses. In April, they thought of poison and nooses, razors and piano wire, a fall from a tall building, a safe falling on him from a tall building. By May, they were discussing the merits and drawbacks of arson, leaving the gas oven on all night, an electric hair curler dropped into the bathtub, and an overdose of sleeping pills. They debated smothering and strangling, knives and ice picks. On Memorial Day, they nearly agreed upon a blow to the head with a blunt object. Whenever she brought up the subject of divorce, he changed the subject back to murder. As the weather improved and all through springtime, all they talked about was murder, murder, murder.

A rumba came over the radio, and the girls twirled their highballs, twisted their hips, and tapped their toes. The baby shook his rattle like a maraca.

It took another accident, another random bit of cosmic mashup, to move from the discussion stage to the execution of the plan. Quite simply, Phil met Woody Pfahl. Standing outside of Bunny's apartment building one morning, wondering whether to take the train uptown or hail a cab or just walk the dozen or so blocks to his office. He'd lit another cigarette and was trying to clear Bunny from his mind, having just left her bed after a particularly athletic romp. Funny how the talk of homicide really revved her motor. Up the block comes this kid, no more than twenty he'd guess, dark shades, wispy beginnings of a goatee, sucking on a Pall Mall like it was an all-day lollipop. The kid seemed lost in thought because he crashed right into Phil despite the lack of foot traffic at that hour.

"Hey man," the kid said, "why don't you watch where you're going?"

Phil brushed the ash from his sportscoat. "You were barreling down the sidewalk like a bull. I was just standing here minding my own business."

"Oh, I'm sorry, man. I didn't realize it was you."

With one hand on the beatnik's chest, he stopped the boy. "What do you mean by that? Do we know each other?"

"Look, man, I don't want no trouble. You're just the cat comes sniffing round here every once in a while."

Phil grabbed the kid by his lapel. "What do you mean by that crack, punk?"

"The situation is getting much too grave. Can we cool it, pops? I'm just trying to get back to my pad, catch a few zees. I've been out all night on Bleecker Street."

"You live in this building?" He suddenly realized the kid's identity. "You called Woody?"

"I don't want no trouble."

Phil laughed and let go of the boy's jacket. "Sure, Woody, go on home." All the way uptown he could not keep from chuckling to himself. The kid could barely sprout a whisker, let alone satisfy Bunny. That's who Jerry thinks is fooling around with his wife? She wouldn't give a kid like that a second look. Bunny was right: Jerry was some kind of psycho nut job, and she deserved better. In Chelsea, he stopped in a shop where he had been told someone might sell him a gun.

. . .

Downstairs the cat clunked the empty saucer across the kitchen tiles, but I dared not move a muscle to see what he wanted. As a matter of fact, I could barely move at all, given the crowd in the tiny bathroom. Who designed such small claustrophobic spaces? Or were people smaller, more compact in their needs and movements at the time this house was built? A good old house, in many ways, but at other times, the shortcomings obverted its charms. I should expand the room or add another powder room downstairs, perhaps off the kitchen. How did the previous owners deal with such inadequacies? Bachelard, I believe, had an interesting passage on the ghosts of former inhabitants of old homes, but I cannot look it up because someone has taken my *Poetics*. Perhaps the cat is to blame. I could hear him creeping about.

On the hot June morning that Phil brought over the gun—a Smith & Wesson revolver, a ".38 Special"—Bunny showered him with kisses and in the bedroom let him do that thing he had always wanted to do to her. Drenched in sweat afterward, they positioned themselves in front of an oscillating fan and let the intermittent breeze dry their skin and cool down their overheated bodies. The gun sat on the end table like a menacing wood and nickel hawk. Bunny rolled over onto her stomach to let the air ride over her legs and back. She could better see his face in profile, the beak of his nose and the pointy cleft chin. His lashes grew longer than hers and curled naturally. "I called her yesterday," she said. "Claire."

He turned partially toward Bunny but found her face too close to focus upon. "Why would you go and do a thing like that?" She had anticipated some anger, but his voice was tired and calm.

"To invite her to lunch, silly. We haven't seen each other since the wedding, your wedding, and I mentioned that Jerry had bumped into you last fall and thought we should all get back in touch."

Raising himself halfway, he rested on his elbows and considered her backside. "I thought we were going to wait—"

"I'm tired of waiting, Phil. There's no reason they both can't die one on top of the other. In fact, the more coincidental, the less likely the police will suspect they had anything to do with each other. I'm meeting Claire day after tomorrow at Moran's, and I read about this drug in an Agatha Christie novel. Imitates food poisoning, but you end up dead. Everyone will think it's bad clams."

"Jeez, Bun, that's not part of the plan."

A fit of giggles passed back and forth between the two, leaving them breathless. Bunny slid from the sheets and hobbled to the end table for a cigarette, and as she exhaled the first puff of smoke, she heard the front door swing open and Jerry's ring of keys jingling like sleigh bells.

They glanced into each other's panicked eyes. "Shit," she said, and he rolled off the mattress, desperate for his pants.

"Bun-ny," her husband called from the foyer. No doubt he saw the man's hat on the sideboard, for he did not call again and did not immediately approach the closed bedroom door at the end of the hallway. There was no time to think. Like a fool, Phil was trying to get dressed. His tie was already roped around his neck. Ripping the sheet from the bed, Bunny wound it around her naked body and then picked up the gat. As Jerry burst into the room, she let him have it, firing aimlessly, the bullet catching him in the right thigh.

He squealed like a schoolgirl at the pain and then clutched at the red carnation blossoming on his seersucker trousers. It never happened like that in the movies. The stiffs usually fell after the first shot—blam—and they were dead, but he was hopping around like a Mexican jumping bean. "What, are you crazy? What are you doing, Bunny?"

She lifted the piece and fired again, this time shattering the lamp on the bureau.

"Bun-Bun, stop. It's me, Jerry. Stop what you're doing. Stop shooting." Jerry sensed the presence of another person in the room and saw the man in trousers and necktie, but no shirt, at the foot of the bed. The sheet was slipping from his wife's shoulders. "Phil? Phil Ketchum?"

Phil grinned and waved meekly.

"Oh jeez," Jerry said. "I only came home because I forgot my wallet. Oh jeez. Bunny, what have you done?"

The shock had worn off, and she found she could now aim straight and true, so she squeezed the trigger and put the third bullet in his chest. Jerry bounced off the edge of the bed before hitting the floor like a sack of potatoes, just like in the movies.

After the noise from the gunshots, the shouting voice, the bodies in motion, after the chaos subsided, they stood quite still, afraid of what might happen next. The droning fan swept back and forth, but the rest of the world went mute for a few seconds, allowing them to catch their hearts from beating through their ribs, to slow the pulse, to steady the heavy breathing. A weak moan floated from the floor.

"Shit," Bunny said. From her side of the bed, she marched round, past the stunned boyfriend, and stopped directly above the victim. She waved the gun at Phil. "See if he's dead."

"Do I have to? I don't want to touch him."

"For cripes' sake, Phil, do I have to do everything myself?"

Since he had only managed to find one shoe, he limped over to the body, which was arranged awkwardly, facedown and partially under the bed. Phil tugged the corpse and rolled him over. A bright red stain seeped through his shirt, and a trickle of blood ran from his mouth. His eyes were open, staring accusingly, but no breath passed his lips and there was no pulse at the carotid artery. He was quite deceased.

"Blood is a dead giveaway," the old man said. "Reminds me of a certain someone."

I reached back to the site of the hole in my head, but there was no blood. From the living room, the cat let loose a plaintive meow. It was only a matter of time before he would come seek me out. I checked my watch, but the hands had not moved.

They wrapped him up like a mummy in a blanket, got dressed, and went to the kitchen to strategize. Phil's hands shook like a dope fiend's when he tried to light a pair of cigarettes. Bunny put on the percolator and grabbed some eggs from the icebox. "Hungry?"

"I couldn't eat a thing," he said.

"Scrambled okay? I'm famished."

"Bunny, what are we going to do with the body?"

Whipping the eggs with a fork, she gathered her thoughts, and as the froth sizzled in the skillet, Bunny cooked up a plan. In the storage locker in the building's basement, she had a trunk big enough, she thought, to hold the body, though they'd have to fold Jerry in half. Phil would have to borrow a car, and they could take the trunk to the river or better yet some deeper water, and weighed down with stones, sink it to the bottom. Jerry had run off, she would say. Probably found another woman. They'd take a few changes of his clothes, empty out a bank account, make it look like he wanted to disappear. Husbands do that all the time.

"But wouldn't it be easier," Phil argued, "to tell the police that you were asleep and you thought he was an intruder who broke into the house, and you shot him by mistake?"

"Shot him three times by mistake? My own husband, I wouldn't recognize?"

In the end, she beat him down, if not by superior logic, then by the sheer absurdity of the situation and her willingness to make decisions.

"I can drag that trunk up from the basement," he said. "But how can I carry the body down?"

"Eat your eggs." She dropped the plate before him. "I'll ask that boy Woody to help you."

Phil started shoveling food into his mouth, wondering the while how well she knew Woody Pfahl.

By the time that question could be answered properly, Phil was exhausted. Carrying the trunk upstairs, packing the body along with some personal effects, borrowing his brother-in-law's Nash station wagon, cashing a forged check while pretending to be Jerry at a midtown branch, and hustling back to Bunny's had taken all day, and it was a few minutes before five that afternoon when they knocked on the door to apartment 2A. High-pitched barking began at once, and then the sound of a woman's voice admonishing the dog to oh, just shut up. A young blonde in a black leotard and dance skirt opened the door with a tiny, trembling dog in her arms.

"Hello," Bunny said. "We're the neighbors from upstairs, and we need some help. I was wondering if Woody was home. We need another man."

"I bet you do," the blonde said. "C'mon in. Woody should be getting out of bed anyhow."

"What kind of dog is that?" Phil asked.

The dog barked fiercely as Bunny stepped inside, but when the blonde girl turned, it wagged its tail at Phil and laid down its pointy ears.

"Pepito? A Mexican chihuahua. He's nervous around strangers. But he likes you." The dog craned his neck to sniff at Phil. "You carrying meat on you?"

Phil held out his fingers and the dog began to lick him with gusto.

The blonde hollered down the hallway, "Woody, get up. Company."

Groggy and disheveled, Woody emerged two minutes later from the bedroom, wearing a robe whose belt trailed behind him like a tail. His T-shirt and boxers were exposed by the open robe. The little dog wagged its tail furiously and leapt from the blonde's arms to run to its master.

"Sherry, baby, what is it?" And as he asked, he saw Phil standing near the doorway. "Hey, man, it's you. From the street."

Phil waved a halfhearted hello. From behind him out popped Bunny, and she was more effusive in her greetings, flashing a big smile and ogling him. Woody gathered in his robe.

"Would you be a dear?" Bunny asked. "Could you give us a hand bringing down a trunk? My husband wants to ship it, but wouldn't you know, he's stuck late at work and can't lend us a hand."

"Sure, Mrs. G. I'd be happy to. Let me throw on some pants."

A few minutes later on the sixth floor landing, they heaved the chest. Phil needed a breather after the first flight of stairs, and on the fourth floor, Woody stopped and set down their burden. "Whatcha got in here, a body?" They made it to the car in twenty minutes, and Phil had laid down the backseat so that the trunk could rest in the bed of the wagon. Sweat dripped from the tips of their noses, and they sat on the front stoop, toweling off and smoking cigarettes. New Yorkers were not interested in their efforts, but hurried by to get out of the heat. Phil offered him a five-dollar bill for his help, but Woody refused all payment. "No problem. I'd do anything in the world for Bunny." He corrected himself. "For Mrs. G."

All the way out to Canarsie, Phil wondered how well Woody knew

her, and how, and what about the blonde with the chihuahua. He drove
the Nash to the piers and with a small bribe to a Negro man sitting on
the docks, they managed to dump the trunk into the deep and silent
waters. As he slid the body over the edge, he almost went in himself,
and later thought of that moment as the last chance he had to save himself from misery. Around eleven, he finally made it home and slept till
noon. The rest of the day he spent reliving the horrors of Jerry's murder and the madness involved in getting rid of the body. Even Claire,
who usually paid no attention to his comings and goings, remarked at
dinner as to how pale and tired Phil looked, as if something was heavy
on his mind. "You'll be all right by yourself tomorrow? It's Saturday, so
you can sleep late again if you like, though I wouldn't make it a habit.
I'll be going out for lunch."

He muttered his approval.

The next morning she bent over him in his bed and kissed him on
the forehead. "Good-bye, sweetheart," Claire said. She was in a new
sundress, a gold chain delicate at her throat, and her hair was newly cut
and styled. "I'll be at Moran's. Back by three, I should think. Try to
make yourself presentable, won't you, darling?"

With a groan, he rolled over and buried his head beneath the pillow. Fifty minutes later, he woke in a panic. Moran's? Wasn't that the
place Bunny had arranged for their lunch? The poisoned seafood? He
slapped some water on his face, jumped into an old suit, and took a cab
across town, arriving well past the appointed hour. The maître d' tried
to stop him, and the waiters and patrons stared at Phil as he burst into
the dining room, searching the tables for his wife and mistress. In the
back corner, farthest from the door, sat Claire, a small grin turning the
corners of her mouth. She was all alone, but another place had been set,
and the appetizer had been served. No murderess sat in the empty chair.
Perhaps she had gone to poison the main course. Phil rushed in like a
madman. "Where's Bunny?"

"Phil, you look a fright. Please sit down, you're making a scene." She nodded to the waiter, who held out a chair. "Have something to eat, you'll feel better. Try the oysters Rockefeller. They're to die for."

Taking the seat next to her, Phil stared at his wife as though he had no idea who she was. A few seconds later, a fat man in a seersucker suit joined them at the table. Claire introduced him as Mr. Rosen, and the two men shook hands.

"Bunny couldn't make it, dear," Claire said. "So I invited Mr. Rosen instead. He's been doing a little work for me. Are you sure you wouldn't like something to eat, Philip? They have other choices besides seafood. How about a nice steak?"

Half her words were inaudible, and he had only a general sense of what she was trying to say. All he could think about was Bunny and her plan to murder Claire, and how he had almost let it happen. He couldn't let it happen. Things had spiraled out of control. One minute he's kissing a beautiful dame behind her ear, the next he's sweating over his life. "Nothing for me, thanks. Maybe just some coffee."

Claire nodded to the waiter, and coffee was served. All the while, she kept talking about something he could not quite follow regarding how she and Mr. Rosen were introduced and came to know each other. ". . . so you see, Phil, Mr. Rosen has been doing a bit of detective work for me. I've suspected, ever since that night you bumped into Katie and her friends outside of *Bridge on the River Kwai,* was it? And who else is there but Bunny. I'd have thought it was a coincidence like you told Kate, but then she said that when she first saw you two, it was like you were a couple of high school kids who got caught out on a date . . ."

Trying to remember that afternoon, Phil sipped at his coffee, which was too hot to drink.

"Mr. Rosen here is what they call a private dick in the movies. Don't you just love the sound of that? Private dick?" She chuckled to herself. "Anyway, he's been following you off and on for the past three months."

The baton was handed to Rosen. His voice was not gruff as Phil had expected, but surprisingly sweet and cheerful, the kind of voice that makes people listening feel gay and carefree. "Standard stuff, really. Philandering husband, happens all the time, and it's just a matter of making a record of your dalliances, taking a few photos, collecting evidence."

Her laugh fairly tinkled with glee. "You see, I was about to divorce you, darling. I knew you were shtupping Bunny, and it was just a matter of Mr. Rosen here putting together his dossier. But you've saved me the trouble. Tell him about the chihuahua, Mr. Rosen."

The thought of the little dog inspired a particular delight, for Mr. Rosen grinned so widely that his gold fillings showed. "Funny story, Mr. Ketchum. Cigarette?" He extended a pack of Luckys, and everyone took a smoke. "When I'm engaged in a surveillance, I like to get some help, see, some people on the margins of my subject's life that don't really have a stake in the matter. You know, doormen are useful people in cases of adultery. So are bartenders and waiters. You remember the peanut vendor down at the park you and Bunny like to visit? He puts you two together six times over April and May. And you're always running out of smokes right around the corner from her building. The Persian fella that runs the newsstand says you never have any coins, just bills. You get the idea. People see you around. Quite a bit."

The coffee had cooled just enough to drink, and the caffeine and nicotine raced through his worn-out system till he felt almost normal.

"So I had the folksinger downstairs, Woody, feeding me bits of info, and it was the dog that proved the most helpful. You ever seen a Mexican chihuahua before, Mr. Ketchum? They are very nervous around strangers, and this little one barked at everyone in the building. Everyone, that is, except Bunny's husband, Jerry. The thing is, Jerry took the trouble to bring that dog a treat when he came home from the deli. A little nosh. Some pastrami, maybe a bit of cheese, a morsel of corned beef."

Lunch arrived. A nice piece of sole for Claire, and a plate of fried clams for Rosen. Smelling the food, Phil wished he, too, had ordered something. He was suddenly ravaged with hunger.

"So the dog loves Jerry and can't trust nobody else. So naturally when Woody is helping you with the trunk, he's wondering what Pepito sees in you. The time before, when you bumped into Woody on the street, you weren't exactly the friendliest guy in Manhattan. So he figures the dog smells you and you're just like Jerry since you been doing his wife—my apologies, Mrs. Ketchum—right, but of course Woody don't know you smell like Jerry cause you got Jerry's blood on your hand and your clothes. Hell, you got Jerry himself in that box he helped you carry six flights." He stopped talking for a moment to squeeze lemon juice on his clams. "The thing is, Mr. Ketchum, I knew it was you since I was watching the joint all day. Jerry goes to work, you come in. Like usual. Jerry comes back home unexpected, but he never comes out. You come out in a hurry. So I figure that's it, he's finally caught you with the wife. But no, you come back with a car a couple hours later, and still Jerry's never left. That's not like him to miss work, and then down you come later to get Woody to help you put a big box in the back of that Nash. Too heavy for one man to lift. What's inside, I ask myself."

Rosen speared a bunch of clams and forked them into his mouth. He did not savor but chewed for sustenance. "Nice car you had for the task, and too bad it was Claire's brother's, now the police know where to look for any blood that may have leaked out of the trunk. And then there's the small matter of the pier at Canarsie. I followed you out there, the whole time wondering what you were going to do with that trunk. You should have gone out farther if you wanted to lose it in the Sound. They've got divers in the water as we speak. Only a matter of time before they find it.

Right off the end of the pier." He attacked the clam strips again, having come to the end.

The look in her eyes revealed just how low Phil had sunk. "Couldn't keep it in your trousers, could you? You and Bunny, both so impetuous. She phoned yesterday, while you were sleeping and muttering in your dreams, by the way. Still wanted to lunch as we'd scheduled, despite the fact that Jerry had gone missing overnight. I asked her if she'd called the police, and no, she hadn't, so I called them for her. Told them everything Mr. Rosen had told me about his suspicions. She hadn't even thought to dig the slug out of the wall. The pistol you bought was right there in the night table. Looks like I won't have to divorce you after all. Not when there's the electric chair. The perfect murder . . ."

His coffee cup was empty, and he wished the waiter would return soon.

Rosen swallowed another mouthful of clams. "Bunny has already confessed. I was just off the phone with my buddy at the precinct right before you came in. She told the police everything. How you planned it, bought the gun, and pulled the trigger. She claims she begged you not to do it, but you couldn't stand waiting any longer."

Through the picture window, red and blue police lights flashed.

"But it wasn't me," Phil said. "It was her. I could never hurt a fly. I came here to save you. She was going to poison you, too. It was Bunny who shot him. Bunny, not me."

Nobody in the bathroom said a word, and the woman in the black dress reached up for the gun atop the medicine cabinet, trembling as she pointed it toward my heart. I froze, my back to the door, and all the women faced me and pressed forward in the tiny space. "What are you going to do with that gat?"

"You coward," Bunny said. "You idiot. You never intended to shoot Jerry, and you never were going to divorce her, were you? And I loved you, yet you wouldn't take the rap for me. It was always about you, just about you. Your lust. Your desires. You, you, you."

"You-you-you," the little boy chimed in.

"Shoot him," Dolly cried from behind Bunny's left shoulder. On the right stood Adele, equally bloodthirsty, vengeance in her eyes. "Do it," Jane hissed. "He deserves it," Alice said. Flo wagged her finger at me, and Marie's eyes widened in anticipation. I looked to the old man to save me, but he was playing peekaboo with the child on his lap.

"Aren't you going to help me like before? Knock the gun from her hand? Intervene?"

The women advanced like a pack of zombies.

"Nothing to be done," he said. "After all, you've not done well by any of them."

"What are you talking about?"

"Surely you know they've come to have their revenge for what you did to each of them in the past. Abandoned Dolly out of pridefulness. Murdered Jane for a few doubloons. Sent Alice to the gallows, kept Marie a slave, drove Flo to the poorhouse. You let your anger get you killed and left poor Adele brokenhearted, and then you ratted out Bunny. Oh, you are a piece of work. I sort of see their point of view."

"But you've always been on my side." I addressed the women. "What about last night and the eight women in the bed?"

Bunny pulled the hammer back on the revolver. She was ready to pump me full of lead.

The old man laughed. "You double-backed from the moment you hit your head, Sonny, and let loose a crack in time. There was no night before, only this one. Let me ask you: which is closer to the truth— your infantile fantasies or the words right out of their mouths?"

CHAPTER FIFTEEN

The Woman Who Stayed in the Bed

A soft push behind me and the door opened a whisker, and I thought for a moment it might be that mysterious eighth woman from the bed come to save me, but instead Harpo the cat squeezed between my legs, purring a greeting. The old man sneezed. Bunny's eyes began to water. She dropped the gun and reached for a tissue. The crowd in the room, upon seeing the cat, panicked. A few more sneezed violently. Shock and terror marked their expressions. Someone squeaked "Eek!" Suddenly the room seemed too small and confining. All of them, the old man and the boy included, tried to squeeze past me to the door. They were mad with conniptions and paroxysms of desire to escape the deadly cat. At the threshold there was a momentary logjam of bodies, and the wooden frame creaked and threatened to crack as we all tumbled through the opening in a rush of knees and elbows, landing in a heap in the hallway. Once they were out of the safety of the bathroom, the women simply vanished, pop-pop-popped into oblivion, as did the child, and, at last, the old man. Not so much as a smile or a wave good-bye. Each person made a small puff like the sound of a kiss upon air as they departed, and the spell was broken. I was quite alone, crumpled on the floor as in the beginning.

The cat crept over like a fog and sat squarely upon my chest. He seemed to be grinning. The show was over, the curtain drawn, and I passed out from sheer exhaustion.

When I came to, it seemed the time had changed at last, but since my wristwatch had gone dead, I could not be certain. Harpo leapt to the floor as I sat up, and he stretched his whole length, a ripple of tension traveling from his front paws to the tip of his tail. The bathroom fan hummed politely, and overhead the light shone on utter empty order. Everything had been restored to its pristine state. There was no gun, no baseball bat, no miner's pick. The war club and the frying pan, the broom and the harpoon had been removed. The martini glasses had been put away, not so much as an olive left behind.

I swiveled on my bum to see if the others had somehow reappeared in the hallway, but they were gone for good, though to where I do not know. Back, I suppose, to where they'd come from, slipping through the cracks, phantoms of time. Perhaps to other space, other lives to right old grievances or guide another transitory visitor from one life to the next. A sense of relief settled like a mist. No gun, no bullet. The threat of my imminent demise had been thwarted once again. But as I sat there, other thoughts haunted the equipoise of the moment.

It hadn't always been so bad. Surely the odd moments of love and affection over the centuries count for something.

Bunny and I had shared some good times. Not just in the sack, though those stolen moments were delicious. No, half the fun had been in anticipation and in the secret thrill of planning our assignations, whether or not we could carry off the whole affair. I may have enjoyed the game more than the final score. What a thrill to seek her on some busy street corner for a rendezvous and suddenly spot her blonde hair bobbing along in a crowd. Or to furtively hold hands on a park bench on a morning in December bright and cold. She had a funny way of pronouncing the letter s—just the hint of a lisp so oddly endearing. I felt sorry for cheating on Claire, of course, and sorrier still for poor Jerry, but in the beginning at least, we were too full of each other to realize that someone was bound to get hurt.

I wished that Adele and I had tasted that same forbidden love, and I wonder now what might have been had we met in a less repressive age. She was such an innocent girl and a good sport to put up with all the baseball. And my temper, too. But there was no one lovelier than Adele in the summer sun at the old ballpark, her face framed beneath some outrageous hat, cheering along with me. Had I known any better, I should have paid her more heed than the sports and the drink. Charlie Wells wasn't such a bad fella after all, but what I wouldn't give to have one more chance at rounding the bases. To her credit, she loved me to the bitter end, and I think Adele was glad to see me, despite that swing of the bat.

Flo, dear Flo, what a helluva gal. Sprightlier than a jenny mule and stronger, too, but the belle of the epoch in her finery. More than all the gold and silver, we had shared something precious in the struggle west and building our empire together. And don't forget our babies, little John and Jess, and the others. What fine young men and women they turned out to be. Surely family is some recompense, though how could I ever repay her for my risk and speculation? Remember old Kentucky, then, and how we tricked your pap, and how far we came from those hills to the grand octagon house in San Francisco? Just lost my will in the end is all, forgive me.

Or perhaps I should save such petitions for absolution from Marie. I can't look back now and condone the tragedy of slavery, but that was the custom in those days, the natural order of things, and I was always a man of my time. But no excuses, eh. We treated her well in New Orleans, as best we knew. We loved her like family, and I can still taste the sweetness she baked into the cornbread, and the spice in her étouffée. Who do that voodoo that you do so well? Surely there is some affection in those menus, a soupçon of love for old LaChance.

I was just playing my part in society, understand, just as I had for poor Alice Bonham. She was the youngest of the witches and fairest of them all, and I can admit now how sorry I was to send her to the gallows. In truth, I envied Mr. Bonham for his pleasures, for I was bewitched, indeed, and carried the memory and curse of her to the end of my days. The whole sad story is one of the madness that sweeps us all when we are afraid of the changing world. And yet, I cannot shake the look in her eyes when she was in the docket, the recognition I daresay that you found me guiltless, and that mercy could be but one kiss away. How can I say I'm sorry, Alice?

Or to Jane, perhaps most deserving of my apologies. Dear boy, dear girl, dear one. Would that the discovery of ambergris had not come between us, nor Waters either. Once upon a time, we were Adam and Eve in our Eden, and looking back upon it, we could have long lingered in the Garden. Would it be any consolation that I had nightmares ever after, that the sound of the blow from the oar lingered in my ears, and I drowned in regret as she drowned in the ocean? I'd give all the riches due me for one more night of her boyish figure, and I know in my heart she loved me better than that old cur Waters.

And there is no doubt about Dolly. She followed me into the rain forest, over the mountains, and into the valley of the grizzlies. How's that for love? Leave hearth and home and enter into the realm of myth. We had two fine cubs together, slept all winter, and made hay in the spring. Not many women could put up with such a bear as me.

After they were all gone, I missed them.

Even the baby, who seemed to grow up in an instant.

The disappearance of the old man left me particularly bereft. Through the unending morning, he had been a true friend, protecting me from harm, and patiently listening to my stories. And we had a few laughs, eh? Couple of tramps wandering through life's comedy. A man is lucky to have even a handful of good friends in one life. How long has it been since I had such a heart-to-heart with my brother? When had I last seen my father? When those we love exit, we are a solitary player upon a bare stage, muttering our lines to ourselves.

Such reveries at five in the morning torture the soul. Disturbed from deep sleep and the uncontrolled dreams of the unconscious and not yet ready to face the day, if we are awakened, we are caught between the mind's dwelling places. Too early to get up, too late to go back to bed. On any other day, I would have padded around the house in my routine, made an early coffee, read the paper, and thought of how to avoid work. But no such comfort came my way. The house itself seemed a foreign place, crouching as if to expel me from this space. The seven women, the baby boy, and the old man had been a big part of my life for such a long time that their sudden absence grieved me most particularly. Despite their nefarious intentions, they were good company with stories to share, and now the house felt both empty yet too small, as though I was trapped within its walls, restricted in time and space. The cat returned and, uncharacteristically, nestled in my lap. I scratched the soft fur behind his ears.

Far off a ticking sound like a heartbeat kept pace with the rhythmic inspiration and exhalation of air, but that just may have been summertime rushing through the windows. I listened to the silence and became a part of it, and the silence filled me with dread.

Everything slowed down. In the absence of the storytellers, the pell-mell of the immediate past ceased, and my mind became my own again. Like the nautilus, I withdrew into my spiral shell and curled up in the fetal position. Once, when I was a boy no more than three years old—perhaps this is my earliest memory or perhaps I have re-created it as a memory out of the telling and retelling of the story by my parents and older brother, so who's to verify its authenticity?—but on this particular occasion, I had invaded my father's forbidden study and sat at my father's desk and found some papers there. Turning over the sheets marked with strange glyphs and letters and symbols, I discovered the obverse gloriously blank. Like some saboteur, I uncapped his fountain pen and proceeded to scribble on page after page, drawing no doubt some design from the shoals of my imagination. At some point, I realized that this creative explosion might be unwelcome by my father, who was in certain respects a fairly stern figure. So I took the papers and threw them in the trashcan, leaving behind some forensic evidence in mislaid sheets and inky splatters. Minding my own business with some wooden blocks in my room upstairs, I was alarmed by the raised voices and commotion when he returned home from work and discovered the crime scene. I sensed I was in trouble, and so found the most hidden spot to crawl into and lie there as snug as in a grave, and there I stayed during their frantic search for me, ignoring the calls of my name, and there I slept till I was discovered hours later and carried to bed in my mother's arms. In memory, that hidey-hole was as dark and safe as a womb.

Someone was crying. The weeping started softly and grew louder and louder till I could discern the source of such sorrow. Behind my closed bedroom door someone wept. Of course, the eighth woman in the bed. I had nearly forgotten she was there. Shooing the cat from my lap, I rose and sought the answer to my questions. Without hesitation this time around, I opened the door and found her there, lying on the bed.

Her back was turned to me as before, but she was no longer naked. Now clad in a simple white sari, the Hindu color of mourning, she appeared to be deep in her grief. Afternoon light streamed through the window and an elongated rectangle illuminated her body from the crown of her black hair to the curve of her hip. I knew who it was, had known I suppose all along, for I was in love with her. "Sita," I called, but she did not stir.

The cat was at my feet, rubbing against my ankle. "Sorry, she can't hear you, mate. Or see you or nuffin. You're not here."

Funny, but I expected some grander special effects. A more spectral nature, the ability to pass my hand through objects, chains to rattle, or the wind creaking through the walls. But it was fairly much the same as it had been since time had stopped. "Like a ghost."

"Exactly like that."

We strolled to the other side of the bed so I could see her face. She was lying atop the quilt of many colors, her bare feet drawn beneath her, arms across her breasts. Her eyes were open, and her makeup was smudged from the tears. Upon one of her hands, she had an intricate henna design that I would have liked to ask her to explain. I crouched down next to her, touched her hair, but I did not feel a thing, and she did not feel a thing, not even a sense of my spirit in the room. She looked sad and beautiful, and I had a thousand things to tell her, but there was no longer any way to talk with Sita. Silence blew right through me. Though it did neither of us any good, I stayed there with her for a long time.

"Why is she crying?" I asked Harpo.

"Because of the hole in your head."

"Because I am dead?"

A figure appeared in the doorway. Tall and thin with hair brushed straight back, he looked like a Giacometti sculpture or a young Samuel Beckett. When he saw Sita crying on the bed, he bowed his head for a moment, and as he lifted it, he revealed his identity at once. Sam. My brother, Sam. As soon as I saw him, I remembered the old man in the bathroom and realized at once that he had been an older version of my brother from some distant future who had slipped in through the same crack of time. Now he was as young as yesterday. He walked into the room without acknowledging me and crouched next to her and said her name. "Sita."

She smiled briefly and held out her hand, which he took and pressed to his face. She smiled again, holding his palm there a beat longer, and then she let him go. "Stay for a while," she said. "Keep me company."

"Everyone was wondering where you went off to." He sat down beside her.

"I couldn't stand another well-wisher. Another person of good intentions but little imagination. He would have wandered off, too, at his own wake. Without saying good-bye. Suddenly I just missed him and wanted to come up here and see if the bed still held his shape. His scent on the pillow."

My brother clearly did not know what to do or say. As he searched the corners of the walls before him, he knitted his fingers together and crossed his legs at the ankles. She had always made him slightly uncomfortable. The cat leapt upon the bed and meandered to my pillow, where he curled like a dish and settled into the dent left by her head.

Sam patted her hand. "You know it was an accident. He was gone right away. Maybe the cat got underfoot, and he fell backward and hit his head. Must have been the cat."

"Don't be absurd," Harpo said from the pillow.

Downstairs there was a party going on. Someone had finished a joke and the punch line released a tide of laughter that rose and fell away and left behind a deeper silence. Stories at funerals seem to me to be the surest sign of our resiliency. That we want to, and can, make each other laugh. I almost wished to be down there among my friends and relatives, to hear what might be said about me and set the record straight, but I could not bear to leave her, even in my brother's good care. As for the cat, I could strangle him, but what's the point? He was forever underfoot. Sita had been there with me all night, not the others, just Sita. I must have risen from the bed, careful not to wake her, and stumbled in the darkness to the bathroom. I tripped over the cat, hit my head, and would not get up.

"I cannot believe Jack is gone," she said.

Jack, of course, she called me Jack. That's my name. My brother's name is Sam. He moved out when things started getting serious between me and my girlfriend, Sita. Who was now speaking of me in the past tense.

The cat read my thoughts. "Because you are definitely not in the present, at present."

"It's like a bad dream," she said. "Wouldn't he have found some humor in the situation? Awakened from his dream only to fall out of the world. Since he was nothing but a dreamer."

I was taken by her flat assertion. I always fancied myself a man of action.

"Come now," said Harpo. "It's just the two of us now. You can be honest with me."

A debate with a cat was out of the question, but at the very least I felt I should express my gratitude. "Thank you, at least, for saving me back there. From the mad woman with the gun."

He coughed on a hairball. "Don't mention it, mate. Just an accident that I showed up at all."

At last, Sam cleared his throat. "He was a dreamer, but such a serious one. When he was a little boy, he liked nothing more than to draw these elaborate designs of his own imagination on this brown paper Mother gave him. From the time Jack could draw, he would sit all day at our father's desk, sketching out his dreams."

I had dreams, all right. Skyscrapers and museums, whole cities, and cities connected to other cities. Or simply the perfect house.

"I often dreamt of something better for myself," Harpo said. "Don't be so incredulous. Cats have nine lives, you know."

"Then there's hope for you yet."

"Even housecats dream of becoming tigers. As long as there's the chance of starting all over again, there's hope, mate." With that, Harpo began to lick at the fur near the base of his tail, the first step in a grooming process that always seemed to last forever. I could not watch, for it made me a little sick to my stomach.

My attention strayed to the commotion going on downstairs. A man's voice, loud with drink, began some apocryphal story to regale the house of mourning. I wondered who else had come to the funeral but knew that I should not leave the room. Part of me wished to reach out and comfort her, say a few words to my brother, but there was no way to do so from this separate plane. This whole ghostly situation—or whatever one calls it—is quite frustrating.

"When we first met," Sita said, "he was so funny and charming and smart. I am so angry that he would leave me all alone like this. What am I to do now?"

My brother had no good answer.

She considered his silence and folded her hands, as if in prayer. "I have a story to tell you," she said. "About your brother and me."

Leaning back against the pillows, in a gesture I had seen before on this night, Sam settled in for the tale.

CHAPTER SIXTEEN

Here We Go Again

My father is old country. He came to America as a young man to study medicine at a time when this was a rarity for a Bengali. But he is a very smart man and hardworking and determined to make a success. The American dream, right? One day, when he was working as a young intern, a patient hobbled in with a broken foot. She smiled at the beautiful doctor. He lingered awhile at her bedside, beguiled by her accent. An immigrant who had escaped Poland, and when the cast came off, she asked him out on a date. I imagine the two of them, struggling with their own cultural differences and then the language and the strange customs of America, and it is still difficult to see what drew them together. Opposites attract and all that.

So they marry, yes. Young Indian doctor and his fair-haired wife. Understand this was a time when such combinations were not as commonplace as today, but they were in love and did not care about stares in the street or the whispers in the grocery store. He had no one at all in the big city. She had room in her heart for every possibility of love. They had each other, and what difference did it make what others might say?

Katya, that is my mother, yes, she was studying poetry of all things at the University of Chicago and Niren was happily in residence at a hospital nearby, and one fine day around Christmas, when all of the decorations are up, and it is cold, and people are bustling about with their shopping and preparations, she casually says, "I'm expecting." "Expecting?" he asks. "What is it you're expecting?" He had in mind a package, perhaps, for the holidays from her folks back in Gdansk, but of course, she beams at his cluelessness. "A baby, Niren," she says, and later, when I was a little girl, he told me that moment he knew how wide the universe was, for it had filled his heart. They both were happiest, I think, in those months before the first child was born, when anticipation and joy and a little fear supersede the inevitable fatigue and reality of caring for a real infant. All the talk was of the coming event, and as such things go, they planned and prepared, found a bigger apartment, bought the necessary accoutrements. Time goes by, the matter of what to call the baby came up. Katya had told him that he was to decide upon the firstborn's name and that she would choose the rest. A wise woman, my mother.

Now my father is not a particularly religious man, not in any formal sense, and I have no real idea what his family back in the old country believes. I've never been to India except once, when I was all of six months old. Nana fell so in love with me that they all moved to Chicago by the very next year. Furthermore, he had by this time adopted nearly all of my mother's customs. There was a Christmas tree in the new apartment. We never spoke of the matter, but I am sure he thought attending the Christian church and so on was part and parcel of becoming a full-fledged American. Or maybe he just wanted to please her. But to my knowledge, his upbringing was secular, so it was a surprise he found my name in the Ramayana. Do you know this story?

. . .

My brother shook his head. In his dark suit and tie, Sam looked incongruous sitting there upon the bed. By now I was more used to him as an old man in a bathrobe, and part of me wished I could speak to him and let him know how he would turn out in the future. The cat stood with an air of mild annoyance and then found his place in the moving patch of sunshine on the floor. I was curious to hear what Sita had to say, since she so rarely spoke about this part of her life.

The Ramayana is the life story of Rama, the seventh incarnation of Vishnu, and I guess you'd call it one of the foundational stories of the Hindu tradition. It's this long, multilayered epic poem about the exiled prince Rama and his wife. She gets abducted by the demon Ravana, a creature with ten heads and twenty arms, who tricks her and takes her to the kingdom of Lanka across the sea. This monkey-god, Hanuman, helps Rama rescue the girl, but Lord, it gets more complicated as it goes. But the point of me telling you this is that Rama's wife is named Sita, incarnation of the goddess Lakshmi, and she is the epitome of beauty, virtue, and loyalty. Follower of the principles of dharma. The ideal wife. Some standard to live up to, eh? How's that a proper name for a baby girl? What was the poor man thinking?

My father used to tell me stories from the Ramayanas—for there are many versions—at bedtime when I was just a little girl, though I don't know how much of it was true and what he may have invented. I don't believe he was secretly trying to make a good Hindu of me, or even much of a Bengali. The bedtime stories were as much for his sake as for putting me to sleep. He seemed to be remembering his own childhood by telling those tales to me, and I enjoyed them for what they were—scary and funny and sad. In one, the monkeys make a bridge from India to Sri Lanka by joining hand to foot and holding on to the next one's tail, and in another, old Ravana sets the monkey-god's tail afire, and he just scoots through the kingdom spreading the blaze from building to building and destroying all.

Whatever the stories meant to him, they were a kind of ritual between us, a private language and a personal bond despite the fact that they're known all around the Hindu world. In that little corner of Chicago, the Ramayana was just ours. None of the other kids had ever heard of such an elaborate myth, and for sure I wasn't going to mention the gods to the nuns at my grammar school. But I liked being the only Sita among all the Mary Margarets and Sean Michael Patrick Francis Joseph Aloysiuses at Our Lady of Grace, the only Sita in the whole neighborhood, or in all of Chicago for all I knew. Although there was a stretch as a teenager when I wished to be Suzie or Rita, but I outgrew all that when I left home for college.

"It's a beautiful name," Sam offered, and Sita blushed at the compliment. She walked to the window and looked out upon the fair summer day. Too nice for a funeral. I was tempted to cross the room and stand behind her, put my arms around her waist, but as neither one of us could feel the gesture, it seemed pointless. In the glass of the windowpanes, her eyes stared straight ahead, not searching the exterior world, but locked upon some inner landscape far away from here.

I began to forget my father's stories and became instead just Sita, a girl with an unusual name. One of many strangers when I went to university in Philadelphia. A boy named Ayodeji from Nigeria. Michiko from Kyoto in my English Composition section. Josip and Baxter and a girl named Feather from Los Lunas, New Mexico. Nothing strange about me, nothing exotic. Just a girl, a little darker than some, but hardly unusual. What's in a name? I was more American than many of these foreign satellites landed on campus, and I became more fully American away from my funny mixed-up parents and their mélange of food and customs, stories and memories.

So in earnest I was determined to say good-bye to the past and become just American like everyone else. My boyfriends were all regular Joes. I hung around with my pixie blonde roommate and the ordinary Janes. In retrospect, it all seems a much more conscious decision, but I had no idea at the time just how much I longed to be just like everyone else. Another eighteen-year-old inventing herself. Funny story, though, I dated this guy a few times, sweet as pie, and one time we got all dolled up for a night on the town and he ends up taking me to an Indian restaurant for dinner, Bombay something or other. And we're sitting there in the red room, the silver samovars and Ganesh and Siva duking it out on the wall, while we waited for our lamb rogan josh or whatever and I must have looked absolutely morose. "What's the matter?" he asks. "Don't you like Indian food?" And that cracks me up for some reason, and I just can't stop laughing. Poor guy didn't even know.

I floundered around for a couple years like a lot of kids, but by senior year, I had decided to study urban design and was going on to graduate school. Ended up at Rhode Island School of Design, and that's where my Americanization project became complete. Nobody blinked when I introduced myself as Sita. I was just one more competitor. We were so focused on doing well and landing a job after graduation, and everyone was so earnest and smart and superior. Lots of pressure to perform, and I felt completely out of my depth for the first time in my life. And just about the worst possible moment, when I'm struggling with school and worrying about the future, along comes Matthew.

. . .

She had told me all about Matthew before. The inevitable dating conversation about our sordid pasts, the litany of exes. We were in the Sculpture Garden of the National Gallery of Art, waiting for a free summer jazz concert to begin, the big fountain spritzing in the middle of the plaza, the tourists staking out their spots along the circle of stone benches. A pair of mallards paddled about, and children of all ages dangled their bare feet in the water. A mob of sparrows hopped on the ground, begging for handouts. Among the dozens of idlers was a scruffy fellow in a black T-shirt and jeans, big hairy feet strapped into sandals, and sunglasses perched atop his head. He strolled along, yakking on his cell, and Sita gasped when he passed by.

"Someone you know?" I asked.

She bent her head and hid her face behind her long dark hair. "Not really. He just reminded me of someone I know. Knew. An old boyfriend."

"Oh."

The tale played out to the syncopated rhythms of the jazz ensemble, in between songs, and later on the Metro home. Not that I wanted the details, but my questions enabled her to sketch out an outline, and the matter over, he was never mentioned again. They had met in grad school at RISD, and apparently this Matthew was touched by the gods, some kind of creative genius, the most brilliant architect ever, and the first love of her life. They moved in together, made plans, but they were just a couple of kids. Months go by, and she told me that he wigs out for some reason and just leaves, and a long time goes by before Sita gets over him. I was surprised that she was bringing up this old flame to Sam at my funeral.

The cat rose to his feet and hissed indignantly. "You've no room to talk, mate. Considering your own checkered past these many centuries."

"True, but still. Some decorum after all. The flowers haven't yet begun to wilt, and the guests are still attacking the canapés downstairs."

"You fink you're the only one wif a broken heart?" Harpo turned his back to me and lay down in the striped sunshine.

Matthew was an architect, like Jack, but there the similarity ends. Where Jack was a dreamer, Matthew was a doer. He had a harder edge, more competitive, downright vicious at times, but he was head of the class, bound for glory at one of the big design firms in New York. We hooked up that first semester and moved in together that first year of school. I loved his manic energy and single-mindedness, and everything started out exciting and dangerous. And Matthew was a creative genius, but some demons often live side by side in such people. His was jealousy. The last few months he grew paranoid about everything I did. One of my partners in a collaborative project was just a nice, friendly boy, and we spent a lot of time together working on a design for a new model for public housing, but Matthew accused me of actually sleeping with this harmless boy, which was ridiculous, and despite my protests, he never truly believed my innocence. I would never do such a thing. And then one night, over the same old argument, Matthew hit me. "Tell me the truth," he said, and I said, "But it's only you," and he hit me with the back of his hand. Have you ever been struck by someone you loved? There was the pain—yes, he drew blood from my lip—but the shock reverberated down to my soul. And the absurdity of the moment, all this because he chose not to trust me. He struck me just once, but that was the end. Somehow I finished up the semester, but that May I packed up all my things and went back to my parents in Chicago.

At first I thought of just going home for the summer. Take some time off and mend. Get over the heartbreak of losing my first love. And what could be safer, more natural than home, for my parents to take care of me while I do nothing, like when I was a child? Do you know your brother's favorite, Bachelard? Somewhere he writes, "All the summers of our childhood bear witness to 'the eternal summer.'" That's what I longed for, what I needed. Another June, another eternal summer stretching out before me and a chance to recover. Centuries of June, life by life, bring the promise of another beginning.

But it did not turn out the way I had planned. Oh, my parents were extraordinary, just angels, really. They understood my anguish and allowed me this retreat, and for the first few weeks, everything was more or less fine. I would take a book and lie in the sun all afternoon, often as not falling asleep rather than reading. And that after lying in all morning long, waking late, and wandering around the old house like a zombie in pajamas. And then after doing nothing more strenuous than sunbathing, I would go to bed early, say nine o'clock, and sleep again for twelve or fourteen hours. My little sibs left me alone, went to their summer jobs, out to movies and so on, and they tried, too, to get some life into me, but I turned down all their offers for a night out. I was just so tired all of the time.

It wasn't just Matthew I was grieving, but something deeper, some fatigue of the soul. We had an old dog at the time, a kind of hybrid shepherd that may have been part wolf. For sure, he looked lupine, is that the right word? Sometimes he would sleep near me, at the foot of the bed or on the floor next to the sofa. Bhedi was an ancient creature, lived a thousand lives, and he knew something was amiss. He'd uncurl his body and poke his muzzle into my hand or just plead with me with those big brown eyes to get up, Sita, get moving, and I would walk him round the block, slowly in respect to his arthritic hips, but I could barely make it back home. So, sorry, Bhedi, and he would whimper when I lay back down on the couch, completely worn-out. Twenty-four and going to pieces.

A month's indulgence, that's what my parents granted me, and come the middle of summer, they were encouraging me to get on my feet, to do something. How would you like to take up swimming? Or we could buy you a horse. Would you like to go out to Lake Michigan for a sail? But everything for me was still at half speed, quarter speed. I could not go when they proposed a vacation to Canada. I did not know the answer when they asked whether I would be going back to grad school in the fall. I hadn't the energy to think about looking for even a part-time job. My mother eventually broached the idea of some professional help. "Not that we think there's something wrong," my mother said. "But just someone to talk to——"

"I'm not crazy."

"No, not crazy. Hurt by that evil boy."

Of course, it wasn't the boy himself, but what he represented, some greater imbalance in the cosmos. The very idea that I, of all people, could not be trusted. What kind of world is this? The notion that some-one would strike me because he believed his suspicions over my truth. What sort of life have I stumbled upon? I was not depressed, but in a state of despair. And I needed something other than a therapist, so I refused to go, despite the anguish in my mother's eyes.

They were not looking at each other, Sam and Sita. Perhaps the mo-ment was too raw and personal, and they were strangers to a degree that made her confession uncomfortable. During the time Sita and I were to-gether, she and Sam probably met no more than a dozen times, so they knew each other primarily through me, and I am a poor vessel for understanding. I didn't know half of Sita's story, never knew the depths of her pain. She was framed by the window, the afternoon backlight-ing her features into obscurity, the sunshine through the silver leaves bestowing a kind of radiance. Sam sat quietly on the bed, studying his shoelaces. In the awkwardness of the conversation, I wished he could

play the fool as he had before. Draw some tattoo upon her eyelids or entertain her with some trick hidden in the pocket of his bathrobe. But Sam
had no magic to lighten the mood. And I could provide little comfort for
her past. Her life before our life. The cat opened one eye and regarded
me with some disdain. "A bit of curiosity wouldn't have killed you," he
said. "For cripes' sake, mate, you should have known before now."

As August ceased, and it became clear that I was in no shape to go
back to school, my parents grew more worried about me. My mother
kept insisting upon a therapist, and I could hear their arguments filtered
through my haze. My brothers and sister were worried, too, not just
about me, but about our mother as well, who was drifting away, lost
in confusion about what to do with me. One late summer night, with
a hint of autumn in the night air, my father knocked on my door and
asked if he might come in.

A cool breeze blew off the lake, and I was already under my covers, though the sun had not set. He motioned for me to give him some
space to sit on the edge of the bed. He has a kind of old-world formality,
a starchy politeness that endeared him to patients and colleagues, but
as a fully Americanized daughter, I found his manners puzzling. Relax,
Daddy. He was not like the American dads and their easy ways with
their children, and as he sat there beside me, I would have given anything just to have him hug me and say everything would be all right. But
that's just not in his makeup, though still, I was grateful for the gesture,
and it had been years since we had been alone together like this since I
was a little girl and he a young man. I bunched my pillows into a cush-
ion and sat up to ask, "Do you remember when you used to come tell
me the old stories?" Searching for words, he looked lost in the thicket,
unsure of the means to rescue his child just beyond.

"Rama," he said, "had heard from the people of his kingdom rumors about what had happened to Sita while she had been kidnapped by Ravana. The demon insisted that she become his bride, and though Sita refused him, the people questioned Sita's chastity during her long captivity. 'She must have given in to him.' Even Rama questioned her honor. So Sita asked Rama's brother to build a huge pyre and set it ablaze, and she told Rama that to prove her purity, she would walk through the fire. If she had been true to him, then she could walk through unscathed. If not, she would perish in the flames. Now, you may think that just proposing the test would be enough, but Sita insisted, and of course, she passed through the fire whole and pure as she had always been."

That was all for the first night's story. Over the next weeks, as summer gave way to autumn, my father would come into my room every so often and tell me more of the Ramayana, all the parts he had left out when I was a small girl. They had a trying marriage, Rama and Sita, predicated on doubt while trying to do the right thing, living the dharma. Rama took her back that first time, after the trial by fire, but he later sent her into exile again because of the persistent rumors in the kingdom. In exile, she bore him twin sons—Lava and Kusha. Sita, the original single mother, raising those children on her own. Years later, Rama chanced upon those boys and they sang to him the song of Rama that their mother had taught them, such was her loyalty, and only then did Rama realize his error and wish to welcome his sons back to his throne. And yet, still, Rama had his doubts about her, so in the end, Sita asked Mother Earth if she could return to her one true home, and Sita went down into an opening in the Earth, back to her Mother's embrace.

"That seems an odd story for a father to tell his daughter under the circumstances," Sam said.

Sita laughed softly. "For sure, if you read it as an allegory for my situation. But my father wasn't recommending trial by fire or a return to Mother Earth for me. I was not the goddess, and Matthew was certainly no god, no incarnation of Rama or anything of the sort. My father had the opposite intent in mind, if any moral is to be drawn, though I am not sure if the purpose of poetry and stories is to provide morals. His point may be: no man is worth such a sacrifice, eh?"

From downstairs came a sudden thud and crash, as if someone had bumped into a sideboard laden with glasses and knocked one to the floor. Judging by the ebb and flow of the conversation below, the guests were busy tidying up the mess. My brother swung his legs and put his feet on the floor. Sita sat beside him.

I got better in time. My father's stories may have helped, more for the teller than the tale. Certainly the chance to be home again and under their care. Do you know Bachelard's concept of the Desire Path? You find them all the time in landscapes, the paths or lines carved into the earth by animals or humans, the path worn by traffic across a park or open space, the most expeditious way from point to point. I loved the sound of it. I followed the desire path home. What I needed. There I found myself again, and by the following term, I went back to school, finished my degree. Took much longer to trust men after that. Lots of first dates, but nobody special. Four years wandering in the desert, and then my desire path led to Jack.

In the book and gift shop at the American Institute of Architects, a lovely unknown place, right around Christmastime. I was looking for a tie for my father, and this guy is the only other person in the shop. Must have been midafternoon on a cloudy December day in the middle of the week. I can't help but notice this man just wandering amid the merchandise. It's not a big shop really, but he passed by me a couple of times, and I can't really tell if he's looking for something in particular or if he's working up the courage to speak to me, so finally I just ask him outright, "Can I help you?" The look of surprise in his eyes is priceless, and then he thinks that I work there. "I don't know what I'm looking for," he says. "Something inspirational, thought-provoking, something to help me dream."

"Are you an architect?" I asked him.

"In a manner of speaking."

He looked just like a small boy caught in a daydream, so I took him by the hand and led him to the bookshelves and pulled out Bachelard's *Poetics of Space*. "You've heard of this?" He shook his head, so I handed him the book, and you'd have thought he was never going to move from the spot, never going to speak again. Just stunned. I suppose I was too forward.

She's right about the book. I never would have found it without her. But I'm not so sure just how shy I was when we met. I mean, I was instantly attracted to her, she's strikingly beautiful. I seem to recall a certain savoir faire on my part—

"Who are you kiddin'?" Harpo asked.

"Ah, what do you know?" Had I a shoe, I would have thrown it at the cat.

Harpo growled at me like the tiger of his dreams.

Jack asked me out for a coffee right then and there, and I thought, whew boy, not another architect. Managed to stay away from that sort for the past couple years, but how much harm in a cup of coffee? Jack was different, it turns out. He seemed to be someone I had always known, like we had met before in a previous life and were meant to meet again. His mannerisms and gestures, the light in his eyes. Even the way he talked. You didn't have an ordinary conversation, chitchat about the weather, but always a little deeper, and I don't know, like a haiku or something Japanese. Philosophical, poetical, straining toward the profound. An old soul. Nobody else talked that way with me. Nobody else treated me that way.

And he lived completely in his own head. Which can be an interesting place when he lets you inside. I used to catch him singing to himself when he thought no one could hear, snatches of opera it turns out. Or I'd come over and see him on a whim and he'd be in the middle of some old cowboy movie or anything with flappers or Buster Keaton or the Marx Brothers. But what was most different was that he was forever off on his own desire path. And his dreams were a symptom of an underlying sorrow, I think, a kind of despair.

"Despair? Jack?" My brother did not recognize me in her description.

"Jack would tell me his dreams. Everything he wished to design and see built, of course, but beyond that. What he hoped to create out of empty space, how to give people the places they needed for work or to study or just live. How to make a home out of a house. He was always reading the *Poetics,* trying to find some key to making it all happen, but I think he truly despaired of ever making it so. Too many hurdles. The bureaucracy of the firm. The conspiracy of other people."

"You have that anywhere," said Sam.

She soothed her grief with a sigh. "I've been there before, so I recognize the signs. Always wishing but never doing. Always desiring but never searching. His dreams of making all those houses and buildings and cities that he had drawn as a boy. He put his life on hold as he waited for his life to begin. All of it, even me. The shame is we were so close."

I saw her face surrounded by fireflies.

"The other night we had a few people over from his firm, a cookout to celebrate the beginning of another summer. The couple across the street were sitting on the porch blowing bubbles for their two girls to chase, and then the fireflies came out by magic in pairs and dozens and hundreds. Those girls were full of joy. And then these two jerks from his office were going on about this and that, and at one moment, I caught Jack's eye and begged him, in my mind, to get me out of here, to take me away from all this. Run off, stare at the ocean together, start a little magic of our own. But I guess he never quite got the signal, and I wonder now if he knew how much he was loved."

She began to cry again, and Sam finally got the signal that I was sending and rose to his feet and draped an arm across her shoulders. She folded herself into his embrace. "One thing I am sure of," he said, "was how much he was loved and how much he loved you."

Thank you, old man, I whispered.

"Perhaps the next time we go around," Sita said.

"Here's to the next life," Sam said. He guided her to the door. She looked back once over her shoulder, and then they left the room. I longed to stop her at the door, hoping to see her one last time, but she did not turn around, so I let it be.

A short while later, the noises downstairs abated as the guests left the house. Good-bye, good-bye, they said to one another. Sam helped Sita with her suitcases, for she was off to Chicago for repair of her heart. When the last one out locked the door, the old empty feeling returned. I was sad to hear them go, of course, but such endings are inevitable.

How much of our lives is spent saying farewell or waiting for someone to say hello? I neither dreaded nor welcomed being alone, but still, one enjoys lively company when it can be found. It had been good to see the girls again. After such a night, I was overwhelmed with sleepiness, and to no great surprise, darkness filled the windows. It would not shock me to learn the clocks read eight minutes until five once more. The cat, perhaps sensing my fatigue, lifted its head from the coil of its body. He appeared curious as to what had transpired during his nap, but no more curious than usual. Unwinding himself, front legs first, then the uncurling tail, and then an invigorating stretch that starts in the claws and ends at the back legs, Harpo woke slowly and meowed once. Inscrutable yet again, he leapt off the bed and swished his tail back and forth. He seemed hesitant to depart, yet anxious to go. I would have preferred he stay but knew better. "Go on," I said. He quick-stepped through the door and into the dark hallway. "I hope you get to be a tiger next time," I said, but he may have been too far gone to have heard.

Where Sita had rested, the comforter lay bunched and ruffled, and her impression remained. I thought I'd lie just for a moment where she had been, for the bed was warm with her memory. I dozed off for a spell. I loved her, perhaps more than I realized at the time when it would have made a difference. Had I any sense that June night of the fireflies, I would have kissed her under the canopy of the great leafy trees or told her how excited I felt just to be near her, but nothing much happened. Her arm brushed against mine every now and then, and I could almost taste her skin. Her hair shone under the string of Christmas lights hung around the railings of the deck. She smelled of cardamom and honey. It was perfect exhilaration, and yet, and yet, I failed to say any of this. And now it is too late. She was good for me, far better than I for her.

I loved them all, in my own way, the women who came to me from the past: Dolly, impetuous and loyal to the end; Jane, from whom I beg forgiveness; Alice, who bewitched me; Marie, most delicious; my darling Flo with whom I struck it rich; my biggest fan, Adele; and Bunny, who brought out the beast in me. I see now how I wronged each of them in one fashion or another. Maybe next time I will get it right. I do not claim innocence or push the blame on any of them. Yet at the same time, I wonder why they bothered to put me to the trial. Is it just possible that they loved me, too, that they came because they missed me and wished for one more day? For I see now that I have been a rascal over centuries, but not without some appeal. And my brother has always been a bit of a rogue as well. These thoughts give me comfort and hope.

Every once in a while, I wake up in the morning in exactly the same position in which I fell asleep. The sheets are barely wrinkled, the pillow holds its shape, and the blanket is merely creased like a flag from where it had been folded before I laid my body down. Following the wake, this is how I slept, as though the bed had been designed to enclose my body and nothing else, and the darkness fell like a lid, reassuring me that I was safe and free to rest. My pounding headache had vanished. Such a peaceful sleep with no thoughts or cares or dreams or anything to wake me.

Recently, though, the space changed, and that changes everything. The light—if one may call it light; perhaps a better term is the shade of darkness—stimulated a nerve cell or two deep in the mind, and by reflex, I kicked and the box smithereened apart. A kind of Big Bang return to consciousness, to a more fluid state of being, yet still somewhat restrictive, as though living in a bubble. It was not an unpleasant transition, somewhere between sleep and wakefulness. The room dark, though not of a smothering sort, but rather an enveloping darkness, and around the edges, a tad cooler. The air itself had become viscous and tasted faintly like the ocean. Life has slowed to a lunar cycle.

The voices, when they became audible, startled me. Emanating from beyond and above yet within the room, they seemed at first to be the gods in conversation, a woman and a man usually, but sometimes a third or fourth person could be heard over some infernal public address system with periodic announcements that buzzed and shook the walls. The actual words were nearly impossible to make out, though every once in a while, a phrase would filter through. "But I don't even like milk," the woman said. And much later, when the man exclaimed, "Hey, look it's snowing," I realized that we were not in June anymore, perhaps not even in the same year, or who knows, the same century. Of course, it was far too dark for me to see anything happening outside, even if I could somehow get up and find a window. For I was trapped in place, barely able to find my thumb with my mouth. And when I finally did manage the trick, that's when I realized what was actually happening in here.

Soon I will forget again everything I ever knew.

I won't remember the night when the seven women from the past came to recount my most grievous sins. Or the old man who led me to think he was the ghost of Beckett. Or the babbling baby boy, the talking cat, the singing windows, the women in the bed. Soon I will forget this very room, my house, and all poetics. I will trade recollections of my brother for some new experience, perhaps with another brother. All that's left of mother and father will vanish, as will every memory of friend and acquaintance. A lifetime of choices and opinions, the carefully constructed persona, vagabond experience, and the hopes and hurts and everything in between passes. Even now, I lose myself, my name escapes me. Sita, love of my life, will disappear from memory.

All of it will be erased completely, and even the simplest things will have to be relearned. Those voices outside will be my new guides to language, to talking and walking and eating solid foods. To make sense again of the material world, to read what's in another's heart by their signs and deeds. Someone will have to show me right from wrong, right from left, how to draw, what to eat, how to tie my shoes, why it is best to keep a cheerful disposition. I sincerely hope that I get reintroduced to the writings of Bachelard. But who will laugh at the Marx Brothers with me? Who will wait with me for Godot? All of it to be learned over and over and over. Here's a kick for you, lady, to remind you I am here. I am filling the last available space, dark as it is, and when all is taken and there is no more, I will fall down, out into the world and light to begin.

Here we go again. Another chance to muck up not only my life but so many others. Another go around, a new desire path to follow with or without the lessons learned. Round and round and round. Soon all this babbling will be just bubble and drool. The stopped watch is now ticking.

Here we go again. Another chance at life.

ACKNOWLEDGMENTS

Thank you to John Glusman and Peter Steinberg. To Bill Pugh and Lee Owens. Rose, for the French, and Melanie, for the red pen and support.

Although some of the characters in this novel actually existed historically, they are fictional representations.

ABOUT THE AUTHOR

KEITH DONOHUE is the author of the bestselling novels *The Stolen Child* and *Angels of Destruction*. For many years a ghostwriter, he has worked at the National Endowment for the Arts and the National Historical Publications and Records Commission. Donohue holds a Ph.D. in English literature, has published literary criticism, and has lectured on literature and writing at several colleges and universities.